"Jennings' ability to marshal the results of considerable re-
search into a smoothly flowing narrative is remarkable; here
he gives appreciators of historical fiction something to relish."

—*Booklist*

Praise for *Aztec*

"A dazzling and hypnotic historical novel."
—*The New York Times*

"A first-class storyteller. . . . Mr. Jennings has achieved true
distinction."

—*Atlantic Monthly*

"Anyone who reads, anyone who still lusts for adventure or
that book you can't put down, will glory in *Aztec*."
—*Los Angeles Times*

"*Aztec* is so vivid that this reviewer had the novel experience
of dreaming of the Aztec world, in Technicolor, for several
nights in a row."

—*Chicago Sun-Times*

"*Aztec* is a magnificent historical saga. . . . The splendor and
the sophistication as well as the sadism of these people come
to life in this novel which is nothing less than a brilliant
evocation of a vanished empire. . . . The true stuff of story-
telling at its height."

—*Houston Chronicle*

"The scope of the book includes the gallantry and barbarism,
sex and nobility, intelligence and folly of historical fiction. . . . [The reader] is amply entertained and caught up in
fascinating history."

—*San Francisco Chronicle*

AZTEC AUTUMN

OTHER BOOKS BY GARY JENNINGS

Aztec

The Journeyer

Spangle

Raptor

·GARY JENNINGS·

AZTEC

AUTUMN

TOR®

A TOM DOHERTY ASSOCIATES BOOK
NEW YORK

This is a work of fiction. All the characters and events portrayed in this
book are either products of the author's imagination or are used ficti-
tiously.

AZTEC AUTUMN

A Tor Book
Published by Tom Doherty Associates, Inc.
175 Fifth Avenue
New York, NY 10010

Tor Books on the World Wide Web:
http://www.tor.com

Tor® is a registered trademark of Tom Doherty Associates, Inc.

ISBN: 0-812-59096-1
Library of Congress Card Catalog Number: 97-5065

First edition: August 1997
First mass market edition: August 1998

Printed in the United States of America

0 9 8 7 6 5 4 3 2 1

To Hugo N. Gerstl

for brotherliness immeasurable

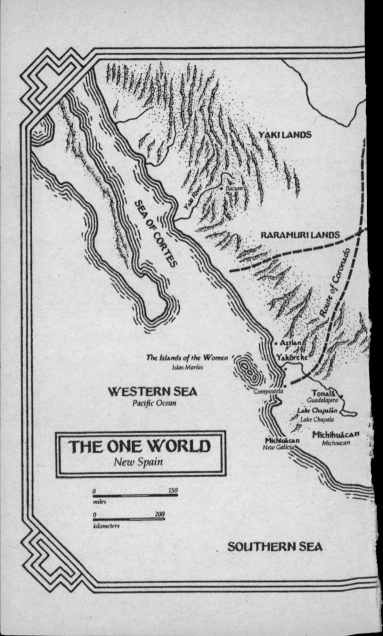

YAKI LANDS

Bacum

Yaki River

SEA OF CORTES

RARAMURI LANDS

Route of Coronado

The Islands of the Women
Islas Marías

Aztlan

Yakoreke

WESTERN SEA
Pacific Ocean

Compostela

Tonalá
Guadalajara

Lake Chapalán
Lake Chapala

THE ONE WORLD
New Spain

Michuácan
New Galicia

Michihuácan
Michoacan

0 ————— 150
miles

0 ————— 200
kilometers

SOUTHERN SEA

I CAN STILL see him burning.

On that long-ago day when I watched the man being set afire, I was already eighteen years old, so I had seen other people die, whether given in sacrifice to the gods or executed for some outrageous crime or simply dead by accident. But the sacrifices had always been done by means of the obsidian knife that tears out the heart. The executions had always been done with the maquáhuitl sword or with arrows or with the strangling "flower garland." The accidental deaths had mostly been the drownings of fishermen from our seaside city who somehow fell afoul of the water goddess. In the years since that day, too, I have seen people die in war and in various other ways, but never before then had I seen a man deliberately put to death by fire, nor have I since.

I and my mother and my uncle were among the vast crowd commanded by the city's Spanish soldiers to attend the ceremony, so I supposed that this event was intended to be some sort of object lesson to all of us non-Spaniards. Indeed, the soldiers collected and prodded and herded so many of us into the city's central square that we were crammed shoulder to shoulder. Within a space kept clear by a cordon of other soldiers, a metal post stood fixed into the flagstones of the square. To one side of it had been built a platform for the occasion, and on it sat or stood a number of Spanish Christian priests, all clad in flowing black gowns, as are our own priests.

Two burly Spanish guards brought the condemned man and roughly shoved him into that cleared space. When we saw that he was not a Spaniard, pale and bearded, but one of our own people, I heard my mother sigh, *"Ayya ouíya . . ."* and so did many others in the crowd. The man wore a loose, shapeless and colorless garment and, on his head, a scraggly crown made of straw. His only adornment that I could see was a pendant of some kind—it flashed when it caught the sun—hanging from a thong about his neck.

The man was quite old, even older than my uncle, and he put up no struggle against his guards. The man seemed, in fact, either resigned to his fate or indifferent to it, so I do not know why he was immediately encumbered by a heavy restraint. A tremendous piece of metal chain was hung upon him, a chain of such dimensions that a single link of it was big enough to be forced over his head to pinion his neck. That chain was then fixed to the upright post, and the guards began piling about his feet a heap of kindling wood. While that was being done, the oldest of the priests on the platform—the chief of them, I assumed—spoke to the prisoner, addressing him by a Spanish name, "Juan Damasceno." Then he commenced a long harangue, naturally in Spanish, which at that time I had not yet learned. But a younger priest, dressed in slightly different vestments, translated his chief's words—to my considerable surprise—into fluent Náhuatl.

This enabled me to comprehend that the old priest was reciting the charges against the condemned man, and also that he was—in a voice alternately unctuous and angry—trying to persuade the man to make amends or show contrition or something of the sort. But even when translated into my native language, the terms and expressions employed by the priest were a bafflement to me. After a long and wordy while of this, the prisoner was given leave to speak. He did so in Spanish, and when that was translated into Náhuatl, I understood him very clearly:

"Your Excellency, once when I was still a small child I vowed to myself that if ever I were selected for the Flowery Death, even on an alien altar, I would not degrade the dignity of my going."

Juan Damasceno spoke nothing more than that, but among the priests and guards and other officials there ensued a great deal of discourse and conferring and gesticulation—before finally a stern command was uttered, and one of the soldiers set a torch to the pile of wood at the prisoner's feet.

As is well known, the gods and goddesses take mischievous delight in perplexing us mortals. They frequently confound our best intentions and complicate our most straightforward plans and thwart even the least of our ambitions. Often they can do such things with ease, simply by arranging what appears to be a matter of coincidence. And if I did not know better, I would have said that it was mere coincidence that brought us three—my uncle, Mixtzin, his sister Cuicáni and her son, myself, Tenamáxtli—to the City of Mexíco on that particular day.

Fully twelve years previous, in our own city of Aztlan, the Place of Snowy Egrets, far to the northwest, on the coast of the Western Sea, we had heard the first startling news: that The One World had been invaded by pale-skinned and heavily bearded strangers. It was said that they had come from across the Eastern Sea in huge houses that floated on the water and were propelled by immense birdlike wings. I was only six years old at that time, with a whole seven years to wait before I could don, beneath my mantle, the máxtlatl loincloth that signifies the attainment of manhood. Hence I was an insignificant person, of no consequence at all. Nevertheless, I was precociously inquisitive and very sharp of ear. Also, my mother Cuicáni and I did reside in the Aztlan palace with my Uncle Mixtzin and his son Yeyac and daughter Améyatl, so I was always able to hear whatever news arrived and whatever comment it provoked among my uncle's Speaking Council.

As is indicated by the -*tzin* suffixion to my uncle's name, he was a noble, the highest noble among us Aztéca, being the Uey-Tecútli—the Revered Governor—of Aztlan. Some while earlier, when I was just a toddling babe, the late Uey-Tlatoáni Motecuzóma, Revered Speaker of the Mexíca, the most powerful nation in all The One World, had accorded our then-small village the status of "autonomous colony of the Mexíca." He ennobled my Uncle Mixtli as the Lord Mixtzin, and set him to govern Aztlan, and bade him build the place into a prosperous and populous and civilized colony of which the Mexíca could be proud. So, although we were exceedingly far distant from the capital city of Tenochtítlan—The Heart of The One World—Motecuzóma's swift-messengers routinely brought to our Aztlan palace, as to other colonies, any news deemed of interest to his under-governors. Of course, the news of those intruders from beyond the sea was anything but routine. It caused no small consternation and speculation among Aztlan's Speaking Council.

"In the ancient archives of various nations of our One World," said old Canaútli, our Rememberer of History, who also happened to be the grandfather of my uncle and my mother, "it is recorded that the Feathered Serpent, the once-greatest of all monarchs, Quetzalcóatl of the Toltéca—he who eventually was worshiped as the greatest of gods—was described as having a very white skin and a bearded face."

"Are you suggesting—?" began another member of the Council, a priest of our war god Huitzilopóchtli. But Canaútli overrode him, as I could have told the priest he would, because I well knew how my great-grandfather loved to talk.

"It is also recorded that Quetzalcóatl abdicated his rule of the Toltéca as a consequence of his having done something shameful. His people might never have known of it, but he confessed to it. In a fit of intoxication—after overindulgence in the drunk-making octli beverage—he committed the act of ahuilnéma with his own sister. Or, some say, with his own daughter. The Toltéca so much adored the Feathered Serpent that they doubtless would have forgiven him that misconduct, but he could not forgive himself."

Several of the councillors nodded solemnly. Canaútli went on:

"That is why he built a raft on the seashore—some say it was made of feathers felted together, some say it was made of interlaced snakes—and he floated off across the Eastern Sea. His subjects prostrated themselves on the beach, loudly bewailing his departure. So he called to them, assuring them that someday, when he had done sufficient penance in exile, he would return. But, over the years, the Toltéca themselves gradually vanished into extinction. And Quetzalcóatl has never been seen again."

"Until now?" growled Uncle Mixtzin. He was almost never of very warm or cheerful temperament, and the messenger's news had not been of a sort to exhilarate him. "Is that what you mean, Canaútli?"

The old man shrugged and said, "Aquin ixnéntla?"

"Who knows?" he was echoed by another elderly councillor. "I know this much, having been a fisherman all my working life. It would be next to impossible to make a *raft* float off across the sea. To get it out past the breakers and the combers and the landward surge of the surf."

"Perhaps not impossible for a god," said another. "Anyway, if the Feathered Serpent had great difficulty in doing that, it seems he has learned from the experience, if now he has voyaged hither in winged houses."

"Why would he need more than one such vessel?" asked another. "He went away alone. But it appears that he returns with a numerous crew. Or passengers."

Canaútli said, "It has been countless sheaves of sheaves of years since he left. Wherever he went, he could have married wife after wife, and begotten whole nations of progeny."

"If this *is* Quetzalcóatl returned," said that priest of the war god, in a voice that quavered slightly, "do any of you realize what the effects will be?"

"Many changes for the better, I should expect," said my uncle, who took pleasure in discomfiting priests. "The Feathered Serpent was a gentle and beneficent god. All the histories agree—never before or since his time has The One World enjoyed such peace and happiness and good fortune."

"But all our other gods will be relegated to inferiority, even obscurity," said that priest of Huitzilopóchtli, wringing his hands. "And so will all us priests of all those gods. We shall be abased, made lower than the lowest slaves. Deposed . . . dismissed . . . discarded to beg and starve."

"As I said," grunted my irreverent uncle. "Changes for the better."

Well, the Uey-Tecútli Mixtzin and his Speaking Council were soon disabused of any notion that the newcomers included or represented the god Quetzalcóatl. During the next year and a half or so, hardly a month went by without a swift-messenger from Tenochtítlan bringing ever more astounding and disconcerting news. From one runner, we would learn that the strangers were only men, not gods or the progeny of gods, and that they called themselves *españoles* or *castellanos*. The two names seemed interchangeable, but the latter was easier for us to transmute into Náhuatl, so for a long time all of us referred to the outlanders as the Caxtiltéca. Then the next-arriving runner would inform us that the Caxtiltéca resembled gods—at least, war gods—in that they were rapacious, ferocious, merciless, and lustful of conquest, because they were now forcing their way inland from the Eastern Sea.

Then the next swift-messenger would report that the Caxtiltéca certainly displayed godlike, or at least magical, attributes in their methods and weapons of war, for many of them rode mounted on giant, antlerless buck deer, and many of them wielded fearsome tubes that discharged lightning and thunder, and others had arrows and spears tipped with a metal that never bent or broke, and all wore armor of that same metal, which was impenetrable by ordinary projectiles.

Then came a messenger wearing the white mantle of mourning, and with his hair braided in the manner signifying bad news. His report was that the invaders had defeated one nation and tribe after another, on their way westward—the Totonáca, the Tepeyahuáca, the Texcaltéca—then had impressed any surviving native warriors into their own ranks. So the number of fighting men did not diminish but continually increased as they marched. (I might mention, from my advantage of hindsight, that many of those native warriors were not too reluctant to join the aliens' forces, because their people had for ages been paying grudging and heavy tribute to Tenochtítlan, and now they had hopes of retaliating against the domineering Mexíca.)

Finally there came to Aztlan a swift-messenger—with white mantle and bad-news hairdress—to tell us that the Caxtiltéca white men and their recruited native allies had now marched right into Tenochtítlan itself, The Heart of The One World, and, inconceivably, at the *personal invitation* of the once-puissant, now-irresolute Revered Speaker Motecuzóma. Furthermore, those intruders had not just marched on through and continued westward, but had occupied the city, and seemed inclined to settle down and stay there.

The one member of our Speaking Council who had most dreaded the coming of those outlanders—I mean that priest of the god Huitzilopóchtli—had lately been considerably heartened to know that he was not about to be deposed by a returning Quetzalcóatl. But he was dismayed anew when this latest swift-messenger also reported:

"In every city and town and village on their way to Tenochtítlan, the barbaric Caxtiltéca have destroyed every teocáli temple, torn down every tlamanacáli pyramid and toppled and broken every statue of every one of our gods and goddesses. In place of them, the foreigners have erected crude wooden effigies of a vapidly simpering white woman holding in her arms a white baby. These images, they say, represent a mortal mother who gave birth to a child-godling, and are the foundations of their religion called Crixtanóyotl.''

So our priest wrung his hands some more. He was apparently doomed to be displaced anyway—and not even by one of our own land's former gods, who had stature and grandeur, but by some new, incomprehensible religion that evidently worshiped an ordinary *woman* and a lackwit *infant*.

That swift-messenger was the last ever to come to us from Tenochtítlan or from anywhere else in the Mexíca lands, bringing what we could assume was authoritative and trustworthy news. After him, we only heard rumors that spread from one community to another and eventually reached us by way of some traveler journeying overland or paddling an acáli canoe up the seacoast. From those rumors, one had to sift out the impossible and the illogical—miracles and omens allegedly descried by priests and far-seers, exaggerations attributable to the superstitions of the common folk, that sort of thing—because, anyway, what remained after the sifting, and could be recognized as at least possible, was dire enough.

In the course of time, we heard and had no reason to disbelieve these things: that Motecuzóma had died at the hands of the Caxtiltéca; that the two Revered Speakers who briefly succeeded him had also perished; that the entire city of Tenochtítlan—houses, palaces, temples, marketplaces, even the massive icpac tlamanacáli, the Great Pyramid—had been leveled and reduced to rubble; that all the lands of the Mexíca and all their tributary nations were now the property of the Caxtiltéca; that more and more floating houses were coming across the Eastern Sea and disgorging more and more of the white men and that those alien warriors were fanning out northward, westward and southward to conquer and subdue still other, farther nations and lands. According to the rumors, everywhere the Caxtiltéca went, they scarcely needed to use their lethal weapons.

Said one informant, ''It must be their gods—that white woman and child, may they be damned to Míctlan—who do the slaughtering. They inflict whole populations with diseases that kill everyone *but* the white men.''

''And horrible diseases they are,'' said another passerby. ''I hear that a person's skin turns to ghastly boils and pustules, and he suffers untold agonies for a long time before death mercifully releases him.''

''Hordes of our people are dying of that blight,'' said yet another. ''But the white men seem impervious. It *has* to be an evil enchantment laid by their white goddess and godling.''

We heard also that every surviving and able-bodied man, woman and child in and around Tenochtítlan was put to slave labor, using what material was salvageable from the ruins, to rebuild that city. But now, by order of the conquerors, it was to be known as the City of Mexíco. It was still the capital of what had been The One World, but *that*, by order of the conquerors, was henceforth to be called New Spain. And, so said the rumors, the new city in no way resembled the old; the buildings were of complex designs and ornamentation that the Caxtiltéca must have remembered from their *Old* Spain, wherever that was.

When eventually we of Aztlan got word that the white men were fighting to subjugate the territories of the Otomí and Purémpecha peoples, we fully expected soon to see those marauders arriving on our own doorstep, so to speak, because the northern limit of the Purémpecha's land called Michihuácan is no more than ninety one-long-runs from Aztlan. However, the Purémpecha put up a fierce and unflagging resistance that kept the invaders embroiled there in Michihuácan for years. Meanwhile, the Otomí people simply melted away before the attackers and let them *have* that country, for what it was worth. And it was not worth much to anybody, including the rapacious Caxtiltéca, because it was and is nothing but what we call the Dead-Bone Lands— arid, bleak, inhospitable desert, as is also all the country north of Michihuácan.

So the white men finally were satisfied to cease their

advance at the southern edge of that unlovely desert (what *they* called the Great Bald Spot). In other words, they established the northern border of their New Spain along a line stretching approximately from Lake Chapálan in the west to the shore of the Eastern Sea, and thus it has remained to this day. Where the southern border of New Spain was finally established, I have no idea. I do know that detachments of the Caxtiltéca conquered and settled in the once-Maya territories of Uluümil Kutz and Quautemálan and still farther south, in the blazing, steaming Hot Lands. The Mexíca had formerly traded with those lands, but, even at the height of their power, had had no craving to acquire or inhabit them.

During the eventful years that I have sketchily chronicled here, there also occurred the more expectable and less epochal events of my own youth. The day I became seven years old, I was taken before Aztlan's wizened old tonalpóqui, the name-giver, so he could consult his tonálmatl book of names (and ponder all the good and bad omens attendant on the time of my birth), to fix on me the appellation I would wear forever after. My first name, of course, had to be merely that of the day I came into the world: Chicuáce-Xóchitl, Six-Flower. For my second name, the old seer chose—as having "good portents," he said—Téotl-Tenamáxtli, "Girded Strong As Stone."

Simultaneous with my becoming Tenamáxtli, I commenced my schooling in Aztlan's two telpochcáltin, The House of Building Strength and The House of Learning Manners. When I turned thirteen and donned the loincloth of manhood, I graduated from those lower schools and attended only the city's calmécac, where teacher-priests imported from Tenochtítlan taught the art of word-knowing and many other subjects—history, doctoring, geography, poetry—almost any kind of knowledge a pupil might wish to possess.

"It is also time," said my Uncle Mixtzin, on that thirteenth birthday of mine, "for you to celebrate another sort of graduation. Come with me, Tenamáxtli."

He escorted me through the streets to Aztlan's finest au-

yanicáti and, from the numerous females resident there,
picked out the most attractive—a girl almost as young and
almost as beautiful as his own daughter Améyatl—and told
her: "This young man is today a *man*. I would have you
teach him all that a man should know about the act of ahuilnéma. Devote the entire night to his education."

The girl smiled and said she would, and she did. I must
say that I thoroughly enjoyed her attentions and the night's
activities, and I was duly grateful to my generous uncle. But
I also must confess that, unknown to him, I already had been
foretasting such pleasures for some months before I merited
the manly loincloth.

Anyway, during those years and subsequent years, Aztlan
never was visited by even a roving patrol of the Caxtiltéca
forces, nor were any of the nearer communities with which
we Aztéca traded. Of course, all the lands north of New
Spain had always been sparsely populated in comparison to
the midlands. It would not have surprised me if, to the north
of *our* lands, there were hermit tribes who had not yet even
heard that The One World had been invaded, or that there
existed such things as white-skinned men.

Aztlan and those other communities naturally felt relief at
being left unmolested by the conquerors, but we also found
that our safety-in-isolation entailed some disadvantages.
Since we and our neighbors did not want to attract the attention of the Caxtiltéca, we sent none of our pochtéca traveling merchants or even swift-messengers venturing across
the border of New Spain. This meant that we voluntarily cut
ourselves off from all commerce with the communities south
of that line. Those had formerly been the best markets in
which to sell our homegrown and homemade products—
coconut milk and sweets and liquor and soap, pearls,
sponges—and from them we had procured items unavailable
in our lands—every sort of commodity from cacao beans to
cotton, even the obsidian needed for our tools and weapons.
So the headmen of various towns roundabout us—Yakóreke,
Tépiz, Tecuéxe and others—began sending discreet scouting

parties southward. These went in groups of three, one of them always a woman, and they went unarmed and unarmored, wearing simple country clothes, seeming to be simple country people trudging to some innocuous family gathering somewhere. They carried nothing to make any Caxtiltéca border guards suspicious or predaceous; usually nothing but a leather bag of water and another of pinóli for traveling provisions.

The scouts went forth with understandable apprehension, not knowing what dangers they might encounter on the way. But they went with curiosity, too, their mission being to report back to their headmen on what they saw of life in the midlands, in the towns and cities, and especially in the City of Mexíco, now that all was ruled by the white men. On those reports would depend our peoples' decision: whether to approach and ally ourselves with the conquerors, in hope of a resumption of normal trade and social intercourse; or to remain remote and unnoticed and independent, even if poorer for that; or to concentrate on building strong forces and impregnable defenses and an armory of weapons, to fight for our lands when and if the Caxtiltéca *did* come.

Well, in time, almost all the scouts returned, at intervals, intact and unscathed by any misadventures either going or coming. Only one or two parties had even seen a border sentry and, except for the scouts having been awestruck by their first sight of a white man in the flesh, they had nothing to report about their crossing of the border. Those guards had ignored them as if they were no more than desert lizards seeking a new feeding ground. And throughout New Spain, in the countryside, in villages and towns and cities, including the City of Mexíco, they had not seen—or heard from any of the local inhabitants—any evidence that the new overlords were any more strict or severe than the Mexíca rulers had been.

"My scouts," said Kévari, tlatocapíli of the village of Ya-kóreke, "say that all the surviving pípiltin of the court of Tenochtítlan—and the heirs of those lords who did not survive—have been allowed to keep their family estates and property and lordly privileges. They have been most leniently treated by the conquerors.''

''However, except for those few who are still accounted lords or nobles,'' said Teciuápil, chief of Tecuéxe, ''there *are* no more pípiltin. Or working-class macehuáltin or even tlacótin slaves. All our people are now accounted equal. And all work at whatever the white men bid them do. So said my scouts.''

''Only one of my scouts returned,'' said Tototl, headman of Tépiz. ''He reports that the City of Mexíco is almost complete, except for a few very grand buildings still under construction. Of course there are no more temples to the old gods. But the marketplaces, he said, are thronged and thriving. That is why my other two scouts, a married couple, Netzlin and Citláli, chose to stay there and seek their fortune.''

''I am not surprised,'' growled my Uncle Mixtzin, to whom the other chiefs had come to report. ''Such peasant oafs would never before in their lives have seen *any* city. No wonder they report favorably on the new rulers. They are too ignorant to make comparisons.''

''*Ayya!*'' bleated Kévari. ''At least we and our people made an effort to investigate, while you and your Aztéca sit lumpishly here in complacency.''

''Kévari is right,'' said Teciuápil. ''It was agreed that all of us leaders would convene, discuss what we have learned and then decide our course of action regarding the Caxtiltéca invaders. But all you do, Mixtzin, is scoff.''

''Yes,'' said Tototl. ''If you so disdainfully dismiss the honest efforts of our *peasant oafs*, Mixtzin, then send some of your educated and refined Aztéca. Or some of your tame Mexíca immigrants. We will postpone any decisions until *they* return.''

''No,'' my uncle said, after a moment of deep thought. ''Like those Mexíca who now live among us, I too once saw the city of Tenochtítlan when it stood in its zenith of might and glory. I shall go myself.'' He turned to me. ''Tenamáxtli, make ready, and tell your mother to make ready. You and she will accompany me.''

So that was the sequence of events that took the three of us journeying to the City of Mexíco—where I would get my uncle's reluctant permission to remain and reside for a time, and where I would learn many things, including the speaking of your Spanish tongue. However, I never took the time to learn the reading and writing of your language—which is why I am at this moment recounting my reminiscences to you, *mi querida muchacha, mi inteligente y bellísima y adorada Verónica*, so that you may set the words down for all my children and all our children's children to read someday.

And the culmination of that sequence of events was that my uncle, my mother and myself arrived in the City of Mexíco in the month of Panquétzalíztli, in the year Thirteen-Reed, what you would call *Octubre*, of the *Año de Cristo* one thousand five hundred thirty and one, on the very day—anyone but the prankish and capricious gods would have deemed it coincidence—that the old man Juan Damasceno was burned to death.

I can still see him burning.

II

To GOVERN AZTLAN during his absence, Mixtzin appointed his daughter Améyatl and her consort Káuri as co-regents—with my great-grandfather Canaútli (who must have been nearly two sheaves of years old by then, but who evidently was going to live forever) to be their sage adviser. Then, without further ado, and without ceremonious leave-takings, Mixtzin and Cuicáni and I departed the city, heading southeastward.

It was the first time I had ever gone very far from the place where I had been born. So, although I was well aware of the serious intent of our venture, still, to me, the horizon was a wide and welcoming grin. It beckoned me to all manner of new sights and experiences. For instance, at Aztlan the dawn had always come late and in full-blown radiance, because it had first to clear the mountains inland of us. Now, when I had crossed those mountains into flatter country, I could really see the dawn breaking—or, rather, unfurling, one colored ribbon after another: violet, blue, pink, pearl, gold. Then the birds began to bubble over in greeting of the day, singing a music all of green notes. It was autumn, so there came no rains, but the sky was the color of wind, and through it wafted clouds that were always the same but never the same. The blowing, dancing trees were music visible, and the nodding, bowing flowers were prayers that said themselves. When twilight darkened the land, the flowers closed, but the stars opened in the sky. I have always been glad that those star blooms are out of the reach of men, else they would have been snatched and stolen long ago. At last, at nightfall, there arose the soft dove-colored mists, which I believe are the grateful sighs of the earth going tired to bed.

The journey was long—more than two hundred one-long-runs—because it could not be done in a direct, straight line of march. It was also sometimes arduous and frequently wearisome, but never really hazardous, because Mixtzin had traveled that route before. He had done that about fifteen years before, but he still remembered the shortest way across scorching patches of desert, and the easiest way to skirt around the bases of mountains instead of having to climb over them and the shallow places where we could ford rivers without having to wait and hope for someone to come by in an acáli. Often, though, we had to veer from the paths he remembered, to make a prudent circuit around parts of Michihuácan where, the local folk told us, there were still battles going on between the unrelenting Caxtiltéca and the proudly stubborn Purémpecha.

When, somewhere in the Tecpanéca lands, we did eventually begin to encounter an occasional white man and the animals called horses, and the other animals called cows and the other animals called staghounds, we did our best to assume an air of indifference, as if we had been accustomed to seeing them all our lives long. The white men seemed equally indifferent to our passing by, as if we too were only commonplace animals.

All along our way, Uncle Mixtzin kept pointing out to my mother and myself landmarks he recalled from his earlier journey—curiously shaped mountains; ponds of water too bitter to be drinkable, but so hot that they steamed even in the sun; trees and cactuses of sorts that did not grow where we lived, some of those bearing delicious fruits. He also kept up a commentary (though we had heard it all before, and more than once) on the difficulties of that earlier excursion toward Tenochtítlan:

"As you know, my men and I were rolling the giant carved stone disk representing the moon goddess Coyolxaúqui, taking it to present as a gift to the Revered Speaker Motecuzóma. A disk is round, true, and you might suppose it would roll easily along. But a disk is also flat on both faces. So an unexpected dip in the ground, or an unnoticed unevenness, could cause it to tilt sideways. And, though my men were sturdy and attentive to their labors, they could not always prevent the tilted stone from falling completely on its back or sometimes, grievous to relate, the dear goddess would fall flat on her face. And *heavy?* To raise that thing up on edge again each time, I swear to Míctlan, required us to beg the aid of every other man we could find in the surrounding area . . ."

And Mixtzin would recollect, as he had done more than once before: "I might never even have got to meet the Uey-Tlatoáni Motecuzóma, because I was apprehended by his palace guards and very nearly imprisoned as a despoiler of the city. As you can imagine, all of us were filthy and fatigued by the time we arrived there, and our raiment was torn and tattered, so no doubt we did resemble savages who had wandered in from some wilderness. Also, Tenochtítlan was the first and only city we traversed that had fine stone-paved streets and causeways. It did not occur to us that our rolling the massive Moon Stone through those streets would so badly crunch and crush the elegant paving. But then the angry guards swooped down upon us . . ." and Mixtzin laughed at the memory.

As we ourselves got closer and closer to Tenochtítlan, we learned—from the people whose communities we passed through—a few things that prepared us so we would not arrive at our destination seeming like absolute country clods. For one thing, we were told that the white men did not care to be called Caxtiltéca. We had been wrong in supposing the two names—*castellanos* and *españoles*—to be interchangeable. Of course,

I later came to understand that all castellanos were españoles, but not all españoles were castellanos—that the latter hailed from a particular *province* of Old Spain called Castile. Anyway, we three made sure, from then on, to refer to the white men as Spaniards and their language as Spanish. We were also advised to be careful about attracting any Spaniard's attention to ourselves:

"Do not simply stroll about the city, gawking," said one country fellow who had recently been there. "Always walk briskly, as if you have a specific objective toward which you are going. And it is wise to be always carrying something when you do. I mean a building brick or block of wood or coil of rope, as if you were on your way to some task already assigned you. Otherwise, if you go about empty-handed, some Spanish overseer of some work project will be sure to *give* you a job to do. And you had better do it."

So, forewarned, we three went on. And even from our first sight of it, from afar, the City of México was awe-inspiring, bulking as large as it did, towering from the floor of the bowl-shaped valley in which it stands. Our actual entry, though, was a little disappointing. As we walked over a long, wide, banistered stone causeway that took us from the town of Tepayáca on the mainland to the city's islands my uncle muttered:

"Strange. This causeway used to vault an expanse of water, busily swarming with acáltin of every size. But now look."

We did, seeing nothing below us but an immense stretch of rather smelly wetland, all mud and weeds and frogs and a few herons—very like the swamps around Aztlan before they were drained.

But, beyond the causeway was the city. And I, even though forewarned, was immediately and often that day tempted to do what we had been told not to do—because the hugeness and magnificence of the City of México were such as to stun me into motionless ogling and admiration. Each time, fortunately, my uncle would prod me onward, because

he himself was not much impressed by the sights of the
place, he having once seen the sights of the vanished Tenochtítlan. And again he supplied a commentary for me and
my mother:

"We are now in the Ixacuálco quarter of the city, the very
best residential district, where lived that friend also named
Mixtli, who had persuaded me to bring the Moon Stone
hither, and I visited in his house while I was here. His house
and the others around it were much more various and handsome then. These new ones all look alike. Friend"—and he
reached out to catch the hand of a passerby (carrying a load
of firewood, with a tumpline about his forehead)—"friend,
is this quarter of the city still known as Ixacuálco?"

"Ayya," muttered the man, giving Mixtzin a suspicious
look. "How is it that you do not know? This quarter is now
called San Sebastián Ixacuálco."

"And what means 'San Sebastián'?" my uncle asked.

The man shrugged his load of wood. "*San* means 'santo,'
a lesser god of the Spanish Christians. Sebastián is the name
of one of the santos, but what he is the god *of*, I have never
been told."

So we moved on, and Mixtzin continued his narration:

"Notice now. Here was a broad canal, always busy and
crowded with a traffic of immense freight acáltin. I have no
idea why it has been filled in and paved over to become a
street instead. And there—*ayyo*, there before you, sister,
nephew"—he made an impressively sweeping gesture of
both arms—"there, enclosed by the undulating Snake Wall
painted in many vivid colors, that was the vast open space—
the bright-shining marble square that was The Center of The
Heart of The One World. And in it, yonder, was the sump-
tuous Palace of Motecuzóma. And yonder, the court for the
ceremonial tlachtli ball games. And yonder, the Stone of Ti-
zoc, where warriors dueled to the death. And yonder"—he
broke off to catch the arm of a passerby (carrying a basket
of lime mortar)—"friend, tell me, what is that gigantic and
ugly structure still a-building over there?"

"That? You do not know? Why, that will be the Christian priests' central temple. I mean cathedral. The Cathedral Church of San Francisco."

"Another of their santos, eh?" said Mixtzin. "And for what aspect of the world is this lesser god responsible?"

The man said uneasily, "As best I know, stranger, he just happens to be the personal favorite godling of Bishop Zumárraga, the chief of all the Christian priests." Then the man scurried away.

"Yya ayya," Mixtzin mourned. "Nínotlancuícui in Teo Francisco. I pick my teeth at the little god Francisco. If that is his temple, it is a poor substitute for its predecessor. For *there*, sister, nephew, *there* stood the most awesome edifice ever erected in all The One World. It was the Great Pyramid, massive but graceful, and so sky-reaching that one had to climb a hundred fifty and six marble stair-treads to attain the top, and there be awed all over again by the brilliantly colored and roofcombed temples of the gods Tlaloc and Huitzilopóchtli. *Ayyo*, but this city had gods worth celebrating in those days! And—"

He was abruptly interrupted, as all three of us were suddenly propelled forward. We might have been standing on a beach with our backs to the sea, and neglecting to count the waves, and thus getting unexpectedly deluged by the always-mountainous seventh wave. What shoved against us from behind was that crowd of people being herded by the soldiers into the open square we had been eyeing. We were in the forefront of the throng, and we managed to stay close together. So, when the square was packed full and the milling had ceased and all was quiet, we had an unimpeded view of the platform onto which the priests were ascending, and the metal post to which the condemned man was led and bound. We had a rather better view than I might, in retrospect, have wished to have. Because I can still see him burning.

As I have told, the old man Juan Damasceno spoke only briefly before the torch was laid to the wood heaped about him. And then he made no moan or scream or even whimper as the fire ate its way up his body. And none of us witnesses made a sound, either, except for my mother, who uttered a single sob. But there were noises, nevertheless. I can still *hear* him burning.

The noises included the familiar crepitations of wood doing its duty as fuel, and the eager lickings and lappings of the flames, and the spitting sounds as the man's skin bulged into blisters that instantly burst, and the crackling and sizzling of his flesh, and the hissing as his blood fumed away, and the snaps and crunches as his muscles tightly contracted in the heat and broke the bones inside him and, toward the end, the indescribably horrid sound of his skull's blowing to fragments from the pressure of the brain boiling within.

Meanwhile, we all could also smell him burning. The aroma of human flesh being cooked is, at first, as deliciously appetizing as that of any other kind of meat being properly broiled. But then this particular cooking became burning, and there was the odor of char and smoke, and the rancid smell of his under-skin fat bubbling and melting, and the lingering scorch odor of his one garment disintegrating, and the briefer but sharper whiff when the hair of his head went away in a flash, and the reek of roasting organs and membranes and viscera, and the cloying sick-sweet smell of blood turning to steam, and after a while the hot metallic odor as the restraining chain seemed trying to catch fire itself, and the powdery smell of bones turning to ashes and the revolting stink when the man's lower guts and their fecal contents were incinerated.

Since the man at the stake could also see, hear and smell those various things happening to himself, I began to wonder what was going on in his mind all that time. He never emitted a sound, but surely he had to be thinking. About what? Regretting the things he had done, or not done, that had brought him to this dreadful end? Or dwelling on and savoring the small pleasures, even adventures he had sometime enjoyed? Or thinking of loved ones left behind? No, at his age, he had probably outlived all of them except children or grandchildren, if he had any, but there must have been women in his life; even old, he had still been a fine-looking man when he came to the stake. Also, he had come to this unspeakable fate unafraid and unbowed; he must have been a man of consequence in his day. Was he now, perhaps, despite the excruciating pain he was enduring, inwardly laughing at the irony of his having once been high and mighty, and today brought so low?

And which of his senses, I wondered, was the first to be extinguished? Did his vision last long enough that he could view the onlooking executioners and his countrymen crowded about, and himself ponder on what the living were thinking at seeing him die? Could he see his own legs shriveling and blackening and, while he hung suspended by the chain, curling up against his belly—and then his arms doing the same, shrinking and crisping and curling across his chest—as if his limbs were trying to protect the torso for which they had worked faithfully during a lifetime? Or had the heat by then burst his eyeballs, so that there would nevermore be any light or any sight to see it?

Then, eyeless, did he go on tracing by sound and smell the remorseless progress of his being corroded? The mud-bubble plopping sounds of his skin's blisters swelling, heaving and viscously erupting—could he hear those? Could he smell his own human meat turning to a nauseous carrion that even the tzopilótin vultures would refuse to feed on? Or did he merely *feel* those things? If so, did he feel them as separate, identifiable pangs or as an all-engulfing agony?

But even when he had been deprived of sight, hearing, smell—and, I hope, feeling—he still for a while had a brain. Did it go on *thinking* until the very last? Did it dread the endless night and nothingness of the Míctlan netherworld? Or did it dream of a new and eternal life in the bright, lush, happy land of the sun god Tonatíu? Or did it simply, desperately try to hold, for just a little longer, the memories of this world and its life that were dearest to him? Of youth, of sky and sunlight, of loving caresses, of deeds and feats, of places once visited and never to be visited again? Had he managed frantically to keep those thoughts and memories for his pathetic last solace until the instant when his whole head shattered and *everything* was ended?

If this spectacle had in fact been intended as some sort of edifying lesson for us who had been commanded to watch, I think we all would have had our fill of it very early on. For one reason, we all saw that the man Juan Damasceno died to no good purpose—not his heart, not even his blood went to nourish any god, none of our own or those of the Christians. But the soldiers would not let us leave before the presiding priests did, and they stayed on their platform until there was little left of their victim but smoke and stench. They watched the entire proceedings with that stern expression of disagreeable-duty-done that any priest of any religion can so righteously assume, but their eyes belied their faces. The priests' eyes were bright with avid enjoyment and approval of what they watched. All but one priest, I should remark—that younger one who had done the translating into Náhuatl.

His face was not stern but sad, his eyes not gloating but pitying. And when the other priests finally stepped down from the platform and went away, and the soldier bade the rest of us disperse, that one younger priest lingered on. He stood before the dangling chain—its links glowing red-hot—and looked sorrowfully down at the small remains of what that chain had held.

Everyone else, including my mother and uncle, made haste to vacate the square. But I too lingered, along with the priest, and approached him and addressed him in the language we both spoke.

"Tlamacázqui," I said, respectfully enough, but he raised a hand to object.

"Priest? I am not a priest," he said. "I can summon one of them, though, if you will tell me why you wish to talk to a priest."

"I wanted to talk to you," I said. "I do not speak the Spanish of the other priests."

"And I say again, I am no priest. Sometimes I am glad of that. I am only Alonso de Molina, notarius to my lord Bishop Zumárraga. And because I troubled to learn your language, I am also His Excellency's interpreter between your people and ours."

I had no idea what a notarius might be, but this one seemed amiable, and he had displayed some human compassion during the execution, which the others officiating had not. So now I addressed him by the honorific that means more than "friend"; it means "brother" or even "twin."

"Cuatl Alonso," I said. "My name is Tenamáxtli. I and some relatives just now came from far away to admire your City of Mexíco for the first time. We did not expect to find a—a public entertainment—provided for us visitors. I would ask only this. Despite your excellent translation, I could not—in my provincial ignorance—understand all the legal-sounding terms you spoke. Would you do me the favor of explaining, in simple words, what that man was accused of and why he was slain?"

The notarius regarded me for a moment, then asked, "You are not a Christian?"

"No, Cuatl Alonso. I have heard of Crixtanóyotl, but I know nothing of that religion."

"Well, Don Juan Damasceno was found guilty of—in simple words, as you request—having pretended to embrace our Christian faith, but all the time remaining an unbeliever. He refused to confess this, refused to renounce his old religion, and so he was sentenced to die."

"I begin to understand. Thank you, cuatl. A man has the choice of becoming a Christian or of being slain."

"Now, now. Not exactly, Tenamáxtli. But once he does become a Christian, he must remain one."

"Or your courts of law order him burned."

"Not exactly that, either," said the notarius, frowning. "The secular courts may adjudge various penalties for various offenses. And if they vote for capital punishment, there are several ways—by shot or sword or the headsman's ax or—"

"Or the most cruel way of all," I finished for him. "The burning."

"No." The notarius shook his head, now looking a trifle uncomfortable. "Only the ecclesiastical Courts of Inquisition can pronounce that sentence. Indeed, that is the sole means of execution the Church *can* specify. You see, the Church is bidden to punish sorcerers and witches and heretics like this late Juan Damasceno, but it is forbidden ever to shed blood. And clearly, burning does not shed blood. Thus it is laid down in canon law, how the Church must execute such persons. By flame . . . and by flame alone."

"I do see," I said. "Yes, laws must be obeyed."

"I am pleased to say that such executions are only infrequently required," said the notarius. "It has been fully three years since a Marrano was burned on this same spot, for having similarly flouted the faith."

"Excuse me, Cuatl Alonso," I said. "What is a Marrano?"

"A Jew. That is, a person formerly a Jew who has converted to Christianity. And Hernando Halevi de León seemed a sincere convert. He even ate pork. So he was given a royal grant of a profitable *encomienda* of his own, at Actópan, north of here. And he was allowed to marry the beautiful Isabel de Aguilar, the Christian daughter of one of the best Spanish families. But then it was discovered that the Marrano was forbidding Doña Isabel to attend Mass at those times of the month when she had her feminine bleeding. Obviously, de León was a false convert, still secretly observing the pernicious strictures of Judaism."

None of this made any sense to me at all, so I returned to the matter nearer to hand, saying, "This man today, cuatl— you did not appear very happy to see this one burned."

"Ayya, make no mistake," he hastened to say. "By all the beliefs and laws and rules of our Church, this Damasceno most certainly deserved his fate. I would not dispute that, not in the least. It is only that . . . well, over the years, I had grown rather fond of the old fellow." He looked down at the ashes one last time. "Now, Cuatl Tenamáxtli, you must excuse me. I have duties. But I shall be pleased to converse with you again, whenever you are in the city."

I had followed his glance down at the ashes with a glance of my own, and had instantly perceived that one other thing besides the metal chain and the upright metal post had survived the flames. It was the pendant I had earlier glimpsed, the light-reflecting object that the dead man had worn about his neck.

As the notarius Alonso turned away, I quickly stooped and picked up the thing, having to toss it from hand to hand for a while, because it was still scorching hot. It was a small disk of some kind of yellow crystal, and it was curiously but smoothly polished, flat on one side, curved inward on the other. The thing had hung from a leather thong, which of course was gone, and it had evidently been set in a circlet of copper, because traces of that still remained, though most had melted.

None of the soldiers patrolling the area or other Spanish persons with errands that took them strolling or hurrying across the vast open square paid any attention to my filching the yellow talisman, or whatever it was. So I tucked it inside my mantle and went in search of my mother and uncle.

I found them standing on a walk-bridge that spanned one of the city's remaining canals. My mother had been weeping—her face was still wet with tears—and her brother had a comforting arm clasped about her shoulders. He was also growling, more to himself than to her:

"Those other scouts gave good report of the white men's rule. They could not have witnessed anything like this. When we get back, I shall most certainly insist that we Aztéca keep our distance from these loathsome—" Then he broke off, to demand crossly of me, "What kept you, nephew? We might well have decided to start for home without you."

"I stayed to pass a few words with that Spaniard who speaks our tongue. He said he had been fond of old Juan Damasceno."

"That was not the man's real name," said my uncle, his voice gruff, and my mother again gave a small sob. I looked at her, in some surmise, and hesitantly said:

"Tene, you sighed and sobbed back there in the square. Of what earthly concern could that man have been to you?"

"I knew him," she said.

"How is that possible, dear Tene? You have never set foot in this city before."

"No," she said. "But he came once, long ago, to Aztlan."

"Even if not for the yellow eye," said my uncle, "Cuicáni and I would have recognized him."

"The yellow eye?" I repeated. "Do you mean this thing?" And I brought out the crystal I had taken from the ashes.

"*Ayyo!*" cried my mother, joyfully. "A memento of the dear departed."

"Why did you call it an eye?" I asked Uncle Mixtzin. "And if this man was not who they said, Juan Damasceno, who was he?"

"I have many times told you about him, nephew, but I suppose I neglected to mention the yellow eye. He was that Mexícatl stranger who came to Aztlan, and it turned out that he had the same name I bore, Tliléctic-Mixtli. It was he who inspired me to begin to learn the art of word-knowing. And he was the cause of my later bringing the Moon Stone to this city—and my being welcomed by the late Motecuzóma, and my being given by Motecuzóma all those warriors and artists and teachers and artisans who went with me back to Aztlan . . ."

"Of course I remember your telling all that, uncle. But what does the yellow eye have to do with anything?"

"Ayya, that poor Cuatl Mixtli had a disability, some weakness of his vision. The thing you hold—it is a disk of yellow topaz, specially and perhaps magically ground and polished. That other Mixtli used to hold it up to his eye whenever he wished to see anything really clearly. But that handicap never deterred his adventuring and exploring. And, if I may say so—in the case of our Aztlan, anyway—his doing good and great deeds.''

"You may indeed say so," I murmured, impressed. "And we ought indeed to mourn him. That other Mixtli gave us much.''

"To you, Tenamáxtli, even more," my mother said quietly. "That other Mixtli was your father.''

I stood stunned and speechless, unable for a long moment to do anything more than stare down at the topaz in my hand, the last remainder of the man who had sired me. At last, though feeling as if I were strangling, I managed to blurt out:

"Why are we all just standing here, then? Are we to do nothing—*am I, his son, to do nothing*—to wreak vengeance on these murderers for my father's gruesome death?''

III

AT THAT TIME, there were many people still alive in Aztlan who remembered the visit of that Mexícatl named Tliléctic-Mixtli, "Dark Cloud." Uncle Mixtzin remembered, of course, and so did his son Yeyac and his daughter Améy-atl, though they were only small children back then. (Their mother, my uncle's wife, who had been the first of all the Aztéca to speak to that visitor, died of a swamp fever not long after.) Another who remembered was old Canaútli, for he had engaged in many and long conversations with that Mixtli, telling him the history of our Aztlan. And Canaútli's granddaughter naturally remembered, because she, Cuicáni, had been the most hospitably welcoming Aztécatl of all, sharing her pallet with the visitor, and becoming pregnant by him, and eventually giving birth to his son, meaning me.

Those and many other Aztéca, too, remembered my uncle's later setting out for Tenochtítlan, with numerous men helping him roll the Moon Stone. And my uncle's triumphant return from that journey is vividly remembered by everyone in Aztlan who was alive at the time—including myself, because I was by then three or four years old. When he went away, he had been only Tliléctic-Mixtli, tlatocapíli of Aztlan. Tlatocapíli was not much of a title—it meant only a "tribal chief"—and his domain was only an insignificant village surrounded by swamps. He himself had on several occasions described Aztlan as "this crack in the buttocks of the world." But he returned to it bedecked in a wondrously beautiful feather headdress and feather mantle, accompanied by many attendants, wearing jewels on his fingers. He was now to be known by the new and noble name of Tliléctic-Mix*tzin*, "Lord Dark Cloud," and bearing the title of Uey-Tecútli, "Revered Governor."

Immediately on his arrival—since the entire adult population had convened to see and admire his new splendor—he addressed his people. I can repeat his words with fair accuracy, because Canaútli memorized them and told them to me when I was old enough to comprehend.

"Fellow Aztéca," said the Uey-Tecútli Mixtzin, loudly and with determination. "As of this day we resume our long-forgotten family connection with our cousins the Mexíca, the most powerful people of The One World. We are henceforth a colony of those Mexíca, and an important one, for the Mexíca have previously had no outpost or stronghold abutting the Western Sea this far north of Tenochtítlan. And a stronghold we shall be!"

He gestured at the considerable train of people who had accompanied him. "The men who came here with me did not come merely to make an impressive show of my return. They and their families will settle among us, will make their homes here, as once their forefathers did. Every one of these stalwarts—from warriors to word-knowers—was chosen for his skill and experience at various arts and trades. They will show you what this farthest bastion of Tenochtítlan can be— a Tenochtítlan in miniature—strong, civilized, cultured, prosperous, and proud."

His voice got even louder, commanding, "And you will hear and heed and obey these teachers. No longer will we of Aztlan be torpid and uncouth and ignorant, and content to be so. From this day on, every man, woman and child of you will learn and work and strive, until we are in every way the equals of our admirable Mexíca cousins."

I remember only vaguely what Aztlan was like in those days. Consider, I was then a child. And a child neither esteems nor disprizes his hometown, does not perceive it as either grand or squalid; it is what he has always known and been accustomed to. But, whether from fragments of memory or from what I was told in later years, I can fairly well describe the Place of Snowy Egrets as it was when that other Tliléctic-Mixtli, the explorer, came upon it.

For one thing, the "palace" in which my tlatocapíli uncle and his two children lived—as did I and my mother, for she became her brother's housekeeper after his wife died—was of numerous rooms but only one story. It was built of wood and reeds and palm leaves, made sturdier and "ornamented" to some extent by having been covered all over with a plaster made from crushed seashells. The rest of Aztlan's buildings of residence and commerce were, if it can be believed, of even flimsier and less handsome construction.

The entire city was set upon an oval-shaped island, perched in the middle of a sizable lake. That lake's farther edges had no real borders or banks. Its brackish, undrinkable waters simply shallowed away in the distance, all around, merging into oozy swampland that, to the west, merged with the sea. Those swamps exuded dank night mists and pestiferous insects and perhaps evil spirits. My aunt was only one of many people who died every year from a consuming fever, and our physicians asserted that the fever was somehow inflicted on us by the swamps.

Notwithstanding Aztlan's backwardness in many respects, we Aztéca at least ate well. Beyond the marshlands was the Western Sea, and from it our fishermen netted or hooked or gaffed or pried from its bottom not only the common and abundant fishes—rays, swordfish, flatfish, liza, crabs, squid—but also tasty delicacies: oysters, cockles, abalone, turtles and turtle eggs, shrimp and sea crayfish. Sometimes, after much violent and prolonged struggling, usually causing the crippling or drowning of one or more fishermen, they would succeed in landing a yeyemíchi. That is a gigantic gray fish—

some can be as big as any palace—and well worth catching. We townsfolk would absolutely gorge ourselves on the innumerable delicious fillets cut from a single one of those immense fish. In that sea, there were also pearl oysters, but we refrained from harvesting them ourselves, for a reason I will tell later.

As for vegetables, besides the numerous edible seaweeds, we had also a variety of swamp-growing greens. And mushrooms could be found sprouting everywhere—frequently even, uninvited, on our houses' ever-damp earthen floors. The only greenery that we actually worked to cultivate was picíetl, dried for smoking. From the meat of coconuts our sweets were confected, and the coconut milk, when fermented, became a drink far more intoxicating than the octli so popular everywhere else in The One World. Another kind of palm tree gave us the coyacapúli fruits, and another palm's inner pulp was dried and ground into a palatable flour. Yet another palm provided us with fiber for weaving into cloth, while shark's skin makes the finest, most durable leather one could want. The pelts of sea otters covered our soft sleeping pallets and made fur cloaks for those who traveled into the high, cold mountains inland. From both coconuts and fish we extracted the oils that lighted our lamps. (I will grant that for any newcomer not inured to the smells of those oils burning, they must have been overpoweringly rank.)

As the Mexíca masters of diverse crafts walked about Aztlan on their first tour of inspection, to see what they might contribute to the city's improvement, they must have had difficulty in containing their laughs or sneers. They surely found our conception of a "palace" ludicrous enough. And our island's one and only temple—dedicated to Coyolxaúqui, the moon goddess, the deity whom in those days we worshiped almost exclusively—was no more elegantly built than was the palace, except for having some conch, whelk, strombus and other shells inset in the plaster around its doorway.

Anyway, the craftsmen were not discouraged by what they saw. They immediately set to work, first finding a place—a

comparatively unsoggy hummock some way around the lake
from Aztlan—on which to put temporary houses for themselves and their families. Their womenfolk did most of the
house building, using what was at hand: reeds and palm
leaves and mud daubing. Meanwhile, the men went inland,
eastward, having to go no great distance before they were in
the mountains. There they felled oak and pine trees, and
manhandled the trunks down to flatter riverside land, where
they split and burned and adzed them into acáltin, far bigger
than any of our fishing craft, big enough to freight ponderous
burdens. Those burdens also came from the mountains, for
some of the men were experienced quarriers, who searched
for and found limestone deposits, and dug deep into them,
and broke the stone into great chunks and slabs. Those they
roughly squared and evened on the site, then loaded them
into the acáltin, which brought them down a river to the sea,
thence along the coast to the inlet leading to our lake.

The Mexíca masons smoothed and polished and used the
first-brought stone to erect a new palace, as was only proper,
for my Uncle Mixtzin. When completed, it might not have
rivaled any of the palaces in Tenochtítlan. For our city,
though, it was an edifice to marvel at. Two stories high, and
with a roof comb making it twice that tall, it contained so
many rooms—including an imposing throne room for the
Uey-Tecútli—that even Yeyac, Améyatl and I had each a
separate sleeping room. That was something almost unheard
of then, in Aztlan, for any person, let alone three children
aged twelve, nine and five, respectively. Before any of us
moved in, however, a swarm of additional workers did—
carpenters, sculptors, painters, weaver-women—to decorate
every room with statuettes and murals and wall hangings and
the like.

Other Mexíca, at the same time, were cleansing and re-
channeling the waters in and around Aztlan. They dredged
the old muck and garbage from the canals that have always
crisscrossed the island, and lined those with stone. They
drained the swamps around the lake, by digging new canals

that drew off the old water and let in new from streams farther inland. The lake remained brackish, being of commingled fresh water and seawater, but it no longer stood stagnant, and the marshes began to dry into solid land. The result was an immediate diminution of the noxious night mists and the former troublesome multitudes of insects and—proving that our physicians had been right—the swamp spirits thereafter vexed only one or two persons each year with their malign fevers.

In the meantime, the masons went straight from building the palace to building a stone temple for our city's patron goddess, Coyolxaúqui, a temple that put the old one to shame. It was so very well designed and graceful that it made Mixtzin grumble:

"I wish now that I had not trundled to Tenochtítlan the stone depicting the goddess—now that she has a temple befitting her serene beauty and goodness."

"You are being foolish," said my mother. "Had you not done that, we would not now have the temple. Or any of the other benefactions brought by that gift to Motecuzóma."

My uncle grumbled some more—he did not like having his convictions disputed—but had to concede that his sister was right.

Next, the masons erected a tlamanacáli, in a manner that we all thought most ingenious, practical and interesting to watch. While the stoneworkers laid inward-slanting slabs, making a mere shell of a pyramid, ordinary laborers brought tumplined loads of earth, stones, pebbles, driftwood, just about every kind of trash imaginable, and dumped that in to fill the stone shell and tamped it firmly down inside. So eventually there arose a perfect tapered pyramid that seemed to be of solid shining limestone.

It was certainly substantial enough to hold high aloft the two small temples that crowned it—one dedicated to Huitzilopóchtli, the other to the rain god Tlaloc—and to support the stairway that led up the height of its front side, and the innumerable priests, worshipers, dignitaries and sacrificial victims who would tread those stairs in the ensuing years. I do not claim that our tlamanacáli was as awesome as the famous Great Pyramid in Tenochtítlan—because, of course, I never saw that one—but ours was surely the most magnificent structure standing anywhere north of the Mexíca lands.

Next, the masons erected stone temples to other gods and goddesses of the Mexíca—to all of them, I suppose, though some of the lesser deities had to group in threes or fours to share a single temple. Among the many, many Mexíca who had come north with my uncle were priests of all those gods. During the early years, they worked alongside the builders, and worked just as hard. Then, after they all had temples, the priests also devoted time—besides attending to their more spiritual duties—to teaching in our schools, which were the next-constructed buildings. And, after those, the Mexíca turned to the erection of less important structures—a granary and workshops and storehouses and an armory and other such necessities of civilization. And finally they set about bringing lumber from the mountain forests and building stout wooden houses for themselves as well as every Aztéca family that wanted one, which included everybody except a few malcontent and misanthropic hermits who preferred the old ways of life.

When I say that "the Mexíca" accomplished this or that, you must realize that I do not mean they did it unaided. Every group of quarriers, masons, carpenters, whatever, conscripted a whole team of our own men (and, for light labor, women and even children) to assist in those projects. The Mexíca showed the Aztéca how to do whatever was required, and supervised the doing of it, and continued to teach, chide, correct mistakes, reprove and approve until, after a while, the Aztéca could do a good many new things on their own. I myself, well before my naming-day, was carrying light loads, fetching tools, dispensing food and water to the workers. Women and girls were learning to weave and sew with new materials—cotton, metl cloth and thread, egret feathers— much finer than the palm fibers they had formerly used.

When our men came to the end of each workday, the Mexíca supervisors did not just let them go home to lie around
and get drunk on their fermented coconut potation. No, the
overseers turned our men over to the Mexíca warriors. Those,
too, might already have put in a full day of hard work, but
they were indefatigable. They put our men to learning drills
and parading and other military basics, then to the use—
eventually the mastery—of the maquáhuitl obsidian sword,
the bow and arrow, the spear, and then to learning various
battlefield tactics and maneuvers. Women and girls were exempted from this training; anyway, not many of them were
inclined, as their men had been, to waste their free time in
drinking and indolence. Boys, myself included, would have
been overjoyed to partake of the military training, but were
not allowed until they were of age to wear the loincloth.

Mind you, none of this total remaking of Aztlan and re-
molding of its people took place all of a sudden, as I may
have made it sound. I repeat, I was a mere child when it all
began. So the clearing away of the old Aztlan and the raising
up of the new seemed—to me—to keep pace with my own
growing up, growing stronger, growing in maturity and sa-
pience. Hence, to me, what happened to my hometown was
equally imperceptible and unremarkable. It is only now, in
retrospect, that I can recall in not too many words all the
very many trials and errors and labors and sweats and years
that went into the civilizing of Aztlan. And I have not bothered to recount the almost-as-many setbacks, frustrations and
failed attempts that were likewise involved in the process.
But the endeavors did succeed, as Uncle Mixtzin had commanded, and on my naming-day, just those few years after
the coming of the Mexíca, there were already built and waiting the telpochcáltin schools for me to start attending.

In the mornings, I and the other boys my age—plus a
goodly number of older boys who had never had any schooling in their childhood—went to The House of Building
Strength. There, under the tutelage of a Mexícatl warrior assigned as Master of Athletics, we performed physical exer-

cises, and learned to play the exceedingly complicated ritual ball game called tlachtli, and eventually were taught elementary hand-to-hand combat. However, our swords and arrows and spears bore no obsidian blades or points, but merely tufts of feathers wetted with red dye to simulate blood marks where we struck our opponents.

In the afternoons, I and those same boys—and girls of the same ages—attended The House of Learning Manners. There an assigned teacher-priest taught us hygiene and cleanliness (which quite a few lower-class children knew nothing about), and the singing of ritual songs, and the dancing of ceremonial dances, and the playing of a few musical instruments—the variously sized and tuned drums, the four-holed flute, the warbling jug.

In order to perform all the ceremonies and rituals properly, we had to be able to follow the tunes and beats and movements and gestures exactly as they had been done since olden times. To make sure of that, the priest passed around among us a roughly pictured page of instructions. Thus we came to grasp at least the rudiments of word-knowing. And when the children went home from school, they taught what they had learned of it to their elders—because both Mixtzin and the priests encouraged that passing-along of knowledge, at least to the grown-up males. Females, like slaves, were not expected ever to have any need of word-knowing. My own mother, though of the highest noble rank attainable in Aztlan, never learned to read or write.

Uncle Mixtzin had learned, beginning back when he was just a village tlatocapíli, and he went on learning all his life long. His education in literacy was begun under the instruction of that long-ago Mexícatl visitor, the other Mixtli. Then, during my uncle's return journey from Tenochtítlan, with all those other Mexíca in his train, at every night's camp he would sit down with a teacher-priest for further instruction. And, from their first arrival in Aztlan, he had kept by him that same priest for his private tutoring. So, by the time I started my schooling, he was already able to send word-picture reports to Motecuzóma regarding Aztlan's progress. And more: he even entertained himself by writing poems— the kind of poems that we who knew him would have expected him to write—cynical musings on the imperfectibility of human beings, the world and life in general. He used to read them to us, and I remember one in particular:

> *Forgive?*
> *Never forgive,*
> *But pretend to forgive.*
> *Say amiably that you forgive.*
> *Convince that you have forgiven.*
> *Thus, devastating is the effect*
> *When at last you lunge*
> *And reach for the throat.*

Even in the lower schools, we students were taught a bit of the history of The One World, and young though I was, I could not help noticing that some of the things we were told were considerably at variance with a few tales that my great-grandfather, Aztlan's Rememberer of History, had occasionally confided to our family circle. For example, from what the Mexícatl teacher-priest taught, one might suppose that the whole nation of Mexíca people had simply sprung up one day from the earth of the island of Tenochtítlan, all of them full-grown, in full strength and vigor, fully educated, civilized, and cultured. That did not accord with what I and my cousins had heard from old Canaútli, so Yeyac, Améyatl, and I went to him and asked for elucidation.

He laughed and said tolerantly, "*Ayya,* the Mexíca are a boastful people. Some of them do not hesitate to contort any uncomfortable facts to fit their haughty image of themselves."

I said, "When Uncle Mixtzin brought them here, he spoke of them as 'our cousins,' and mentioned some kind of 'long-forgotten family connection.' "

"I imagine," said the Rememberer, "that most of the

Mexíca would have preferred not to hear of that connection. But it was one fact that could not be avoided or obscured, not after your—not after that other Mixtli stumbled upon this place and then took the word of our existence back to Motecuzóma. You see, that other Mixtli asked me, as you three have just done, for the true history of the Aztéca and their relation to the Mexíca, and he believed what I told him."

"We will believe you, too," said Yeyac. "Tell us."

"On one condition," he said. "Do not use what you learn from me to correct or contradict your teacher-priest. The Mexíca are nowadays being very good to us. It would be wicked of you children to impugn whatever silly but harmless delusions it pleases them to harbor."

Each of us three said, "I will not. I promise."

"Know then, young Yeyac-Chichiquíli, young Patzcatl-Améyatl, young Téotl-Tenamáxtli. In a time long ago, long sheaves of years ago—but a time known and recounted ever since, from each Rememberer to his successor—Aztlan was not just a small seaside city. It was the capital of a territory stretching well up into the mountains. We lived simply—the folk of today would say we lived primitively—but we fared well enough, and seldom suffered the least hardship. That was thanks to our moon goddess Coyolxaúqui, who saw to it that the dark sea's tides and the mountains' dark fastnesses provided bountifully for us."

Améyatl said, "And you once told us that we Aztéca worshiped no other gods."

"Not even those others as beneficent as Coyolxaúqui. Tlaloc, to name one, the rain god. For look about you, girl." He laughed again. "What need had we to pray that Tlaloc give us water? No, we were quite content with things as they were. That does not mean we were hapless weaklings. *Ayyo*, we would fiercely defend our borders when some envious other nation might try to encroach. But otherwise we were a peaceable people. Even when we made sacrificial offerings to Coyolxaúqui, we never chose a maiden to slay, or even a captured enemy. On her altar we offered only small creatures of the sea and of the night. Perhaps a strombus of perfectly shaped and unblemished shell . . . or one of the big-winged, soft-green moon moths . . .''

He paused for a bit, apparently contemplating those good old days, long before even *his* great-grandfather was born. So I gently prompted him:

"Until there came the woman . . .''

"Yes. A woman, of all things. And a woman of the Yaki, that most savage and vicious of all peoples. One of our hunting parties came upon her, wandering aimlessly, high in our mountains, alone, infinitely far from the Yaki desert lands. And those men fed and clothed her and brought her here to Aztlan. But, *ayya ouíya*, she was a bitter woman. When our ancestors thus befriended her, she repaid them by turning Aztéca friends against friends, families against families, brothers against brothers.''

Yeyac asked, "Had she a name?''

"An ugly-sounding Yaki name, yes, G'nda Ké. And, what she did—she began by deriding our simple ways and our reverence for the kindly goddess Coyolxaúqui. Why, she asked, did we not instead revere the war god, Huitzilopóchtli? He, she said, would lead us to victory in war, to conquer other nations, to take prisoners to sacrifice to the god, who would thus be persuaded to lead us to other conquests, until we ruled all of The One World.''

"But why,'' asked Améyatl, "would she have sought to foment such alien passions and warlike ambitions among our peaceable people? What profit to her?''

"You will not be flattered to hear this, great-granddaughter. Most of the earlier Rememberers simply attributed it to the natural contrariness of all women.''

Améyatl only wrinkled her pretty nose at him, so Canaútli grinned toothlessly and went on:

"You should be glad to learn, then, that I hold a slightly different theory. It is a known fact that the Yaki men are as inhumanly cruel to their own women as they are to every non-Yaki human being alive. It is my belief that that one woman was obsessed with having every man treated as she must have been treated by those of her own nation. To set all the men of The One World to butchering one another in war, and bloodily sacrificing one another to the lip-smacking satisfaction of this or that god.''

''As almost every community in The One World does now,'' said Yeyac. ''And as the Mexíca priests and warriors would teach us to do. Except that we are on good terms with all our neighbors. We would have to march far beyond the mountains to wage a battle or take a prisoner for sacrifice. Nevertheless, the despicable G'nda Ké did indeed succeed.''

''Well, she very nearly did not,'' said Canaútli. ''She convinced hundreds of Aztlan's people to emulate her in worshiping the bloody-handed god Huitzilopóchtli. But other hundreds sensibly refused to be converted. In time, she had split the Aztéca into two factions so inimical—as I said, even brothers against brothers—that she and her followers crept away to take up residence in seven caverns in the mountains. There they armed themselves, and practiced at the skills of war, and awaited the Yaki woman's command to go forth and commence conquering other peoples.''

''And surely,'' said softhearted Améyatl, ''the first to suffer would have been the still-peaceable dissidents of Aztlan.''

''Most assuredly. However. However, by good fortune, Aztlan's tlatocapíli of the time was about as irascible and fractious and intolerant of fools as is your own father Mixtzin. He and his loyal city guard went to the mountains and surrounded the misbelievers and slew many of them. And to the survivors he said, 'Take your contemptible new god and your families and begone. Or be slain to the last man, last woman, last child, last infant in the womb.' ''

''And they went,'' I said.

''They did. After sheaves of years of wandering, and new generations of them being born, they came at last to another island in another lake, where they espied the symbol of their war god—an eagle perched on a nopáli cactus—so there they settled. They called the island Tenochtítlan, 'Place of the Tenoch,' which was, in some forgotten local dialect, the word for the nopáli cactus. And, for what reason I have never troubled to inquire, they renamed themselves the Mexíca. And in the course of many more years they thrived, they fought and overwhelmed their neighbors, and then nations farther afield.'' Canaútli shrugged his bony old shoulders, resignedly. ''Now, for good or ill, Tenamáxtli, through the efforts of your uncle and that other Mexícatl, also named Mixtli—we are reconciled again. We shall see what comes of it. And now I tire of remembering. Go, children, and leave me.''

We started away, but I turned back to ask, ''That Yaki woman—G'nda Ké—whatever became of her?''

''When the tlatocapíli stormed the seven caves, she was among the first slain. But she was known to have coupled with several of her male followers. So there is no doubt that her blood still runs in the veins of many Mexíca families. Perhaps in all of them. That would account for their still being as warlike and sanguinary as she was.''

I will never know why Canaútli refrained from telling me right then: that I *myself* very likely contained at least a drop of that Yaki woman's blood, that I could certainly claim to be Aztlan's foremost example of an Aztéca-Mexíca ''family connection'' since I had been born of an Aztécatl mother and sired by that Mexícatl Mixtli. Maybe the old man hesitated because he deemed it his granddaughter's place to disclose or withhold that family secret.

And I really do not know, either, why she did withhold it. When I was a child, the population of Aztlan was so small and close-knit that my illegitimacy had to have been widely known. An ordinary woman of the macehuáli class would have been severely censured and probably chastised if she had borne a bastard. But Cuicáni, being sister to the then tlatocapíli and later the Uey-Tecútli, hardly had to fear gossip and scandal. Still, she kept me in ignorance of my paternity until that horrific day in the City of Mexíco. I can only suspect that she must have hoped, during all the intervening years, that that other Mixtli would someday return to Aztlan, and to her embrace, and that he would rejoice in finding that the two of them had a son.

To be honest, I do not even know why I never, in childhood or later, evinced any inquisitiveness about my parentage. Well, Yeyac and Améyatl had a father but no mother; I had a mother but no father. I must have reasoned that a situation so self-evident could only be normal and commonplace. Why ponder on it?

My mother would occasionally make a motherly proud remark—"I can see, Tenamáxtli, that you will grow up to be a handsome man, strong of features, just like your father." Or, "You are getting very tall for your age, my son. Well, so was your father much taller than most other men." But I paid little heed to such comments; every mother fondly believes that her hatchling will prove an eagle.

Of course, if anyone at all had ever voiced an insinuating hint, I would have been prodded to ask questions about that absent father. But I was the nephew and the son of the lord and the lady occupying Aztlan's palace; no one with good sense would ever have risked Mixtzin's displeasure. Neither was I ever taunted by playmates nor neighbor children. And, at home, Yeyac and Améyatl and I lived together in amity and harmony, more like half brothers and sister than like cousins. Or so we did, I should say, until a certain day.

IV

Y EYAC WAS THEN fourteen years old and I was seven, newly named and newly attending school. We were living in the splendid new palace by then, each of us young ones glorying in having his or her own sleeping room, and being childishly jealous of our separate privacies. So I was vastly surprised when one day, about twilight, Yeyac stepped into my room, uninvited and without asking permission. It happened that he and I were alone in the building—except for any servants who may have been working in the kitchen or elsewhere downstairs—because our elders, Mixtzin and Cuicáni, had gone to the city's central square to watch Améyatl participate in a public dance being performed by all the girls of The House of Learning Manners.

What mainly surprised me was that Yeyac entered, quietly, while my back was turned to the room door, so I did not even know he was there until his hand reached under my mantle, between my legs, and—as if weighing them—gently *bounced* my tepúli and olóltin. As startled as if a claw-clacking crab had got under my mantle, I gave a prodigious jump in the air. Then I whirled and stared at Yeyac, bewildered and disbelieving. My cousin had not only breached my privacy, he had handled my private *parts*.

"Ayya, touchy, *touchy!*" he said, half smirking. "Still the little boy, eh?"

I spluttered, "I was not aware . . . I did not hear . . ."

"Do not look so indignant, cousin. I was but comparing."

"Doing what?" I said, mystified.

"I daresay mine must have been as puny as yours when I was your age. How would you like, small cousin, to have what I have got now?"

He raised his mantle, unloosed his máxtlatl loincloth, and there emerged—sprang forth, actually—a tepúli like none I had ever seen before. Not that I had seen many, only those in evidence when I and my playmates frolicked naked in the lake. Yeyac's was much longer, thicker, erect, engorged and almost glowing red at its bulbous tip. Well, his full name was Yeyac-Chichiquíli, I reminded myself—Long Arrow— so perhaps the name-bestowing old seer had been truly pre- scient in this case. But Yeyac's tepúli looked so swollen and angry that I asked, sympathetically:

"Is it sore?

He laughed a loud laugh. "Only hungry," he said. "This is the way a man's is *supposed* to be, Tenamáxtli. The big- ger, the better. Do not you wish you possessed the like?"

"Well," I said hesitantly, "I expect I will. When I am of age. Like you."

"Ah, but you should start exercising it now, cousin, be- cause it improves and enlarges, the more it is employed. That way, you can be *sure* to have an impressive organ when you are man-grown."

"Employ it how?"

"I will show you," he said. "Take mine in your grasp." And he took my hand and put it there, but I yanked it back again, saying severely:

"You have heard the priest warn that we should not play with those parts of ourselves. You are in the same cleanliness class as I at The Learning Manners House."

(Yeyac was one of those older boys who had had to start, along with us really young ones, at the most elementary school level. And now, though he had worn the máxtlatl for a year or more, he had not yet qualified to go on to a calmécac.)

"Manners!" he snorted scornfully. "You really are an innocent. The priests warn us against pleasuring ourselves, only because they hope that sometime we will pleasure them."

"Pleasure?" I said, more befuddled than ever.

"Of course the tepúli is for pleasure, imbecile! Did you think it was only to make water with?"

"That is all mine has ever done," I said.

Yeyac said impatiently, "I *told* you—I will show you how to have pleasure with it. Watch. Take mine in your hand and do this to it." He was briskly rubbing his own clasped hand up and down the length of his tepúli. Now he let go of it, hugged me to him and closed *my* hand on it—though mine only barely encircled the girth of it.

I imitated, as well as I could, what he had been doing. He closed his eyes, and his face got almost as red as his tepúli bulb, and his breathing became quick and shallow. After a while of nothing else happening, I said, "This is very boring."

"And you are very awkward," he said, his voice quavery. "Tighter, boy! And faster! And do not interrupt my concentration."

After another while I said, "This is *extremely* boring. And how is my doing this supposed to benefit mine?"

"*Pochéoa!*" he growled, which is a mildly dirty word. "All right. We will exercise them both at once." He let me take my hand away, but with his own resumed the stroking of his tepúli. "Lie down here on your pallet. Lift up your mantle."

I complied, and he lay down beside me, but opposite— that is, with his head near my crotch and my head near his.

"Now," he said, still vigorously stroking himself. "Take mine in your mouth—like this." And, to my amazement and incredulity, he did just that with my small thing. But I said vehemently:

"I most certainly will not. I know your japeries, Yeyac. You will make water in my mouth."

He made a noise like "arrgh!" in a rage of frustration, but without releasing my tepúli from his mouth, or breaking the rhythm of his hand stroking his own, close before my face. For a moment, I feared that he might be angry enough to bite my thing right off. But all he did was keep his lips tight about it, and suck at it and wiggle his tongue all over it. I confess that I felt sensations that were not at all unpleasant. It even seemed that he might be right—that my small organ was actually lengthening under these ministrations. But it did not stiffen like his, it merely let itself be played with, and that did not go on for long enough for me to get bored again. Because suddenly Yeyac's whole body convulsed, and he widened his mouth to gobble into it also my sac of olóltin, and sucked hard at all those parts of mine. Then his tepúli gushed a stream of white matter, liquid but thick, like coconut-milk syrup, that splashed all over my head.

Now it was I who bellowed "arrgh!"—in disgust—and frantically wiped at the stickiness befouling my hair, eyebrows, lashes and cheeks. Yeyac rolled away from me and, when he could cease his gasping and catch his breath, said, "*Ayya*, do not go on behaving like a timid child. That is only omícetl. It is the spurting of the omícetl that gives such sublime pleasure. Also, omícetl is what creates babies."

"I do not want any babies!" I croaked, wiping even more desperately.

"Fool of a cousin! The omícetl does that only to females. Exchanged between men it is an expression of—of deep affection and mutual passion."

"I have no affection for you, Yeyac, not any more."

"Come, now," he said, wheedlingly. "In time you will learn to like our playing together. You will *yearn* for it."

"No. The priests are right to forbid such play. And Uncle

Mixtzin seldom agrees with any priest, but I wager he would,
if I told him about this."

"Ayya—touchy, touchy," Yeyac said again, but not jo-
vially this time.

"No fear. I will not tell. You are my cousin, and I would
not see you beaten. But you are nevermore to touch my parts
or show me yours. Do your exercises elsewhere. Now kiss
the earth to that."

Looking disappointed and disgruntled, he slowly bent
down to touch a finger to the stone floor and then to his lips,
the formal gesture signifying that I-swear-to-it.

And he kept that promise. Not ever again did he try to
fondle me or even let me see him except when he was fully
clothed. He evidently found other boys who were not, like
me, averse to learning what he taught, because when the
Mexícatl warrior in charge of our House of Building Strength
assigned students to the tedious duty of standing guard in
remote places, I noticed that Yeyac and three or four boys
of varying ages were always eager to step forward. And
Yeyac may have been right in what he had said about the
priests. There was one who, whenever he wanted something
carried to his room, would always ask Yeyac to do it, and
then neither of them would be seen again for a long while.

But I did not hold that against Yeyac, or hold any lingering
resentment about his behavior with me. True, relations between the two of us were strained for some time, but they
gradually relaxed to mere coolness and perhaps overpolite
politeness. Eventually I, at least, quite forgot the episode—
until much, much later, when something occurred to make
me remember it. And meanwhile, my tepúli grew on its own,
without requiring any outside assistance, as the years passed.

Over those years, we Aztéca got accustomed to the crowded
pantheon of gods the Mexíca had brought with them and
raised temples to. Our people began to join in the rites for
this or that god—at first, I think, just to show courtesy and
respect to the Mexíca now residing among us. But, in time,

our Aztéca seem to have found that they were deriving something—security? uplift? solace? I do not know—from sharing in the worship of those gods, even some of the ones they
might otherwise have found repellent, such as the war god
Huitzilopóchtli and the frog-faced water goddess Chalchi-
huítlicué. Nubile girls prayed to Xochiquétzal, the Mexíca's
goddess of love and flowers, that they might snare a desirable
young man and make a good marriage. Our fishermen, before
setting out to sea, besides uttering their usual prayers to Coyolxaúqui for a bounteous catch, prayed also that Ehécatl, the
Mexíca's wind god, would not raise a gale against them.

No person was expected, as are Christians, to confine his
or her devotion to any particular god. Nor were people punished, as Christians are, if they switched their allegiance at
whim from one deity to another, or impartially among many
of them. Most of our folk still reserved their truest adoration
for our longtime patron goddess. But they saw no harm in
giving some, too, to the Mexíca deities—partly because
those newcome gods and goddesses provided them with so
many new holidays and impressive ceremonies and causes
for song and dance. The people were not even much deterred
by the fact that many of those deities demanded compensa-
tion in the form of human hearts and blood.

We never, during those years, engaged in any wars to provide us with foreign prisoners for sacrifice. But, surprisingly,
there was never any lack of persons—Aztéca as well as
Mexíca—to *volunteer* to die and thereby nourish and please
the gods. Those were the people convinced by the priests
that if they simply lolled about and waited to die of old age
or in some other ordinary way, they risked an instant plunge
into the depths of Míctlan, the Dark Place, there to suffer an
eternal afterlife devoid of delight, diversion, sensation, even
misery, an afterlife of absolute nothingness. To the contrary,
said the priests, anyone undergoing the Flowery Death, so-
called, would instantly be wafted to the lofty realm of the
sun god, Tonatíu, there to enjoy a blissful and ever-lasting
afterlife.

That is why numerous slaves offered themselves to the priests, to be sacrificed to any god—the slaves cared not which—believing they would thus be improving their lot. But flagrant gullibility was not limited to the slaves. A young male *freeman* would volunteer to be slain, after which his body would be flayed of its entire skin, and that would be donned by a priest to imitate and honor Xipe Totec, the god of seedtime. A freeborn young maiden would volunteer to have her heart torn out, to represent the mother-goddess Teteoínan's dying while giving birth to Centéotl, the maize god. Parents even volunteered their infant children to be suffocated in sacrifice to Tlaloc, the rain god.

Myself, I never felt the least inclination to self-immolation. No doubt influenced by my irreverent Uncle Mixtzin, I never cared much for any god, and cared even less for priests. Those dedicated to the Mexíca's new-brought deities, I found especially detestable, because, as a mark of their high calling, they performed various mutilations on their own bodies and, worse, never washed themselves or their garments. For some while after their arrival in Aztlan, they had worn rough work clothes and, like every other worker, cleaned themselves after a day of hard labor. But later, when they were excused from the work teams and donned their priestly gowns, they never so much as took a dip in the lake—let alone enjoyed a really good purification in a steam hut—and very soon were repulsively filthy, the air around them almost visibly mephitic. If I had ever taken the trouble to meditate on my cousin Yeyac's curious sexual tastes, I probably would have done no more than wonder, with a shudder, how he could possibly bring himself to embrace such an abhorrent thing as a priest.

However, as I have said, it was a long time—fully five years—before I again had occasion to think, and then only briefly, of Yeyac's having made advances to me. I was now twelve years old, my voice just beginning to change, alternating between rumble and squeak, and I was looking forward to putting on my own loincloth of manhood before long. And what happened, absurdly enough, happened just as it had the other time.

As I keep remarking, the gods derive their merriest entertainment from putting us mortals in situations that could *seem* to be mere coincidence. I was in my room at the palace, my back to the door, when again a hand stole under my mantle, gave my genitals an affectionate squeeze—and propelled me to another prodigious leap.

"*Yya ouíya*, not again!" I squealed, as I went up in the air and came down again, and spun to face my molester.

"Again?" she said, herself surprised.

It was my other cousin, Améyatl. If I have not earlier mentioned that she was beautiful, well, she was. At sixteen, she was more fair of face and form than any other girl or woman I had seen in all of Aztlan, and, at that age, probably at her veriest pinnacle of beauty.

"That was most unseemly," I chided her, my voice now coming out as a growl. "Why would you do such a thing?"

She said forthrightly, "I hoped to tempt you."

"Tempt me?" I piped, like a wee child. "To what?"

"To prepare for the day when you will wear the maxtlatl. Would you not like to learn, before that day, how to perform like a man?"

"Perform?" I grunted. "Perform what?"

"The private act that a man and woman do together. I confess, I should very much like to learn. I thought we might teach one another."

"But—why me?" I said in a thin peep.

She smiled mischievously. "Because, like me, you have not yet learned. But that one touch I gave you, just now, tells me that you are full-grown and able. So am I. I shall undress and you will see."

"I *have* seen you undressed. We have bathed together. Sat in the steam hut together."

She waved that away. "When we were sexless children. Since I donned my own undergarment of womanhood, you have not seen me naked. You will find me much different

now, both here . . . and here. You can touch, too, and so will
I, and we will go on to do whatever we are next inclined to
do.''

Now, I and my childhood companions had often solemnly
discussed, as I imagine even Christian youngsters do, the
differences between male and female bodies, and what we
believed men and women did in private, and how it was
done, and with which on top, and with what variations, and
how long did the act take, and how often could it be done
in succession. Each of us, first in secret, later in competitive
gatherings, found out how to verify that our tepúltin were
reliably erectile and that our olóltin eggs contained manly
omícetl in a quantity and projectile capability not inferior to
that of our fellows.

Also, whenever we were put to assist at one of the city's
never-finished works of improvement, we listened with avid-
ity to the adult workers' bawdy banter, and their reminiscences of their adventures with women, almost certainly
exaggerated in the telling. So I, and every other boy I knew,
possessed only vague and secondhand information, a good
deal of it *mis*information, ranging from the implausible to
the anatomically impossible. If we boys came to any con-
sensus at all in our discussions, it was simply that we were
more than eager to delve into those mysteries ourselves.

And here was I, being offered the body of the loveliest
maiden in Aztlan—not a cheap and common maátitl or even
an expensive auyaními, but a veritable princess. (As the
daughter of the Uey-Tecútli, she was entitled to be addressed—and was by the common folk—as Améyatzin.)
Any of my usual companions would have snatched at the
offer without demur, but with glee and gratitude and fulsome
thanks to all the gods that be.

But remember, even though she was four years my senior,
I had grown up with this princess. I had known her when
she was just a grubby girl-child, her nose often running, her
knobby knees frequently skinned, and sometimes her picking
at the scabs on them, and her occasional crying fits and tem-

per tantrums and being a general nuisance, and, later, her spiteful older-sister teasing and tormenting of me. She had, of course, become more ladylike since those days, but I still regarded her as a big sister. So, to the same degree that she held no mystery for me, she held no compelling attraction. I could not look at her, as I could at just about any other pretty woman I encountered, and think: *Now . . . what if we two . . . ?*

Nevertheless, this was an opportunity I could hardly—as we say—pick my teeth at. Even if coupling with this cousin should prove as boring, even distasteful, as my long-ago brief experience with her brother, I *was* being offered the chance to explore an adult female body and all its secret places, and to find out what no one yet had credibly explained to me: how the act of coupling was actually *done*. Still, to my credit, I put up an argument, however feebly:

"Why me? Why not Yeyac? He is older than us both. He should be able to teach you more than—"

"*Ayya!*" she said with a grimace. "Surely you must have realized that my brother is a cuilóntli. That he and his lovers indulge only in cuilónyotl."

Yes, I did know that, and by now I had learned the words for that sort of man and that sort of indulgence, but I was fairly astonished that a cloistered maiden would know such words. I was even more astonished that a cloistered maiden could, as Améyatl was now doing, so casually take off her blouse, leaving herself bare to the waist. But suddenly her expression of pleased expectancy turned to one of dismay, and she cried:

"Is that what you meant when you said 'again'? That you and Yeyac—? Ayya, cousin, are you a cuilóntli, *too*?"

I could not reply on the instant, for I was dumbstruck, gaping at her divinely round, smooth, inviting breasts, each tipped with a russet bud that I was sure would taste like flower nectar. Améyatl was right; she was different now. She had used to be as flat there as I was, and her nipples as indistinct as mine. But, after that spellbound moment, I hastened to say:

"No. No, I am not. Yeyac did once grab at me. As you did. But I repulsed him. I have no interest in cuilónyotl lovemaking."

Her face cleared and she smiled and said, "Then let us get on with the right sort of lovemaking." And she let her skirt drop to the floor.

"The right sort?" I repeated, like a parrot. "But that is the sort by which babies are made."

"Only when babies are wanted," she said. "Do you think I am a baby myself? I am a grown woman, and I have learned from other grown women how to avoid pregnancy. I daily take a dose of the powdered tlatlaohuéhuetl root."

I had no notion of what that might be, but I took her at her word. Still—again to my credit, I think—I tried one last argument:

"You will want to be married one day, Améyatl. And you will wish to marry a píli of your own rank. And he will expect you to be a virgin." My voice went up into a squeak again, as she began slowly, almost teasingly, to unwind the felted tochómitl garment that wrapped her loins. "I am told that a female, after even one single time of lovemaking, is *not* a virgin, and that the fact is manifest on her wedding night. In which case you would be fortunate if you were accepted as a wife by even a—"

She sighed as if much exasperated by my nervous maundering. "I told you, Tenamáxtli, I have been taught by other women. If ever I do have a wedding night, I shall be prepared. There is an astringent ointment to make me tighter than a virgin only eight years old. And a certain sort of pigeon's egg to insert inside me. Unnoticed by my husband, it will break at the proper moment."

My voice gone gruff again, I said, "You certainly seem to have given this considerable thought before you invited me to—"

"Ayya, *will* you be quiet? Are you afraid of me? Cease

your blithering, idiot cousin, and come *here*!'' And she lay back on my pallet and drew me down beside her, and I surrendered utterly.

I found that she had spoken truthfully, also, about her being different in that place, too. The earlier times that I had seen her naked, there had been only a small, barely defined crease at her groin. The tipíli there now was rather more than a crease, and within it were marvels. *Marvels.*

I am sure that anyone observing our inexperienced fumblings, even a totally disinterested cuilóntli, would have been overcome with laughter. In my unreliable voice, which wavered through every tone from reed flute to conch trumpet to turtleshell drum, I kept stammering inanities like ''Is this the right way?'' and ''What do I do with this?'' and ''Would you prefer that I do this . . . or this?'' Améyatl, more calmly, was saying things like ''If you gently spread it open with your fingers, as if it were an oyster shell, you will come upon a little tiny pearl, my xacapíli . . .'' and, not calmly at all, ''Yes! There! *Ayyo, yes!*'' And, of course, after a while she abandoned all calm, and I was no longer nervous, and we were both crying inarticulate noises of rapture and delight.

The thing I remember best, about that coupling and all the subsequent others, is how well Patzcatl-Améyatl personified her name. It means ''Fountain of Juice,'' and when we lay together, that is what she was. I have known many women since then, but have found none who was so copious of juices. That first time, my first mere touch of her started her tipíli exuding its water-clear but lubricant fluid. Soon we were both—and the pallet, too—slick and shiny with it. When we finally got to the act of penetration, Améyatl's virginity-protecting chitóli membrane gave way without resistance. She was virginly tight, but there was no forcing or frustration at all. My tepúli was welcomed by those juices, and it glided right in. On later occasions, Améyatl started her fountaining as soon as she unwound her tochómitl—and later still, as soon as she entered my room. And sometimes, still later, when we were both fully dressed and in the company of others and were behaving with impeccable propriety, she would cast me a certain look that said, "I see you, Tenamáxtli . . . and I am moist beneath my clothes."

That is why, on my thirteenth birthday, I was secretly a little amused when Améyatl's father, my uncle, inelegantly but with good intentions, bade me accompany him to the foremost house of auyaníme in Aztlan, and selected for me an auyaními of prime quality. Smug young sprig that I was, I thought I already knew everything a man could know about the act of ahuilnéma with a female. Well, I soon discovered—with delight, with several moments of real surprise, even now and then with mild shock—that there were a great many things I did not know, things that my cousin and I would never once have thought to try.

For example, I was briefly taken aback when the girl did to me with her mouth what I thought only cuilóntli males did between themselves, because it was what Yeyac had once tried to do to me. But my tepúli was more mature now, and the girl so expertly excited it that I erupted with glorious gratification. Then she showed me how to do the same to her xacapíli. I learned that that inconspicuous pearl, though so much tinier than a man's organ, can likewise be mouthed and tongued and suckled until, all by itself, it impels a female to virtual convulsions of joy. On learning this, I began to suspect that no woman ever actually *needed* a man—that is to say, his tepúli—since another woman, or even a child, could give her that same sort of joy. When I said so, the girl laughed, but agreed, and told me that that lovemaking between females is called patlachúia.

When I left the girl the next morning and returned to the palace, Améyatl was impatiently waiting for me, and urgently hustled me off to where we could converse in private. Though she knew where I had spent the night, and what I had been doing all the night long, she was neither jealous nor distressed. Quite the contrary. She was almost aquiver to find out if I had learned any novel or exotic or voluptuously wicked things to impart to her. When I grinned and said that

I certainly had, Améyatl would that instant have dragged me off to her room or mine. But I pleaded for time to rest and recover and revitalize my own juices and energies. My cousin was no little annoyed at having to wait, but I assured her that she would much more enjoy the new things she would learn when I had regained the vigor necessary to teach them.

And so she did, and so did I, and we went on enjoying one another at every possible private moment during the next five years or so. We never were caught in the act, never even suspected, as far as I knew, by her father or brother or my mother. But neither were we ever really in love. Each of us simply happened to be the other's most convenient and ever-willing utensil. Just as on my thirteenth birthday, Améyatl never evinced any displeasure or indignation on the few times when surely she was aware that I had sampled the charms of a servant wench or a slave girl. (*Very* few times, and I kiss the earth to that. None of those compared with my dear cousin.) And I would not have felt betrayed if ever Améyatl had done the same. But I know she did not. She was a noble, after all, and she would never have hazarded her reputation with anyone she could not have trusted as she did me.

Nor was I heartbroken when, in her twenty-first year, Améyatl had to forsake me and take a husband. As with most marriages between young pípiltin, this one was arranged by the fathers involved, Mixtzin and Kévari, tlatocapíli of Ya-kóreke, the community nearest ours to the southward. Améy-atl was formally betrothed to become the wife of Kévari's son Káuri, who was about her own age. It was obvious to me (and to Canaútli, our Rememberer of History) that my uncle was thus allying our people and Yakóreke's as a subtle step toward making Aztlan again—as it long ago had been— the capital city of all the surrounding territories and peoples.

I did not know whether Améyatl and Káuri had even got to know one another very well, not to say love one another, but they would have been obliged to obey their fathers' wishes in any case. Besides, in my view, Káuri was a passably personable and acceptable mate for my cousin, so my only emotion on the day of the ceremony was some slight apprehension. However, after the priest of Xochiquétzal had tied the corners of their separate mantles in the wedding knot, and all the traditional festivities were over, and the couple had retired to their finely furnished quarters in the palace, none of us wedding guests heard any scandalized uproar from there. I assumed, with relief, that the tight-making ointment and the tucked-inside pigeon's egg, as prescribed by Améyatl's old-crone advisers all those years before, had sufficed to satisfy Káuri that he had wed an untarnished virgin. And no doubt she had further convinced him with a maidenly show of ineptitude at the act she had so artfully been practicing during those years.

Améyatl and Káuri were married only shortly before the day that I and my mother Cuicáni and Uncle Mixtzin departed for the City of Mexíco. And I deemed that my uncle showed perspicacity in appointing not his son and presumptive heir Yeyac, but his clever daughter and her husband to govern in his place. It would be a long, long time before I would see Améyatl again, and then in circumstances that neither of us could remotely have imagined when she waved good-bye to us wayfarers that day.

V

SO I STOOD in what had been The Heart of The One World, my knuckles white from clenching tight in my hand the topaz that had belonged to my late father, my eyes probably fiery, and I demanded of my uncle and mother that we do *something* to avenge that Mixtli's death. My mother merely sniffled miserably again. But Mixtzin regarded me with sympathy tempered by skepticism, and asked sardonically:

"What would you have us do, Tenamáxtli? Set the city aflame? Stone does not readily catch fire. And we are but three. The whole of the all-powerful Mexíca nation was unable to stand against these white men. Well? What would you have us do?"

I stammered witlessly, "I . . . I . . ." then paused to collect my thoughts, and after a moment I said:

"The Mexíca were taken by surprise because they were invaded by a people never previously known to exist. It was that surprise and the ensuing confusion that caused the downfall of the Mexíca. They simply did not recognize the white men's capabilities and cunning and lust for conquest. Now all of The One World does. What we still do not know is in what way the Spaniards may be vulnerable. They must have a weak point somewhere, a soft underbelly where they can be attacked and gutted.''

Mixtzin made a gesture encompassing the city about us, saying, ''Where is it? Show it to me. I will gladly join you in the disemboweling. You and I against all of New Spain.''

''Please do not mock me, uncle. I quote to you a bit of one of your own poems. 'Never forgive . . . at last you lunge and reach for the throat.' The Spaniards surely have a pregnability somewhere. It has only to be found.''

''By you, nephew? In these last ten years, no other man of any of the defeated nations has found a penetrable crack in the Spanish armor. How will you?''

''I have at least made a friend among the enemies. That one called a notarius, who speaks our tongue. He invited me to come and talk to him at any time. Perhaps I can pry from him some useful hint of—''

''Go then. Talk. We will wait here.''

''No, no,'' I said. ''It is bound to take me a long time to gain his full confidence—to hope for any helpful disclosures. I ask your permission, as my uncle and my Uey-Tecútli, to remain here in this city for as long as that may require.''

My mother murmured dolefully, ''Ayya ouíya . . .'' and Mixtzin pensively rubbed his chin.

At last he asked, ''Where will you live? How will you live? The cacao beans in our purses are negotiable only in the native markets. For any other purchase or payment, I have already been told that things called *coins* are necessary. Gold and silver and copper pieces. You have none and I have none to leave with you.''

''I shall seek some kind of work to do, and be paid for it. Perhaps that notarius can assist me. Also—remember—the tlatocapíli Tototl said that two of his scouts from Tépiz are still here somewhere. They must have a roof over them by now, and may be willing to share it with a onetime neighbor.''

''Yes.'' Mixtzin nodded. ''I remember. Tototl told me

their names. Netzlin and his wife Citláli. Yes, if you can find them . . .''

"Then I may stay?"

"But, Tenamáxtli," my mother whimpered. "Suppose you should come to accept and adopt the white men's ways . . .''

I snorted and said, "Not likely, Tene. Here I shall be as the worm in a coyacapúli fruit. Making it nourish me only until it is dead itself.''

We inquired of passersby whether there was any place we might spend the night, and one of them directed us to the House of Pochtéca, a meeting hall and warehouse for the traveling merchants who brought their wares to the city. But there was a steward at the door, and he apologetically but firmly declined to let us enter.

"The building is reserved to the use of pochtéca only," he said, "which you obviously are not, since you bear no bundles and lead no train of tamémime porters.''

"All we seek is a place to sleep," growled Uncle Mixtzin.

"The thing is," explained the steward, "the original House of Pochtéca was almost of the size and grandeur of a palace, but it suffered the same demolition as the rest of the city. This replacement is but small and poor by comparison. There simply is no room for anyone not a member.''

"Then where, in this warmly hospitable city, *do* visitors find lodging?''

"There is an establishment the white men call a *mesón*. It is provided by the Christian Church, to house and feed itinerant or indigent persons. The Mesón de San José.'' And he told us how to find it.

My uncle said, through his teeth, "By Huitzli, another of their trifling *santos*!'' but we went there.

The mesón was a large adobe structure that was an annex to an even larger and much more substantial building called the Colegio de San José. I learned later that the word *colegio* means much the same as our calmécac—a school for advanced students, taught by priests, though in this case Christian priests, of course.

The mesón, like the colegio, was in the charge of what we took to be priests, until some others converging on the building told us that these were only friars, a lowly grade of the Christian clergy. We arrived about sundown, just as some of those friars were spooning food from huge cooking vats into bowls held by the many people who got in line for it. Most of those people were not travel-stained like ourselves, but only ragged and defeated-looking inhabitants of the city itself. Evidently they were so impoverished that they depended on the friars for their sustenance as well as shelter, because none made any offer of any kind of payment when his bowl was filled, and the friars gave no sign of expecting payment.

Under the circumstances, I would have expected the charity fare to be some cheap and filling gruel like atóli. But what was poured into our bowls was, surprisingly, duck soup, thick with meat, hot and tasty. Each of us also was handed a warm, globular, brown, crusty thing. We watched what others did with theirs, and saw that they were eating them in bites and using them to sop up their soup, just as we always had done with our round, thin, flat tláxcaltin.

"Our maize-flour tláxcaltin the Spaniards call *tortillas*," said a scrawny man who had been in the line with us. "And this bread of theirs they call a *bolillo*. It is made of flour from a kind of grass they call wheat, which they deem superior to our maize, and which can be grown in places where maize cannot."

"Whatever it is," my mother said timidly, "it is good."

She had been right to speak with timidity, for Uncle Mixtzin instantly and sharply told her, "Sister Cuicáni, I wish to hear no approving words about *anything* to do with these white people!"

The scrawny man told us his name, Pochotl, and sat with us while we all dined, and continued helpfully to inform us:

"It must be that the Spaniards have only few and puny ducks in their own country, for here they devour ducks in preference to all other meats. Of course, our lakes support such multitudes of these birds, and the Spaniards have such a strange but effective means of slaughtering them—" He paused and held up a hand. "There. Did you hear that? Twilight is when the flocks come homing to the water, and the Spanish fowlers kill them by the hundreds every evening."

We had heard several claps of what might have been distant thunder, off to the eastward, and it went on rumbling for a time.

"That is why," Pochotl went on, "duck meat is so abundant that it can even be fed free to us paupers. Myself, I would prefer pitzóme meat, if I could afford to buy it."

Uncle Mixtzin said, with a snarl, "We three are not paupers!"

"You are newcomers, I assume. Just stay awhile, then."

"What is a pitzóme?" I asked. "I never heard the word before."

"An animal. Brought by the Spaniards, and bred by them in great numbers. It is very like our familiar wild boar, only tame and much fatter. Its meat, called by them *puerco*, is as tender and savory as a well-cooked human haunch." My mother and I both winced at that, but Pochotl took no notice. "Indeed, so close is the similarity of pitzóme and human meat that many of us believe the Spaniards and those animals must be blood relations, that the white men and their pitzóme both propagate their kind by mutual copulation."

Now the friars were waving all of us out of the big bare room where we had been eating, up the stairs to the sleeping quarters. It was the first time in my recollection that I had ever gone to bed without steaming or bathing myself, or at least taking a swim in the nearest available water. Upstairs were two separate big rooms, one each for men and women, so my uncle and I went one way and my mother the other, looking unhappy at being parted from us.

"I hope we see her safe and sound in the morning," muttered Mixtzin. "Yya, I hope we see her at all. These white priests may well have a rule that giving a woman a meal entitles them to the use of the woman."

To soothe him, I said, "There were women being fed down there who are rather younger and more tempting than Tene."

"Who knows what tastes these aliens may have, if, as that man said, they are thought to couple even with sows? I would put nothing past them."

That man, Pochotl—so scrawny as to belie his name, which means a certain tree, a very bulky one—was again joining us, taking the straw pallet next to mine, whence he continued to regale us with information about the City of México and its Spanish masters.

"This," he said, "was once an island entirely surrounded by the waters of Lake Texcóco. But now that lake has dwindled so much that its nearer shore is fully one-long-run eastward from the city—except for the canals that must repeatedly be dredged to provide access for the freight acáltin. The causeways that link the city to the mainland used to cross expanses of clear lake water, but now, as you must have seen yourselves, those expanses are more weed than water. The other lakes, too, back then were interconnected with Lake Texcóco and with each other. In effect, one single great lake. A man could row an acáli from the island of Tzumpánco in the north to the flower gardens of Xochimílco in the south, some twenty one-long-runs—or twenty leagues, as the Spanish would say. Now that man would have to plod through the wide bogs that have put those shrunken lakes far apart from each other. Some people say the trees were responsible."

"The *trees?!*" exclaimed my uncle.

"This valley is ringed by mountains, all around the horizon. And all those mountains bore thick forests—were almost *furred* with forests—before the white men came."

Mixtzin said slowly, remembering, "Ye-es, you are right. It did strike me, on this visit, that the mountains look more brown than green."

"Because they are barren of trees," said Pochotl. "The Spaniards chopped them down—all of them—for timbers and lumber and firewood. Truly, that could well have angered Chicomecóatl, the goddess of green growing things. She may have taken revenge by persuading the god Tlaloc to send his rain only meagerly and sporadically, as he has been doing, and by persuading Tonatíu to blaze more hotly, as he has been doing. Whatever the reason, our weather gods have behaved most peculiarly ever since the coming of the Crixtanóyotl deities."

"Excuse me, friend Pochotl," I said, changing the subject. "I hope to find employment here. Not to make any fortune, but work that will pay me enough to live on. Can I expect to do that?"

The scrawny man looked me up and down. "Have you any skills, young man? Can you write the white men's language? Are you talented at any craft? Do you possess any artistic ability?"

"None of those. No."

"Good," he said bleakly. "Then you will not balk at hard labor. Hefting stone blocks and baskets of mortar for the new buildings. Or drudging as a tamémi porter. Or mucking out silt and excrement and trash from the canals. Whether such work will enable you to live depends, of course, on how skimpily you *can* live."

"Well," I said, gulping, "I had hoped for something rather more . . ."

Uncle Mixtzin interrupted, "Friend Pochotl, you are a well-spoken man. I take you to have some intelligence, even education. And clearly you do not love the white men. Why, then, do you subsist on their charity?"

"Because I do have skills," said Pochotl with a sigh. "I was a master worker in gold and silver. Delicate jewelry—necklaces, bracelets, labrets, diadems, anklets—things for which the Spaniards have no use. They want their gold and silver melted down into featureless ingots, for sending home to their king, or for stamping into crude coins. Barbarians!

Their other metals, what they call iron and steel, copper and bronze, they entrust to brawny smiths, to forge into horseshoes, armor plates, swords and the like.''

Mixtzin asked, "You could not do that?"

"Any muscular lout could do that. I think such strong-arm work beneath me. Also, I do not care to callus and gnarl my artist's fingers. Someday, somehow, there may again be decent work for them to do."

I was only half listening to them. I sat cross-legged on my rancid pallet—it smelled of numberless earlier unwashed occupants—and contemplated the extremely unappealing careers the scrawny man had suggested for me. I had sworn to myself that I would do anything the gods might require in the furtherance of my vengeance against the white men, and I would keep that oath. The prospect of hard and ill-paid labor did not affright me. But the whole object of my staying in this city was to search out some hitherto unnoticed weakness in the Spaniards' grip on The One World, some flaw in their system of governing and controlling New Spain, some blind spot in their allegedly all-seeing preparedness against any kind of overthrow. It seemed unlikely that I could do much successful spying while spending most of my time among other laborers at the bottom of a canal ditch, or bent under the tumpline of a tamémi porter. Well, maybe the notarius Alonso de Molina could provide for me some better line of work, where I would have more opportunity for employing my eyes and ears and instincts.

Now Pochotl was telling my uncle, "The white men have brought us several new and very flavorsome foods. Their chicken, for instance, yields a much more tender and juicy meat than does our bigger huaxolómi fowl that they call the *gallipavo*. And they grow a cane from which they extract a powder called sugar, much sweeter than honey or coconut syrup. And they brought a new kind of bean called an *haba*, and other vegetables called cabbage, artichoke, lettuce and radish. Good eating, for those who can afford to buy them, or still have a plot of ground in which to grow them. But I think the Spaniards found here many more things new to them. They are ecstatic over our xitómatl and chili and cho-cólatl and ahuácatl, which they say do not exist in their Old Spain. Oh, and also they are learning how to take pleasure in smoking our picíetl.''

Gradually I became aware of other voices around me in the dark room, other people staying awake to converse as Mixtzin and the scrawny man were doing. Most of those voices were speaking Náhuatl, and not saying anything much worth my listening to. But other conversations were in languages incomprehensible; they could have been conveying the wisdom of the world, or the deepest secrets of the gods, for all I could make out. At that time, I was unable to sort out the nationalities of those various speakers. But after a few more nights in the guest house, I would learn something interesting—that almost every man of them, except those native to this City of Mexíco itself, had come to this San José mesón from somewhere *north* of the city, often *far* north.

It stood to reason. As I have said, all the nations and peoples south of the City of Mexíco—also to the east—had early succumbed to the Spanish conquest, and by now had well adapted to the presence and puissance of the Spaniards, in all their social and commercial dealings with them. So any visitors from the south or east would be envoys or swift-messengers or pochtéca bringing goods to the city to sell or barter, or coming here to buy merchandise imported from Old Spain. Those visitors, then, would be lodging at the House of Pochtéca, where we three had been turned away—or, not impossibly, they would even be guests in some high-ranking Spaniard's mansion or palace.

Meanwhile, the less favored lodgers in this charitable mesón were, if not homeless local townsfolk, all from the still-unconquered northern lands of The One World. They had come either as scouts, like Uncle Mixtzin, to take the measure of the white men and determine what their own peoples' future might be—or they had come, like those other scouts, Netzlin and Citláli, to seek a living among the luxuries of the white men's city. Or perhaps some, I thought, might have come here to do both, like me and like the worm in the coyacapúli fruit—hoping to delve and burrow and hollow out this New Spain from within. If there *were* others of similarly subversive intent, I must find them and join them.

The friars woke us at sunrise and directed us downstairs again. My uncle and I were pleased to see that my mother had passed the night unharmed, and all three of us were pleased to find that the friars now ladled out bowls of atóli mush with which to break our fast, and even a cup of frothy chocólatl for each person. Evidently my mother, like Mixtzin, had spent much of the night awake and in converse with other lodgers, for she reported, with more vivacity than she had shown all during our journey:

"There are women here who have served some of the best Spanish families, in some of the best homes, and they have marvelous things to tell. Especially of some new fabrics that have never before been known in The One World. There is a stuff called wool, which is shorn from curly-furred creatures called *ovejas*, which are being raised in great herds all over New Spain. The fur is not felted, but made into yarn— much as is done with cotton—and that is woven into cloth. Wool can be as warm as fur, they say, and colored as vividly as if it were of quetzal feathers."

I was happy to see that my Tene had encountered novelties enough to erase—or at least to dim—her memory of what we had seen the day before, but my uncle only grunted as she prattled on.

I looked about the dining chamber, trying not to be too obvious about it, wondering which of these people—if any— might be future allies in my campaign of prying and plotting. Well, yonder squatted the scrawny man, Pochotl, swilling his bowl of atóli. He could be useful in that he was a native of this city and knew it intimately, though I could not envision him acting the warrior, if my campaign ever came to that. And of the others around the room, which? There were children, adults and oldsters, male and female. I might recruit one or more of the latter, because there are places a female can go, without arousing suspicion, where a male cannot.

"And there is an even more wonderful fabric of which they tell," my mother was saying. "It is called silk, and they say it is as light as a cobweb, but lustrous to the eye, voluptuous to the touch and as long-wearing as leather. It is not made here; it comes from Old Spain. And what is truly incredible, they say its thread is spun by *worms*. They must mean spiders of some sort."

"Trust women to be beguiled by trifles and trinkets," muttered Mixtzin. "If this One World were all of women, the white men could have had it for an armload of baubles, and never a weapon raised against them."

"Now, brother, that is not so," she said virtuously. "I detest the white men as much as you do, and I have even more reason, having been widowed by them. But, as long as they *did* bring such curiosities . . . and as long as we *are* here where they can be seen . . ."

Mixtzin expectably erupted, "In the name of Míctlan's uttermost darkness, Cuilcáni, would you engage in *trade* with these loathsome trespassers?"

"Of course not." And she added, with womanly practicality, "We have no coins to trade with. I do not wish to acquire any of those fabrics, only to see and touch them. I know you are in a hurry to be gone from this alien city. But it will not be much out of our way to go past the marketplace and let me browse a bit among the stalls."

My uncle mumbled and balked and grumbled, but of course he would not deny her that one small pleasure, which would never be within her reach again. "Then, if you *must* dawdle, let us be on our way this instant. Fare you well, Tenamáxtli." He clapped a hand on my shoulder. "I wish you success with your foolhardy notion. But I wish even more that you come home safely, and not too long from now."

Tene's leavetaking was rather lengthier and more emotional, with embraces and kisses and tears and admonitions to stay healthy and eat nourishing foods and tread cautiously among the unpredictable white men and, above all, have nothing whatever to do with any white women. They went off toward the northern end of the city, where was situated the largest and busiest market square. And I went off toward a different square, the one in which yesterday my father had been burned alive. I went alone but not empty-handed; as I was leaving the Mesón de San José, I saw outside its door a large, empty clay jar that no one was using or guarding. So I lifted it up onto my shoulder, as if I were carrying water or atóli for the laborers in a construction party somewhere. I pretended it was heavy, and I walked slowly, in part because that was the way I imagined an ill-paid laborer would walk, but mainly because I wanted to examine thoroughly every person, place and thing I passed.

The day before, I had been inclined to gape at whole, wide aspects of the city, taking each scene at one eye-gulp, so to speak—the broad, long avenues lined with immense buildings of alien architecture, their stone or gesso-plastered fronts adorned with sculptured friezes, convoluted and complicated but meaningless, like the embroidery with which certain of our peoples hem their mantles; and the much narrower side streets, where the buildings were smaller, crammed side by side, and not so fancily decorated.

This day, I concentrated on details. Thus I could now discern that the grand edifices fronting on the avenues and open squares were mostly workplaces for the functionaries of the government of New Spain, and *their* numerous subordinates and councillors and clerks and scribes and such. I also now noticed that among the many men wearing Spanish attire who went in and out of those buildings—bearing books or papers or messenger pouches or just facial expressions of haughty self-importance—a number were of the same dark complexion and beardlessness as myself. Other grand buildings were clearly inhabited by the dignitaries of the white men's religion, and *their* numerous subordinates and minions. And among those, too, wearing clerical garb and

blandly complacent expressions, were more than a few men
with coppery and beardless faces. Only at the buildings hous-
ing military men—the headquarters of high officers, the barracks of the lower ranks—did I see none of my own people
in formal parade dress or in everyday working uniform or in
armor or bearing arms of any sort. A few of the *really* large
and ornate structures, of course, were palaces in which resided the uppermost quality folk of the government, the
Church and the military, and at every door of them stood
armed and alert-looking soldier sentries, usually holding on
a leash one of their fierce staghound war dogs.

I saw other dogs, too, of various shapes and sizes and
unfierce mien, though one could hardly believe that they are
related to the pudgy little techíchi dogs that we of The One
World had for ages been breeding for no other use than as
emergency rations. Indeed, there were no more techíchime
to be found in the City of Mexíco, because all of the native
citizens had become so fond of puerco meat and there was
such an abundance of it here, and the Spaniards never *would*
eat techíchi meat. There were other animals here that were
totally new to me, though I assume they must be Old Spain's
peculiar variety of our jaguar, cuguar and océlotl. They are
ever so much smaller than those cats, however, and tame and
gentle and soft of voice. And as only the cuguar, of all our
cats, can do, these miniature versions even purr.

The elbow-to-elbow buildings on the narrower side streets
were both working and living quarters for their occupants,
all of them white. At ground level might be a shop selling
some kind of merchandise, a smithy, a stable for horses or
an eating establishment open to the public—the white public.
The one or two or three floors above would be where the
proprietors and their families lived.

Except for those I have mentioned, the dark-skinned persons I saw on those streets and avenues were mostly swift-
messengers going somewhere at a trot or tamémime trudging
along under yokes or tumplines bearing bales and bundles.
Those men were dressed as I was, in tilmatl mantle, máxtlatl

loincloth and cactli sandals. But there were some others who had to be servants of white families, because they were dressed like Spaniards, in tunics and tight-fitting breeches and boots and hats of one shape or another. Some of the older of those men had curious scars on their cheeks. The first such man that I saw I assumed had come by his scar in some war or duel, because its shape—like this: *G*—conveyed nothing to me. But then I saw several more men whose cheeks were marked with that same figure. And I saw others, younger men, similarly scarred but with different symbols. It was clear that all of them had deliberately been so marked. Whether any of the city's women had been treated the same, I could not determine, because I saw on those streets no women at all, neither white nor dark.

I learned later that this portion of the city through which I was plodding was called the *Traza*, a vast rectangle comprising many streets and avenues in extent, the entire center of the City of Méxíco. The Traza was reserved for the residences, churches, commercial establishments and official buildings of the white men and their families. There were exceptions. The copper-skinned men in clerical garb lived in the church residences along with their white fellow churchmen. And a few of the white families' native servants ate and slept in the houses where they worked. But all other native citizens—even those who worked for the governing functionaries—had to go home at night to the *colaciones*, the several parts of the city that extended out from the Traza to the edges of the island. And those sections ranged in quality and appearance and cleanliness from respectable to tolerable to vile.

Just looking at the fine, large buildings that composed the Traza, I wondered if the Spaniards were ignorant of the natural disasters that this city was prone to, and which were well known to everybody else in The One World. Tenochtítlan had frequently been inundated by floods of the surrounding lake waters, and two or three times had been all but washed away. I supposed that there was no longer much

danger of floods, with Lake Texcóco's being now so diminished.

However, the entire island, because it was simply an up-
cropping of the lake's unstable bed, had often also been
racked by what we called the tlalolíni—the *terremoto* in
Spanish. On some of those occasions, just one or a few of
Tenochtítlan's structures had shifted position slightly or had
leaned sideways or had sunk below ground level to some
degree. On other occasions, the whole island had violently
shaken and heaved, making buildings fall down as suddenly
as did the people on the streets. That was why, by the time
my Uncle Mixtzin first saw Tenochtítlan, its major buildings
were all firmly broad-based, and the lesser ones were built
on pilings that would merely sway or give a little, to com-
pensate for the island's settling or quaking.

Another thing that I learned later was that the Spaniards
were beginning to realize this propensity of the island, and
from experience. The looming Cathedral Church of San
Francisco, the biggest, therefore the heaviest, structure yet
attempted by the white builders—and not even completed
yet—was already perceptibly and lopsidedly sinking. Its
stone walls were cracking in places, its marble floors buck-
ling.

"It is the spiteful doing of the pagan demons," declared
the priests who inhabited the place. "We should never have
built this house of God on the site of the red heathens' mon-
strous temple, and even used that temple's stones in the process. We must start again, and rebuild elsewhere."

So the Cathedral's architects were frantically putting
wedges under the building, and buttresses about it, trying
every means to keep it upright and intact at least until it was
finished. At the same time, they were drawing plans for a
whole *new* Cathedral to be erected some distance away, with
an extensive underground foundation that they hoped would
hold it up.

I knew none of that on the day, still carrying the empty
jar on my shoulder, I crossed the immense open square

beside which the Cathedral stood. I set the jar down beside the big main door, so that I might look less like an itinerant laborer and more like an estimable caller. I waited while several clerically gowned white men went in or came out, addressing each of them and asking if I might enter their temple. (I also knew nothing then of the rules regarding respectful entrance; for instance, whether I should kiss the ground before or after going through the door.) What soon became evident was that not a one of these white priests, friars, whatever they were—and some had been resident in New Spain for as long as ten years—could speak or comprehend a word of Náhuatl. And none of our people-turned-Crixtanóyotl came by. So I tried repeating over and over, as best I could pronounce the words, "notarius" and "Alonso" and "Molina."

Finally one of the men snapped his fingers in recognition of what I was asking, and led me through the portal—no kissing the ground at all, by either of us, though he did give a sort of reverential little dip at one point—through the cavernous interior and along aisles and corridors and up stairways. Inside the church, I noticed, all the churchmen removed their hats—they wore quite an assortment, from small and round to large and puffy—and every one of them had a circle of his hair shaved bald at the crown of his head.

My guide stopped at an open door and motioned for me to enter, and in that small room sat the notarius Alonso at a table. He was smoking picíetl, but not in the way we do, with the dried, shredded herb rolled in a tube of reed or paper. He held between his lips a long, stiff, thin thing of white clay, the far end of which was bent upward and packed with the slow-burning picíetl, and he inhaled the smoke from the other, narrower end.

The notarius had one of our native pleated bark-paper books before him, and was copying from its many colored word-pictures. I should say translating from it, because the copy he was writing on another paper was not in word-pictures. He was doing it with a sharpened duck quill that he dipped in a small jar of black liquid, and then scribbled on his paper only wiggly lines of that one color—what I know now, of course, is the Spanish style of writing. He finished a line and looked up, and looked pleased, but had to fumble for my name:

"Ayyo, it is good to see you again . . . er . . . Cuatl . . ."

"Tenamáxtli, Cuatl Alonso."

"Cuatl Tenamáxtli, to be sure."

"You told me I might come and talk to you again."

"By all means, though I did not expect you so soon. What can I do for you, brother?"

"Teach me to speak and understand Spanish, if you would, brother notarius."

He gave me a long look before he asked, "Why?"

"You are the only Spaniard I have met who speaks *my* language. And you said it makes you useful as a communicator between your people and mine. Perhaps I could be equally useful. If none other of your countrymen can manage to learn our Náhuatl—"

"Oh, I am not the only one who speaks it," he said. "But the others, as they become fluent, get variously assigned to other parts of the city or out in the farther reaches of New Spain."

"Then will you teach me?" I persisted. "Or if you cannot, maybe one of those others . . ."

"I can and I will," he said. "I cannot make time to give you private lessons, but I do teach a class every day at the Colegio de San José. That is a school established solely for the education of you *indios*—of you people. Every priest-teacher at the Colegio speaks at least a passable Náhuatl."

"Then I am in luck," I said, pleased. "As it happens, I am lodging in the friars' mesón next door."

"Even better luck, Tenamáxtli, there is a beginners' class just starting. That will make the learning easier for you. If you will be at the front gate of the Colegio tomorrow at the hour of Prime—"

"Prime?" I said blankly.

"I was forgetting. Well, never mind. As soon as you have broken your night's fast—that would be the hour of Lauds—simply step over to the Colegio gate and wait for me. I will see that you are properly admitted and enrolled and told when and where your classes will be."

"I cannot thank you enough, Cuatl Alonso."

He picked up his quill again, expecting me to depart. When I hesitated there before his table, he asked, "Was there something else?"

"I saw something today, brother. Can you tell me what it means?"

"What sort of something?"

"May I borrow your quill for a moment?" He gave it to me, and I wrote with that black liquid on the back of my hand (not to spoil any of his paper) the figure _G_. "What is that, brother?"

He looked at it and said, "Hay."

"Hay?"

"That is the name of the character. Hay. It is a _letra inicial_—well, there is no word in Náhuatl for it. You will learn these things in your Colegio class. Hay is a particle of the Spanish language, as is _ahchay, ee, hota_ . . . and so on. Where did you see this?"

"It was scarred into a man's face. Cut or burned, I could not tell."

"Ah, yes . . . the brand." He frowned and looked away. It seemed that I had a faculty for making Cuatl Alonso uncomfortable. "In that case, the letra inicial stands for _guerra_. War. It means the man was a prisoner of war, therefore now a slave."

"I saw several wearing that mark. I saw others—like these." Again I wrote on the back of my hand, the figures _HC_ and _JZ_ and perhaps others that I do not now remember.

"More letras iniciales," he said. "_Ahchay thay_, that would be the Marqués Hernán Cortés. And _hota thaydah_, that would be His Excellency, the Bishop Juan de Zumárraga."

"Those are names? The men's own names are branded onto them?"

"No, no. The names of their owners. When a slave is not a prisoner taken during the conquest of ten years ago, but is simply bought and paid for, then the owner may brand him— like a horse—as a permanent claim on him, you see."

"I see," I said. "And female slaves? They are branded, too?"

"Not always." He looked uncomfortable yet again. "If she is a young woman, and comely, her owner may not wish to disfigure her beauty."

"I can understand that," I said, and gave his quill back to him. "Thank you, Cuatl Alonso. You have taught me some things of the Spanish nature already. I can hardly wait to learn the language."

VI

HAD INTENDED to ask the notarius Alonso for another favor—his suggestion of some work I might do that would pay me a living wage. But as soon as he mentioned the Colegio de San José, I decided on the instant not to ask that question. I would go on living at the mesón for as long as the friars would let me. It was right next to the school, and not having to work for my food and lodging would enable me to take advantage of all the kinds of education the Colegio could teach me.

I would not be living luxuriously, of course. Two meals a day, and not very substantial meals, were hardly enough to sustain one of my age and vigor and appetite. Also, I would have to contrive some way to keep myself clean. In my traveling pack, I had brought only two changes of apparel besides what I was wearing; those clothes would have to take turns being laundered. Just as important, I would have to make some arrangement for washing my body. Well, if I could find that Tépiz couple, perhaps they would accommodate me in the matter of hot water and amóli soap, even if they had no steam hut. Meanwhile, I had a fair number of cacao beans in my purse. For a time, at least, I could buy from the native markets the amenities that were indispensable, and an occasional morsel to supplement the friars' charity fare.

"You can reside here forever, if you wish," said the scrawny man, Pochotl, whom I found at the mesón when I returned there, both of us getting into the line for the evening meal. "The friars will not mind, or probably even notice. The white men like to say that they 'cannot tell one of the filthy indios from another.' I myself have been sleeping here for months, and gleaning my two skimpy meals a day, ever since I sold the last few granules of my stock of gold and silver." He added wistfully, "You may not believe it, but I once was admirably fat."

I asked, "What do you do with yourself during the rest of the day?"

"Sometimes, feeling guilty about being a parasite, I stay here to help the friars clean out the cooking vessels and the men's sleeping chamber. The women's quarters are cleaned by some nuns—those are female friars—who come over from what they call the Refugio de Santa Brígida. But most days, I merely amble about the city, remembering what used to be where in the bygone days, or just gazing at things in the market stalls that I wish I could buy. Idling, nothing but idling."

We had shuffled our way to the vats and a friar was ladling our bowls full—again with duck soup—handing us each a bolillo when, as on the previous afternoon, there came that distant thunder rumble from the eastward.

"There they go," said Pochotl. "Collecting ducks again. The fowlers are as punctual as those misbegotten church bells that mark divisions of the day by beating us on the ears. But, *ayya*, we must not complain. We get our share of the ducks."

I carried my bowl and bread into the building, thinking that I must sometime soon go to the eastern side of the island at twilight and see what was the method the Spanish fowlers employed to harvest the ducks.

Pochotl joined me again and said, "I have confessed to

being a mendicant and an idler. But what about you, Tena-máxtli? You are still young and strong and not work shy, I think. Why are you planning to stay on here among us pauper wretches?"

I pointed toward the Colegio next door. "I shall be going to classes yonder. Learning to speak Spanish."

"Whatever for?" he asked, in mild surprise. "You do not even speak Náhuatl very well."

"Not the modern Náhuatl of this city, that is true. My uncle told me that we of Aztlan speak the language as it was spoken long ago. But everyone I have met here understands me, and I, them. You, for instance. Also, you may have noticed that many of our fellow lodgers—those who come from the Chichiméca lands far to the north—speak several different dialects of Náhuatl, but all of them understand each other without great difficulty."

"Arrgh! Who cares what the Dog People speak?"

"Now there you are mistaken, Cuatl Pochotl. I have heard many Mexíca call the Chichiméca the Dog People . . . and the Téochichiméca the Wild Dog People . . . and the Zácachi-chiméca the Rabid Dog People. But they are wrong. Those names do not derive from chichíne, the word for dog, but from chichíltic—red. Those people are of many different nations and tribes, but when they call themselves collectively the Chichiméca, they mean only red-skinned, which is to say akin to all of us of The One World."

Pochotl snorted. "Not akin to me, thank you. They are an ignorant and dirty and cruel people."

"Because they live all their lives in the cruel desert lands up north."

He shrugged. "If you say so. Still, why would you wish to learn the Spaniards' language?"

"So I can learn about the Spaniards themselves. Their nature, their Christian superstitions. Everything."

Pochotl used the last of his bolillo to sop up the last of his soup, then said, "You saw the man burned to death yesterday, yes? Then you know all that anyone could possibly *want* to know about Spaniards and Christians.''

"Well, I know one thing. My jar disappeared from right outside the Cathedral. It must have been a Christian who stole it. I had only borrowed it. Now I owe these mesón friars a jar.''

"What in the name of all the gods are you talking about?''

"Nothing. Never mind.'' I looked long at this self-described mendicant, parasite, idler. But Pochotl did possess a lifetime's knowledge of this city. I decided to trust him. I said, "I wish to know everything about the Spaniards because I want to overthrow them.''

He laughed harshly. "Who does not? But who can?''

"Perhaps you and I.''

"I?!'' Now he laughed uproariously. *"You?!''*

I said defensively, "I have had the same military training as did those warriors who made the Mexíca the pride and terror and overlords of The One World.''

"Much good their training did those warriors,'' he growled. "Where are they now? The few who are left are walking around with brands etched into their faces. And you expect to prevail where they could not?''

"I believe a determined and dedicated man can do anything.''

"But no man can do everything.'' Then he laughed again. "Not even you *and* I can.''

"And others, of course. Many others. Those Chichiméca, for instance, whom you so despise. *Their* lands have not been conquered, nor have they. And theirs is not the only northern nation still defying the white men. If all of those were to rise up and charge southward . . . Well, we will talk more, Pochotl, when I have begun my studies.''

"Talk. Yes, talk. I have heard much of *talk.*''

I was waiting at the Colegio entrance for only a short while before the notarius Alonso arrived and greeted me warmly, adding:

"I was a little concerned, Tenamáxtli, that you might have changed your mind."

"About learning your language? Why, I am sincerely determined—"

"About becoming a Christian," he said.

"What?" Taken aback, I protested, "We never discussed any such thing."

"I assumed you understood. The Colegio is a *parroquial* school."

"The word tells me nothing, Cuatl Alonso."

"A Christian school. Supported by the Church. You must be a Christian to attend."

"Well, now . . ." I muttered.

He laughed and said, "It is no painful thing to do. *Bautismo* involves only a touch of water and salt. But it cleanses you of all sin, and qualifies you to partake of the Church's other sacraments, and assures the salvation of your soul."

"Well . . ."

"It will be a long while before you are sufficiently instructed and prepared for *Catecismo* and *Confirmación* and first *Comunión*."

All those words were also meaningless to me. But I gathered that I would be merely a sort of apprentice Christian during that "long while." If in the meantime I could learn Spanish, no doubt I could escape from here before I was totally committed to the foreign religion. I shrugged and said, "As you will. Lead on."

Which he did, leading me into the building and to a room he said was "the office of the *registrador*." That personage was a Spanish priest, bald on top like all the others I had seen, but very much fatter below, who eyed me with no great show of enthusiasm. He and Alonso exchanged a fairly lengthy conversation in Spanish, and then the notarius spoke to me again:

"At bautismo a new convert is given a Christian name, and the custom is to bestow the name of the saint on whose feast day the bautismo is administered. Today being the feast day of Saint Hilarion the Hermit, you will therefore be styled Hilario Ermitaño.''

"I had rather not."

"What?"

I said tentatively, "I believe there is a Christian name called Juan . . . ?"

"Why, yes," said Alonso, looking puzzled. I had mentioned that name because—if I had to have one—that had been the Christian name inflicted on my late father Mixtli. Apparently Alonso made no connection with the man who had been executed, because he said with approval, "Then you *do* know something about our faith. Juan was that *discípulo* whom Jesús loved best." I made no reply, for that was just more gibberish to me, so he said, "Then Juan is the name you would prefer?"

"If there is not some rule forbidding it."

"No, no rule . . . but let me inquire . . ." He turned again to the fat priest and, after they had conferred, said to me, "Father Ignacío tells me that this is also the feast day of a rather more obscure saint called John of York, once the prior of a priory somewhere in Inglaterra. Very well, Tenamáxtli, you will be christened Juan Británico."

Most of that speech was also incomprehensible to me. And when the priest Ignacio sprinkled water on my head and had me lick a taste of salt from his palm, I regarded the whole ritual as so much nonsense. But I tolerated it, because it clearly meant much to Alonso, and I would not disappoint a friend. So I became Juan Británico and—while I could not know it at the time—I was again being a dupe of those gods who prankishly arrange what seem to be coincidences. Though I very seldom in my life called myself by that new name, it would eventually be heard by some foreigners even more alien than the Spaniards, and that would cause some occurrences most odd.

"Now then," said Alonso, "besides Spanish, let us decide what other classes you will avail yourself of, Juan Británico." He picked up a paper from the priest's table and scanned it. "Instruction in Christian doctrine, of course. And, should you later be blessed with a calling to holy orders, there is also a class in Latin. Reading, writing—well, those must wait. Several other classes are taught only in Spanish, so those must wait, too. But the teachers of handicrafts are native speakers of Náhuatl. Do any of these appeal to you?" And he read from the list, "Carpentry, blacksmithing, tanning, shoemaking, saddlery, glassworking, beer-brewing, spinning, weaving, tailoring, embroidery, lacemaking, begging of alms—"

"Begging?!" I exclaimed.

"In case you should become a friar of a mendicant order."

I said dryly, "I have no ambition to become a friar, but I think I could already be called a mendicant, living at the mesón as I do."

He looked up from the list. "Tell me, are you competent at reading the Aztec and Maya books of word-pictures, Juan Británico?"

"I was well taught," I said. "It would be immodest of me to say how well I learned."

"Perhaps you could be of help to me. I am attempting to translate into Spanish what few native books are left in this land. Almost all of them were purged—burned—as being iniquitous and demonic and inimical to the true faith. I manage fairly well with those books whose word-pictures were drawn by speakers of Náhuatl, but some were done by scribes who spoke other languages. Do you think you might be able to help me fathom those?"

"I could try."

"Good. Then I shall ask His Excellency for permission to pay you a stipend. It will not be lavish, but you will be spared the feeling that you are a disgraceful drone, living on charity." After another exchange with the fat priest Ignacio, he said to me, "I have registered you for only two classes, for now. The one I teach in basic Spanish and the one in Christian instruction taught by Father Diego. Any other classes can wait. In the meantime, you will spend your free hours at the Cathedral, helping me with those native books—what we call the *códices*."

"I shall be pleased," I said. "And I am greatly obliged to you, Cuatl Alonso."

"Let us go upstairs now. Your other classmates should already be seated on their benches and waiting for me."

They were, and I was abashed to find that I was the only grown man among some twenty boys and four or five girls. I felt as my cousin Yeyac must have felt, years ago, back in Aztlan's lower schools, when he had to commence his education with so many classmates who were mere infants. I do not believe there was a single male in the room old enough to wear the máxtlatl under his mantle, and the few girls appeared even younger. Another thing immediately noticeable was the range of skin coloration among us. None of the children was Spanish-white, of course. Most of them were of the same complexion as myself, but a good number were much paler of hue, and two or three were much darker. I realized that the lighter-skinned ones must be the offspring of couplings between Spaniards and us "indios." But whence came those very dark ones? Obviously one of the parents of each had been of my people . . . but the other parent?

I asked no questions right then. I dutifully sat down on one of the benches set in rows and—while those youngsters craned and leaned around to gawk at this hulking adult in their midst—waited for the first lesson to begin. Alonso stood behind a table at the front of the room, and I must say that I admired his clever approach to the teaching of us.

"We will start," he said in Náhuatl, "by practicing the open *sounds* of the Spanish language—ah, ay, ee, oh, oo. They are the same sounds as in these words of your tongue. Listen. Ac*á*li . . . *te*ne . . . *ix*tlil . . . *po*chotl . . . calp*ú*li."

The words he had uttered were recognizable by even the youngest in the class, since they meant "canoe," "mother," "black," "ceiba tree" and "family."

He continued, "You will hear the very same sounds again

in these Spanish words. Listen. Ac*á*li . . . *banca. Te*ne . . . *dente. I*x*t*lil . . . *piso. Po*chotl . . . *polvo. *Calp*ú*li . . . *muro.*"

He led us in repeating those ten words again and again, stressing the sameness of the "open sounds." Only then— not to confuse us—did he demonstrate what the Spanish words stood for.

"Banca," he said, and reached down to pat one of the front-row benches. "Dente," and he pointed to one of his own teeth. "Piso," and he pointed to and stamped his foot on the floor. "Polvo," and he swept his hand across the table, raising a puff of dust. "Muro," and he pointed to the wall behind him.

Then he made us repeat those Spanish words again and again, and join him in pointing to the things meant. *Banca,* "bench." *Dente,* "tooth." *Piso,* "floor." *Polvo,* "dust." *Muro,* "wall." Now he returned to our own tongue, saying:

"Very good, class. Now—which of you bright students can tell me five other Náhuatl words that contain those sounds of ah, ay, ee, oh, oo?"

When nobody, including myself, volunteered to do so, Alonso motioned for a small girl on a front bench to stand up. She did, and began timidly, "Ac*á*li . . . te*ne . . ."

"No, no, no," said our teacher, wagging his finger. "Those are the same words I gave you. There are many, many others. Who can speak five of them for us?"

The students, including myself, all sat silent and glanced shyly sideways at each other. So Alonso pointed at me.

"Juan Británico, you are older and I know you have a good store of words in your head. Tell us five of them that contain those various open sounds."

I had already been meditating on this and—I do not know why—a certain five had come into my mind. So now, as mischievously as a schoolboy half my age, I grinned and spoke them:

"*Maá*titl . . . ahuil*né*ma . . . ti*pí*li . . . chi*tó*li . . . te*pú*li."

A few of the younger children looked blank, but most of the older ones recognized at least some of the words, and gasped with horror or giggled behind their hands, because those were words that any teacher—especially a Christian one teaching in a church school—would not often hear or care to hear.

Glowering at me, Alonso snapped, "Very comical, you impudent *babalicón.* Go and stand in that corner with your face to the wall. Stay there, and be ashamed of yourself, until class is dismissed."

I did not know what a babalicón was, but I could hazard a guess. So I stood in the corner, feeling that I had been rightfully chastised, and regretting having spoken so to a man who had been kind to me. Anyway, the whole of that day's lesson was given over to repeating, again and again, *innocuous* words containing those open sounds. I had already mastered the sounds, and memorized those five Spanish words, so I did not miss much by being ostracized and ignored. Also, after the class, Alonso said to me:

"It *was* a rude and unseemly and infantile thing you did, Juan. And I had to be strict with you as a caution to the others. But I must confide that your wicked caprice did relax the stiffness of those children. Most of them were tense and nervous at this commencement of a new experience. They and I will get along more easily and familiarly from now on. So I forgive your deviltry. This time."

I said, and meant it, that there would not be any more such times. Then Alonso led me along the hall to the room where my next class was assembling. This was where I would be subjected to my first instruction in Christianity, and I was pleased to see that here I was not the oldest pupil. My classmates ranged in age from adolescents to mature adults. There were no children, and only a few females, and among these students there was none of that disturbing diversity of skin color displayed by the youngsters in the other room. However, this was not a class where beginners were being taught the very simplest rudiments of their subject. It had clearly been going on for some time, maybe months, before I joined it. Therefore I was plunged into what, for me, were depths that defied my comprehension.

On that, my first day, the teacher-priest was expounding on the Christian concept of *trinity*. Padre Diego was bald of hair, not shaven just on the crown of his head, and was pleased when addressed as Tete, our people's fond diminutive of "father." He was very nearly as fluent in Náhuatl as was the notarius Alonso, so I understood everything he *said*, but not what the words and phrases *meant*. For example, the word *trinity* in our tongue is yeyíntetl, and it denotes a group of three, or three things in company, or three entities acting together, or a set of three *somethings*—such as the three points of a triangle or the three-lobed leaf of certain plants. But Tete Diego kept urging us listeners to adore what is plainly a group of *four*.

To this day, I have never met a Christian Spaniard who does not wholeheartedly worship a trinity comprising one God, who has no name, and the God's son, who is named Jesucristo, and that son's mother, named María Virgen, and an Espíritu Santo, who, though he has no name, is apparently one of those godling Santos, like San José and San Francisco. However, that makes four to be adored, and how four could constitute a trinity I never *could* understand.

VII

THAT DAY, AND each day thereafter—except for the days called Sunday—when I had finished with my two classes at the Colegio, I would report to Alonso de Molina at the Cathedral. We would sit among his heaps of bark-paper books, metl-fiber books, fawnskin books, and discuss the interpretation of this or that page or passage or sometimes just a single pictured symbol.

Of course, the notarius was already well acquainted with such basic matters as the Aztéca's and Mexíca's method of counting numbers, and the differing methods used by other peoples—in the Tzapotéca and Mixtéca languages, for example—and those used by older nations that no longer existed, but had left records of their times—the ancient Maya and Olméca, for example. He also knew that in any book drawn by any scribe of any nation a person depicted with a náhuatl—that is, a tongue—near its head meant the person was speaking. And if the pictured tongue was curly, it meant the person was singing or speaking poetry. And if the pictured tongue was pierced by a thorn, it meant the person was lying. Alonso could recognize the symbols that all our peoples employed to indicate mountains and rivers and the like. He knew many such features of our picture writing. But I was able to correct him, now and then, in some misapprehension.

"No," I might say, "the southernmost inhabitants of The One World—the peoples of Quautemálan—do not call the god Quetzalcóatl by that name. I have never visited those lands but, according to my calmécac teachers, in those southern languages the god has always been known as Gúkumatz."

Or I might say, "No, Cuatl Alonso, you are misnaming these several gods shown here. These are the itzceliúqui, the *blind* gods. That is why you will find them always pictured, as here, with all-black faces."

That particular remark of mine, I remember, led to my asking Alonso why some of the younger pupils at the Colegio had skin so dark that *they* were almost black. The notarius enlightened me. There existed certain men and women, he said, called in Spanish *Moros* or *Negros*, a pitiably inferior race inhabiting some place called Africa. They were brutish and savage, and could be civilized and domesticated only with great difficulty. But those who *could* be tamed, the Spanish made into slaves—and a favored few of the Moro men had even been allowed to enlist as Spanish soldiers. Several of those had been among the original troops who had conquered The One World—and those were, like their white comrades, rewarded with grants of tribute here in New Spain, and with slaves of their own, "indio" prisoners of war, the men I had seen with the figure *G* branded into their faces.

"I have seen two or three of the black men, too, on the streets," I said. "They seem to be fond of rich apparel. They dress even more gaudily than the upper-class white men. Perhaps it is because they are so ugly in the face. Those broad, splayed noses and immense, everted lips and the tight-kinked hair. I have seen no black women, though."

"Just as ugly, believe me," said Alonso. "Most of the Moro *conquistadores* who were given grants settled on the east coast, around the Villa Rica de Vera Cruz. And some of those have imported black wives for themselves. But they generally prefer the lighter—and much more handsome—native women."

All warriors, of course, are inclined and expected to rape the womenfolk of their defeated foes, and the white Spanish conquerors naturally had done much of that. But, according to Alonso, the Moro soldiers were even more lustfully inclined to seize and rape *anything* female that could not outrun them. Whether this had resulted in the birth of such brute creatures as tapir-children or alligator-children, Alonso could not say for sure. But, in New Spain and in older Spanish colonies, too, he said, both Spanish and Moro *patrones* were still making use, at whim, of their female slaves. Also, though it was not much talked about, there was ample evidence that some Spanish *women* had done the same; not just the sluts imported from Spain to be whores for hire, but some of the wives and daughters of the highest-born Spaniards. Out of perversity or prurience or simple curiosity, they occasionally copulated with men of any color or class, even their own male slaves. What with this abundance of licentious miscegenation, said Alonso, there resulted an abundance of children with skins ranging from near-black to almost-white.

"Ever since Velázquez took Cuba," he said, "we have found it convenient to apply names of classification to the variously colored offspring. The product of a coupling between a male or female indio and a male or female white person we call a *mestizo*. The product of a coupling between Moro and white we call a *mulato*, meaning 'mulish.' The product of a coupling between indio and Moro we call a *pardo*, a 'drab.' Should a mulato or a pardo and a white person mate, their child is a *cuarterón*, and a child with that mere one-quarter of indio or Moro blood can sometimes appear to be pure white."

I asked, "Then why bother with such minute specifics of degree?"

"Oh, come now, Juan Británico! Because it can happen

that the father or mother of a bastard of mixed blood may come to feel some responsibility for it, or actually become fond of it. As you have noticed, they sometimes enroll such mongrels for an education. Sometimes, too, the parent may bequeath to the child a family title or property. There is nothing to forbid the doing of that. But the authorities—especially Holy Church—must keep precise records, to prevent the adulteration of the pure Spanish blood. Just suppose a cuarterón should pass himself or herself off as white, and thereby trick some unsuspecting real Spaniard into marriage . . . well . . . that *has* happened."

"How could anyone else possibly know?" I asked.

"Recently, in Cuba, an apparently white man and wife bore a—what we call a *turna atrás*—an unmistakably black baby. The woman of course pled innocence and immaculate Castilian lineage and unblemished wifely fidelity. And later the local gossips said that if records had been properly kept since the first Spaniards settled in Cuba, the white *husband* could very well have proved to be the guilty possessor of the black blood. But the Church had, of course, by that time sent the woman and her child to the burning stake. Hence our now-punctilious attention to records. Because the merest trace of non-white blood, evident or not, taints the bearer of it as inferior."

"Inferior," I said. "Yes, of course."

"We Spaniards even observe some distinctions among ourselves. The indisputably white Spanish children you see in your Colegio classrooms we call *criollos*, meaning that they were born on this side of the Ocean Sea. The older children and their parents, who, like myself, were born in Mother Spain are called *gachupines*—which is to say, the 'spur-wearers'—the most *Spanish* Spanish of all. In time, I daresay, the gachupines will look down on the criollos, as if being born under different skies made some difference in their social status. All it means to me is that I am bidden to list them that way in my census and cadastral records."

I nodded, to show that I was following him, though I had

no least idea what words like "spur" and "census" meant.

"However," he continued, "of the others, the mongrels, I have mentioned only a very few of the fractional classifications. If, for instance, a cuarterón mates with a white, their child is an *octavo*. The divisions of classification extend to *decimosexto*, which would be a child probably indistinguishable from white, though New Spain is too young a colony yet to have spawned any. And there are other names for those of every possible combination of white, indio and Moro blood. *Coyotes, barcinos, bajunos*, the unfortunate mottled-skin *pintojos*, and many more. Keeping records of those can be vexatiously complicated, but maintain the records we must, and we do, to distinguish every person of every quality, from noblest to basest."

"Of course," I said again.

It would eventually be evident on any city street, and not at all ambiguously, that many of my own people came to accept, even to agree with, that Spanish-imposed notion of their being less-than-human beings. Their acceptance of that evaluation, that they were inherently inferior, they expressed with—of all things—hair.

The Spaniards have long known that the majority of our peoples of The One World are markedly less hairy than they. We "indios" have abundant hair on our heads, but except for the people of one or two anomalous tribes, we have no more than a trace of hair on our faces or bodies. Our male children, from their birth throughout their infancy, have their faces repeatedly bathed by their mothers with scalding lime water. So, at adolescence, they do not sprout even a fuzz of beard. Female children, of course, do not have to endure that preventative treatment. But, male or female, we grow no hair on the chest or in armpits, and only a few of us have even the merest wisp of ymáxtli in the genital region.

Very well. White Spaniards are hairy, and white Spaniards, by their own definition, are immeasurably superior to indios. And I gather that the blood of a white forebear, however much diluted down the generations, confers on every

descendant a tendency to hairiness. So, in time, our men
ceased to be proud of having a smooth and clean visage.
Mothers no longer scalded the faces of their male infants.
Those adolescent boys who found the least tufts of down on
their cheeks let it grow and did whatever they could to en-
courage it to full beardedness. Any who sprouted hair on
their chests or under their arms refrained from plucking or
shaving it.

Worse yet, young women—even women who were otherwise comely—if they found themselves growing hair on
their legs or under their arms, they were not ashamed of it.
Indeed, they began to wear their skirts short, to display those
hairy legs, and they cut the sleeves from their blouses, to
show the little bushes in their armpits.

To this day, any of our men and women who grow hirsute
of face or body—whether just a few sparse hairs or near to
furriness—he or she flaunts that. Of course, it marks them
as having the taint of bastardy somewhere in their lineage,
but they do not mind that, because it proclaims to the rest
of us:

"You smooth-skinned persons may be of the same complexion as myself, but you and I are no longer of the same
lowly and despised race. I have an excess of hair, meaning
that I have Spanish blood in me. You can tell just by looking
at me that I am superior to you."

But I am getting ahead of my chronicle. At the time I
settled in the City of Méxíco, there were not so many mestizos and mulatos and other mongrels to be seen. I had passed
my nineteenth birthday some while back—though exactly
when, by the Christian calendar, I could not say, since I was
not then very familiar with that calendar. Anyway, the white
and black conquerors had not yet been among us for long
enough to have produced more than those very young offspring, such as I saw in my Colegio classes.

What I did see on the streets, though, from my first arrival
and ever afterward, was a much greater number of drunken
people than I had ever seen even at the most licentious re-

ligious festivals in Aztlan. Many men, and more than a few
women, could be seen at all hours, day or night, staggering
about or even collapsed unconscious where sober passersby
had to step over them. Our people, even our priests, had
never been totally abstemious, but neither had they often
overindulged—except at festivals—in the intoxicating beverages like Aztlan's fermented coconut milk or the tesgúino
that the Rarámuri make from maize or the chápari that the
Purémpecha make from bees' honey or the everywhere-
common octli, which the Spaniards call *pulque*, made from
the metl plant, which the Spaniards call *maguey*.

I could only suppose that the Mexíca citizens had taken
to drinking to excess in order to forget for a while their utter
defeat and despair, but Cuatl Alonso disagreed with that notion.

"It has been amply evidenced," he said, "that the entire
race of indio peoples is susceptible to the gross effects of
drink, and fond of those effects, and desirous of attaining
those effects at every least opportunity."

I said, "I cannot speak for the inhabitants of this city, but
I have never known the indios elsewhere to be so."

"Well, we Spaniards have subdued many other peoples,"
he said. "Berbers, Mohammedans, Jews, Turks, Frenchmen.
Not even the Frenchmen took to mass drunkenness as a result
of their defeat. No, Juan Británico, from our years-ago landing in Cuba to the farthest extent that we have secured this
New Spain, we have found the natives to be natural-born
sots. De León reported the same of the red men in Florida.
It appears to be an inherent physical failing in your people,
much the same as their so easily dying from such trivial
diseases as measles and the small pocks."

"I cannot deny that they sicken and die," I said.

"The authorities, especially Mother Church," he said,
"have compassionately tried to lessen the temptation that
drink holds for the weakling indios. We have tried to convert
them to Spanish brandies and wines, in the hope that those
more highly intoxicating beverages would lead people to

drink *less* of them. But of course only the rich nobles could afford them. So the *gobernador* set up a brewery in San Antonio de Padua—what used to be Texcóco—hoping to wean the indios onto the cheaper and weaker intoxicant called beer, but to no avail. Pulque remains the easiest available liquor, almost dirt-cheap, since anyone can make it even at home, hence it remains the most-favored way for an indio to get drunk. The authorities' only recourse has been to make a law against any native's drinking to excess, and jailing those that do. But even the law is impracticable. We should have to lock up almost the entire indio population.''

Or kill them, I thought. I had recently watched as a middle-aged and very drunk woman, reeling and shouting incoherently, was seized by three soldiers of the force that regularly patrolled the city. They had not bothered to jail the woman. They had set upon her with the stocks of their thunder-stick weapons, and with seeming glee, until she was beaten unconscious. Then they used their swords, not to stab and kill but only to slash her repeatedly, crisscross-wise, all over her body, so that when the woman awoke from the beating—if she ever did—she would be conscious just long enough to realize that she was irremediably bleeding to death.

''Speaking of pulque,'' I said, to change the subject, ''it is made from the metl, or maguey. And while we have been translating this newest text, Cuatl Alonso, I heard you speak of the maguey as a *cacto*. It is not. The maguey has spines, yes, but every cactus also has an internal woody skeleton, and the maguey does not. It is a *planta*, the same as any bush or grass.''

''Thank you, Cuatl Juan. I am making a note. So—let us get on with our work, then.''

I continued to sleep every night and to take my morning and evening meals at the Mesón de San José, while I passed my free Sundays in the several city markets, asking stall-keepers and passersby if they knew any persons named Netzlin and Citláli, formerly of the town of Tépiz. For a long while, my search was unsuccessful. But I was not wasting what time I spent, either at that endeavor or at the mesón.

Mingling with the city folk in the markets helped me refine my old-fashioned way of speaking Náhuatl and acquire the more modern vocabulary of the Mexíca. Also I associated as much as possible with those prosperous, far-traveled pochtéca who had brought goods from the south to sell in the city—and with the burly tamémime who had actually carried those goods—and thereby learned a useful number of words and phrases of the southern tongues: the Mixtéca language of the people who call themselves Men of the Earth, and the Tzapotéca of those who call themselves the Cloud People, even many words of the tongues spoken in the Chiapa and Quautemálan lands.

At the mesón, every night I was in the company of foreigners from the north, as I have said. Of those, as I have also said, the Chichiméca lodgers spoke a Náhuatl about as archaic as my own, but understandable. So I consorted mainly with foreigners of the Otomí and Purémpecha and the so-called Runner People, thereby learning useful fragments of the Otomíte and Poré and Rarámuri languages. I had never before had any occasion, back home in my own land, to discover my considerable facility for learning other tongues, but now it was evident to me. And I supposed that I must have inherited the ability from my late father, because *he* must have acquired it during his extensive travels throughout The One World. I will say this, however: the languages of our peoples, though they might be very different from Náhuatl, and sometimes difficult for me to enunciate, none was so *very* different and difficult as the Spanish, or took me as long to gain fluency in.

At the mesón, also, on any night I could engage in conversation that long-time city dweller, the former jewelsmith Pochotl, who obviously *had* determined to spend the rest of his life battening on the hospitality of the San José friars. Some of our talks consisted of my merely listening, and trying not to yawn, as he recited his innumerable grudges and grievances against the Spanish, against the tonáli that from his birth had predestined his present misery, and against the gods who had laid that tonáli on him. But more often I listened more attentively, for he had really informative things to tell. For example, Pochotl provided my first knowledge of the orders and ranks and authorities by which New Spain was ruled and governed.

"The very topmost personage," he said, "is a certain man named Carlos, who resides back in what the Spaniards call the Old World. He is sometimes referred to as 'king,' sometimes as 'emperor,' sometimes as 'the crown' or 'the court.' But clearly he is the equivalent of a Revered Speaker, such as we Mexíca once had. A good many years ago, that king sent ships full of warriors to conquer and colonize a place called Cuba, which is a very large island in the Eastern Sea, somewhere beyond the horizon."

"I have heard of it," I said. "It is now populated by varicolored mongrel bastards."

He blinked and said, "What?"

"No matter. Go on, please, Cuatl Pochotl."

"From that Cuba, about twelve or thirteen years ago, came hither that Carlos's captain-general Hernán Cortés, to lead the conquest of our One World. Cortés naturally expected that the king would make him lord and master of all he conquered. However, it is now common knowledge that there were many dignitaries in Spain, and many of his own officers, who were jealous of Cortés's presumption. They persuaded the king to clamp a firm restraining hand on him. So now Cortés holds only the grand but empty title of Marqués del Valle—of this Valley of Mexíco—and the real rulers are the members of what they call the *Audiencia*, or what in the old days would have been a Revered Speaker's Speaking Council. Cortés has retired in disgust to his estate south of here, in Quaunáhuac—"

I interrupted. "I understand that place is no longer called Quaunáhuac."

"Well, yes and no. Our name for it, Surrounded by Forest,

is pronounced by the Spaniards *Cuernavaca,* which is ridiculous. It means 'Cow's Horn' in their tongue. Anyway, Cortés now sits sulking on his fine estate there. I do not know why he should sulk. His herds of sheep and his plantations of the sugar-yielding cane and the tribute he still receives from numerous tribes and nations—all of that has made him the wealthiest man in New Spain. Perhaps in *all* the dominions of Spain.''

''I am not much interested,'' I said, ''in the intrigues and exploitations that the white men concoct and inflict among themselves. Nor in the riches they have laid up for themselves. Tell me the details of the hold they have on *us.*''

''There are many who do not find that grip too onerous,'' said Pochotl. ''I mean those who have always been the lower classes. Peasants and laborers and such. They so seldom raise their eyes from their toil that they may not yet have noticed that their masters have changed color.''

He went on to elaborate. New Spain was governed by the councilmen of the Audiencia, but, every so often, their King Carlos would send across the sea a royal inspector called a *visitador,* to make sure the Audiencia was properly attending to its business. The visitadores reported back to a council in Old Spain, the *Consejo de los Indios.* That council was purportedly responsible for protecting the rights of all in New Spain, natives and Spaniards alike, so it could change or amend or overrule any laws made by the Audiencia.

''I personally believe, though,'' said Pochotl, ''that the Consejo exists mainly to make sure that the *quinto* gets paid.''

''The quinto?''

''The King's Fifth. Every time a quill measure of gold dust or a handful of sugar is extracted from our land—or cacao beans or cotton or anything else—one fifth of it is set aside for the king, before any others get their share of it.''

The Audiencia's laws and regulations made in the City of Mexíco, Pochotl continued to explain, were passed along for enforcement by Spanish officials called *corregidores,* posted in the major communities throughout New Spain. And those officials, in turn, enjoined the *encomenderos* residing in their districts to abide by those laws and see that they were obeyed by the native population.

"The encomenderos, of course, are usually Spanish," he said, "but not all of them. Some are the survivors or descendants of our own onetime overlords. The son and two daughters of Motecuzóma, for instance, as soon as they converted to Christianity and took Spanish names—Pedro, Isabel and Leonor—they were given *encomiendas*. So was Prince Black Flower, the son of Nezahualpíli, the late, great and sincerely lamented Revered Speaker of Texcóco. That son fought on the side of the white men during their conquest, so he is now *Hernando* Black Flower, and a wealthy encomendero."

I said, "Encomendero. Encomienda. What are those?"

"An encomendero is one who has been granted an encomienda. And that is a territory of varying size, within which the encomendero is master. The cities or towns or villages within that area pay him tribute in money or goods, all who grow or produce anything give him a share of it, all are subject to his command, whether to build him a mansion, to till his fields for him, to tend his livestock, to hunt or fish for him, even to lend him their wives or daughters, if he demands. Or their sons, I suppose, if it is a female encomendera of lascivious tastes. An encomienda does not include the land, only everything and everybody on it."

"Of course," I said. "How could anyone own *land*? Own a piece of the *world*? The notion is beyond belief."

"Not to the Spaniards," said Pochotl, raising a cautionary hand. "Some of them were granted what is called an *estancia*, and that *does* include the land. It can even be bequeathed from one generation to the next. The Marqués Cortés, for example, owns not just the people and produce of Quaunáhuac, but also the very ground under the whole of it. And his former concubine Malinche, that traitress to her own people, is now respectfully entitled the Widow Jaramillo and owns an entire, immense river island as her estancia."

"It is against all reason," I growled. "Against all nature. No person can claim to possess the smallest fragment of the world. It was put here by the gods, it is managed by the gods. In times past, it has been purged of people by the gods. It belongs only to the gods."

"Would that the gods would purge it again, then," said Pochotl with a sigh. "Of white people, I mean."

"Now, the encomienda I can understand,'' I went on. "It is no more than our own rulers did. Collect tribute, conscript workers. I do not know of any who demanded partners for their beds, but I suppose they could have done, if they had wanted to. And I can understand why you say that many persons nowadays do not perceive any difference in the change of masters from—"

"I said the lower classes," Pochotl reminded me. "What the Spaniards call *indios rústicos*—clods, bumpkins, priests of our old religion, other persons easily dispensable. But I am of the class called *indios pallos*—persons of quality. And, by Huitztli, *I* perceive the difference. So does every other artist and artisan and scribe and—"

"Yes, yes," I said, for I could recite his lamentations almost as well as he, by now. "And what of this city, Pochotl? It must constitute the biggest and richest encomienda of all. To whom was it granted? To the Bishop Zumárraga, perhaps?"

"No, but sometimes you would *think* he owned it. Tenochtítlan—excuse me, the City of Mexíco—is the encomienda of the crown. Of the king himself. Carlos. From the things made here and the things traded here—every commodity from slaves to sandals, and every last copper *maravedí* of profit realized therefrom—Carlos takes not just the King's Fifth, but *everything*. Including all the precious gold and silver I had worked all my life to—"

"Yes, yes," I said again.

"Also, of course," he went on, "any citizen can be commanded to cease his occupation of earning his livelihood, to help dig or build or pave for the king's city's improvement. Most of Carlos's buildings are completed now. But that is why the bishop had to wait impatiently for the start of his Cathedral Church, and why it is still under construction. And I believe Zumárraga works his laborers harder than ever the king's builders did.''

"So . . . as I see it . . ." I said pensively, "any revolt would best be fomented first among the so-called rústicos. Stir them up to overthrow their masters on the estancias and encomiendas. Only then would we persons of the higher classes turn against the *Spanish* higher classes. The pot must start to boiling—as a pot does in actuality—from the bottom up.''

"*Ayya,* Tenamáxtli!" He grabbed at his hair in exasperation. "Are you again thumping that same flabby drum? I assumed you would abandon that nonsensical idea of rebellion, now that you are such a darling of the Christian clergy."

"And glad I am to be that," I said, "for thereby I can see and hear and learn much more than I could otherwise. But no, I have not abandoned my resolution. In time, I shall tighten that flabby drumhead so that it can be heard. So that it thunders. So that it deafens with its defiance.''

VIII

FOR SOME TIME, I had had enough grasp of the Spanish tongue that while I was yet too timorous to attempt speaking it anywhere outside the notarius Alonso's classroom, I could understand much of what I heard spoken. So Alonso, aware of that, obviously warned all the clerics of the Cathedral where he and I worked together—and warned any other persons whose duties brought them there—not to discuss anything of a confidential nature within my hearing. I could hardly help but notice that whenever two or more Spanish speakers got to talking in my presence, they would at some point give me a glance askance and then move elsewhere. However, when I walked anonymously about the city, I could eavesdrop shamelessly and undetected. One conversation that I overheard, as I browsed over the vegetables displayed at a market stall, went like this:

"Just another damned meddling priest," said one Spaniard, a person of some importance, I judged from his dress. "Feigning to weep tears over the cruel *mistreatment* of the indios, his excuse for making rules that benefit himself."

"True," said the other man, equally richly attired. "Being a bishop makes him no less the cunning and hypocritical priest. He *agrees* that we brought to these lands a gift beyond price—the Gospel of Christianity—and that the indios

therefore owe us every obedience and exertion we can wring
from them. *But,* he says, we must work them less rigorously
and beat them seldomer and feed them better.''

"Or risk their dying," said the first man, "as did those
indios who perished during the Conquest and in the plagues
of disease that followed—before the wretches could be confirmed in the Faith. Zumárraga pretends that what he wants
saved is not the indios' lives, but their souls.''

"So," said the second man, "we strengthen them and cod-
dle them, to the detriment of the work we need them for.
Then *he* conscripts them, to build more churches and chapels
and shrines, all over the damned country, and for all of which
he takes credit. And any indio that displeases *him,* Bishop
Zurriago can *burn.*''

They went on for some while in this wise, and I was
pleased to hear them do so. It was the Bishop Zumárraga
who had condemned my father to his terrible death. When
these men called him Bishop Zurriago, I knew they were not
mispronouncing his name; they were making play on it, and
mocking him, for the word *zurriago* means "a scourge."
Pochotl had told me how the Marqués Cortés had been dis-
credited by his own officers. Now I was hearing stalwart
Christians defaming their own highest priest. If both soldiers
and the citizenry could openly dislike and malign their superiors, it was evidence that the Spaniards were not so like-
minded that they would spontaneously present a united and
solid front to any challenge. Nor were they so secure in their
vaunted authority as to be invincible. These glimpses into
Spanish thought and spirit I found encouraging, possibly useful to me in the future, therefore worth remembering.

On that same day, in that same market, I finally found the
scouts from Tépiz that I had been seeking for so long. At a
stall hung all over with baskets woven of rushes and reeds,
I inquired of the man attending it—as I had been inquiring
everywhere—whether he knew of a Tépiz native named Netzlin or his wife named—

"Why, I am Netzlin," the man said, eyeing me with some

wonderment and a little of apprehension. "My wife is named Citláli."

"*Ayyo*, at last!" I cried. "And how good it is to hear someone talking with the accents of the Aztéca tongue again! My name is Tenamáxtli, and I come from Aztlan."

"Welcome, then, former neighbor!" he said with enthusiasm. "It is indeed good to hear Náhuatl spoken in the old way, not in the city manner. Citláli and I have been here for nearly two years now, and yours is the first voice I have heard from our homeland."

"Mine may be the only such voice for a long while," I said. "My uncle has decreed that no one from Aztlan or its surrounding communities shall have anything to do with the white men."

"Your *uncle* has decreed?" Netzlin said, looking puzzled.

"My Uncle Mixtzin, the Uey-Tecútli of Aztlan."

"*Ayyo*, of course, the Uey-Tecútli. I knew he had children. I apologize for not knowing that he had you for a nephew. But if he forbids familiarity with the Spaniards, what are you doing here?"

I glanced about before I said, "I should prefer to speak of that in private, Cuatl Netzlin."

"Ah," he said, and winked. "Another secret scout, eh? Then come, Cuatl Tenamáxtli, let me invite you to our humble home. Just wait while I collect my stock of wares. The day latens, so there will likely be few customers disappointed."

I helped him stack the baskets for carrying, and each of us hefted a load that, combined, must have been a considerable weight for him to bring to market unaided. He led me through back streets, out of the white men's Traza and southeast toward a colación of native dwellings—the one called San Pablo Zoquípan. As we walked, Netzlin told me that after he and his wife decided to settle in the City of Méxíco, he had been straightway put to work at repairing the aqueducts that brought fresh water to the island. He had been paid only barely enough to buy maize meal, from which

Citláli made atóli, and they lived on that mush and nothing else. But then, when Netzlin was able to demonstrate to the tepízqui of his *barrio* that he and Citláli had a better means to earn their livelihood, he was given permission to set up on his own.

"Tepízqui," I repeated. "That is clearly a Náhuatl word, but I never heard it before. And barrio, that is Spanish for a part of a community—a small neighborhood within it—am I right?"

"Yes. And the tepízqui is one of us. That is to say, he is the Mexícatl official responsible for seeing that his barrio observes all the white men's laws. He, of course, is answerable to a Spanish official, an *alcalde*, who governs that whole colación of barrios and their several tepízque and their people."

So Netzlin had shown his tepízqui how adept and artful he and his wife were at the weaving of baskets. The tepízqui had gone and reported that to the Spanish alcalde, who in turn passed the word to the corregidor who was his superior, and that official in turn reported it to the gobernador of the king's encomienda, which, as I already knew, comprised all the barrios and quarters and inhabitants of the City of Mexíco. The gobernador took up the matter with the Audiencia, when next it met in council, and finally, trickling back down through all those twisty channels, came a *concesión real* granting Netzlin leave to utilize the stall in the market where I had found him.

I said, "It seems an almighty lot of conferring and dawdling for a man to put up with, just to sell the work of his own hands."

Netzlin shrugged, as well as he could under his load. "For all I know, things were just as complicated back when this was the city of Motecuzóma. Anyway, the concesión exempts me from being snatched away to do foreign labor."

"What decided you to do baskets instead?" I asked.

"Why, it is the same work that Citláli and I did back in Tépiz. The reeds and canes that we plucked from the brackish bogs up north were not much different from the ones that grow in the lake beds here. Reeds and swamp grass are, in fact, about the only greenery that *does* grow around the shore here, though I am told that this was once a most fertile and verdant valley.''

I nodded. ''Now it merely stinks of mud and moldiness.''

Netzlin continued, ''At night, I slog about in the muck and pick the rushes and reeds. Citláli weaves during the day, while I am at the market. Our baskets sell well, because ours are much tighter and more handsome than those done by the few local weavers. The Spanish householders, especially, prefer our wares.''

This was interesting. I said, ''So you have had dealings, then, with the Spanish residents? Have you learned much of their tongue?''

''Very little,'' he said, not regretfully. ''I deal with their servants. Cooks and scullions and laundresses and gardeners. They are of our own people, so I need none of the white men's gabbling language.''

Well, I thought, to have access to their domestics might be even more useful to my purpose than to have acquaintance with the Spanish householders themselves.

''Anyway,'' Netzlin went on, ''Citláli and I earn a rather better living than most of our neighbors in our barrio. We eat meat or fish at least twice in a month. Once, we even shared one of those strange and expensive fruits the Spaniards call a *limón*.''

I asked, ''Is that all you ever aspire to be, Cuatl Netzlin? A weaver and peddler of baskets?''

He looked genuinely surprised. ''It is all I have ever been.''

''Suppose someone offered to lead you to war and glory. To rid The One World of the white men. What would you say to that?''

''*Ayya*, Cuatl Tenamáxtli! The whites are my basket-buyers. They put the food in my mouth. If ever I wish to rid myself of them, I have only to return to Tépiz. But no one there ever paid as well for my baskets. Besides, I have no experience of war. And I cannot even imagine what glory might be.''

I gave up any idea of recruiting Netzlin as a warrior, but he still could come in handy if I wanted to infiltrate the servants' quarters of some Spanish mansion. I am sorry to say, though, that Netzlin would not be the last potential recruit to decline to join in my campaign, on the ground that he had become dependent on the white men's patronage. Each of those who did so might have quoted at me—if he ever had heard it—the old Spanish proverb: in effect, that a cripple would have to be crazy to break his own crutch. Or, to describe more accurately a man pleading that reason to dodge service in my cause, I might have said of him what I have heard some uncouth Spaniards say: that he preferred instead to *lamer el culo del patrón.*

We arrived at Netzlin's barrio in San Pablo Zoquípan, which was one of the not *too* squalid outskirts of the city. He told me, with some pride, that he and Citláli had built their own house—as had most of their neighbors—with their own hands, of the sun-dried mud brick that is called *adobe* in Spanish. He also proudly pointed out the adobe steam hut at the end of the street, which all the local residents had joined together to build.

We entered his little two-room abode through a curtain closing the doorway, and he introduced me to his wife. Citláli was about his own age—I guessed them both to be thirty or so—and sweet-faced and of a merry disposition. Also, I soon realized, she was as intelligent as he was obtuse. She was busily working at a just-begun basket when we arrived, although she was enormously pregnant and had to squat *around* her belly, so to speak, on the earthen floor that was her workplace. Tactfully, I think, I inquired whether in her delicate condition she should be doing manual labor.

She laughed and said without embarrassment, ''Actually, my belly is more help than hindrance. I can use it as a form—a mold—for shaping any size basket from small and shallow to voluminous."

Netzlin asked, "What sort of lodgings have you found, Tenamáxtli?"

"I am living on the Christians' charity. At the Mesón de San José. Perhaps you know of it?"

"Yes, we do," he said. "Citláli and I availed ourselves of that shelter for a few nights when we first came here. But we could not endure being put into separate chambers every night."

Netzlin might not be a willing warrior, I thought, but he was evidently a devoted husband.

Citláli spoke again, "Cuatl Tenamáxtli, why do you not make your home here with us until you can afford quarters of your own?"

"That is wondrously kind and hospitable of you, my lady. But if being separated at the mesón was unacceptable to you, having a stranger under this same roof would be even more intolerable. Especially since another and smaller stranger is about to join you."

She smiled warmly at that. "We are all of us aliens in this city. You would be no more a stranger than the small newcomer will be."

"You are more than gracious, Citláli," I said. "But the fact is that I *could* afford to move elsewhere. I have employment that pays me at least better than laborer's wages. But I am studying the Spanish language at the Colegio right next door to the mesón, so I will stay there until it becomes too wearisome."

"Studying the white men's tongue?" said Netzlin. "Is that why you are here in the city?"

"That is part of the reason." I went on to tell him how I intended to learn everything possible about the white men. "So that I can effectively raise a rebellion against them. Drive them out of all the lands of The One World."

"Ayyo . . ." Citláli breathed softly, regarding me with what could have been awe or admiration—or maybe suspicion that she and her husband were entertaining a madman.

Netzlin said, "So that was why you asked me about going to war and glory. And you can see"—he indicated his wife—"why I was less than eager. With my first son about to be born."

"First son!" said Citláli, laughing again. To me she said, "First *child*. I care not, son or daughter, so long as it is hale and whole."

"It will be a boy," said Netzlin. "I insist on it."

"And of course," I said, "you are right, not wanting to go adventuring at such a time. There is, though, one favor I would ask of you. If your neighbors have no objection, might I have your permission to use the local steam hut now and again?"

"Surely so. I know the mesón has no bathing facilities at all. How do you keep even passably clean?"

"I have been bathing from a pail. And then washing my clothes in it. The friars do not mind my heating my water over their fire. But I have not enjoyed a good, thorough steaming since I left Aztlan. I fear I must smell like a white man."

"No, no," they both assured me, and Netzlin said, "Not even a brute Zácachichimécatl just come from the desert smells as bad as a white man. Come, Tenamáxtli, we will go to the steam hut this instant. And after our bath we will drink some octli and smoke a poquíetl or two."

"And when next you come," said Citláli, "bring all your spare garments. I will take care of your laundering from now on."

So thereafter I spent as much time visiting those two pleasant persons—and their steam hut—as I did in conversation with Pochotl at the mesón. And all the while, of course, I was still spending much time with the notarius Alonso—in his Colegio classroom each morning, in his Cathedral workroom each afternoon. We often interrupted our task of rooting through the old word-picture books to sit back and smoke while we discussed unrelated topics. My Spanish had im-

proved to the point where I had a better grasp of those words
he frequently had to use because there simply were no equivalent terms in Náhuatl.

"Juan Británico," he said to me one day, "are you acquainted with Monseñor Suárez-Begega, the *arcediano* of
this Cathedral?"

"Acquainted? No. But I have seen him in the halls."

"He has evidently seen you, too. As archdeacon, you
know, he is in charge of administration here, assuring the
fitness of all things pertaining to the Cathedral. And he bids
me give you a message from him."

"A message? For me? From someone so important?"

"Yes. He wants you to start wearing *pantalones*."

I blinked at him. "The lofty Suárez-Begega can stoop to
concern himself with my bare shanks? I dress the same as
all the Mexíca working around here. The way we men have
always dressed."

"That is the point," said Alonso. "The others are laborers,
builders, artisans at best. All very well for them to wear
capas and *calzoncillos* and *guaraches*. Your work entitles
you—obliges you, according to the monseñor—to dress like
a white Spaniard."

I said with asperity, "I can, if he likes, array myself in a
fur-trimmed doublet, tight-fitting trousers, a feather-topped
hat, some fobs and bangles, tooled-leather boots, and pass
for a swaggering *Moro* Spaniard."

Stifling a smile, he said, "No fur, fobs or feathers. Ordinary shirt, trousers and boots will suffice. I will give you the
money to buy them. And you need wear them only at the
Colegio and here. Among your own people, you can dress
as you please. Do this for me, Cuatl Juan, so I do not have
the archdeacon pestering me about it."

I grumbled that my posing as a Spanish white man was
almost as distasteful as trying to pass for a Moro, but at last
I said, "For you, of course, Cuatl Alonso."

He said, with asperity to match my own, "This distaste-
fully white Spaniard thanks you."

"I apologize," I said. "You personally are certainly not so. But tell me this, if you would. You always speak of white Spaniards or of Spanish whites. Does that mean that there are Spaniards somewhere who are not white? Or that there are other white people besides the Spanish?"

"Be assured, Juan Británico, that all Spaniards are white. Unless perhaps one excepts the Jews of Spain who converted to Christianity. They are somewhat dark and oily of complexion. But yes, indeed, there are many other white peoples besides Spaniards. Those of every nation in Europe."

"Europe?"

"It is a large and capacious continent, of which Spain is only one country. Rather as your One World used to be—a single sweeping terrain occupied by numerous different nations. However, all the native peoples of Europe are white."

"Then are they all equal in quality to each other—and to you Spaniards? Are they all Christians? Are they all equally superior to people who are not white?"

The notarius scratched his head with the duck quill with which he had been writing.

"You pose questions, Cuatl Juan, that have perplexed even philosophers. But I will do my best to answer. All whites are superior to all non-whites, yes, that is certain. The Bible tells us so. It is because of the differences among Sem and Cam and Jafet."

"What or who are they?"

"The sons of Noé. Your instructor, Padre Diego, can explain that better than I. As to the matter of all Europeans being equal, well . . ." He laughed in a slightly self-mocking way. "Each nation—including our beloved Spain—likes to *regard* itself as superior to every other. As no doubt you Aztéca do here in New Spain."

"That is true," I said. "Or it was heretofore. But now that we and all others are lumped together as mere indios, we may discover that we all have more in common than we formerly believed."

"To your other question—yes, all of Europe is Christian—bar some heretics and Jews here and there, and the Turks in the Balkans. Sad to say, though, in recent years there has been disquiet and dissatisfaction even among the Christians. Certain nations—England, Germany, others—have been contesting the dominion of Holy Church."

Astonished to hear that such a thing could be possible, I asked, "They have ceased to worship the four of the Trinity?"

Alonso, preoccupied, evidently did not hear me say "four." He replied somberly, "No, no, all Christians still believe in the Trinity. What some of them nowadays refuse to believe in is the pope."

"The pope?" I echoed wonderingly. I was thinking, but not saying aloud: A fifth entity to be adored? Is such queer arithmetic conceivable? A trinity of *five?*

Alonso said, "El Papa Clemente Séptimo. The Bishop of Rome. The successor to San Simón Pedro. Jesucristo's vicar on earth. The head of the entire Roman Catholic Church. Its supreme and infallible authority."

"This is not another santo or espíritu? This is a living person?"

"Of *course* a living person. A priest. A man, just like you or me, only older. And vastly more holy, in that he wears the shoes of the fisherman."

"Shoes?" I said blankly. "Of the fisherman?" In Aztlan, I had known many fishermen. None wore shoes, or was the least bit holy.

Alonso sighed with exasperation. "Simón Pedro had been a fisherman before he became Jesucristo's most prominent disciple, the foremost among the Apostles. He is regarded as having been the first pope of Rome. There have been ever so many since then, but each succeeding pope is said to have stepped into the shoes of the fisherman, thereby acquiring the same eminence and authority. Juan Británico, why do I suspect that you have been idly daydreaming during Padre Diego's instruction?"

"I have not," I lied, and said defensively, "I can recite the Credos and the Pater Noster and the Ave María. And I have memorized the ranks of the Church's clerics—nuns and friars, *abades* and *abadesas, padres, monseñores, obispos.* Then . . . uh . . . is there anything higher than our Bishop Zumárraga?"

"Archbishops," Alonso snapped. "Cardinals, patriarchs. And then the pope over all. I strongly recommend that you pay closer attention in Padre Diego's class, if you wish ever to be confirmed in the Church."

I forbore to tell him that I wanted nothing more to do with the Church than was absolutely necessary to my private plans. And it was mainly because my own plans were still so nebulous that I continued attending the class of instruction in Christianity. That consisted almost entirely of our being taught to recite rules and rituals and invocations, most of those—the Pater Noster, for instance—in a language that even the Spaniards did not pretend to understand. When the class, at Tete Diego's insistence, made visits to the church service called Mass, I went along with them a few times. That, too, was totally incomprehensible to anybody except, I suppose, the priests and *acólitos* who conducted the Mass. We natives and mestizos and such had to sit in a separate upper gallery, but still the smell of many unwashed Spaniards crowded together would have been intolerable but for the heady clouds of incense smoke.

Anyway, since I had never taken a great deal of interest in my native religion—except for enjoying the many festivities it provided—I was no more interested in adopting a new one. I was particularly inclined to pick my teeth in disdain of a religion that seemed unable to count higher than *three*, since its objects of adoration, by my count, totaled at least four, maybe five, but were called a trinity.

Despite that numerical eccentricity of his own faith, Tete Diego frequently inveighed against our old religion as *overcrowded* with gods. His pink face purpled perceptibly when one day I pointed out to him that while Christianity purported to recognize only a single Lord God, it actually accorded almost equal prestige to the worshipful beings called santos and *angeles* and *arcángeles*. They were easily as numerous as our gods, and several of them seemed as vicious and vindictive as those darker gods of ours that Christians called demons. The chief difference I could see between our old religion and Tete Diego's new one, I told him, was that we *fed* our gods, while Christians *eat* theirs, or pretend to, in the ritual called Communion.

I went on to say:

"There are many other ways in which Christianity is no improvement on our old *paganismo*, as you call it. For example, Tete, we too confessed our sins, to the kindly and forgiving goddess Tlazoltéotl, meaning 'Filth Eater,' who thereupon inspired us to acts of contrition or gave us absolution, just as your priests do. As for the miracle of virgin birth, several of our deities came into existence just that way. And so did even one of the Mexíca's mortal rulers. That was the First Motecuzóma, the great Revered Speaker who was grand-uncle to the lesser Motecuzóma who reigned at the time you Spaniards came. He was conceived when his mother was still a virgin maiden and—"

"That will do!" said Tete Diego, his entire bald head gone purple. "You have an antic sense of humor, Juan Británico, but you have made mock and jest enough for one day. You verge on blasphemy, even heresy. Leave this classroom and do not return until you have repented *and made confession*, not to some Filthy Glutton but to a Christian *confesor sacerdote*!"

I never did that, then or since, but I did do my best to look chastened and repentant when I returned to class the next day. And I continued to attend the class, for a reason that had nothing whatever to do with comparing religious superstitions, or with plumbing the Spanish ways of thought and behavior, or with furthering my plans for revolution. I was now attending that class just to see and be seen by Rebeca Canalluza. I had not yet done the act of ahuilnéma with either a white female or a black one, and perhaps would never have a chance at either. But, in the person of Rebeca Canalluza, I could, in a sense, sample both kinds of female at once.

That is to say, she was what Alonso had classified as a mulato—"mulish"—the offspring of a coupling between a Moro and a white.

There being so very few black women, as yet, in New Spain, Rebeca's father had to have been the black party to the coupling, and her mother some sluttish or perversely curious Spanish woman. But the mother had contributed little to Rebeca's configuration, and that was hardly surprising; no more does coconut milk poured into a cup of chocólatl lighten it at all.

At least the girl had inherited from her mother decently long and wavy hair, not the moss-kinks of a full-blooded Moro. But in everything else—*ayya*, she had the broad, flat nose with wide nostrils, the overfull and purplish lips, and the rest of what I could see of her was precisely the color of a cacao bean. Also, I had to assume that Moro females mature at a very early age, because Rebeca was only a child of eleven or twelve, and small even for that age, but she already had the curves of a woman, and estimable breasts, and buttocks that could only be called protuberant. Furthermore, the looks she gave me were the covetous appraisals of a woman ripe for mating.

Those things I could see for myself. What I could not divine was the reason for her name, which was derogatory, derisive and even demeaning. Not so much her Christian name, Rebeca. Among the edifying little Bible stories that Tete Diego told us from time to time, he had mentioned the biblical Rebeca, and the only bad thing I could remember about that one was that she seemed easily bribed with gold and silver trinkets. But the name *Canalluza* means "vagrancy, roguery, wantonness." If that was Rebeca's mother's surname, well, it had certainly fit her. But how, I wondered, would Rebeca's mother have acquired that name *before* she bedded with a black man?

Anyway, this little brown-black Rebeca Canalluza had long been following me with avid brown-black eyes, and when I first appeared at the Colegio in long-sleeved *camisa*, pantalones, and calf-high *botas*, her eyes became fervid— possibly because she had always worn Spanish attire and may have thought that I was now emulating her—and she began following me *literally*, sitting down beside me on whatever schoolroom bench I occupied, standing close to me on the infrequent occasions when I attended Mass. I did not mind. I had not enjoyed so much as a street-woman since leaving Aztlan, and aside from that, I was as perversely curious as Rebeca's mother must have been with *her* black, thinking, *What would it be like?* I only wished that Rebeca were a bit older and a lot prettier. Nevertheless, I returned her looks and then her smiles and eventually we were conversing, though her Spanish was much more fluent than mine.

"The reason for my awful name," she said, when I asked her, "is that I am an orphan. Whatever were the names of my father and mother, I will never know. I was abandoned, as are many other infants, at the door of the Refugio de Santa Brígida, the *convento de monjas*, and there I have lived ever since. The nuns in charge of us orphans take some queer delight in bestowing on us undignified names, to mark us as children of shame."

Here was an aspect of Spanish custom that I had not encountered before. Among us indios, there were of course children who suffered the loss of father or mother or both— to disease or war or some other disaster. But we had no word for *orphan* in any of the native languages that I knew. And that was simply because no child was ever abandoned or cast away or foisted upon the community. Every child was dear to us, and any one of them left alone in the world was instantly, eagerly adopted by some man and wife, whether they were forlornly childless or had a home teeming with other children.

"At least I was given a decent first name," Rebeca went on. "But that 'drab' yonder"—she discreetly indicated him—"the pardo boy, the ugly one, being also an orphan living at the Refugio, was named by the nuns Niebla Zonzón."

"*Ayya!*" I exclaimed, half laughing, half pitying. "*Both* his names mean 'dim, foggy, stupid'!"

"And *ay de mí*, so he is," said Rebeca with a pearly grin. "Well, you have heard him stutter and stammer and flounder when he speaks here in class."

"At any rate, the nuns provide you orphans with an education," I said. "If religious instruction can be called education."

"For me it is," she said. "I am studying to become a Christian nun myself. To wear the veil."

"I thought it was shoes," I said confusedly.

"What?"

"No matter. What does it mean—wearing the veil?"

"I become the bride of Christ."

"I thought he was dead."

"You really do not listen very closely to our Tete, do you, Juan Británico?" she said, sounding as severe as Alonso. "I will become Jesucristo's bride *in name*. All nuns are called so."

"Well, it is better than the name Canalluza," I said. "Will the ugly pardo Niebla Zonzón get to change his name, too?

"*¡Vaya al cielo—no!*" she said, laughing. "He has not the brains to become a religious of any order. From this class here, poor witless Zonzón goes to a cellar room where he is training to be an apprentice tanner. That is why he smells so bad all the time."

"Tell me, then," I said, "what does it entail—becoming a dead godling's bride?"

"It means that, like any bride, I devote myself only to him for the rest of my life. I renounce every mortal man, every pleasure, every frivolity. As soon as I am confirmed and

make my first Communion, I become a novice in the convent. From that time on, I am dedicated to duty, to obedience,
to service.'' She dropped her eyes from mine. "And to chastity.''

"But that time is not yet," I said gently.

"Soon, though," she said, her eyes still downcast.

"Rebeca, I am nearly ten years older than you are."

"You are handsome," she said, still without raising her
eyes. "I will have you—to remember—during all the years
of having no one else but Jesucristo."

In that wistful moment, the little girl was very nearly lovable, certainly pitiable. I could not have refused such a shy
and tender plea, even had I wanted to. So we arranged to
meet in a private place, after dark, and there I gave her what
she wanted to remember.

Even with her eager collaboration, however, our coupling
did not come easily. First, as I should have expected, I found
that Spanish-style clothes—both mine and hers—were difficult to doff with any grace. It required awkward contortions
that considerably lessened the gratification of two persons
getting themselves naked. Next, the size of her body and
mine proved to be a disadvantage. I am rather taller than
almost every other Aztécatl and Mexícatl man—according to
my mother, I inherited my height from my father Mixtli—
and, as I have said, for all her womanly proportions, Rebeca
was a very small child. This was her first attempt at the act,
and it might as well have been the first for me, so bumblingly
did we go about it that night. She simply could not spread
her legs far enough apart for me to get properly between
them, so my tepúli could put no more than its tip end into
her tipíli. After much mutual frustration, we finally settled
for doing it rabbit-fashion, she on elbows and knees, I cov-
ering her from above and behind—though even then, her
extraordinary buttocks were something of a hindrance.

I did learn two things from that experience. Rebeca was
even blacker of skin at her private parts than elsewhere, but
when the black lips down there opened, she was as flower-

pink inside as any other female I ever knew so intimately. Also, because Rebeca was a virgin when we began there was a little smear of blood when we were done, and I discovered that her blood was as red as that of anyone else. I have, ever since then, been inclined to believe that all persons, whatever their outer color, are made of the very same meat within.

And Rebeca so delighted in her first ahuilnéma that we did it thereafter at every opportunity. I was able to show her some of the more comfortable and pleasurable expedients that I had learned from that auyaními in Aztlan and then had perfected in practice with my cousin Améyatl. So Rebeca and I enjoyed one another often, and right up until the night before the day that Bishop Zumárraga anointed her and several of her sister orphans in the rite of Confirmation.

I did not attend that ceremony, but I did get a glimpse of Rebeca in her ceremonial gown. I have to say that she looked rather comical—the brown-black head and hands in stark contrast to the gown as white as the only white feature of Rebeca, her teeth, gleaming in a smile of commingled excitement and nervousness. And, from that day on, I never again touched her or even saw her, for she never again emerged from the Refugio de Santa Brígida.

IX

"¿**A** CUÁNTOS PATOS ha matado hoy?" I asked, with some diffidence.

"*¡Caray, cientos! ¡Y a tenazón!*" he said, grinning proudly. "*Unos gansos y cisnes además.*"

Well, he had understood my asking how many ducks he had slain that day, and I had understood his reply: "Hah, hundreds! And without even aiming. Also some geese and swans."

It was the first time I had tested my command of Spanish on anyone but my teacher and classmates. This young man was a soldier doing fowler duty at the lakeside, and he seemed amiable, perhaps because I was in Spanish garb and he took me to be a domesticated and Christianized manservant of some sort. He went on:

"*Por supuesto, no comemos los cisnes. Demasiado duro a mancar.*" And he took pains to make that clear to me, waggling his jaw in an exaggerated manner. "Of course, we do not eat the swans. Too tough to chew."

I had come here to the lakeside on other occasions, to watch what Pochotl had called the "strange but effective means" employed by the Spaniards to harvest the waterfowl that descended onto the lake at every dusk. It was indeed a strange method, and it was done with the thunder-stick (properly called an *arcabuz*) and it was indeed effective.

A considerable number of the arcabuces were tied firmly to posts sunk in the lake's bank, the weapons pointing straight out across the water. Another battery of arcabuces was similarly tied to stakes, but pointing upward at various angles and in various directions. All those weapons could be tended and set off by a single soldier. First, he pulled a string and the leveled arcabuces boomed their flashes and smokes directly across the lake surface, killing many of the birds floating there and frightening the rest into sudden flight. At which, the fowler pulled another string, and those severally aimed, uptilted arcabuces fired all together, knocking whole swarms of the birds out of the air. Then the soldier would go about to all the weapons, doing something at the front of their tubes and something else at the rear of them. By the time he had completed that task, the birds would have calmed and resettled on the water, and the twofold slaughter would commence again. Finally, before full darkness came, the fowler would send out boatmen in acáltin canoes to collect the drifts of dead birds.

Though I had witnessed that procedure several times, this was the first time I had nerved myself to ask questions about it.

"We indios never used anything but nets," I told the young soldier, "into which we drove the birds. Your method is much more rewarding. How does it work?"

"Very simple," he said. "A string is tied to the *gatillo* of each of the leveled arcabuces." (I was already puzzled, for gatillo means a "little cat" or a "kitten.") "All those strings are tied to a single string for me to pull and fire those weapons all at once. Likewise, strings are tied to the gatillos of all the upward-aimed—"

"I could see that," I said. "But how does the arcabuz *itself* work?"

"Ah," he said, and pridefully led me to one of the staked weapons, knelt beside it and began to point. "This little thing here is the gatillo." It was a bit of metal protruding from under the rearward part of the arcabuz, crescent-shaped to be pulled by a finger or, in this case, a string, and the kitten was inside a metal guard, evidently to prevent its being pulled accidentally. "And this thing here is the wheel, which is spun by a spring that you cannot see, inside the lock there." The wheel was just that—a wheel—but small, about the size of an *ardite* coin, made of metal and grooved with tiny teeth all around.

"What is a spring?" I asked.

"A narrow leaf of thin metal, wound into a tight coil by this key." He showed me the key, then used it to sketch a small, tight spiral in the earth at our feet. "That is what the spring looks like, and every *arcabucero* carries a key." He inserted his into a hole in what he had called "the lock," turned the key a time or two, and I heard a faint grating noise. "There, the wheel is ready to spin. Now, this thing here we call a cat's-paw." It was another small metal piece, not like a cat's paw at all, but shaped more like a bird's head, gripping in its beak a bit of gravel. "That stone," the soldier explained, "is a *pirita*." And I recognized it as a tiny fragment of what we call the "false-gold."

"Now, we cock the cat's-paw back, ready to strike," he went on, thumbing it backward with a click, "and another spring holds it there. Then—observe—I squeeze the kitten, the wheel spins and at the same instant the cat's-paw slaps its pirita against the wheel and you will see a spray of sparks."

Which is exactly what occurred, and the soldier looked more proud than ever.

"But," I said, "there was no flash or noise or smoke from the tube."

He laughed indulgently. "That is because I had not yet loaded the arcabuz or primed its *cazoleta*."

He produced two large leather pouches and, from one of them, dribbled a small pile of dark powder into my palm. "That is the *pólvora*. See, now I pour a measured amount of it down the mouth of the *cañon* here, and shove in behind it a small piece of cloth. Then, from this other pouch, I take a *cartucho*." He showed me a small, transparent sac—like a bit of tied-off animal intestine—packed with little metal pellets. "For shooting enemies or large animals, of course, we use a heavy round *bala*. But for birds we use a cartucho of *perdigones*." Then, with a long metal rod, he tamped all the contents tightly down in there. "Last of all, I put a mere touch of the pólvora here on the cazoleta." That was a little pan sticking out shelflike from the lock, where the sparks from the wheel and the false-gold would strike it. "You will notice," he concluded, "that there is a narrow hole going from the cazoleta into the cañon where the charge of pólvora is packed. Now, here, I wind the spring and *you* squeeze the gatillo."

I knelt down to the charged weapon with commingled curiosity, timidity and dread. But the curiosity was foremost, because I had come here and accosted the young soldier with precisely this end in mind. I put my finger through the guard beneath the arcabuz's lock, hooked it around the kitten and squeezed.

The wheel spun, the cat's-paw snapped down, the sparks sprayed, there was a noise like an angry little snarl and a puff of smoke from the powdered pan . . . and then the arcabuz rocked backward, and I flinched wildly away, as its mouth roared and spewed a flame and a bloom of blue smoke and, I had no doubt, all those death-dealing metal pellets. When I had recovered from the shock and the ringing in my ears, the young soldier was laughing heartily.

"¡Cáspita!" he exclaimed. "I will wager that you are the first and only indio ever to fire such a weapon. Do not let anyone know that I let you do it. Come, you can watch me load all the arcabuces for the next fusillade."

As I followed him, I said, "Then the pólvora is the absolute essential component of the arcabuz. The lock and wheel and cats and such are simply to make the pólvora work as you wish it to."

"Indeed, yes," he said. "Without the pólvora there would

be no firearms at all in the world. No arcabuces, *granadas, culebrinas, petardos. Ni siquiera triquitraques. Nada.*''

"But what *is* the pólvora?" I asked. "What is it made of?"

"Ah, now *that* I will not tell you. It was rash enough of me to let you play with the arcabuz. The orders are that no indio be allowed to handle any weapon of the white men, and my punishment for that would be dire. I certainly cannot reveal the composition of the pólvora."

I must have looked downcast, because he laughed once more and said, "I will tell you this much. The pólvora is obviously very much a *man's* property, for manly uses. But, oddly enough, one of its ingredients is a very *intimate* contribution from the *ladies.*"

He went on laughing as he went on working, and as I drifted away. He took no notice of my departure, nor had he noticed that the small amount of the pólvora he had poured into my hand had gone into my own belt pouch, nor that I had picked up one of the wheel-winding keys I found lying beside one of the other arcabuces.

Bearing those items, I made my way to the Cathedral—hurrying thence, before I might forget any detail of the contrivances I had been shown. It was past the hour of Compline when I got to Alonso's workroom, so the notarius was not there, probably busy at his devotions. I found a blank piece of bark paper and, with a stick of charcoal, began to draw: the kitten and its guard, the cat's-paw, the wheel, the spiral of spring . . .

"Are you returned to work late this evening, Juan Británico?" said Alonso, coming through the door.

I managed not to jump or act startled. "Only practicing some word-pictures of my own," I said offhandedly, crumpling the paper but holding on to it. "You and I do so much translating of other scribes' work that I feared I might be forgetting the craft. So, having nothing better to do, I came back here to practice."

"I am glad you did. I would like to ask you something."

"*A su servicio*, Cuatl Alonso," I said, hoping I did not look wary.

"I have just come from a meeting of Bishop Zumárraga, Archdeacon Suárez-Begega, the Ostiarius Sánchez-Santoveña and various other custodians. They are all agreed that it is time the Cathedral was provided with more dignified and resplendent furnishings and vessels. We have been using makeshift paraphernalia only because a whole new Cathedral must be built before long. However, since such articles as chalice and monstrance, pyx and stoup—even larger things, like a rood screen and a font—can be easily moved to the new building, it has been agreed that we procure all those things, and of a quality befitting a Cathedral."

"Surely," I said, "you are not seeking *my* agreement?"

He smiled. "Hardly. But you may be of assistance, since I know you wander widely about the city. These fixtures and appurtenances must be of gold and silver and precious gems. Your people used to be sublimely accomplished at such works. Before we send a crier through the streets, calling for a master jewelsmith to come forward, I thought you might be able to suggest someone."

"Cuatl Alonso," I said, gleefully clapping my hands together, "I know the very man."

Back at the mesón, I said to Pochotl, "You are acquainted with the Spanish weapon we call the thunder-stick?"

"The arcabuz, yes," he said. "At any rate, I have seen what it can do. One of them put a hole—as if it had thrown an invisible javelin—clear through my elder brother."

"Do you know how the arcabuz works?"

"How it works? No. How should I?"

"You are an artist of great ingenuity. Could you make one?"

"Make a device that is both outlandish and prodigious? A thing I have seen only from a distance? Without even knowing how it works? Are you tlahuéle, friend, or merely xolopítli?"

There are two Náhuatl words meaning "deranged." Tlahuéle refers to a person who is violently and dangerously insane. Xolopítli refers to one who is witless in only a moony and harmless degree.

I said, "But could you build one if I show you pictures of the parts that make it work?"

"How can you possibly do that? None of us is allowed anywhere near the white men's arms or armor."

"I *have* done that. Here, look." I showed him the paper of drawings I had made, and, right there, with a bit of charcoal, I completed a couple of the pictures that had been left unfinished when Alonso interrupted me. I told Pochotl what the drawings represented and how the various pieces performed to make an arcabuz do its death-dealing.

Pochotl mumbled, "Well, it would not be impossible to forge and shape the pieces, and to fit them together as you have described. But this is work for a common smith, not for an artificer of delicate jewelry. All of it, anyway, except for these strange things you call springs."

"Except the springs, exactly," I said. "That is why I come to you."

"Even assuming I can lay hands on the iron and steel required, why should I waste my time fooling with such a complicated contraption?"

"Waste *what* time?" I asked sardonically. "What are you spending your time on, beyond eating and sleeping?"

"Be that as it may, I told you I want nothing to do with your ludicrous idea of revolution! Making an unlawful weapon for you would involve *me* in your tlahuéle delirium, and I would stand yoked beside you at the burning stake!"

"I shall absolve you and go to the stake alone," I said. "Meanwhile, suppose I offer you a reward irresistible in payment for the arcabuz?"

He said nothing, only glared darkly at me.

"The Christians are looking for an artist to sculpture for their Cathedral numerous items of gold and silver and gems." Pochotl's eyes went from dark to brightly glowing.

"Dishes and cups and other vessels, also articles that I cannot describe to you, all to be most ornately worked. Splendiferous things. The man who makes those will leave a heritage to posterity. An outlandish posterity, of course, but—"

"But artistry is artistry!" Pochotl exclaimed. "Even in the service of an alien people and an alien religion!"

"Indubitably," I said, complacent. "And, as you yourself have remarked, I am something of a darling of the Christian clergy. Were I to put in a word on behalf of a certain incomparable artificer . . ."

"Would you? *Yyo ayyo*, Cuatl Tenamáxtli, *would* you?"

"Should I do so, I believe that artist would be assured of the commission to do the work. And all I would ask in return would be that he waste his *free* time in the construction of my arcabuz."

Pochotl snatched up the paper of my drawings. "Let me take and study this." He started away, muttering, ". . . Have to contrive some way to procure the metals . . ." But then he turned back, frowning, and said, "When you explained the workings of the arcabuz, Tenamáxtli, you made it plain that the secret powder called pólvora is the one vital component. What is the use of my building this weapon if you have no pólvora?"

"I have a pinch of it," I said, "and I think I may be able to divine the separate constituents. By the time you have made the weapon, Pochotl, I hope to have the pólvora in abundance. That young soldier was indiscreet enough to give me a hint that may help."

"The hint," I said to Netzlin and Citláli, "was that *women* make some contribution to this powdery mixture. An *intimate* contribution, he called it."

Citláli widened her eyes at that, as she and her husband and I, squatting on the earthen floor of their little house, regarded the pinch of pólvora I had carefully put onto a piece of bark paper.

"As you can see," I went on, "the powder appears gray in color. But, working very meticulously with the tip of a tiny feather, I have succeeded in separating the almost impalpable grains of it. As best I can determine, there are only three different sorts mixed together. One kind is black, one is yellow and one is white."

Netzlin grunted skeptically. "So much painstaking and ticklish labor, and what do you learn from that? The specks could be pollens from any number of different flowers."

"But they are not," I said. "I have already identified two of them, simply by touching a few grains of each to my tongue. The black specks are nothing but common charcoal. The yellow ones are the dust of that crusty excretion found around the vents of any volcano. The Spaniards use that for several other purposes as well—for preserving fruits, for making dyes, for caulking their wine casks—and they call it *azufre*."

"So those two would be easy for you to procure," said Netzlin. "But the white grains defy your so-clever investigation?"

"Yes. All I can tell about those is that they taste something like salt, only more sharp and bitter. That is why I brought the pólvora here"—I turned to Citláli—"because that soldier spoke of women."

She smiled with good humor but shrugged helplessly. "I can discern the white grains in that little pile, but I certainly do not recognize them. Why should a woman's eyes see more to them than yours do, Tenamáxtli?"

"Perhaps not the eyes," I said. "A woman's other senses and intuitions are known to be much more acute than a man's. Here, I will separate out a number of those specks." I had brought the little feather, and delicately employed it, so that I teased a minute quantity of the white grains apart from the rest. "Now, taste them, Citláli."

"Must I?" she asked, eyeing them askance. Then she leaned forward—with considerable effort, because her protuberant belly was in the way—lowered her head to the paper and sniffed. "Must I really taste them?" she asked again, sitting back on her heels. "They smell exactly like xitli."

"*Xitli?*" said both Netzlin and myself, blinking at her, because that word means "urine."

Citláli blushed with embarrassment and said, "Well, like *my* xitli, anyway. You see, Tenamáxtli, we have only a single public retiring-closet here on this street, and only immodest women go there to urinate. Most of us use axixcáltin pots and, when they are full, go and empty them in that closet's pit."

"But nobody—not even a Spanish woman, I am sure—urinates *powder*," I said. "Unless, Citláli, you are one uncommon human being."

"I am no such thing, you simpleton!" she said, in mock anger, but blushing again. "However, I have noticed that while the xitli sits undisturbed between emptyings, at the bottom of the axixcáli there come into being some little whitish crystals."

I stared at her, cogitating.

"The way a moss or a scale sometimes develops at the bottom of a water jar," she elaborated, as if she thought me so dense that I needed a simple illustration.

I continued staring at her, making her blush redder yet.

"Those crystals I speak of," she said, "if they were ground very fine on a metlatl stone, they would be a powder just like those white grains you have there."

Almost breathlessly, I said, "You may have hit on it, Citláli."

"What?!" her husband exclaimed. "You think that is why the soldier mentioned women in connection with the secret powder?"

"In an *intimate* connection," I reminded him.

"But would a female's xitli be any different from a male's?"

"In one respect, I *know* it is, and so do you. You must have seen that when a man urinates outdoors, on the grass,

the grass is not at all affected. But wherever a woman urinates, the grass goes brown and dead.''

"You are right," he and his wife said together, and Netzlin added, "It is such a commonplace occurrence that no
one ever even speaks of it.''

"And charcoal is also a commonplace thing," I said.
"And so is the volcanic yellow azufre. It stands to reason
that something as common as a female's xitli could provide
the third ingredient of the pólvora. Citláli, forgive my audacious rudeness, but may I borrow your axixcáli pot for a
while, and do some experimenting with its contents?"

She went still redder in the face, maybe by now all the
way down to her taut belly, but her laugh was unabashed.
"Do with it what you like, you preposterous man. Only do
bring back the pot, please. I have ever more frequent need
of it now that the child is due to be born at any moment.''

It took both hands to carry the clay container, covered but
audibly sloshing, back to the mesón—and I got some queer
looks from passersby along the way, because everyone
knows an axixcáli by sight.

Yes, I had been living all this while at the mesón—or at least
sleeping and taking meals there—and so had Pochotl, while
many other lodgers had come and gone in the meantime. So,
feeling guilty about my leechlike dependence on the friars
of San José, I had often joined Pochotl in helping them clean
the place, fetch wood to stoke the fires, stir and serve the
soup, things like that. I might have thought that the friars
were lenient about my staying on and on because they knew
of my attending classes next door. But they were equally
lenient about the perpetual residence of Pochotl, so obviously
they were not showing me any partiality. In my opinion, they
were kindheartedly carrying charity to an extreme of benev-
olence. Even though I was one of its chief beneficiaries, that
day I returned from visiting Netzlin and Citláli, I made bold
to ask one of the soup-ladling friars about that.

To my bewilderment, the friar actually sneered at me.

"You think we do this for love of you shiftless layabouts?" he snarled. "We do this in God's name, for our own souls' sake. Our order bids us to debase ourselves, to work among the lowest of the lowly, the filthiest of the filthy. I am here at this mesón only because so many other brothers of the order had already volunteered for the leprosery that there was no room there for me. I had to settle for serving you indio sluggards. And that I do, and in doing that I lay up for myself credits in heaven. But one thing I do not have to do is *associate* with you. So get back to your lazy fellow redskins."

Well, I thought, charity comes in some strange guises. I wondered if the nuns of Santa Brígida felt similar contempt for the multicolored orphans in their charge—caring for them ostensibly in the name of their God, but really in the expectation of reward in the afterlife. I wondered also if Alonso de Molina had been kind and helpful to me only for that same reason. Such thoughts naturally strengthened my resolve not to adopt such a crass religion. Bad enough that my tonáli had decreed that I be born into The One World precisely when I would have to share my lifetime with these Christians; I certainly did not intend to spend my afterlife among them.

No longer feeling guilty, but feeling *ashamed* of myself for having partaken of the friars' grudging charity, I decided to move away from their mesón. The Cathedral elders had been paying me only a pittance for my work with notarius Alonso—barring whatever extra they had paid for my three articles of Spanish attire: shirt, trousers and boots. Still, of my wages I had spent only the occasional bit for a midday meal, so my savings should enable me to take lodging at one of the cheap native hostelries situated in the colación neighborhoods. I went to my pallet determined that this was the last night I would sleep there, that in the morning I would pack up my few belongings—which now included Citláli's axixcáli—and be gone. However, no sooner had I made that decision than it turned out that the decision had already been made for me, doubtless by those same mischievous, interfering gods who had for so long been persistently at my heels.

In the middle of the night I was awakened—as was every-one else in the men's chamber—by the shouting of the aged warder whom the friars left to watch over the premises after they had departed:

"¡Señor Tennamotch! ¿Hay aquí un señor bajo el nombre de Tennamotch?"

I knew he meant me. My name, like so many other Ná-huatl words, was always a tongue-twister for the Spaniards, particularly because they are unable to pronounce the soft "sh" sound represented by the letter *x* with which they write my name. I scrambled up from my pallet, threw on my man-tle, and went down the stairs to where the old man stood.

"¿Señor Tennamotch?" he barked, angry at having been disturbed himself. "Hay aquí una mujer insistente e impor-tuna. La vejezuela demanda a hablar contigo."

A woman? Insistently demanding to speak to me? The only female I could think of, who might come seeking me at midnight, was the mulata child Rebeca, and that was highly unlikely. Anyway, the warder had called her an "old hag." Mystified, I followed him out the front door, and there stood a woman, old indeed, and no one I had ever seen be-fore. Tears were flowing down along the many wrinkles of her face as she said in Náhuatl:

"I am midwife to the young woman friend of yours, Cit-láli. The baby is born, but the father has died."

I was shocked, but not too shocked to correct her. "You mean the mother, surely." Even I knew that even the healthiest-appearing woman could die in giving birth, but it gave me a heart pang that dear Citláli should have done so.

"No, no! The father. Netzlin."

"What? How could that be?" Then I remembered his ex-treme eagerness to see a son born to him. "Did he die of the excitement? Of a stroke of the hands of a god?"

"No, no. He waited in the front room, pacing. The instant the baby gave its first cry in the other room, Netzlin roared triumphantly and went crashing out the door into the street, bellowing, 'I have a son!' though he had not yet even seen the child.''

"Well? Did he come back and find it was a daughter? And *that* killed him?''

"No, no. He gathered all the men of the barrio, and bought much octli for them, and they all got drunk, but he much more drunk than the others.''

"And *that* killed him?'' I demanded in frustration. "Old mother, you will never make a storyteller. Best stick to midwifing.''

"Well . . . yes. But, after tonight, I think I may even give up that humble profession and—''

"*Will* you get on?'' I shouted, almost dancing in impatience.

"Yes, yes. You could say the drinking did kill poor fuddled Netzlin. He was caught by the soldiers on night patrol. They beat and cut him to death.''

I was too stunned to say anything. The old midwife went on:

"The neighbors came to tell us. Citláli was already near to frenzy, and the news of Netzlin's death on top of everything else drove her near to madness. But she was able to tell me where to find you and—''

"What do you mean—on top of everything else? Did the birthing cause injury to her? Is she in pain? In danger?''

"Just come, Tenamáxtli. She needs comforting. She needs you.''

Rather than go on asking frantic questions and getting dotard answers that were nearly sending *me* into a frenzy, I said, "Very well, old mother. Let us hurry.''

As we approached the unlighted house, we heard no screams or moans or other sounds of distress coming from within. But I let the old woman precede me, and waited in the front room while she tiptoed into the other. She returned with a finger held to her lips, whispering: "She sleeps at last.''

"She is not dead?" I asked, in a sort of a shout of a whisper.

"No, no. Only sleeping, and that is good. But come now—quietly—and see the infant. It sleeps also."

With a tongs, she plucked an ember from the cooking hearth and used it to light a coconut-oil lamp, and with that led me into the room where Citláli slept. In a straw-padded box beside her pallet lay the child, neatly swathed, and the midwife held the lamp so I could look down at it. To me it looked like any other newborn: red and raw and as wrinkled as the midwife, but apparently entire, with all the requisite appendages, the proper number of ears and fingers and toes and such. It lacked hair, true, but there was nothing unusual about that.

"Why did you want me to see it, old mother?" I whispered. "I have seen babies before, and this one appears no different."

"Ayya, friend Tenamáxtli, it has no eyes."

"The child is blind? How could you tell?"

"Not just blind. *It has no eyes.* Look more closely."

Since the child was asleep, I had taken for granted that its eyelids were closed. But now I could see that there was no line of closed lashes. Where there should have been lids, each eye socket was closed over—from the faint little eyebrows down to the cheekbones—with the same delicate skin that covered the rest of the face, only slightly indented where the eyeballs should have been.

"By all the darkness of Míctlan," I muttered, horrified. "You are right, old mother. It is a monster."

"That is why Citláli was so distraught, even before she heard the news about Netzlin. At least he was spared knowing of this." She hesitated, then asked, "Shall I throw it into a canal?"

That would have been the kindest thing, for both Citláli and the infant. It would indeed have been the *obligatory* thing, according to the customs of The One World. Children born defective in either body or intellect were disposed of, immediately as the defect was discovered. It was the natural and expected thing to do, in order that such creatures not grow up to be a burden to themselves and to the community, or, worse, perhaps to bear similarly blighted children themselves. No one wept or regretted or disputed the quick disposal of such unfortunates. It was too plainly necessary, to maintain undiluted the best physical and mental qualities of the race. One nation, the Cloud People of Uaxyácac, renowned for their beauty, even disposed of infants who were merely *ugly*.

But, I reminded myself, this was no longer The One World, free to follow its age-old, wise traditions. I knew that the Christians let their own varicolored and despised mongrel offspring live and grow up—even those wretched ones of splotched brown-and-white complexion that they called *pintojos*, from whom *everyone* of every other color turned his gaze away in revulsion. So there was probably a Christian law requiring that *any* child—though misbegotten and, for whatever reasons of practicality, unwanted—must be kept and reared, at whatever cost in misery to itself, its parents and all the rest of society. I was not *sure* that such a law existed; I would have to remember to ask Alonso if the Christians truly were that insensitive and pitiless and unmerciful. Anyway, this one poor creature's fate need not be decided this very night, so I told the midwife:

"It is not for me to say. Netzlin would assuredly have told you to get rid of it. But he is gone, and Citláli is its only parent. We will wait for her to wake."

X

"I WISH TO keep the child," said Citláli when she had awakened and I had spoken some consoling and encouraging words, and she was able to regard the two sudden disasters in her life with more composure than she had the night before.

I asked her, "Have you considered what you will have to bear? Besides staying in constant and vigilant attendance on the child—perhaps even until it is full grown, or even until one of you dies—you will suffer the scorn and derision of all our people, especially our priests. And to what sort of tonáli has your baby been destined? A life of abject dependence on its mother. A life of inability to deal with the commonest happenings of every day, let alone any real difficulty that may come along. Practically no hope of its ever doing anything in life to earn a place in the happy afterworld of Tonatíucan. Why, no tonalpóqui will even deign to consult his book of omens to give the child an auspicious name."

"Then its birthday name will have to serve as its only name," she murmured, undeterred. "Yesterday was the day Two-Wind, was it not? So—Ome-Ehécatl its name will be, and that is fitting. The wind has no eyes, either."

"There," I said, "you have spoken it. Ome-Ehécatl will never even see you, Citláli; never know what its own mother looks like; never marry and give you grandchildren; never support you in your old age. You yourself are still young and comely and talented in your craft, and sweet of nature, but you will not likely attract another husband, not with such a gross impediment hung upon you. Meanwhile—"

"Please, Tenamáxtli, no more," she said sadly. "In my sleep I confronted all those obstacles in my dreams, one after another. And you are right. They are formidable. Nevertheless, little Ehécatl is all that I have left of Netzlin and our life together. That little I wish to keep."

"Very well, then," I said. "If you *must* persist in this folly, I insist on helping you to do so. You will need a friend and an ally against those obstacles."

She looked at me unbelievingly. "You would encumber yourself with both of us impediments?"

"For as long as I can, Citláli. Mind you, I do not speak of marriage or of permanence. There will come a time when I expect to be doing—other things."

"That plan of which you have spoken. To drive the white men out of The One World."

"Yes, that. But, for right now, I had already decided to move out of the mesón and seek private lodgings. I will stay here with you—if you agree—and contribute my savings to the household. I think I need no further classes in my study of Spanish, and I *know* I want no more in the study of Christianity. I will continue to do my work with the Cathedral's notarius, to keep on earning those wages. In my free time I will occupy Netzlin's concesión stall in the market. I see there is a supply of baskets yet to be sold, and when you regain your strength, you can make more. There will be no need for you ever to leave Ehécatl's side. In the evenings, you can assist me in my experiments at making pólvora."

"It is more than I could have hoped for, and you are kind to offer it, Tenamáxtli." But she looked vaguely troubled.

"You have been kind to me, Citláli, ever since we met. And already helpful, I believe, in that matter of the pólvora. Have you some objection to my offer?"

"Only that I, too, have no intention of marrying anyone. Or to be anyone's woman. Even if that is the price of survival."

I said stiffly, "I suggested no such thing. Nor did I expect you to infer it."

"Forgive me, dear friend." She reached out a hand and held mine. "I am sure you and I could easily become . . . and I know the powdered root that safeguards against . . . but it does not *always* avert mishaps . . . Ayya, Tenamáxtli, I am trying to say that I very well might yearn someday to have you—but *not* to chance having another deformed child like—"

"I understand, Citláli. I promise, we shall live together as chastely as brother and sister, bachelor and spinster."

Which is what we did, and for quite a long time, during which many things occurred, of which I shall try to tell in sequence.

That first day, I removed my belongings—and the sloshing axixcáli pot—from the Mesón de San José, never to go there again. I also took away with me the artificer Pochotl, and led him to the Cathedral, and introduced him to the notarius Alonso, and highly recommended him as the one man best qualified to devise all those sacramental baubles that were wanted. Before Alonso, in turn, led him off to meet the clerics who would instruct and supervise him, I told Pochotl where I would be living from now on, and then told him in an undertone:

"I will, of course, be seeing you here at the Cathedral, and will be much interested in your progress with this work. But I trust you will report to me at my new lodgings your progress in that *other* work."

"I will, to be sure. If all goes well for me here, I shall be immeasurably indebted to you, Cuatl Tenamáxtli."

And that very night I began my attempts at concocting pólvora. All the traveling the axixcáli had endured had not dissolved or disturbed the little whitish crystals that, true to Citláli's word, had formed in the bottom of the pot. I gingerly

extracted those from the xitli, and set them to dry on a piece
of bark paper. Then, simply at a venture, I set the pot itself
on the hearth fire until the remaining urine came to a boil.
It produced a fearful stink and made Citláli exclaim, in mock
horror, that she was sorry she had let me move into the
house. However, my venture proved worthwhile; when all
the xitli had boiled away, it left still more of the little crystals.

While all of those were drying, I went off to the market
and easily found lumps of charcoal and of the yellow azufre
for sale, and brought home with me a quantity of each. While
I pounded those lumps into powder with the heel of my
Spanish boot, Citláli, though still abed, ground the xitli crystals on a métlatl stone. Then, on my piece of bark paper, I
thoroughly mixed the black, yellow and white grains together
in equal measure. For the sake of caution against accident, I
took the paper to the muddy alley outside the house. A number of the neighborhood children, already attracted by the
stench I had inflicted on the locality, watched with curiosity
as I touched an ember from the hearth to that powder mixture. And then they cheered, though the result was no thunder
or lightning, merely a small, sparkly fizzle and a cloud of
smoke.

I was not too disappointed to make a gracious bow to the
children in thanks for their applause. I had already perceived,
in the pinch of pólvora I had got from the young soldier-
fowler, that the mixture was not compounded equally of
black, white and yellow. But I had to start *somewhere*, and
this first attempt had been a success in one important respect.
Its cloud of blue smoke smelled exactly like the smoke that
had erupted from the arcabuces at the lakeside. So the crystal
derived from female urine *must* be the third ingredient of
pólvora. Now I had only to try various proportions of those
ingredients to achieve the proper balance. My chief problem,
obviously, would be the procurement of enough of those xitli
crystals. I half thought of asking the gathered children to run
home and bring me all their mothers' axixcáltin. But I dis-

missed that idea; it would cause questions from the neighbors—the first, probably, being their asking why a demented man was at large in their streets.

Some months went by, during which I kept boiling urine at every opportunity, until I think the neighborhood in general had got used to the smell, but I personally was getting thoroughly sick of it. Anyway, that labor did yield the crystals, though still in minute quantities, making it difficult for me to try differing measures of the white powder and the other two colors. I kept track of all my experiments, recording them on a piece of paper that I was careful not to misplace—listing them like this: two parts black, two yellow, one white; and three parts black, two yellow, one white; and so on. But no mixture I tried gave any more heartening result than the very first, when the proportions had been one and one and one. That is to say, most mixtures provided only a sparkle, fizzle and smoke, and some gave no result at all.

Meanwhile, I had explained to the notarius Alonso why I was ceasing to attend the classes at the Colegio. He agreed with me that my fluency in Spanish would be best improved, henceforward, by my actually speaking and hearing it, rather than studying the rules of it. He was not so approving, however, of my retirement from Tete Diego's teachings about Christianity.

"You could be imperiling the salvation of your immortal soul, Juan Británico," he said solemnly.

I asked, "Would not God count it a good deed that I hazard my salvation in order to support a helpless widow woman?"

"Well . . ." he said, uncertain. "But only until she is able to support herself, Cuatl Juan. Then you must resume your preparation for Confirmation."

At intervals thereafter, he would inquire as to the health and condition of the widow, and every time I could tell him honestly that she was still housebound, having to care for her crippled child. Thereafter, too, I believe Alonso kept me employed long beyond the time that I was really of any use

to him—finding ever more obscure, even dull and valueless
pages of word-pictures made far away and long ago, for me
to help him translate—just because he knew that my wages
went mostly for the upkeep of my little household.

Whenever I was not occupied with that, I visited the several workrooms that the Cathedral had provided for Pochotl.
His clerical employers had first tested his skill by giving him
a very small amount of gold in a lump, to see what he might
do with it. I forget what it was that he created, but it made
the priests ecstatic. From then on, they allowed him increasing quantities of gold and silver, and gave him instructions
as to what to make—candlesticks and censers and various
urns—and left the actual design of those things to him, and
were vastly pleased with every one of them.

So now Pochotl was master of a smelter room where all
the metals he used were melted and refined; a forging room
where the coarser metals—iron, steel, brass—were hammered into shape; a room of mortars and crucibles in which
the precious metals were liquefied; a room of workbenches,
all strewn with tools of the utmost delicacy. And of course
he had many assistants, some of them who had previously
also been jewel-artificers in Tenochtítlan. But most of the
helpers were slaves—and most of those were Moros, because
those people are immune to the hottest heat—who did the
heavy drudgery requiring not much skill.

Naturally, Pochotl was as happy as if he had been transported alive to the blissful afterworld of Tonatíucan—"Have
you noticed, Tenamáxtli, how I am becoming enviably fat
again, now that I am well paid and well fed?"—and he enjoyed showing me his every new production, and he took
pleasure in my admiring them as much as the priests did.
But there at the Cathedral he and I never spoke of his other
work; that project we discussed only when he came to the
house, to ask questions about various parts of the arcabuz
that I had sketched for him:

"Is this piece supposed to move like so? Or like so?"

And in time he began to bring actual metal pieces to show, for my approval or comment.

"It is a good thing," he said, "that you got me appointed to the Cathedral's enterprise at the same time you asked me to build this weapon. Just the making of the arcabuz's long, hollow tube would have been impossible without the tools I now have. And only today, I was trying to bend a thin metal strip into that spiral you called a spring, and fumbling at it, when I was unexpectedly interrupted by a certain Padre Diego. He startled me by speaking to me in Náhuatl."

"I know the man," I said. "Caught you, did he? And he would hardly believe a spring to be any kind of church decoration. Did he scold you for neglecting your proper work?"

"No. But he did ask what I was fooling with. Cunningly, I told him that I had had an idea for an invention, and I was struggling to bring it into reality."

"An invention, eh?"

"That is what Padre Diego said, too, and he laughed in ridicule. He said, 'That is no invention, *maestro*. It is a contrivance that has been familiar to us civilized folk for ages and ages.' And then—can you guess what he did, Tenamáxtli?"

"He recognized it as a piece of an arcabuz," I groaned. "Our secret project is exposed and thwarted."

"No, no. Not at all. He went away somewhere and came back, bringing me a whole handful of different sorts of springs. The spiral coil that I require to spin the grooved wheel." He showed me the spring. "Also the flat kind that bends back and forth, which I need for snapping what you called the cat's-paw." He showed me that one, too. "In brief, I now know how to make those things, but I do not need to. The good priest made me a gift of them."

I let out my breath in a sigh of relief. "Marvelous!" I exclaimed. "For once, the coincidence-loving gods have been gracious. I must say, Pochotl, you are having more success than I." And I told him of my discouraging experiments with the pólvora.

He thought for a moment, then suggested, "Perhaps you are not experimenting under the right conditions. From what you have described as the workings of the arcabuz, I think you cannot judge the efficacy of the pólvora until you pack it into a tightly constricted space before you touch fire to it."

"Perhaps," I said. "But I have only pinches of the powder to work with. It will be a long time before I can fabricate enough of it to *pack* into anything."

However, the very next day the gods of coincidence arranged another happy furtherance of my project.

As I had promised Citláli, I was spending some part of every day at the late Netzlin's market stall. That required little of me except to be there standing among the baskets whenever a customer wished to buy one, because Citláli had told me the price she expected to be paid for each one—in cacao beans or snippets of tin or maravedí coins—and the customer could judge the quality without my needing to point it out. He or she could even pour water into any of Citláli's baskets to test it; they were all so tightly woven that they would not leak water, let alone seeds or meal or whatever else they were destined to contain. Since there was nothing else for me to do, between customers, I spent the time conversing with passersby or smoking picíetl with other stallkeepers or—as I was doing on the day of which I speak—pouring onto my stall's shopboard small mounds of charcoal, azufre and xitli powders, so I could morosely meditate on them and their infinite number of possible combinations.

"*Ayya*, Cuatl Tenamáxtli!" boomed a hearty voice in a pretense of dismay. "Are you going into competition with *my* wares?"

I looked up. It was a man named Peloloá, a pochtécatl trader whom I knew from previous encounters. He regularly came to the City of Mexíco, bringing the two prime products of his native Xoconóchco, that coastal Hot Land far to the south, whence had come most of our cotton and salt since long before the white men set foot in The One World.

"By Iztocíuatl!" he exclaimed, invoking the goddess of

salt, as he pointed at my pathetic pile of white grains on the shopboard. "Are you intending to trounce me at my own trade?"

"No, Cuatl Peloloá," I said, smiling ruefully. "This is not a salt that anyone would wish to buy."

"You are right," he said, touching a few grains to his tongue, before I could stop him and tell him it was purely essence of urine. Then he surprised me, saying, "It is only the bitter first-harvest. What the Spaniards call *salitre*. It sells so cheaply that it would hardly pay you a living."

"Ayyo," I breathed. "You recognize this substance?"

"But of course. Who from the Xoconóchco would not?"

"Do you boil women's urine in the Xoconóchco, then?"

He looked blank and said, "What?"

"Nothing. No matter. You called the powder 'first-harvest.' What does that mean?"

"What it says. Some people think we simply dip a scoop into the sea and strain the salt directly from it. Not so. The making of salt is a more complicated process. We dike off the shallows of our lagoons and let them dry, yes, but then those chunks and lumps and flakes of dry matter must be rid of their many impurities. First, in fresh water, they are sieved clean of sand and shells and weeds. Then, again in fresh water, the substance is boiled. From that initial boiling come crystals that are also sieved out. Those are the first-harvest crystals—salitre—exactly what you have there, Tenamáxtli, only yours has been pulverized. To get to the goddess's invaluable *real* salt takes several more stages of refinement."

"You said this salitre sells, but cheaply."

"The Xoconóchco farmers buy it merely to spread it on their cotton fields. They claim it enhances the ground's fertility. The Spanish employ salitre in some manner in their tanneries. I know not what use you might be thinking of making of it—"

"Tanning!" I lied. "Yes, that is it. I contemplate adding fine leather goods to my stock here. I was only puzzled as to where to get the salitre."

"I shall be glad to bring you a whole tamémi load, on my next trip north," said Peloloá. "Cheap it is, but I shall charge you nothing at all. You are a friend."

I raced home to announce the good news. But in my excitement, I did it awkwardly. I dashed through the doorway curtain, shouting:

"You can cease urinating now, Citláli!"

My inelegant entrance threw her into such a paroxysm of laughter that it was a while before she could gasp out, "I once—called you—preposterous. I was wrong. You are—totally xolopítli!" And it was a while longer before I could gather my wits and rephrase my announcement, and tell her what great good fortune had befallen me.

Citláli said shyly, and she was seldom shy, "Perhaps we should make a small celebration. To show gratitude to the salt goddess Iztocíuatl."

"A celebration? Of what sort?"

Still shyly, and blushing now, she said, "I have been taking the powdered root tlatlaohuéhuetl throughout the past month. I believe we need worry about no mishap if we were to give its vaunted impregnability a trial."

I looked at her—"with new eyes," I was about to say, but that would not be true. During all this time that we had been sleeping apart, on pallets in the separate rooms, I had been desiring her, but virtuously had given no sign of it. Also, it had been so very long since I had lain with a female—the tiny brown Rebeca—that I might soon have resorted to the services of a maátitl. Citláli must have taken my brief hesitation as reluctance, for now she said boldly, with laughter, and made me laugh, too:

"Niez tlalqua ayquic axitlinéma." Which means, "I promise not to urinate."

And so we embraced laughing, which, I now learned for the first time, is the very best way to begin.

All this while, Ome-Ehécatl had been growing, from a babe in arms, to an infant that crawled, to a weanling learning wobblily to walk. I kept expecting Ehécatl to die any day, and no doubt Citláli did, too, because a child afflicted with a physical deformity so evident at birth usually has other defects that are not visible, and dies very young. During Ehécatl's infancy, the only other deficiency that became apparent was the child's never learning to speak, and possibly that indicated deafness as well. That may have troubled Citláli more than it did me; I was frankly pleased that the child never cried, either.

Anyway, its brain appeared to function well enough. While learning to walk, Ehécatl also learned to make its way most adroitly around the house and learned early on to veer clear of the cooking hearth. Whenever Citláli decided to give the child some outdoor exercise, she would stand it in the street and point it and give it a gentle shove. Ehécatl would dauntlessly toddle straight along the middle of that street, confident that its mother had made sure nothing was in the way. Of course, Citláli was always gentle and kindly toward everyone, but I believe she also had maternal feelings, even for such an offspring as Ehécatl. She kept the child clean, and tidy of dress—and well fed, though at first it had difficulty in finding her teat and, later, in wielding a spoon. The other neighborhood children rather surprised me with their attitude. They seemed to regard Ehécatl as a kind of plaything—not human like themselves, certainly, but not as inert as a straw or clay doll—and played almost affectionately with the child, without ever being abusive or derisive. All in all, while getting to live for more years than such monstrosities usually do, Ehécatl passed those years as pleasantly as an incurable cripple could ever have hoped to do.

I knew that Citláli's chief worry about the child was the question of its afterlife, whether Ehécatl went there young or old. Citláli probably had some concern for her own afterlife, as well. No person of The One World is necessarily damned to the nothingness of Míctlan after death—as Christians are to hell—simply because he or she has been born, has lived and has died. Still, to *assure* that one does not get plunged to Míctlan, one should have done *something* in one's lifetime to merit residing afterward in the sun god's Tonatíucan or one of the other beneficent gods' similarly appetizing afterworlds.

A child's only hope of doing that is to sacrifice itself—that is, have its parents sacrifice it—to appease the hunger and the vanity of one god or another. But no priest would have accepted a useless object like Ehécatl as an offering to even the least of gods. A grown man can best attain his desired afterworld by dying in battle or on the altar of a god, or doing some deed noteworthy enough to please the gods. A grown woman can also die in sacrifice to a god, and some have done deeds as praiseworthy as any man's, but most have deserved their places in Tonatíucan or Tlálocan, or wherever, simply by being the mothers of children whose tonáli has destined *them* to be warriors or sacrifices or mothers. Ome-Ehécatl could never be any of those things, which is why I say Citláli must have had some anxiety about her own prospects after death.

XI

SOME MONTHS AFTER our earlier encounter in the market, the pochtécatl Pololoá came again from the Xoconóchco, and brought along one tamémi laden with nothing but a big sack of the "first-harvest" salitre, and grandly presented that to me, and even bade the porter continue carrying it as far as my house. And there I began devoting every free moment to trying the black, white and yellow powders in mixtures of varying proportions, and noting down every experiment I made. I now had a good deal more free time than before, because both Pochotl and I had been dismissed from our duties at the Cathedral.

"It is because the Church has a new pope at Rome," the notarius Alonso explained in a tone of apology. "The old Papa Clemente Séptimo has died and been succeeded by the Papa Paulo Tercero. We have just been informed of his accession and his first directives to all the world's Catholic Christian clergy."

I said, "You do not sound pleased by the news, Cuatl Alonso."

He grimaced sourly. "The Church commands that every priest be celibate and chaste and honorable—or at least that he pretend to be. That certainly should apply to the pope, the highest priest of all. But it is well known that while he

was still just the Padre Farnese, he began his climb through
the Church hierarchy by what the coarser folk call *'lamiendo
el culo del patron.'* That is to say, he put his own sister,
Giulia the Beautiful, to bed with the earlier Papa Alessandro
Sexto, thereby winning for himself substantial preferments.
And this Papa Paulo himself has by no means been celibate
during his life. He has numerous children and grandchildren.
And one of those, a grandson, Paulo has already—immedi-
ately on attaining the papacy—made a *cardinal* at Rome.
And that grandson is only *fourteen years old.*''

"Interesting," I said, though I did not find it very much
so. ''But what has this to do with us here?''

''Among his other directives, Papa Paulo has decreed that
every diocese commence to conserve on its expenditures.
That means we can no longer finance even such a small
luxury as your work with me on the codices. Also, the pope
has addressed Bishop Zumárraga *specifically* in the matter of
what he calls 'squandering' gold and silver on 'fripperies.'
All the precious metals the Church has acquired here in New
Spain he decrees must be shared among less fortunately endowed bishoprics. Or so he says.''

''You do not believe him?''

Alonso blew out a long breath. ''Doubtless I am predis-
posed to distrust him, because of what I know of his personal
life. Nevertheless, it sounds to me as if Papa Paulo is appro-
priating his own private King's Fifth from the treasures of
New Spain. Anyway, that is why Pochotl must leave off his
wondrous jewelsmithing for us, and you your help with the
translations.''

I smiled at him. ''You and I both know, Cuatl Alonso,
that for a long while you have been merely—and compassionately—inventing work for me to do. But I have some
savings put by. I think that I and the widow and orphan I
support will not suffer much hardship from my leaving this
post.''

''I shall be sorry to see you go, Juan Británico. But I
strongly recommend, now that you will not be occupied here,

that you put those hours to good advantage by resuming your Christian studies under Padre Diego.''

''It is thoughtful and caring of you to tell me that,'' I said, and meant it, but I made no promise.

He sighed, then said, ''I should like to bestow on you a small gift, by way of saying farewell.'' He took up a bright object that was holding down the papers on his table. ''Everybody owns a thing like this nowadays—I mean every Spaniard—but this particular one was given to me by that poor wretched heretic whom you and I saw executed outside the Cathedral here.''

Ayyo, I thought, a gift to him from my own father, and now from him to me. Alonso handed it over, a piece of crystal the size of my palm, circular and smoothly polished. I still had that other crystal that my father had involuntarily bequeathed, tucked safely among my belongings. But that was a yellow topaz, and this was clear quartz. Also, this one was differently shaped, being gently rounded on both surfaces.

''That old man recounted how he discovered these objects, somewhere in the southern lands,'' said Alonso, ''and made them popular utensils among all his people. They are now much used by us Spaniards—very useful things they are, indeed—but they seem to have been forgotten by you indios.''

''Useful?'' I asked. ''How?''

''Observe.'' He took it from me and held it in a shaft of sunlight from the window. In his other hand he took a piece of bark paper and held it so the sunlight came through the crystal onto the paper. Moving the paper and crystal back and forth, he gradually brought that spot of light down to a bright point on the paper. And, after a very brief moment, the paper began to emit smoke there—then, amazingly, broke into a small but real flame. Alonso blew it out and handed the crystal back to me. ''A burning-glass,'' he said. ''We also call it a *lente*, from the shape of it, like the bean of the same name. With it, a person can kindle a fire without any need for steel and pirita, or without the drudgery of drill-stick and block. When the sun is shining, anyway. I trust you will find it useful, too.''

I certainly would, I was thinking exultantly. It was like a gift from the gods. No—a gift from my father Mixtli, now surely a dweller in Tonatíucan. He must have been watching me from that afterworld as I struggled to master the making of pólvora—and must know *why* I was doing so—and decided to make the struggle easier for me. Even long gone and far removed from mortal concerns, my father Mixtli *must* be in accord with my intention to rid The One World of its alien masters. And this was his way of telling me so, from beyond the immeasurable distances that separate us living from the dead.

I said nothing of that to Alonso de Molina, of course, but only, ''I thank you very much, indeed. I will think of you every time I make use of the lente.'' And then I said good-bye.

Pochotl was no more woebegone than I at being dismissed from the Cathedral roster of workers. He had cannily invested the wages he had been paid, having built for himself a more than decent house and workshop in one of the better colaciones of the city set aside for native settlement. His house was, in fact, right on the edge of the Traza reserved for the Spaniards. And such numbers of those Spaniards had been dazzled by the articles Pochotl had crafted for the Cathedral that he was already being solicited to do private commissions.

''The white men are finally striving to emulate us in culture and refinement and good taste,'' he said. ''Have you noticed, Tenamáxtli? They no longer even *smell* so bad as before. They have acquired our habit of bathing, though perhaps not so frequently or thoroughly as we do. And now they have learned to appreciate the kind of jewelry that I have always done—much finer and more ingenious works than those of their own clumsy artificers. So they bring me their gold, their silver, their gems, and tell me what they want—a necklace, a finger ring, a sword hilt—and leave me to determine the design. None yet has been less than overjoyed at the results or failed to pay me handsomely. And none has yet remarked on my always somehow having a bit of the metal left over to keep for my own.''

"I am mightily glad for you," I said. "I only hope that you have some time free for—"

"Ayyo, yes. The arcabuz is almost complete. I have finished the metal works of it, and now have only to mount those properly in the wooden stock. I was much aided, odd though it may seem, by the order of my dismissal from the Cathedral. The bishop bade me empty and clean my workrooms, and he set guards to make sure that I did not carry off any of the valuables with which I had been entrusted. And I did not, but I did take the opportunity, seeing the soldiers' weapons up close, to ogle every detail of the way those arcabuces are put together. Now—how are you faring in the making of the pólvora?"

I was still engaged in the seemingly never-to-end process of trying different mixtures of the powders, and I will not recount all the dreary time and infuriating attempts I had to endure. I will merely say that *I finally achieved success*—with a mixture that was two-thirds salitre and one-third comprising equal measures of charcoal and azufre.

When, one afternoon, I used my new lente to bring a dot of sunlight down to ignite that little heap of grayish powder—what would prove to be the ultimate and conclusive trial—the alley outside our house was empty of any of the local children. They all had got even more bored than I by the repeated puny fizzles. On this occasion, however, the powder absolutely *spewed* sparks, and only a modest puff of the acrid blue smoke. But, most important, it uttered that angry sound like a muted snarl—what I had heard when the young soldier let me pull the gatillo and fire his arcabuz. At last, *I knew how to make pólvora*, and could make it in significant quantities. After doing a small, private victory dance and giving silent but heartfelt thanks to the war god

Huitzilopóchtli—and to my revered late father Mixtli—I hurried off to Pochotl's house to announce my grand achievement.

"*Yyo ayyo*, I stand in awe of you!" he exclaimed. "Now, as you can see, I too am very nearly done." He gestured at his workbench, bearing the metal components I had already examined, and now also the wooden stock that he was shaping. "While I finish my work, I suggest that you do what I suggested before: test the pólvora in some kind of firmly constricted container."

"I intend to," I said. "Meanwhile, Pochotl, make for the arcabuz also some round lead balls for it to discharge. They must be of a size to ram down into the hollow tube, but must fit *snugly* in there."

I went again to the market and begged a lump of common clay from a potter there. I took it home and, while Citláli watched pridefully, poured onto that a very modest measure of pólvora, rolled the clay tightly around it to make a ball about the size of a nopáli fruit, punched a tiny hole in that with a quill, then set the ball to dry near the hearth. The next day, it was as hard as any pot, and I took it out to the alley.

This being something new to them, the local children did gather around again, and were equally interested by the lente I was about to use. But I waved them off to a respectful distance—and also put an arm up to shield my face—before I touched the crystal's hot spot to the quill-hole. I am glad that I took those precautions, because the ball disappeared on the instant, with a flash that was dazzling even in the daylight, a cloud of the pungent blue smoke, a noise almost as loud as was made by the arcabuz I had once discharged—and a spray of sharp fragments that stung my raised arm and bare chest. Two or three of the children uttered small yelps, but none of us was more than slightly nicked. Rather too late, it occurred to me that there might have been a roving patrol somewhere near enough to have heard the report. No one came to investigate, but I decided to do my experimenting, from then on, well away from the city.

So, a few days later, carrying a pólvora-packed hard pottery ball as big as my fist, and some of the powder carried loose in a pouch, I took a ferry acáli at the western edge of the island and crossed to the mainland bluff called Chapultépec, Grasshopper Hill. I could easily have walked there; this part of the lake was only about knee-deep, green-brown and fetid. The rocky front of the bluff had formerly, so I was told, been carved with gigantic faces, the many-times-magnified visages of four of the Revered Speakers of the Mexíca. But the faces were gone, because Spanish soldiers had boisterously used them for practice in firing the immense, wheel-mounted, big-mouthed thunder-tubes called *culebrinas* and *falconetes*. The bluff was now just a rocky-fronted bluff again, its only notable feature being the aqueduct that jutted out from it, carrying the water from Chapultépec's springs to the city.

All about, the parkland that the last Motecuzóma had laid out—with gardens and fountains and statues—likewise had been obliterated. There existed now only grass, wildflowers, underbrush and, here and there, the great, towering oldest-of-old trees, the ahuehuétquin cypresses, too invulnerably tough for even the Spaniards to chop down. The only people I saw anywhere around were the slaves who were at work every day, repairing the ever-occurring leaks and fractures in the aqueduct. I had to trudge but a short way inland to find myself alone, and to find a spot of ground clear of underbrush, on which to place the object I carried.

This time, I had made the clay ball with a flattened base, and had put there the quill-hole, so the hole was on a level with the ground when I set down the thing. I opened my pouch, and starting from that quill-hole, I dribbled a thin stream of the pólvora to a considerable distance and around the root spread of a big cypress. There, safe behind the tree's trunk, I took out my burning-glass, held it in a sunbeam that had made its way through the foliage, and kindled a small flame at the very end of my powder train. As I had hoped, the loose pólvora began sparking and snarling, and the sparks danced merrily back the way I had come. I realized that this would not always be a practical way to ignite my experimental balls; any breath of wind would interrupt its progress; but that day no wind did. The sparking went around the cypress's bole and out of my sight, but I could still smell the distinctive sharp odor of the pólvora trail's burning.

Then, though I had anticipated it, or at least fervently hoped for it, there erupted such a roar of noise that I jumped in spite of myself. The tree that shielded me seemed to rock, too. Countless birds burst from the greenery all about, screeching and cawing, and the underbrush rustled violently to the scampering of unseen animals. I heard the whizzing sound of the pottery shards flying in all directions, and a few of them going *thunk* against the limbs of my sheltering tree, while leaves and twigs cut loose by them came fluttering down, and the blue smoke spread its pungent miasma far and wide in the windless air.

From somewhere in the distance, I heard human shouts, too. So, as soon as there was no more patter of things falling roundabout, I left my tree and went to where the ball had been. A patch of the earth as big as a petatl mat was scorched black, and the nearby bushes were charred to shriveling. At the edge of the clearing, a rabbit lay dead; it had been pierced right through by one of the shards.

The shouts were getting nearer and more excited. I only then remembered that the Spaniards had built, on the heights of Grasshopper Hill, a fort-and-stockade structure they called the *Castillo*, and that it was always full of soldiers, because that was where new army recruits were trained. Even the rawest recruit would, of course, have recognized the sound of a pólvora explosion and—it having come from the depths of a usually uninhabited forest—would dash out with his comrades to find out where and how it had happened, and by whose doing. I did not want to leave any evidence for those soldiers. I had no time to try to erase the burn mark, but I did pick up the rabbit before I scurried off toward the lakeside.

That night, Pochotl visited the house, with an oily rolled-up mantle under his arm and a many-creased grin on his face. With the sly, secretive mien of a conjuror, he laid the bundle on the floor and very slowly unrolled it, while Citláli and I watched bright-eyed. There it was: the replica arcabuz, and very authentic it looked.

"Ouiyo ayyo," I murmured, genuinely pleased and genuinely admiring of Pochotl's artistry. Citláli smiled from one to the other of us, pleased *for* us both.

Pochotl handed me the key for winding the spring inside. I inserted it in its place, turned it and heard the ratcheting noise I had heard once before. Then, with my thumb, I pulled back the cat's-paw holding its flake of false-gold, and it clicked and stayed back. Then, with my forefinger, I tugged the gatillo. The cat's-paw snapped down, the false-gold struck the grooved wheel just as the wheel was spun by its wound-up spring—and the resultant sparks sprayed right across the little cazoleta pan as they were supposed to do.

"Of course," said Pochotl, "the crucial test will be to try it fully charged with pólvora and one of these." He handed me a pouch of the heavy lead balls. "But I advise you to go far away from here, Tenamáxtli, to do that. The word is already abroad. An unaccountable blast was heard today by the Chapultépec garrison." He winked at me. "The white men fear—as well they might—that someone besides themselves possesses some quantity of the pólvora. The street patrols are stopping and searching every indio carrying pots or baskets or any other possibly suspicious container."

"I expected that," I said. "I will be more circumspect henceforth."

"One other thing," said Pochotl. "I still regard your idea of revolution as foolish in the extreme. Consider, Tenamáxtli. You know how long it has taken me to make this one arcabuz. I believe it will work as warranted. But do you expect me or anyone to construct the thousands you would need to equal the weaponry of the white men?"

"No," I said. "No more need be made. If this one works as warranted, I shall use it to—well—acquire another from some Spanish soldier. Then use those two for the acquisition of two more. And so on.'' Pochotl and Citláli stared at me, either aghast or struck with admiration, I could not tell. ''But now,'' I cried, jubilant, ''let us celebrate this auspicious occasion!''

I went out and bought a jar of the best octli, and we all drank happily of it—even little Ehécatl was given some—and we adults got sufficiently inebriated that, come midnight, Pochotl bedded down in the front room rather than risk encountering a patrol. And Citláli and I reeled and giggled as we went to our pallet in the other room, there to continue the celebration in an even more enthusiastic fashion.

For my next series of experiments I made only clay balls no bigger than quails' eggs, each containing a mere thumbnail's measure of pólvora. These all burst asunder with little more noise than a castor pod makes when it explodes its seeds, so the local children soon lost interest in those, too. But they enjoyed a different amusement I gave them—asking them to be lookouts for me, prowling all the streets around, to run and warn me if they espied a patrolling soldier anywhere. Since I already knew I had made a satisfactory pólvora and had observed its nicely destructive behavior when ignited in tight confinement, what I was trying now was to find a way to set off a pólvora-packed ball, small or large, from a *distance*—some means more reliable than laying a trail of loose powder.

I have mentioned the manner in which our people generally smoked our picíetl: rolled inside what we called a poquíetl, a tube of reed or paper that slowly burned along with the herb—not in a nonburning clay pipe, as the Spaniards do.

Occasionally we, and the white men, too, liked to mix with the picíetl some other ingredient—powdered cacao, certain seeds, dried blossoms—to change its taste or fragrance. What I did now was to roll numbers of very thin paper poquíeltin that contained the herb mixed with varying traces of pólvora. An ordinary poquíetl burns slowly as a smoker puffs on it, but is likely to extinguish itself when laid down for a while. I thought the addition of pólvora would keep an unattended tube alight but still let it burn only slowly.

And I was right. Trying these tiny paper poquíeltin in varying circumferences and lengths and content of picíetl plus pólvora, I eventually hit on the right combination. Inserted into the quill-hole of one of my miniature pottery balls, such a poquíetl could be lighted and would burn for a time—brief or prolonged, depending on its length—before reaching the hole and demolishing the ball with that clap of noise. There was no way I could *accurately* time such things—for instance, to make a number of balls burst simultaneously. But I *could* make and trim a poquíetl to a length that, when lighted, would give me ample time to be far away from the scene when it burned down to the ignition hole. I could also be sure that no vagrant breeze or the footstep of some passerby would disrupt its burning, as could so easily happen with a loose powder trail.

To verify that, I next did something so daring, hazardous and downright wicked that I did not even tell Citláli about it beforehand. I made another fist-size, pólvora-packed clay ball and inserted into its quill-hole a lengthy poquíetl. On the next sunny day, I put it into my waist pouch and walked from the house to the Traza, to the building I had long ago identified as the barracks of the lesser-ranking Spanish soldiers. There was, as always, a sentry on duty at the entrance, armed and armored. Looking as stupid and inoffensive as I could manage, I sauntered past him to the corner of the building, and there stopped and knelt as if to dislodge a pebble from my sandal.

I was able, both quickly and silently, to light the protruding end of the poquíetl, then to wedge the hard ball into the space between the corner stone and the street's cobblestones. I glanced at the guard; he was paying me no attention; nor was anyone else on the crowded street; so I stood up and sauntered on my way. I had gone at least a hundred paces before I heard the bellow of the blast. Even at that distance,

I also heard the whizzing of the flying shards, and one of them actually tapped me lightly on my back. I turned and looked, and was gratified to see the commotion I had caused.

There was no visible damage to the building, except for a black, smoking blotch on its side, but two people were lying supine and bleeding near it—a man in Spanish dress and a tamémi whose yoke lay beside him. From out of the barracks came scampering not only the sentry but also numerous other soldiers, some of them only half-dressed, but all carrying weapons. Four or five of the indios on the street began running, from sheer terror at this unprecedented occurrence, and the soldiers went pelting after them. So I casually returned, to join the numerous others who stood about and gawked, obviously innocent of any involvement.

The Spaniard on the ground writhed and moaned, still alive, and a soldier brought the barracks *médico* to attend him. The unoffending tamémi, however, was quite dead. I was sorry, but I felt sure that the gods would regard him as having fallen in battle, and would treat him kindly. This had not really been a battle, of course, but I *had* struck a second blow against the enemy. Now, after two such inexplicable happenings, the white men had to have realized that they were suddenly beset by subversion, and they had to be disconcerted, perhaps even frightened, by that realization. As I had promised my mother and uncle, I had become the worm in the coyacapúli fruit, eating it from within.

During the rest of that day, the soldiers—every one in the city, I think—fanned out among the colación neighborhoods, searching houses, market stalls, the bags or bundles carried by native men and women, even making some of those strip off their clothes. But they gave that up after only the one day, their officers probably having decided that if illicit pólvora existed anywhere, it could easily be hidden (as I had hidden mine), and that the pólvora's separate ingredients, if any could be found, were totally innocuous and easily explainable. Anyway, they never got to our house, and I simply sat back and enjoyed the white men's discomfiture.

The next day, however, it was my turn to be discomfited, when a messenger came from the notarius Alonso—who knew where I lived—bidding me to appear before him at my earliest convenience. I dressed in my Spanish attire and went to the Cathedral and greeted him, again trying to look stupid and inoffensive. Alonso did not return my greeting, but gazed morosely at me for several moments before saying:

"Do you still think of me every time you use your burning-glass, Juan Británico?"

"Why, of course, Cuatl Alonso. As you said, it is a most useful—"

"Do not call me 'cuatl' any more," he snapped. "I fear we are no longer twins, brothers, even friends. I also fear that you have shed all pretense of being a Christian, meek and mild, respectful and obedient to that creed and to your superiors."

I said boldly, "I never *was* meek or mild, and I never have regarded Christians as my superiors. Do not call me Juan Británico any more."

Alonso glowered, but held his temper. "Hear me now. I am not officially involved in the army's hunt for the perpetrator of certain recent disturbances of the peace of this city. But I am as concerned as any decent and dutiful citizen should be. I do not accuse you personally, but I know you have a wide acquaintance among your fellows. I believe you could find the villain responsible for those acts as quickly as you found for us that goldsmith when we needed one."

Still boldly, I said, "I am no more a traitor to my own people, notarius, than I am obedient to yours."

He sighed and said, "So be it, then. We once *were* friends, and I will not directly denounce you to the authorities. But I give you fair warning. From the instant you leave this room, you will be followed and watched. Your every move, your every encounter, every conversation, every *sneeze* will be monitored and noted and reported. Soon or later, you will betray either yourself or another, perhaps even some person dear to you. If you do not go to the burning stake, be assured that someone will.''

"That threat," I said, "I cannot abide. You give me little choice but to depart from this city forever.''

"I think that would be best," he said coldly, "for you, for the city and for all who have ever been close to you.''

He dismissed me forthwith, and one of the Cathedral's tame indio servants made no attempt to be unobtrusive as he trailed me all the way home.

XII

▌ HAD RESOLVED to quit the City of Mexíco even before
Alonso so coldly recommended that I do so. That was because I had despaíred of ever raising an army of rebellion
from among the city's inhabitants. Like the late Netzlin—
and now Pochotl—the local men were too dependent on their
white masters to want to rise up against them. Even had they
wanted to, they were by now so enervated and unwarlike
that they would not have dared to make the attempt. If I was
to recruit any men like myself, resentful of the Spaniards'
domination and bellicose enough to challenge it, I must re-
trace my journey hither. I must go again northward, into the
unconquered lands.

"You are more than welcome to come with me," I told
Citláli. "I truly have treasured the blessing of your nearness,
your support and—well, everything you have meant to me.
But you are a woman, and some years older than I, so you
might find that I set too brisk a pace on the road. Especially
since you would have to be leading Ehécatl by the hand."

"You are definitely going, then," she murmured unhap-
pily.

"But not forever, despite what I said to the notarius. I
fully intend to come back here. At the head of an armed
force, I trust, sweeping the white men from every field and

forest, every village, every city, including this one. However, that cannot be soon. So I will not ask you to wait for me, dear Citláli. You are still an exceedingly handsome woman. You may attract another good and loving husband, aquín ixnentla? At any rate, Ehécatl is old enough now for you to take the child with you when you tend the market stall. With what you earn there, and with the sum we have put by, and without my being an extra mouth to feed—''

She interrupted, "I *would* wait, dearest Tenamáxtli, however long. But how can I hope that you will ever be back? You will be risking your life out there.''

"As I would, Citláli, even if I stayed here. As you have been risking yours. If I had been caught in the crime of experimenting with the pólvora, you would have been dragged to the stake along with me.''

"I risked that because it was a chance we were taking together. I would go anywhere, do anything, if only we did it together.''

"But there is Ehécatl to consider . . .''

"Yes," she whispered. Then, suddenly, she burst into tears and demanded, "*Why* are you so determined to pursue this folly? Why can you not resign yourself to recognize reality, and bear with it, as others have done?''

"*Why?*" I echoed, dumbfounded.

"Ayya, I know what the white men did to your father, but—''

"That is not reason enough?" I snapped. "I can still see him burning!''

"And they slew your friend, my husband. But what have they done to *you*? Tenamáxtli, you have suffered neither injury nor insult, beyond those few words spoken long ago by the mesón friar. Every other white man you have mentioned, you have said only good things of him. The kindness of the man Molina, the other teachers who gave of their knowledge, even that soldier who started you on your quest for the pólvora . . .''

"Crumbs from their table! The richly laden table that used

to be ours! Whether my tonáli dictates that I shall succeed in restoring that table to our people, I do not know. But I am sure it bids me try. I refuse to believe that I was born to settle for crumbs. And I am wagering my life on that.''

Citláli sighed so deeply that she seemed to shrink a bit. ''How much longer will I have you by me? Or how little longer? When do you plan to go?''

''Not immediately, for I will not slink away, like a techíchi dog, with its head hung low and its tail tucked under. I want to leave something for the City of Mexíco—for all of New Spain—to remember me by. And what I have in mind, Citláli, is one final crime that you and I can commit together.''

I cannot refute what Citláli had said: that I myself had never had pain, deprivation, imprisonment or even indignity inflicted on me by the Spaniards. But, during my years in the city, I had met or become aware of a multitude of my fellows who *had*. There were, as I have mentioned, the one-time warriors branded with the *G*, and the other slaves branded with the mark of their owners. There were the wretched, drunken men and women I had seen beaten and minced to death by the patrols, as Netzlin had been. And I had seen the once-pure blood of our race diluted, dirtied and disgraced in the varicolored mongrel offspring of the Spaniards and Moros.

Also I knew—not from personal experience, I rejoice to say, but from those very few who had somehow escaped—the horrors of the *obrajes*. These were vast, stone-walled, iron-gated workshops where cotton or wool was washed, carded, spun, dyed and woven into fabrics. The obrajes had first been established by the Spanish corregidores as a means of making a profit from convicted criminals. Criminal indios, I mean. Rather than just being locked up in idleness, such miscreants were put to that filthy, dreary and laborious work (and a cruelly demeaning work, for a man). They were paid no wages at all, were given only squalid quarters and no privacy whatever, were poorly fed, barely clothed, never let to bathe—and never let to leave the obraje until the expiration of their prison sentence, which few of them lived long enough to enjoy.

And the obrajes *were* profitable, so much so that individual Spaniards set up their own, and were freely given state prisoners to work in them, until eventually there were not enough prisoners to go around. At which time, the obraje owners began wheedling our people into handing over their children. Those boys and girls, the owners promised, would be apprenticed to learn a trade that they could follow in later life, and meanwhile the parents would be saved the cost of their upbringing. Worse yet, the abbots and abbesses of Christian orphan asylums, such as that at the Refugio de Santa Brígida, were easily persuaded to give their indio wards a choice, as soon as the children were old enough to understand: either take holy orders, to become a Christian nun or friar, or be damned to go and live and labor in an obraje. (The orphans of mixed blood, such as Rebeca Canalluza, were exempted from that damnation, because the Christian asylum-keepers could not be sure that some Spanish parent might not someday come looking to acknowledge and claim them.)

Whether or not the enslaved criminals had been deservedly convicted, those were at least grown men. The conscripted orphans and "apprentices" were not. But, just like the criminals, those boys and girls were almost never seen outside the obraje gates again. Like the criminals, they were worked unmercifully, often to death, and they suffered degradations and defilements that the grown men were spared. The obrajes were guarded and overseen not by their Spanish owners, but by cheaply hired Moros and mulatos. Those creatures delighted in showing their superiority to mere indio rústico children by beating and starving them, when they were not repeatedly forcing ahuilnéma upon the girls and cuilónyotl upon the boys.

The Christian corregidores and alcaldes and the Christian owners of obrajes and the converted-Christian native tepísque all colluded in these atrocities, and the Christian Church connived at them, for their own aggrandizement, of course, but for another reason as well. The Spaniards had firmly convinced themselves that every single one of our people was a lazy, shiftless layabout who would never work unless compelled by imminent punishment, starvation or violent death.

That was not and never had been true. In the old days, our able-bodied men and women had often been commandeered by their lords—whether local nobles or Revered Speakers— to do unpaid labor, much of it drudging, on many a public project. In this city, for example, those had ranged from the building of the Chapultépec aqueduct to the erection of the Great Temple of Tenochtítlan. And our people did such work willingly, eagerly, because they regarded communal labor as just another way of getting together for cheerful social intercourse. They would undertake any task assigned to them if it was presented—not *as* a task—as an opportunity for convivial mingling. The Spanish masters could profitably have taken advantage of that trait in our people, but they preferred to use the lash and the sword and the prison and the obraje and the threat of the burning stake.

I grant that there were some good and admirable men among the whites—Alonso de Molina, for one, and others whom I would meet in time to come. There was even one among the black Moros who would become my staunch ally, friend and fellow adventurer. And then there was you, mi querida Verónica. But of our encounter I will tell in its place.

I grant, too, that my hoped-for overthrow of the white men's regnancy was in truth intended, at least partly, as my personal revenge for the murder of my father. My aim may also have been partly ignoble—in that I, like any young man, would have gloried in being acclaimed by the populace as a conquering hero, or, if I died in the striving, being exuberantly welcomed by all the warriors of the past when I arrived in the Tonatíucan afterworld. However, I maintain that, even more, my aim was to upraise *all* our downtrodden peoples and to bring our One World back from oblivion.

* * *

To make memorable my taking leave of the City of Mexíco, I had conceived a veritably temptestuous parting salute. Though I had already twice caused the Spaniards some alarm and agitation, that furor subsided after several days in which no more disturbances occurred. Only an occasional, really suspicious-looking person on the street was being stopped and searched or stripped, and only in the precincts of the Traza. I had to assume that *I* was still under the watchful eye of a Cathedral spy at all times, but I made sure that he never *saw* me do anything that would reward his vigilance.

When I told Citláli what I had in mind, she laughed approvingly, even while she shivered with mixed emotions of trepidation and gleeful anticipation—and enthusiastically agreed to assist me. So, as I set about preparing fully four of the clay balls, each as big as the ball used in a tlachtli game, each tightly packed with pólvora, I instructed her in all the details of my plan.

"The last time," I said, "I managed only to put a black smudge on the outside of the Spanish soldiers' building, and in the process slew a passing tamémi. This time, I wish to explode the pólvora *inside* a building—I am confident that it will cause great destruction—and *not* to kill any innocents. Well, admittedly, there are always several maátime about the place, selling their favors to the soldiers, but I do not regard such women as innocents."

"Do you mean that same barracks building in the Traza?"

"No. The street there is forever crowded with passersby. But I know of one place in which and around which there are never any persons but Spaniards. And the maátime. You will take the pólvora balls in there for me. The military school and stronghold called the Castillo, high on Grasshopper Hill."

Citláli exclaimed, "I am to carry these death-dealing objects *inside*? Inside a building full of soldiers, surrounded by soldiers?"

"Its stockade is ringed about by oldest-of-old trees, and it is very loosely guarded. I recently spent a whole day prowling its environs, unobserved, peering from behind one after another of those trees, and I am satisfied that you can easily get into and out of the Castillo without any danger of harm or capture."

She said, "I should very much like to be satisfied of that, myself."

"The stockade gates are always wide open, and the *cadetes*, as the recruits are called, wander in and out. So do their soldier-teachers. So do ordinary Spaniards, those who bring food and supplies and such. So do the maátime. And the one lone armed guard at the gate simply lolls about, uncaring. He challenges no one, not even the whores. I suppose the Spaniards feel they can be lax about protecting such a place, because what person in his right mind would try to wreak damage inside a *military garrison*?"

"Only I? Citláli the Brave and Foolhardy?" she said archly. "Please do assure me, Tenamáxtli, that I *am* doing this in my right mind."

"When I have explained everything," I said, "you will see how practical is my plan. Now, I myself cannot get through that stockade gate without being challenged and doubtless arrested. But you can."

"I pretend to be a maátitl? *Ayya*, do I look that much like a slut?"

"Hardly. You are far prettier than any of those. And you will be carrying a basket of fruit by its handle, and leading Ehécatl. Nothing could look more innocent than a young mother strolling through the greenwood with her child. If anyone *does* ask, you say that one of the maátime is your cousin, and you are bringing her a gift of fruit. Or that you hope to sell your fruit to the cadetes. That you need the money to support your obviously disabled child. I will teach you enough of the Spanish words for you to make those remarks. You will not be stopped. Then, once you are inside the Castillo, you simply set down your fruit basket and stroll out again. Set it near something combustible, if possible."

"A basket of fruit? These clay things do not much resemble fruit."

"Let me finish. Right now—you see?—into the quill-hole of this one of the balls I am inserting a thin poquíetl as long as my forearm. I will light it before you approach the stockade gate, and it will take a long, slow while to burn down and ignite the ball, by which time you and Ehécatl will be safely outside with me again. That one ball, when it bursts, will ignite the other three. All together, they should make a really spectacular explosion. Very well. When these have dried rock-hard and we are ready to go, I will place them in one of your elegant baskets, then cover them with fruits from the market." I paused and said, half to myself, "Those ought to be coyacapúli fruits. And I must try to find some with worms—like me—inside them."

"What?" said Citláli, puzzled.

"A private jest. Pay it no mind. Coyacapúli fruits are light of weight, not to make the basket too heavy. Anyway, I shall be carrying it until we get to the Castillo. Well, then. On the first sunny day, we three will leave this house and amble casually westward across the island, I with the basket, you leading Ehécatl . . ."

So that is what we did, a few days later, all of us dressed in immaculate white clothing and acting innocently carefree. To any onlooker we would have appeared to be only a happy family going off to enjoy an outdoor meal in the open air somewhere. And I assumed that there had to *be* an interested onlooker, some one of the Cathedral hirelings.

Besides the basket, I was carrying my arcabuz beneath my mantle, its stock clamped under my free arm so it hung vertically. It forced me to walk a bit stiffly, but it was invisible. And I had loaded it beforehand, exactly as I had once seen it done—a good measure of pólvora and a cloth patch and a lead ball rammed down the tube, a chip of false-gold held by the cat's-paw, the whole weapon awaiting only a pinch of pólvora on the little cazoleta pan to be ready to fling its lethal missile. I really had no notion of how to aim the thing, beyond vaguely pointing it. But, if the arcabuz also worked, and if fortune favored me, my swift-flying ball of lead might actually strike and wound some Spanish soldier or cadete.

If there was anyone following us, he was at least temporarily balked when, at the island's edge, I beckoned to a ferryman and we got aboard his acáli. I had him pole us first southward, toward the flower gardens of Xochimilco—where even Spanish families sometimes go for a day's outing—until I was sure no other acáli was pursuing us. Then I directed the ferryman to turn, and we landed at the mudflats bordering what was once the Chapultépec park. We climbed uphill, encountering no one, until the Castillo's roof was in sight. Then we dodged from tree to tree, going ever closer, until we could see the gate and the numerous figures going in and out, or to and fro, or just idling about, and still no one raised any outcry. At last we came to the tremendously thick-trunked ahuéhuetl I had earlier chosen, no more than a hundred paces distant from the gate, and we crouched behind that.

"It appears to be just another routine day at the Castillo," I said, as I disencumbered myself of the arcabuz and laid it beside me. "No extra guards, no one looking particularly wary. So the more quickly we do this, the better. Are you and the child ready, Citláli?"

"Yes," she said, her voice steady. "I did not tell you, Tenamáxtli, but last night we both went to a priest of the good goddess Tlazoltéotl, and I confessed all the misdeeds of our lifetimes. Including this one, if this *is* one." She saw the expression on my face and hastily added, "Just in *case* anything should go wrong. So, yes, we are ready."

I had winced at Citláli's mention of that goddess, because one does not usually invoke Filth Eater until one feels death is near—hence asks her to take and swallow all one's sins, in order to go purged and clean to one's afterlife. But, if it made Citláli feel better . . .

"This poquíetl will go on emitting its trail of smoke and smell while it burns," I said, as I used my lente and a stray sunbeam to light the paper that protruded slightly from the basket. "But there is a breeze up here today, so it will not be too noticeable. If anyone does smell it, he will doubtless think some cadetes have been practicing with their arcabuces. And I say again, the poquíetl will give you plenty of time to—"

"Let me have it, then," she said, "before I am overcome by nervousness or cowardice." She took the basket's handle and Ehécatl's hand. "And give me a kiss, Tenamáxtli, for . . . for encouragement."

I would have done that anyway, and gladly, lovingly, without her asking. She hesitated, peering around the tree, only until she was sure no one was looking our way. Then she stepped from behind the trunk and, the child beside her, walked sedately, serenely out from the tree's dense shade into the bright sunlight—as if they had just then come up the hill through the deep wood. I took my eyes off them only long enough to prime the arcabuz's cazoleta with a pinch of pólvora and to click the cat's-paw rearward, ready for firing. But when I looked again at the mother and child, what I saw was disconcerting.

Many of the men outside the gate were glancing with smiles of approval at the handsome woman approaching them. There was nothing unnatural about that. But then their gaze dropped to the eyeless Ehécatl, and their smiles turned to expressions of disbelief and distaste. Their focused attention caught the attention, too, of the armed guard leaning against the gate. He stared at the approaching pair, then straightened from his slouch and moved to intercept them. This was a contingency that I should have foreseen and prepared for, but I had not, or I most certainly would have instructed Citláli to desist from our plan if she were challenged.

Citláli stopped in front of him and they exchanged some words. I supposed that the guard said something like, "In God's name, what kind of freak is this you have in tow?" But Citláli would not have understood that, nor been able to make coherent reply. What she was saying—or trying to say—I assumed was one of the remarks in which I had drilled her: that she was visiting a maátitl cousin, or that she was peddling fruit. She *could* simply have set down her basket and stalked away, as if offended.

Anyway, the guard, seeing this comely woman up close, appeared to lose interest in her malformed little companion. As well as I could tell from my hiding place, he grinned and uttered a command, gesturing ominously with his arcabuz, for Citláli let go the child's hand and—to my astonishment— gave the basket to Ehécatl! That small person had to use both arms to hold it. Then Citláli turned Ehécatl to face the gate and gave a gentle push. As Ehécatl toddled obediently and directly toward the open entrance, Citláli raised her hands and began slowly undoing the knots that closed her huipil blouse. Not the guard nor the other men roundabout gave any notice to the child carrying the basket through the gate. All eyes were salaciously fixed on Citláli as she undressed.

Obviously, the guard had ordered her to strip for a thorough search—he had that authority—and she was doing it slowly, as voluptuously as any maátitl, to divert everyone's attention from Ehécatl, now out of my sight inside the stockade somewhere. Here was another distressing contingency for which we had not prepared. What was I to do? I knew from previous observation that the Castillo's fort door was in a line with the gate; presumably little Ehécatl would continue on, straight through it and into the fort. But then what?

I was now standing erect behind my tree, only my head extended far enough to keep watching, and I was uncertainly fingering the gatillo of my arcabuz. Should I discharge it now? I certainly was tempted to kill *some* one of the white men, who were clustered now and staring avidly, for Citláli had bared herself above the waist. All I could see was her shapely back, but I knew well that her breasts were lovely things to look upon. She began, still slowly, provocatively, undoing the waistband of her long skirt. It seemed to me—

and perhaps also to those smirking onlookers—a sheaf of years before that skirt dropped to the ground. Then Citláli commenced another sheaf of years of unwinding her tochómitl undergarment. The guard took a step closer to her, and all the other men crowded close behind him, when at last Citláli tossed the cloth away and stood totally naked before them.

At that instant came a bellow of noise and a billow of smoke from some remote place inside the stockade, inside the fort itself, making every one of the watching men flinch even farther toward Citláli, then turn to gape openmouthed— as another and louder thunder boomed inside their fort, and another, louder yet. The red tiles of the fort's roof jittered and danced, and several fell off. Then, as if those still-reverberating roars had been only preliminary ebullitions— as occasionally the great volcano Citlaltépetl clears its throat three or four times before belching up a devastating eruption—so did the fort erupt with a blast that must have been heard all over the valley.

Its entire roof lifted high into the air, and disintegrated there, so the tiles and timbers soared even higher. From under them rose a tremendous, roiling, yellow-and-red-and-black cloud of commingled flames, smoke, sparks, unidentifiable pieces of the fort's interior furnishings, flailing human bodies and limp fragments of human bodies. I was quite sure that even my extravagant employment of *several* pólvora balls could not have caused such a cataclysm. What must have happened—little Ehécatl must have toddled, unhindered, as far as some storeroom of the fort's own pólvora or its cache of some other terribly sensitive combustible, just at the moment my basketful ignited and blew apart. I briefly wondered—could the child have been guided by our war god Huitzilopóchtli? By the spirit of my dead father? Or was it simply Ehécatl's own tonáli?

But I had other things to wonder about. Simultaneously with the fort's flying all to pieces, every person between it and me staggered as if by a heavy blow—including the guard and his captive Citláli—and several of the men lost their

footing and fell down. Also, Citláli's discarded garments
went whisking away from around her feet. I could not see
anything to account for those happenings. But then I felt a
shock as if cupped hands had abruptly slammed hard against
both my ears. A mighty gale of wind, with the force of a
stone wall falling, dashed against my ahuéhuetl and every
other tree in the vicinity. Leaves, twigs, small branches, all
went hurtling away from the site of that awesome explosion.
The wall of wind was gone as suddenly as it had come, but
had I not been behind my tree, my cazoleta would have been
blown clean of pólvora and my arcabuz made useless.

When those people between me and the gate regained their
balance, they stared horrified at the destruction within the
stockade, and the fiercely blazing fire, and at the pieces of
stone, wood, weapons—and their fellows—dropping from
the sky. (Some of the men who had fallen did not get up;
they had been hit by the things hurled straight outward by
the blast.) The gate guard was the first to realize who was
responsible for the disaster; he whirled again to face Citláli,
a snarl contorting his visage. Citláli turned and ran, toward
me, and the guard pointed his arcabuz at her back.

I pointed mine, too—at him—and squeezed the gatillo.
My arcabuz performed exactly as it was supposed to, with a
roar and a jolt that numbed my shoulder and rocked me backward a step or two. Where my lead ball went, whether it
struck the guard or any of the others, I have no idea, because
my view of them was clouded by the blue smoke I had created. Anyway, regretfully, I had not prevented the guard
from discharging his own weapon. One moment Citláli was
running toward me, her fine breasts bouncing lightly. The
next moment, those breasts, her whole upper body, opened
out like a red flower bursting into blossom. Gouts of blood
and gobbets of flesh spewed out ahead of her to spatter on
the ground, and onto those shreds of herself she fell face
forward and lay still.

*   *   *

There was no sign or sound of pursuit as I fled down the hill. Evidently the discharge of my weapon had gone unheard, as I had expected, in the general tumult. And if I *had* hit anybody with the lead ball, his fellow soldiers probably assumed that he had been felled by one of the far-flung pieces of the fort. When I reached the lakeside, I did not stand about, waiting for an acáli to come along. I strode straight out across the mudflats and then, knee-deep in the turbid water, waded all the way back to the city, staying close under the aqueduct's tree-trunk piles to avoid being seen from either shore. Once I got to the island, though, I had to wait awhile before I had an opportunity to slip unnoticed in among the crowds of people that had gathered there, buzzing excitedly as they gazed at the tower of smoke still hanging over Grasshopper Hill.

The streets were all but empty as I scuttled to our familiar colación of San Pablo Zoquipan and to the house Citláli and I had shared for so long. I doubted that any Cathedral spy was still keeping watch—he would be down beside the lake with almost every other city resident—but if he *was* on duty, and if he challenged me or even followed me, I was fully prepared to kill him. Inside the house, I recharged my arcabuz, to be ready for that necessity or any other. Then I lifted to my back, with a tumpline around my forehead, the bale of my belongings that I had prudently packed beforehand. The only other things I took from the house were our little hoard of money—in cacao beans, tin snippets, a variety of Spanish coins—and my sack of salitre, the one pólvora ingredient that might be hard to find elsewhere. With a piece of rope, I made a sling for my arcabuz, so it could be carried inconspicuously under my pack and sack.

On the street again, I saw none of the few passersby take any interest in my doings and, glancing back from time to time, saw no one following me. I did not head north to the Tepeyáca causeway by which my mother, my uncle and myself had so long ago entered the City of Mexíco. If soldiers should be sent chasing me, the notarius Alonso would be in conscience bound to tell them that I was most likely going directly homeward, toward the Aztlan I had told him about. So I went west through the city instead, and across the causeway that leads to the town of Tlácopan. And there, as I stepped onto the mainland, I turned just long enough to shake my clenched fist back at the city—the city that had slaughtered both my father and my lover—swearing an oath that I *would* be back, to avenge them both.

Many things have happened in my lifetime that have forever hung heavy in my heart. The death of Citláli was one of those occurrences. And I have known many regrettable losses, leaving voids in my heart that never would be filled again. The death of Citláli was one of those occurrences, too.

I have just now spoken of her as my lover, and of course, in the physical sense, she was certainly that. She was also most lovable and loving—and for a very long while I would be desolate, bereft of her dear presence—but in truth I never loved her unreservedly. I knew it then, and I know it even better now, because, at a later time in my life, I *would* love with all my heart. Even if I had been totally and utterly smitten with Citláli, I could not have brought myself to marry her. For one reason, she had been the wife of another before me. I had been a second-best, so to speak. For another reason, I could never have hoped for children of my own, not by her, not with the sad example of Ome-Ehécatl always in view.

Though I am sure that Citláli was well aware of my feelings—or my insufficiency of them—she never gave the least hint of that awareness. She had said, "I would do anything . . ." meaning that, if need be, she would die for me. And she had done just that, and more than that. With her successful accomplishment of my taunting farewell insult to the City of Mexíco, she had won for both Ehécatl and herself not only my gratitude, but also that of the gods.

As I have said, Ehécatl would have had no hope of escaping damnation to the eternal nothingness of Míctlan—and neither would Citláli, since she had given birth only to a child too dreadfully defective for any of our priests to have accepted it for sacrifice to any god. But now Citláli had contrived to make sacrifices of both mother and child—and at the same time to annihilate many of the alien white men. That deed, worthy of a warrior hero, was certain to please *all* our old-time gods, so she and Ehécatl were assured of an afterlife of ease and opulence. I knew they both would be happy during that eternity, and I could even hope that the gods would benignantly bestow on Ehécatl the eyes to see the splendors of whichever afterworld they had gone to.

XIII

OUR PEOPLE HAVE a saying: that a man who goes he knows not where does not need to fear losing the road. My only aim was to get well away from the City of Mexíco before I turned northward into the unconquered lands. So, from Tlácopan, I took the roads that continued to lead me westward. In time, I found myself in Michihuácan, the homeland of the Purémpe people.

This nation was one of the few in The One World that had never been subsumed or put under tribute by the Mexíca. The chief reason for Michihuácan's sturdy independence in those days was that the Purémpe artisans and armorers knew the secret of compounding a brown metal so hard and sharp that, in battle, the blades made of it easily prevailed over the brittle obsidian weapons of the Mexíca. After just a few tries at subduing Michihuácan, the Mexíca were satisfied to settle for a truce, and thereafter the two nations engaged freely in trade—or almost freely; the Purémpecha never *did* let any other people of The One World learn the secret of their marvelous metal. Of course, that metal is no longer a secret; the Spaniards recognized it on sight as what they call *bronce*. And those brown blades could not prevail against the white men's even harder and sharper steel—nor their softer metal, the lead propelled by pólvora.

Nevertheless, even with inferior weaponry, the gallant Purémpecha fought more fiercely against the Spaniards than had any other nation thus invaded. As soon as those white men had conquered and secured what is now New Spain, one of the most cruel and rapacious of their captains, a man named Guzmán, led a force westward from the City of México— the same way I had just now come. His intent was to seize for himself as much land and as many subjects as his commandér Cortés had acquired. Though the word *Michihuácan* means only "Land of the Fishermen," Guzmán soon found— as the Mexíca had found before him—that it could as well have been called Land of Defiant Warriors.

It cost Guzmán several thousand of his soldiers to advance—and advance only creepingly—across the lush fields and rolling hills of that eye-pleasing countryside. Of the Purémpecha, many *more* thousands fell, but there were always some remaining to go on fighting, undeterred. To slash and blast and burn his way to Michihuácan's northern border, where it abuts the land called Kuanáhuata, and to its western edge, which is the coast of the Western Sea, took Guzmán nearly fifteen years. (As I have mentioned, back when my mother, my uncle and I journeyed to the City of México, we often had to circle warily around parts of Michihuácan in which bloody battles were still being waged.) As a warrior myself, I must concede, considering what it had cost Guzmán in years and casualties, that he had fairly won the right to claim all that land and to give it a new name of his own choosing—New Galicia, honoring his home province back in Old Spain.

But he also did things inexcusable. He herded together the few Purémpe warriors he had taken prisoner alive and all the *other* Purémpe men and boys throughout New Galicia who might someday decide to turn warriors, and he shipped them off as slaves, over the Eastern Sea, to the island of Cuba and another island somewhere out there called Isla Española. Thus Guzmán could be sure that those men and boys, unable to speak the tongues of the islands' native slaves and the imported Moro slaves, would be helpless to foment any further defiance against their Spanish masters.

So it was that, by the time I arrived in Michihuácan, the population consisted entirely of females young and old, aged males and barely adolescent boys. I being the first adult-but-not-elderly man seen thereabouts in recent memory, I was regarded as a curiosity, and a welcome one. During my travel westward across what had been the Mexíca lands, I had had to request food and shelter in the villages and farmsteads I had come upon. The menfolk of those places always agreeably accorded me that hospitality, but I had had to *ask*. Here in Michihuácan, I was positively besieged with *offers* of food, drink, a place to sleep and "stay as long as you like, stranger." When I passed homesteads along the road, their womenfolk—because there *were* no menfolk—would actually run out from their doorways to tug at my mantle and invite me inside.

If I was a novelty to them, so were the Purémpecha a novelty to me—even though I had expected them to be the kind of people they were. That was because I had met a number of their elderly (hence surviving) men in the City of Mexíco—pochtéca merchants or messengers or mere vagabonds—at the Mesón de San José or in the marketplaces. The heads of those men were as bald as huaxolómi eggs, and, they told me, so was the head of every man, woman and child in Michihuácan, because the Purémpecha regarded sleek, shiny baldness as the crowning touch of human beauty. Still, my having seen those men with their heads shaved clean of everything but eyelashes had not made much impression on me; after all, they were old enough to be bald in any case. It was quite different when I got to Michihuácan, to see every single soul—from infants to children to grown women and grandmothers—as hairless as the old men among them.

Most of The One World's people, including myself, took pride in our hair and wore it long. We men let it grow to shoulder length, with a heavy fringe across our foreheads;

women's hair might reach to their waists or below. But the Spaniards, deeming their beards and mustaches the only true symbols of virility, thought our men looked effeminate and our women slatternly. They even coined a word, *balcarrota* (roughly "a haystack"), with which to speak of our hairstyle, and spoke it disparagingly. They also—since they were continually accusing us of petty pilferage from their belongings—assumed that we hid such stolen items under all that hair. So Guzmán and the other Spanish lords of New Galicia doubtless highly approved of the Purémpe custom of total baldness.

However, there were in Michihuácan other customs of which I am certain the Spaniards, being Christians, could *not* have approved. That is because Christians are disquieted even by any mention of sexual acts, and are veritably horrified by any out-of-the-ordinary sexual behavior—far more so than they are repelled by, say, human sacrifices to "pagan gods." Those Purémpe men in the city, when I was learning what I could of their Poré language, had taught me many Poré words and phrases relating to sexual matters. Those men, I repeat, were old, long past any capacity for coupling or the least cravings of that sort. Nevertheless, they lustfully smacked their gums as they recounted the various and remarkable, even unseemly and scandalous ways in which they had slaked the sexual appetites of their youth—*and had been allowed by local custom to do so.*

I say "unseemly and scandalous" not because I myself have ever been any paragon of chastity or modesty. But my Aztéca people, and the Mexíca, and most others, always had been almost as prudish as Christians in regard to sex. We had no written laws and regulations and shall-nots, as the Christians do, but tradition taught us that certain things simply were not to be done. Adultery, incest, promiscuous fornication (except during certain fertility ceremonies), the conceiving of bastards, rape (except by warriors in enemy territories), the seduction of the underaged, the act of cuilón-yotl between males and patlachúia between females, all those were forbidden. While we, unlike the Christians, acknowledged that any person might be of a deviant or even depraved nature, and that any *normal* person might misbehave when overwhelmed by lust, we did not sanction such doings. If anything of that sort was discovered, the perpetrator (or participants) would at the very least be shunned by all decent people forever after, or be banished into exile, or be severely punished, or even be put to death with the "flower garland" noose.

But, as those aged Purémpe men in the city had so gleefully and bawdily forewarned me, the customs of Michihuácan could not have been more different. Or more lenient. Among the Purémpecha, not *any* imaginable kind of sexual congress was prohibited, so long as both (or all) the participants concurred in the act—or at least did not vociferously complain of the act, as in the case of animals employed by men and women who had a taste for that sort of coupling. In former days, said the old men, only the native doe and buck deer had satisfactorily met those people's two requirements: namely, that the creature be catchable and that it have a usable feminine orifice or masculine protuberance. Indeed, they said, copulation with a buck or a doe was regarded by everyone, especially the priests, as a praiseworthy act of religious devotion, because the Purémpecha believe that deer are earthly manifestations of the sun god. Since the coming of the Spaniards, however, said the old men, more than a few Purémpe females and the surviving adolescent males had found reason to be glad for the white men's introduction of embraceable jack and jenny asses, rams and ewes, billy and nanny goats.

Well, I had no predilections of that sort, and, if any of the many females I encountered in Michihuácan had previously been entertaining themselves with bestial surrogates for their vanished menfolk, they were happy enough to discard the animals when I came along. There being such an abundance of women and girls eager for my attentions, everywhere I wandered in that land, I could take my pick of the comeliest, and I did. At first, I admit, it was a trifle hard for me to get accustomed to bald women. It was even hard sometimes to tell the younger among them from the younger *males*, because both sexes of the Purémpecha dress almost exactly alike. But I gradually developed an almost Purémpe admiration for their baldness, as, over time, I learned to perceive that the facial beauty of some women is actually enhanced by being otherwise unadorned. And in their having shed their tresses, they had by no means diminished any of their feminine fervors and amative abilities.

Only once did I make a misjudgment in that respect, and I blame that occurrence on chápari, the beverage that the Purémpecha make from the honey of their land's wild black bees, a drink incalculably more inebriating than even Spanish wines. I had stopped for a night at a travelers' inn, where the only other guests were an elderly pochtécatl and a messenger almost as old. The inn's owner was a bald woman, and her three bald helpers were apparently her daughters. Over the course of the evening I partook indiscreetly of the inn's delicious chápari. I got sufficiently sodden that I had to be helped to my cubicle and undressed and deposited on my pallet by the smallest and most beautiful of the servants, who then, unbidden, lavished on my tepúli that wonderfully ardent ingurgitation I had first experienced with my birthday auyaními in Aztlan and later, many times, with my cousin Améyatl and other women. No man is ever too drunk to enjoy that experience to the utmost.

So, afterward, I bade the servant undress and let me gratefully reciprocate with the same attention to her xacapíli. Muddled as I was, I had it well within my mouth before I realized it was rather too prominent to *be* a xacapíli. It got spit out of my mouth, not in revulsion, but because I gave such a sudden laugh at my own befuddled mistake. The beautiful boy looked hurt, and backed away, and his tepúli instantly wilted very nearly to xacapíli stubbiness—which sight inspired in me some drunken ideas of experimentation, so I beckoned him to me again. When he finally departed, I gave him a drunkenly extravagant maravedí coin by way of thanks, then fell drunkenly asleep, to wake the next day with an earthquake of a headache and only the dimmest recollection of what experiments the boy and I had engaged in.

Considering Michihuácan's abundance of available womanhood and girlhood—not to mention boys and domestic animals, should I ever get so very drunk as to essay further experimentation—and the land's bounty of other good things, I could have supposed myself prematurely transported to Tonatíucan or one of the other afterworlds of eternal joyfulness. Besides its limitless sexual license and opportunity, Michihuácan offered also a voluptuous variety of food and drink: the delicate lake and river fish that can be found nowhere else, eggs and stews of the turtles that abound on its seacoast, clay-baked quail and toasted hummingbirds, vanilla-flavored chocólatl and of course the incomparable chápari. In that land, one could even feast with only one's eyes: on the profusely flowered rolling meadows, the sparkling streams and limpid lakes, the richly fruiting orchards and farm fields, all bordered by the blue-green mountains. Yes, a man young, healthy and vigorous might well be tempted to stay in Michihuácan forever. And so I might have done, had I not dedicated myself to a mission.

"Ayya, I will never recruit any warlike men here," I said. "I must move on."

"What about warlike women?" asked my consort of the moment, a radiantly lovely young woman, whose feather-fan eyelashes seemed even more luxuriant in contrast to her otherwise hairless and glowing visage. Her name was Pakápeti, which means "Tiptoe." When I only looked blankly at her, she added, "The Spaniards committed an oversight when they killed or abducted only our menfolk. They ignored the capabilities of us women."

I snorted in amusement. "Women? Warriors? Nonsense."

"It is you who speak nonsense," she snapped. "You might as well claim that a man can ride a horse faster than a woman can. I have seen both Spanish men and women on

horseback. As to which can ride the faster, much depends on
the *horse*.''

"I have no men *or* horses," I said ruefully.

"You have that," said Tiptoe, indicating my arcabuz. I
had been practicing with it all afternoon, trying with only
middling success to knock individual ahuácatin fruits off a
tree near her hut. "A woman could use it as expertly as you
do," she said, trying hard not to sound sarcastic. "Make or
steal more of those thunder-sticks and . . ."

"That is my intention. As soon as I have enough of an
army to warrant the need of them."

"I would not have to travel very far hereabout," she said,
"to recruit for you a considerable number of strong and willing and vengeful women. Except for those whom the Spaniards took for household slaves—or bed-warmers—the rest
of us would not even be missed, if we disappeared from our
customary abodes."

I knew what she meant. On my way westward, thus far, I
had carefully stayed clear of the many Spanish estancias, all
of which, naturally, encompassed Michihóacan's prime
growing and grazing lands. There being no more Purémpe
men, and the Purémpe women having been judged suitable
only for indoor services, the outdoor work of the farms and
ranches and orchards was done by imported male slaves.
From a distance, I had seen the black Moros laboring, overseen by Spaniards on horseback, each usually with whip in
hand. The new masters of Michihuácan had planted the fields
mostly with marketable crops—the alien wheat and sweet
cane and a greenery called *alfalfa*, and the trees that grow
alien fruits called *manzanas, naranjas, limónes* and *aceitu-
nas*. Less tillable fields were thick with herds of sheep or
cows or horses, and there were pens full of pigs, chickens
and gallipavos. Even places so swampy they had never been
tilled before were planted with a foreign water-growing grain
called *arroz*. Since the Spaniards managed to wrest harvests
and profits from almost every piece of Michihuácan, the plots

left to the surviving Purémpecha were few and small and only grudgingly productive.

Pakápeti said, "You have spoken of eating well in this land, Tenamáxtli. Let me tell you why that is. What patches we have of maize and tomatoes and chilis are tended by our old men and women. The children gather fruits, nuts, berries, the wild honey for making sweets and chápari. It is we women who bring in the meat. Wild fowl, small game, fish, even the occasional boar and cuguar."

She paused, then added wryly, "We do not do that with thunder-sticks. We use the ancient means of fowling nets and fishing lines and obsidian hunting weapons. Also, we women continue the ancient Purémpe crafts of making lacquerware and glazed pottery. Those objects we barter for other foods from the seacoast tribes, and for pigs or chickens or lambs or kids from the Spaniards. We live, even without menfolk, and we live not badly, but we live only by the sufferance of those white masters. That is why I say we would not be missed if we marched off to war."

"At least you live," I said. "You would assuredly not live so well if you went to war. If you lived at all."

"Other women have fought the Spaniards, you know. The Mexíca women, during the final battles in the streets of Tenochtítlan, stood on the rooftops and threw down on the invaders stones and nests full of wasps and even lumps of their own excrement."

"Much good it did them. I knew an even braver Mexícatl woman in more recent times. She actually *slew* a number of the white men, and much good it did *her*. She lost her own life in consequence."

Tiptoe said urgently, "We, too, would gladly give our lives if we could take some of theirs." She leaned close, those extraordinary eyelashes wide, fixing me with eyes as dark and lovely as the lashes. "Only *try* us, Tenamáxtli. It would be the last thing the Spaniards would ever expect. An uprising of *women*!"

"And the last thing I should ever hope to be involved in,"

I said with a laugh. "Me—at the head of an army of females. Why, every dead warrior in Tonatíucan would be convulsed, either with hilarity or with horror. The idea is ludicrous, my dear. I must seek men."

"Go then," she said, sitting back and looking extremely vexed. "Go and get your men. There still *are* some in Michihuácan." She waved an arm vaguely northward.

"Still some men here?" I said, surprised. "Purémpe men? Warriors? Are they in hiding? In ambuscade?"

"No. They are in swaddling," she said contemptuously. "Not warriors and not Purémpecha. They are Mexíca, imported here to settle new colonies around the lake Pátzcuaro. But I fear you will find those men much less stalwart and much more meek than myself and the women I could gather for you."

"I grant, Tiptoe, that you are anything but meek. Your name-giver must have badly misread his tonálmatl book of names. Tell me about those Mexíca. Imported by whom? For what purpose?"

"I know only what I have heard. Some Spanish Christian priest has founded colonies all around that Lake of Rushes, for some peculiar purpose of his own. And there being no Purémpe men still in existence, he had to bring men—and their families—from the Mexíca lands. I hear also that the priest coddles all those settlers as tenderly as if they were his children. His babes in swaddling, just as I said."

"Family men," I muttered. "You are probably right about their not being very much disposed to rebellion. Especially if they are being so well treated by their overlord. But if that is so, he sounds little like a Christian."

Pakápeti shrugged, and that made my heart smile, for she happened to be naked at the time, and her darling breasts bounced with the movement. Not at all heart-smilingly, but frostily, she said, "Go and see. The lake is only three one-long-runs from here."

*　　　*　　　*

The Lake of Rushes is the exact color of the chalchíhuitl, the jadestone, the gem that is held sacred by every people of The One World. And the low, rounded mountains enclosing Pátzcuaro are a darker shade of that same blue-green color. So, as I crested one of the mountains and looked down, the lake appeared to be a bright jewel that had been dropped upon a bed of moss. There is an island in the lake, Xarák-uaro, that must once have been the brightest facet of that gem, for I am told that it was covered with temples and altars that glowed and coruscated with colored paints and gold leaf and feather banners. But Guzmán's soldiers had razed all those edifices and scoured the island down to the barrenness that it still is.

Gone, too, were all the original communities that had ringed the lake, including Tzintzuntzaní, "Where There Are Hummingbirds." That had been the capital city of Michi-huácan, a city composed entirely of palaces, one of them the seat of Tzímtzicha, last Revered Speaker of the vanquished Purémpecha. From my mountaintop, I could see only one thing remaining from olden days. That was the pyramid, east of the lake, notable for its size and form, not tall but lengthy, combining both round and square shapes. And that iyákata, as a pyramid is called in Poré, I knew was a survivor from a *really* olden time, erected by a people who lived here long before the Purémpecha. Even in Tzímtzicha's day, it had been ruinously crumbled and overgrown, but it was still an awesome sight to see.

There were again villages scattered around the lake's rim, replacing those that had been leveled by Guzmán's men, but these were in no way distinctive, all their houses having been built in the Spanish style, low and flat, of that dried adobe brick. In the nearest village, directly below the height where I stood, I could see people moving about. All were clad in Mexíca fashion and were of my own skin color; I saw no Spaniards anywhere among them. So I descended thither, and greeted the first man I came upon. He was seated on a bench before the doorway of his house, painstakingly whittling and shaping a piece of wood.

I spoke the customary Náhuatl salute, "Mixpantzínco," meaning "In your august presence . . ."

And he replied, not in Poré, but also in Náhuatl, with the customary polite "Ximopanólti," meaning "At your convenience . . ." then added, cordially enough, "We do not have many of our fellow Mexíca coming to visit *Utopía*."

I did not want to confuse him by saying that I was actually an Aztécatl, nor did I ask the meaning of that strange word he had just spoken. I said only, "I am a stranger in these parts, and I only recently learned that there were Mexíca in this vicinity. It is good to hear my native tongue spoken again. My name is Tenamáxtli."

"Mixpantzínco, Cuatl Tenamáxtli," he said courteously. "I am called Erasmo Mártir."

"Ah, after that Christian saint. I too have a Christian name. Juan Británico."

"If you are a Christian, and if you are looking for employment, our good Padre Vasco may make room for you here. Have you a wife and children somewhere?"

"No, Cuatl Erasmo. I am a solitary wayfarer."

"Too bad." He shook his head sympathetically. "Padre Vasco accepts only settlers with families. However, if you care to stay for a time, he will most hospitably afford you guest lodging. You will find him in Santa Cruz Pátzcuaro, the next village west along the lake."

"I will go there, then, and not keep you from your work."

"Ayyo, you are no hindrance. The padre does not make us labor unceasingly, like slaves, and it is pleasant to converse with a newcome Mexícatl."

"What is it that you are making, anyway?"

"This will be a mecahuéhuetl," he said, indicating some nearly finished parts behind the bench. They were pieces of wood about the size and gracefully curvaceous shape of a woman's torso.

I nodded, recognizing what the parts would be when assembled. "What the Spaniards call a *guitarra*."

Of the musical instruments that the Spanish introduced to New Spain, most were at least basically similar to those already known in our One World. That is to say, they made music by being blown through or shaken or struck with sticks or rasped with a notched rod. But the Spaniards had also brought instruments totally different from ours, such as this guitarra and the *vihuela*, the *arpa*, the *mandolina*. All of our people were much amazed—and admiring—that such instruments could make sweet music from mere strings, tightly strung, being plucked with the fingers or rasped with an *arco*.

"But why," I asked Erasmo, "are you copying a foreign novelty? Surely the white men have their own guitarra makers."

"Not so expert as we are," he said proudly. "The padre and his assistants taught us how to make these, and now he says we make these mecahuéhuetin superior even to those · brought from Old Spain."

"We?" I echoed. "You are not the only maker of guitarras?"

"No, indeed. Every man here in San Marcos Churítzio concentrates on this one craft. It is the particular enterprise assigned to this village, as other villages of Utopía each produce lacquerwork or copperware or whatever."

"Why?" was all I could think to say, for I had never before known of any community devoted to doing just one thing and nothing else.

"Go and talk to Padre Vasco," said Erasmo. "He will be happy to tell you all about his engendering of our Utopía."

"I will do that. Thank you, Cuatl Erasmo, and mixpantz-ínco."

Instead of saying "ximopanólti" in farewell, he said, "*Vaya con Dios,*" and added cheerfully, "Come again, Cuatl Juan. Someday I intend to learn to play music from one of these things."

I trudged on westward, but halted in an uninhabited area and went among some bushes to change from my mantle and loincloth into the shirt and trousers and boots I carried in my pack. So I was Spanishly attired when I arrived at Santa Cruz Pátzcuaro. On inquiry, I was directed to the small adobe church and its attached *casa de cura*. The padre himself answered the door there; he was in no wise so aloof and inaccessible as most Christian priests are. Also, he was dressed in sturdy, heavy, work-stained shirt and breeches, not a black gown.

I made bold to introduce myself, in Spanish, as Juan Británico, lay assistant to Fray Alonso de Molina, notarius of Bishop Zumárraga's Cathedral and said I was presently engaged, at my master Alonso's behest, in visiting Church missions in these hinterlands, to evaluate and report on their progress.

"Ah, I think you will give good report of ours, my son," said the padre. "And I am pleased to hear that Alonso is still toiling so assiduously in the vineyards of Mother Church. I remember the lad most fondly."

So I and my prevarication were instantly accepted, without question, by the good priest. And good I found him truly to be. Padre Vasco de Quiroga was a tall, thin, austere-looking but really merry-humored man. He was old enough to be bald enough that he required no tonsure, but he was still vigorous, as was attested by his work clothes, for which he humbly apologized.

"I should be properly cassocked to welcome an emissary of the bishop, but I am today helping my friars build a pigsty behind this house."

"Do not let me interrupt—"

"No, no, no. *Por cielo*, I am glad to take a respite. Sit down, son Juan. I can see that you are dusty from the road." He called to someone in some other room to bring us wine. "Sit, sit, my boy. And tell me. Have you yet seen much of what the Lord has helped us to accomplish hereabouts?"

"Only a little. I talked for a while to an Erasmo Mártir."

"Ah, yes. Of all our skillful guitarra makers, perhaps the most skillful. And a devout Christian convert. Then tell me also, Juan Británico. Since you are named for an English saint, are you perhaps acquainted with the late saintly Don Tomás Moro, also of England?''

''No, padre. But—excuse me—I was given to understand that the men of England are white men.''

''So they are. Moro was this man's name, not his race or color. He was but lately and unjustly and vilely slain—his Christian piety his only crime—executed by the king of that England, who is an odious and despicable heretic. Anyway, if you do not know of Don Tomás, I suppose you do not know of his far-famed book, *De optimo Reipublicae statu . . .*''

''No, padre.''

''Or of the Utopía he prefigured in that book?''

''No, padre, except that I heard the artisan Erasmo speak the word.''

''Well, Utopía is what we are trying to create here, around the shores of this paradisal lake. I only wish I could have undertaken it years ago. But I have not been that long a priest.''

A young friar came in, bringing two exquisitely carved and lacquered wooden cups, clearly Purémpe products. He handed one to each of us and silently withdrew, and I drank gratefully of the cool wine.

''For most of my life,'' the padre went on, sounding contrite, ''I was a judge, a man of the legal profession. And any practice of the law—let me tell you, young Juan—is a venal and corrupt and loathly occupation. At last, thanks be to God, I realized how I was so foully defiling myself and my soul. That is when I tore off my judicial robe, took holy orders and eventually was ordained to wear the cassock instead.'' He paused and laughed. ''Of course, many of my former adversaries in the courts have gleefully quoted to me the old proverb: *Hartóse el gato de carne, y luego se hizo fraile.*''

It took me a moment to translate that in my head: ''The cat got a gutful of meat before it turned friar.''

He went on, ''The Utopía envisioned by Tomás Moro was

to be an ideal community whose inhabitants would exist under perfect conditions. Where the evils bred by society—poverty, hunger, misery, crime, sin, war—would all have been done away with.''

I forbore from commenting that there would be some people, even in an ideal community, who might wish to retain the right to enjoy sinning or waging war.

"So I have repopulated this pleasant piece of New Galicia with colonist families. Besides instructing them in the tenets of Christianity, I and my friars show them how to use European tools and how to employ the most modern methods of agriculture and husbandry. Beyond that, we strive *not* to direct or meddle in the colonists' lives. True, it was our Brother Agustín who taught them how to make guitarras. But we found elderly Purémpe men who could be persuaded to lay aside old rivalries and teach the colonists the age-old Purémpe handicrafts. Now each village devotes itself to perfecting *one* of those arts—woodwork, ceramics, weaving and so on—in the finest tradition of the Purémpecha. Any colonists incapable of learning such artisanry make their contribution to Utopía by farming or fishing or raising pigs, goats, chickens and such.''

"But, Padre Vasco,'' I said. "What use have your settlers for such things as guitarras? That Erasmo to whom I spoke, he did not even know how to play music on it.''

"Why, those are sold to merchants in the City of Méxíco, my son. The guitarras and the other crafted objects. Many of them are bought by brokers who, in turn, export them all the way back to Europe. We get handsome prices for them, too. The bulk of our farmers' and herders' produce also is sold. Of the money received, I pay a portion to the village families, equally divided among them. But most of our income is spent on new tools, seeds, breeding stock—whatever will improve and benefit Utopía as a whole.''

"It all sounds most practical and laudable, padre,'' I said, and sincerely meant it. "Especially since, as Erasmo said, you do not make your people drudge like slaves.''

"¡Válgame Dios, no!" he exclaimed. "I have seen the infernal obrajes in the city and elsewhere. Our colonists may be of an inferior race, but they are human beings. And now they are Christians, so they are not brute animals without souls. No, my son. The rule here in Utopía is that the people work communally for just six hours a day, six days a week. Sundays, of course, are for devotions. All the rest of the people's time is theirs to spend as they like. Tending their own home gardens, private doings, socializing with their fellows. Were I a hypocrite, I could say that I am simply being Christian in being no tyrannical master. But the truth is that our people work harder and more productively than any whip-driven slaves or obraje laborers."

I said, "Another thing Erasmo told me is that you allow only men and women already married to settle in this Utopía. Would you not get even more work out of single men and women, unburdened with children?"

He looked slightly uncomfortable. "Well, now, you have broached a rather indelicate subject. We do not presume to have re-created Eden here, but we do have to contend with both Eve and the serpent. Or with Eve *as* the serpent, I might better say."

"Ayya, forgive my having asked, padre. You must mean the Purémpe women."

"Exactly so. Bereft of their own menfolk, and learning that there were young, strong men here in Utopía, they have frequently descended on us to—how shall I say?—entice our men into performing at stud. They were absolutely pestiferous when we first settled here, and still to this day we get the occasional female visiting and importuning. I fear our family men are not all—or always—able to resist the temptation, but I am sure that unmarried ones would be much more easily seduced. And such debaucheries could lead to the ruin of Utopía."

I said approvingly, "It appears to me, Padre Vasco, that you have everything well thought out and well in hand. I shall be pleased to report that to the bishop's notarius."

"But not solely on my unsupported word, son Juan. Go all the way around the lake. Visit every village. You will need no guide. Anyway, I would not want you to suspect that you were being shown only the exemplary aspects of our community. Go alone. See things plain and unvarnished. When you return here, I shall be gratified if *then* you can say, as San Diego once said, that by works a man is justified, and not by faith only."

XIV

SO I WENT on westward, stopping for at least a night in each village I came to, and then northward, eastward, southward, until I had circled the entire Lake of Rushes and come westward again to the very first village I had visited, San Marcos Churítzio, that one where Erasmo Mártir resided.

I found it to be true, what Padre Vasco had said, that the lakeside people all lived in amity and prosperity and conviviality, and were understandably content to live so. And they had indeed mastered the ancient crafts of the Purémpecha. One village produced hammered copperware: dishes and platters and pitchers of graceful design and dimpled finish. Another village produced similar utensils, but of a kind of pottery to be seen nowhere else, colored a lustrous black by an admixture of powdered lead in the clay. Another made the long-famous Purémpe lacquerware: trays, tables, huge folding screens, all of a rich, shiny black, inset with gold and many vivid colors. Another made mats and pallets and baskets of braided rushes from the lake; they were, I had to admit, even more elegant than those woven by my lost Citláli. Another village made intricate jewelry of silver wire; another did jewelry of amber; another with the pearly nacre of mussel shells. And so on and on around the lake. Between and about the villages were the tilled fields, growing the newcome sweet cane and a sweet grass called *sorgo*, as well as the more familiar crops like maize and beans. All the fields were bearing far more lushly than any known in former times, before our farmers had the advantages of Spanish-imported tools and ideas.

There was no denying that these Mexíca colonists had benefited hugely from their association with the Spaniards. I asked myself: did the virtues of their winsome Utopía, then, counterbalance the miseries and degradations being suffered by their fellow Mexíca in the abominable obrajes? I thought they did not, for the latter Mexíca numbered in the many thousands. No doubt there existed other white men like Padre Vasco de Quiroga, who took the word Christianity to mean "loving kindness." But I *knew* that any men of his kind were vastly outnumbered by the vicious, greedy, deceitful, cold-hearted white men who likewise called themselves Christians and even priests.

At the time, I admit, I was being as deceitful as any white man. I was not, as Padre Vasco supposed, touring the villages of his Utopía just to assess or admire them; I was combing them for any inhabitants who might collaborate in my planned sedition. To every village smith who worked with metals, I showed my arcabuz and inquired whether he could make a copy of such a contrivance. They all, of course, recognized a thunder-stick—and made loud praise of the Mexícatl who had crafted mine. But all were unanimous in saying that even if they were inclined to imitate that talented artisan, they had not the necessary tools. And the replies I got when I asked *all* the men whether any would rally to me in rebellion against the Spanish oppressors could be summed up in the response I got from Erasmo Mártir, the last one I queried.

"No," he said flatly.

We were sitting together on the bench before his house door, where, this time, he was not shaping a woman-formed piece of guitarra. He went on:

"Do you take me for a raving tlahuéle? I am one of the fortunate few Mexíca who have ample food, secure shelter, freedom from any master's abuse, freedom to come and go as I please. I have even real prosperity and a promising future for my family.''

Yet another man drained of manhood, I thought bitterly, "lamiendo el culo del patrón." I growled, "Is that *all* you desire to have, Erasmo?"

"All?! Are *you* tlahuéle, Juan Británico? What more could a man want in this world as it is today?"

"Today, you say. But there was a day when the Mexíca also had pride."

"Those who could afford to. The tlátoantin rulers, and those with the noble *-tzin* to their names, and the pípiltin upper classes and the cuáchitin knights and such. They were *so* proud, in fact, that they gave no thought to us macehuáltin commoners who fed and clothed and attended them. Except when they needed us on the battlefield."

I said, "Most of the cuáchitin of whom you speak were likewise mere macehuáltin, who rose from the common class to the knighthood because they fought the enemies of the Mexíca, and were proud to do so, and showed it in their prowess on the battlefield."

Erasmo shrugged. "I have here everything that any Mexícatl knight ever had, and I won it without fighting."

"You did not win it!" I snapped. "It was given to you."

He shrugged again. "If you like. But I work hard to be worthy of it and to keep it. And to show my gratitude to the good Padre Vasco."

"The padre is good and gracious, that is true. But do you not see, Cuatl Erasmo? He is degrading your Mexícatl manhood just as would a cruel, whip-wielding white master. He is treating all of you as if you were only domesticated wild beasts. Or drooling xolopítlin. Or swaddled infants."

This appeared to be Erasmo's day for shrugging. "Even the manliest man can appreciate being treated with tender solicitude." Now he sniffled, as if near to weeping. "The way a good wife treats a good husband."

I blinked. "What has wifeliness to do with—?"

"Hush. No more, please, Cuatl Juan. Come, walk with me. I would speak with you on something of a different nature."

Wondering, I went with him. When we were some distance from his house, I ventured to say, "You do not seem nearly so cheerful as when I last saw you, and that was not too long ago."

He sniffled again, and said gloomily, "That is certain. My head is bowed, my heart bleeds, my hands tremble so that my work suffers."

"Are you ill, Erasmo?"

"Best you address me by my pagan name—Ixtálatl—for I am no longer fit to be a Christian. I have sinned most irredeemably. I am . . . afflicted with cháhuacocolíztli." That long word means "the shameful disease caused by adultery." He went on, still sniffling, "Not only does my heart leak. So does my tepúli. For some time now, I have not dared to embrace my good wife, and she keeps plaintively asking why."

"Ayya," I murmured sympathetically. "Then you have lain with one of those importunate Purémpe women. Well, a tícitl of our own people—or probably even a Spanish médico,—can alleviate the ailment. And any priest of our kindly goddess Tlazoltéotl can absolve you of the transgression."

"As a Christian convert, I cannot resort to the goddess Filth Eater."

"Then go and confess to Padre Vasco. He told me that the sin of adultery is not exactly unknown here in Utopía. Surely he has forgiven others, and has let them continue being Christians."

Erasmo muttered guiltily, "As a man, I am too ashamed to confess to the padre."

"Then why, may I ask, are you confessing to me?"

"Because she wants to meet you."

"Who?" I exclaimed, mystified. "Your wife?"

"No. The adulterous woman."

Now I was nonplussed. "Why in the name of all the gods should I consent to meet a slut of polluted tipíli?"

"She asked for you by name. By your pagan name. Tenamáxtli."

"It must be Pakápeti," I said, even more confounded, because if Tiptoe had been diseased when she and I so often and so enjoyably coupled, I too would be hurting and leaking by now. And there had hardly been time since then for some other male passerby to have—

"Her name is not Pakápeti," said Erasmo, and astounded me again by announcing, "Here she comes now."

This was too coincidental to be coincidence. The woman must have been observing our approach from some nearby hiding place, and now stepped forward to meet us. She was no one I had ever seen before, and I hoped I would never again see such a cold and gloating smile as she was smiling at me. Erasmo, speaking Náhuatl, not Poré, said without enthusiasm:

"Cuatl Tenamáxtli, this is G'nda Ké, who expressed a fervent wish to meet you."

I spoke no courteous salutation to her, saying only, "G'nda Ké is not a Purémpe name. And you have abundant hair on your head."

Clearly she understood Náhuatl, for she said, "G'nda Ké is Yaki," and gave a haughty toss of her dead-black mane.

Erasmo mumbled, "I must go. My wife . . ." and scampered back toward his home.

"If you are a Yaki," I said to the woman, "you are far from home."

"G'nda Ké has been many years away from that home."

That was the way she talked, not ever saying "I" or "me." She spoke always as if she were standing apart from her own physical presence. She appeared to be no older than myself, and she was fair of face and form; I could understand how easily she must have seduced Erasmo. But whether G'nda Ké smiled, frowned or wore no expression whatever, her visage never ceased to seem *gloating*. It implied that she possessed some private, secret, unclean bit of knowledge with which she could damage or even damn to Míctlan any person she chose. There was one other feature of her face that was only rarely seen among our people.

"You have a profusion of freckles," I said, not caring if I was being rude, because I supposed it was a manifestation of her detestable disease.

"G'nda Ké is freckled all over her body," she said with a gloating grin, as if inviting me to have a look.

I ignored that, and asked, "What brought you so far south from the Yaki lands? Are you on a quest of some sort?"

"Yes."

"What do you seek?"

"You."

I laughed, without humor. "I did not realize that my attractiveness had such a long reach. Anyway, you found Erasmo instead."

"Only to find you."

I laughed again. "Erasmo has good reason to wish you had never found *him.*"

She said indifferently, "Erasmo does not matter. G'nda Ké hopes that he will convey the disease to every other Mexícatl here. They deserve the agony and the shame. They are as flabby and cowardly as their forebears who refused to leave Aztlan with me."

My memory stirred. And, I think, so did the roots of my back hair. I recalled how my great-grandfather, Canaútli the Rememberer, had told of the long-ago Yaki woman—and yes, her name had been G'nda Ké—who turned some of the peaceable early Aztéca into the bellicose Mexíca who battled their way to greatness.

"That was sheaves of sheaves of years ago," I said, certain that she did not need my explaining of what "that" was. "If you did not die then, as reported, Yaki woman, how old must you be?"

"That does not matter either. What matters is that you, too, Tenamáxtli, have left Aztlan. And now you are of a disposition to accept G'nda Ké's gift of her *other* disease."

I blurted, "By Huitzli, I want none of your afflictions!"

"*Ayyo*, but you do! You just spoke the word—the name of him—Huitzilopóchtli, god of war. For that is G'nda Ké's other disease, and one she will happily help you spread through all The One World. *War!*"

I could only stare at her. I had not lately partaken of chápari, so this awful creature was hardly a drunken hallucination.

"You will recruit no warriors here, Tenamáxtli. Do not be tempted to loiter in this easeful Utopía. Your tonáli has destined you to a harder life, and a more glorious one. Go north. You and G'nda Ké will meet again, probably many times, along the way. Wherever you need her, she will be there, to help infect others with the sublime disease that you and she share."

She had been walking backward away from me as she spoke, and was now at some distance, so I shouted, "I need you not! I want you not! I can make war without you! Go back to the Míctlan you came from."

Just before she disappeared around a corner of one of the village houses, she spoke a last time, not loudly but audibly, and ominously:

"Tenamáxtli, no man can ever repulse or elude a woman bent on spite and malice. You will never be rid of this one while she still lives and hates and schemes."

Padre Vasco said, "I never even heard of the Yaki."

I told him, "They abide in the very farthest northwest corner of The One World. In forests and mountain ranges far beyond the desert wastes that our people call the Dead-Bone Lands. The Yaki are reputed to be the fiercest, most bloodthirsty of savages, loathing every other human being, including their own nearest relatives. I am quite ready to give credence to that reputation, after meeting my first Yaki yesterday. If the women are all like her, the men must be fiends indeed."

It was because I liked and admired Vasco de Quiroga that I had troubled to revisit his capital village of Santa Cruz

Pátzcuaro. Leaving out any mention of the Yaki woman's warlike aspirations—those she had expressed yesterday as well as those imputed to her in Canaútli's tales of long ago— I recounted to the padre what else I knew of her evil doings and intentions.

"It happened in a time before imagining," I said, "but the happenings were never forgotten. The words were repeated from one aged Rememberer to the next. How that mysterious Yaki woman insinuated herself into our serene Aztlan, preaching the worship of an alien god, and thereby setting brother against brother."

"Hmmm," mused the padre. "Lílith comes to Cain and Abel."

"Pardon?" I said.

"Nothing. Go on, my son."

"Well, either she did not die, all those ages ago, and became a demoness immortal, or she spawned a long line of demoness daughters. For there is most certainly just such a Yaki woman trying to disrupt your Utopía. This G'nda Ké is far more of a menace to your colonists here than any number of Purémpe women merely hungry for a man's embrace. It was my great-grandfather's belief that because the Yaki males are notorious for cruelly abusing their females, this particular Yaki woman is out to wreak revenge on *every* man alive."

"Hmmm," the padre murmured again. "Ever since Lílith, every country of the Old World has known a similar female predator, eager to rip the entrails out of any male. Real woman or mythical, who can say? In various languages she is the harpy, the lamia, the witchwife, the nightmare hag, *la bella dama sin merced*. But tell me, Juan Británico. If I am to thwart this demoness, how do I find and recognize her?"

"It might be difficult," I admitted. "G'nda Ké could pass as a transient young woman of any nation—except the bald Purémpecha, of course—even as a Spanish señorita, if she • chose to disguise herself. I confess I cannot remember her face well enough to describe her. It was handsome enough, but it seems to blur in my memory. Except for three things. I can tell you that her hair is of no living color. And her skin is flyspecked with freckles. And her eyes are like those of the axólotl lizard. However, if she saw me take the road hither, padre, she would know I intended to warn you about her, and she may well have gone into hiding or fled Utopía altogether.''

We were interrupted by the sudden entry of that young friar I had seen before, now agitated and shouting:

''Padre! Come quickly! A terrible fire to the eastward! San Marcos Churítzio—the guitarra village—it seems to be all ablaze!''

We dashed outdoors and looked where he pointed. An immense column of smoke was rising there, much like the one I had once caused to rise over Grasshopper Hill. But this mischief was none of my doing, so I stayed where I stood when Padre Vasco, his friars and everyone else of Santa Cruz went running to help their neighbors in San Marcos. I of course assumed that the fire was the work of that malevolent G'nda Ké—until I felt a tug at my mantle and turned to find that Tiptoe, this time having personified her name, had slipped up noiselessly behind me. She was smiling broadly, triumphantly, so I said:

''*You* did that! Set that village afire.''

''Not I, but my warrior women. Ever since I assembled them, we have been searching for you, Tenamáxtli. I saw you in that village yonder. When you departed, I gave orders to my women, then I followed you here.'' She added, with some scorn, ''I could see that you had acquired no other followers.''

I gestured toward the smoke. ''But why do that? Those Mexíca are a harmless lot.''

''*Because* they are a harmless lot. To show you what we mere women can do. Come, Tenamáxtli, before the Spaniards return. Come and meet the first recruits of your army of rebellion.''

* * *

I accompanied her to a mountainside overlooking the lake, where her "warriors" had regrouped to wait for her after their torch-bearing foray among the buildings of Erasmo's village. Besides Tiptoe, there were forty-two females, of all ages from barely nubile to matronly. Though they were also of varying degrees of sightliness—uniformly bald, of course—all looked healthy, sturdy and determined to show their mettle. I was resignedly thinking, "Well, they are only women, but they are forty-three more allies than I have had until now . . . ," when suddenly my masculine presumptuousness was rebuked.

"Pakápeti," one of the older women barked at her. "It was *you* who enlisted us in this venture. Why now do you ask us to accept this stranger as our leader?"

I expected Tiptoe to say something about my masterly qualities of leadership, or at least to mention the fact that this "venture" was originally my idea, but all she said was, turning to me, "Tenamáxtli, show them how your arcabuz works."

Though considerably exasperated, I did as she said—charging the weapon, then discharging it at a squirrel perched on a tree limb not too far distant (and this time, happily, hitting what I aimed at). The ball of lead fairly disintegrated the little animal, but the women excitedly fingered the remaining scraps of fur and handed them around, and clucked admiringly at the destructiveness of the thunder-stick, and marveled at my possessing such a thing. Then, all together, they began to clamor that I show *them* how to wield the arcabuz, and that I let them take turns at practicing with it.

"No," I said firmly. "If and when each of you procures a thunder-stick of your own, then I will teach you how to use it."

"And how do we manage that?" demanded that same older woman, who had the voice (and visage) of a cóyotl. "The white men's weapons are not procurable just for the asking."

"Here is one who will tell you how," said a new voice.

We had been joined by a forty-fourth woman, this one not bald, not Purémpe—this one the Yaki G'nda Ké again, and again obtruding herself into my affairs. Evidently, in just the short time since I had last seen her, the demoness had somehow joined this troop of women and ingratiated herself with them, for they listened respectfully when she spoke. And even I could not find fault with what she had to say:

"There are comely girls among you. And there are numerous Spanish soldiers here in Michihuácan, manning army outposts or guarding the estancias of Spanish landowners. You have only to catch the eye of those men and, with your beauty and your seductive wiles—"

"Are you suggesting that we *go astraddle the road*?" cried one of the comely young women, using the phrase that connotes prostitution or wanton promiscuity. "You would have us couple with our avowed enemies?"

I was tempted to say that even hateful, unwashed Christian white men ought to be preferable to billy goats and such other mates as were currently available in Michihuácan. But I kept silent and let G'nda Ké reply:

"There are many ways of besting an enemy in war, young woman. And seduction is one way denied to male combatants. You should take pride in having a weapon unique to our female sex."

"Well . . ." said the girl who had objected, sounding somewhat mollified.

G'nda Ké continued, "Besides, as *Purémpe* women, you have another unique advantage. The Spaniards' own females are repellently hairy of head and body. The Spanish soldiers will be curious to—shall we say?—*explore* any woman totally and temptingly hairless."

Most of the bald heads nodded agreement.

"Go to each guard or to each post," the Yaki woman went on, "singly or severally, and exercise your charms. Do whatever is necessary, either to addle the soldiers with lust or— if you care to go so far—to wring them limp and helpless. Then steal their thunder-sticks."

"And any other weapons they may have," I hastened to put in. "Also the pólvora and lead for those weapons."

"Now?" asked several of the women, almost eagerly. "Do we go this instant to seek those soldiers?"

I said, "I do not see why not, if you are indeed ready to employ your womanly attractions in our cause. But you will appreciate that I have not had time yet to think out any extensive plan of action. Most assuredly, there must be more of us. And to find more, I must go far beyond this land."

"I will come with you," Tiptoe said decisively. "If I could rally this many women in such a short time, surely I can do the same among other peoples and nations."

"Very well," I said, having no objection to the company of such an enterprising (and enjoyable) consort. "And since you and I will be traveling," I added, magnanimously according her the rank of leader equal to myself, "I suggest, Pakápeti, that we jointly appoint a second in command here."

"Yes," she said, and looked over the gathering. "Why not you, newcome comrade?" She pointed to the Yaki woman.

"No, no," said that one, trying to look modest and self-effacing. "These gallant Purémpe women should be led by one of their own. Besides, like you and Tenamáxtli, G'nda Ké will have work to do elsewhere. For the cause."

"Then," said Tiptoe, "I recommend Kurúpani." She indicated the cóyotl-looking woman—another one egregiously misnamed, for that Poré word means "Butterfly."

"I concur," I said, and spoke directly to Butterfly. "It may be a long time before we can wage real warfare against the white men. But while Pakápeti and I are scouring the country for further recruits, you will be in charge of mounting that campaign to procure weapons."

"No more than that?" the woman asked, and showed me the bowl of hot embers that was their only weapon at present. "Cannot we do some burning, as well?"

I exclaimed, "Ayyo, by all means! I am heartily in favor

of anything that will harass and worry the Spaniards. Also, your burning of army posts or hacienda buildings should distract their attention from whatever larger war preparations Pakápeti and I may be making elsewhere. Just one thing, though, Butterfly. Please do not molest any more of these villages here around Pátzcuaro. Neither Padre Vasco nor his tame Mexíca are our enemies.''

The woman assented, if grudgingly. G'nda Ké frowned and looked ready to challenge my instructions, but I turned my back on her and spoke to Tiptoe:

''We will go north from here, and we can start right now, if you are ready. I see you already have a traveling pack. Is there anything else you might require, anything I can provide for you?''

''Yes,'' she said. ''As soon as possible, Tenamáxtli, I want a thunder-stick of my own.''

XV

"**I** INSIST," SHE said, some ten or twelve days later. "I want a thunder-stick of my own. And this will probably be our last opportunity for me to get one."

We were crouched in some bushes on a knoll overlooking a Spanish guardhouse. That consisted of only a small wooden shack, in which were posted two soldiers, armed and armored, with a fenced pen alongside, containing four horses, two of them saddled and bridled.

"We could also steal a horse for each of us," Tiptoe urged. "And surely we could learn to ride them."

We were at the northern border of New Galicia. Everything south of here was comfortably called by the Spaniards their Tierra de Paz, everything to the north was known as the Tierra de Guerra, and this area along the border was somewhat hazily described as the Tierra Disputable. From east to west along here, there was an army outpost like this one situated every few one-long-runs, and mounted patrols continuously prowled between them. All the soldiers were on the alert against any forays by war parties from the nations of the Tierra de Guerra.

Years earlier, these same or similar guards had paid little heed when my mother, my uncle and I—obviously innocuous travelers—had crossed some part of this border, going southward. But I dared not assume that the soldiers would be so inattentive this time. For one reason, I was sure that even the most negligent guardsman would happily detain and search a young woman as conspicuously unusual and attractive as Tiptoe—and probably would do more than that to her.

"Well?" she said, digging an elbow into my ribs.

I grumbled, "I am not too eager to share you with someone else, especially a white someone else."

"Ayya!" she scoffed. "You did not hesitate to tell those *other* women to prostrate and prostitute themselves."

"I was not so intimately acquainted with those other women. Nor did they have any consorts to object to their going astraddle the road. You do."

"Then my consort can also rescue me before I am soiled beyond redemption. Shall we wait until one of those men leaves and you have only the one to deal with?"

"I suspect that neither man gets relieved until a patrol arrives from some other post. If you are really determined on this, we might as well act now. My weapon is charged. Go and employ yours. Your seductive self. When you have got your victim thoroughly bedazzled, and the other gawking, give a cry—of ecstatic admiration, anticipation, whatever—loud enough for me to hear, and I will come bursting through the door. Be prepared to seize and entangle your man while I slay the onlooker. Then together we will overpower yours."

"The plan sounds simple enough. Simple plans are best."

"Let us hope so. Just do not get so carried away that you neglect to utter that shout."

She asked teasingly, "Are you afraid that I might perhaps *enjoy* the embrace of a white man? Even come to *prefer* it?"

"No," I said. "Once you have got close enough to a white man to smell him, I doubt that you will prefer him. But I want this done quickly. There *will* be a patrol arriving sometime."

"Then . . . ximopanólti, Tenamáxtli," she said, mockingly taking her leave with utmost formality.

She stood up from among the bushes and walked down the slope—slowly, but not at *all* formally—undulating her hips as if she were doing what our people call the quequez-cuícatl, "the ticklish dance." The soldiers must have glimpsed her through some peephole in their shack wall. They both came to the door, and except for one significant look that passed between them, they leeringly ogled her progress all the way, then very politely stepped aside for her to enter, and the door closed behind all three of them.

I waited, then, and waited and waited, but heard no summoning cry from Tiptoe. After a considerable while, I began cursing myself for having made my plan *too* simple. Did the soldiers suspect that the comely young woman had not been traveling alone? Were they simply holding her hostage while they waited, weapons at the ready, for her presumed companion to appear? Eventually I decided that there was only one way to find out. Risking the chance that one of the men was still keeping a lookout at the peephole, I stood up in plain view of the shack. When there came no explosion of pólvora or shout of challenge, I scurried down the knoll, my own arcabuz at the ready. When still it seemed I had been unnoticed, I crossed the level ground before the shack and leaned an ear against the door. All I could hear was a sort of chorus of voices *grunting*. This puzzled me, but evidently Tiptoe was not being tortured to screaming, so I waited a little longer. At last, unable to bear the suspense, I gave the door a push.

It was not fastened in any way, and swung loosely inward, letting daylight into the dark interior. Against the shack's rear wall, the guards had built a shelf of planks, probably used by them alternately as a dining board and sleeping cot, but now being used for something else. On that shelf Tiptoe was stretched, her bare legs splayed apart and her mantle bunched up around her neck. She was silent, but she was squirming desperately, because both of the soldiers were raping her simultaneously. Standing at opposite ends of the shelf, one man had rammed his tepúli into her nether orifice, the other into her upper, and they were grinning lasciviously at one another while they pumped and grunted.

Instantly I discharged my arcabuz, and at that close distance I could not miss my aim. The soldier standing between Tiptoe's legs was slammed away from her and against the shack wall, his leather cuirass torn open and his chest abruptly bright red. Though the room was as instantly clouded with blue smoke, I could see the second soldier also lurch back, away from Tiptoe's head, and he also, curiously, was wet with much blood. Clearly he was still alive—he was shrieking like a woman—but he obviously posed no immediate danger to me, for he had both hands clutched to what remained of his tepúli, while it hosed out blood like a fountain's spout. I did not take time to grab for my other weapon—the obsidian knife I wore at my belt—but merely reversed my arcabuz in my one hand, holding it like a club. I reached out my other hand to the agonized soldier, who stood teetering and screeching in my face, snatched off his metal helmet and beat his head with the arcabuz's butt until he fell dead.

When I turned from him, Tiptoe had clambered off the plank shelf and stood, also unsteady on her feet, letting her mantle fall to clothe her nakedness, while she choked and coughed and spat onto the dirt floor. Her face, where it was not slick with juices, was a sickly greenish color. I took her arm and hurried her out into the open air, starting to say, "I would have come sooner, Pakápeti—"

But she only reeled away from me, still making strangling noises, to lean on the fence of the horse pen, where a hollowed-out log trough held water for the animals. She plunged her head under the water, then several times tilted her head back to gargle the water in her mouth and spit it out, and meanwhile, with her cupped hands, scooped water up under her mantle to wash her nether parts. When finally she felt clean enough or composed enough to speak, she did so, but disjointedly, gagging and retching between words:

"You saw . . . I could not . . . shout . . ."

"Do not talk," I said. "Stay here and rest. I must hide the bodies."

The very mention of the men made her face go ill and greenish again, so I left her and went into the shack. As I dragged one dead man, then the other, by the feet out of the door, I was struck by an idea. I ran again to the top of the knoll, and could espy no patrol or any other moving being either east or west. So I ran back down to the soldiers and clumsily, but as quickly as I could, I unstrapped their various pieces of metal and leather armor. When I could get to the heavy blue canvas uniforms beneath, I stripped those garments off the bodies, too. Several pieces of the clothing were ruined, either rent by the blast of my arcabuz or drenched with blood. But I salvaged and set aside one shirt, one pair of trousers, and a pair of stout military boots.

When they were unclad, the corpses were easier to move, but I was panting and sweating heavily by the time I had dragged each of them around to the far side of the knoll. There was thick underbrush there, and I thought I did a creditable job of hiding them and the remainder of their weapons in it. Then, with a torn shirt of theirs, I went back over the traces of our passage—my own tracks, their smeared blood, the broken twigs and disarranged greenery—doing my best to make them unnoticeable.

The smoke had cleared from the shack by then, so I went in and picked up the two arcabuces the soldiers had had no chance to use, and the leather pouches in which they kept balls and pólvora, and two metal water flasks and one fine, sharp steel knife. There was also a pouch of dried, fibrous meat that I thought worth taking, and some leather straps and lengths of rope. While I was collecting these things, I saw that the dirt floor was much splotched with clotting blood, so I used the knife to chop up the earthen surface, then started stamping it flat again. I was busy at that when something occurred to me, and I paused to look more closely around me on the ground.

"What are you doing?" Tiptoe asked urgently. She was leaning against the doorjamb, limp, looking still sick and wretched. "You have hidden them. We must get away from here." I could see that she was bravely trying to suppress those gut-wrenching spasms of nausea, but her breast throbbed with the effort of it.

"I want to hide *everything* of them," I said. "There is—er—one piece missing."

Tiptoe suddenly looked even sicker than before, and the heaves of her breast became again violent retches between her words: "Did not mean to ... but ... the thunder-noise ... I bit ... and then I ..."

She swallowed, with a phlegmy gulp, to fight down the gagging that strangled her next words. I did not need to hear the words. I had to swallow several times myself, to keep from vomiting most unmanfully.

Tiptoe disappeared from the doorway, and I hurried to finish tamping the shack floor. Then I ran once more to the top of the knoll to make sure that we were not yet in hazard of being interrupted by any patrols or passersby. Though I was by now getting very tired, I continued trying to behave manfully, to inspirit poor Tiptoe, who was again gargling water at the horse trough. Manfully, I overcame what would have been *anybody's* natural timidity around such huge and alien animals as horses, and approached those in the fenced pen. I was somewhat surprised, and much emboldened, when they did not recoil from me or strike out at me with their massive hooves. All four of them merely regarded me with deerlike looks of mild curiosity, and one of the barebacked animals stood submissively still while I bundled onto its back the various things I had plundered from the soldiers and the shack, tying them on with the bits of rope and straps I had found there. When the horse still showed no signs of objecting, I added to its burden my traveling pack and that of Tiptoe. Then I went to where she sat huddled and miserable

beside the trough, and bent to help her to stand. She flinched
away from my hand and said, almost snarling:

"Please, do not touch me again. Not ever again, Tenamáxtli."

I murmured encouragingly, "Just get up and help me lead
the horses, Pakápeti. As you said, we must be away from
here. And when we are safely distant, I will teach you how
to kill Spaniards with your very own thunder-stick."

"Why should I stop with Spaniards?" she muttered, and
spat on the ground, and added disgustedly, *"Men!"*

She was now sounding uncomfortably like that Yaki
witchwife, G'nda Ké. But she stood up and, evincing no
nervousness at all, took the reins of one saddled horse and
the rope I had tied around the neck of the pack animal. I led
the other two horses, and kicked down a fence rail so we
could get out, and away we all went.

I was trusting that when a patrol *did* arrive at that outpost,
those men would be confounded by the inexplicable absence
of the guards and all their animals, and would waste some
time waiting for the truants to reappear, before going to
search for them. Whether or not the patrol found the two
corpses, they would almost certainly assume that the outpost
had been attacked by some war party from the north. And
they would hardly dare to go chasing after them into the
Tierra de Guerra until they had assembled a considerable
force of other soldiers. So Tiptoe and I and our acquisitions
should be able to put ample distance between ourselves and
any pursuit. Nevertheless, I did not take us straight to the
north. I had already calculated, from where the sun stood in
the sky at every time of day, that we must be almost directly
eastward of my home city of Aztlan. If I was to start recruiting warriors from the still-unconquered lands, where better than there? So it was in that direction that we went.

On our first night in the Tierra de Guerra, we stopped
beside a spring of good water, tied the horses to nearby
trees—each on a long tether, so it could graze and drink—

laid only a small fire and ate of the dried meat I had brought along. Then we spread our blankets side by side, and because Tiptoe was still being disconsolate and untalkative, I reached out a hand to give her a comforting caress. She irritably brushed the hand away and said firmly:

"Not tonight, Tenamáxtli. We both have too many other things to think about. Tomorrow we must learn to ride the horses and I must learn to wield the thunder-stick."

Very well, next morning we loosed the two saddled horses from their tethers, Tiptoe doffed her sandals and put a bare foot into the dangling wooden piece provided for that purpose. We both had seen many Spaniards on horseback, so we were not entirely ignorant of the method of mounting. Tiptoe required a boost from me to get up there, but I clambered onto my horse by using a tree stump for a mounting block. Again the horses made no complaint; evidently they were accustomed to being ridden not by a single master but by anyone who had need of them. I kicked my bare heels to make mine walk, and then tried to turn it leftward in a circle, to stay close to our camping place.

I had seen other riders do that, apparently by pulling one rein to tug the horse's head in the desired direction. But when I yanked hard on the left rein, I succeeded only in getting a sidewise stare from the horse's left eye—an almost school-masterish look, mingling "you are wrong" and "you are stupid." I took heed that the horse was trying to teach me a lesson, so I paused to reflect. Perhaps the riders I had watched had only *seemed* to jerk their horses' heads this way and that. After a little experimenting, I discovered that I had to do no more than lay the right-side rein gently against the horse's neck and it would turn left as I wished. I imparted that information to Tiptoe, and we both sat our saddles proudly as our horses sauntered around in leftwise circles.

Next, I brushed my horse's sides with my heels to make it move faster. It commenced the rocking gait that the Spanish call the *trote*, and I learned another lesson. Until now, I had supposed that sitting on a leather saddle, nicely curved to cup one's backside, would be more comfortable than sitting on something stiff, like an icpáli chair. I was wrong. This was excruciating. After the trotting gait had jounced me for only the briefest while, I began to fear that my backbone was being driven through the top of my head. And clearly the horse did not enjoy being under my thumping rump; it turned its head to give me another look of reproach and slowed to a walk again. Tiptoe had endured the same brief experience of being painfully hammered from underneath, so we mutually decided to postpone any attempt to proceed at speed until we had sufficiently practiced just sitting astride for some time.

So, all the rest of that day, we rode at the walk, leading the two other horses behind, and all six of us were satisfied with that leisurely pace. But then, near sundown, when we found another watering place at which to stop for the night, both Tiptoe and I were shocked to find ourselves so stiff that we could only slowly and creakily get down from our saddles. We had not noticed until then how our shoulders and arms ached, just from holding the reins; how our ribs hurt as if they had been cudgeled; how our crotches felt as if they had been split with wedges. And our legs were not only cramped and trembly from their having clutched the horses' sides all day, they were also almost bloodily raw from having rubbed against the saddles' leather flaps. These pains I found hard to understand, since we had ridden so slowly and easefully. I was beginning to wonder why the white men had ever found horses useful as their means of transport. At any rate, Tiptoe and I were too sore even to think of taking up practice with the arcabuces right then, and that night Tiptoe had no need to fend off any amative overtures from me.

But the next day we dauntlessly determined to try riding again, and I was at least able to provide us with clothing more protective than the mantles that left our legs bare and abradable. I got out the various items of Spanish costume that I had packed. Though Tiptoe angrily refused to wear anything that the two frontier guards had bequeathed to us,

I did persuade her to put on the shirt, trousers and boots that I had acquired at the Cathedral. They were far too big for her, of course, but they served. And I donned the military boots, the blue shirt and the trousers of one of those soldiers' uniforms. When we set off, I tried riding the unsaddled horse that was carrying no pack, thinking that maybe I could better adapt to its bare back. I could not. Even at the walking gait, I soon began to fear that the horse's rooftree backbone was cleaving me asunder from my buttocks all the way upward. I abandoned the trial and remounted my saddled horse.

Ayya, I will not dwell on all the painful trials and errors that Tiptoe and I made during the next several days. Suffice it to say that we did at last get used to riding astride the animals, and so did our muscles and skins and buttocks. In fact, in time—as if to prove the truth of a remark she had once made to me—Tiptoe became a much better rider than I, and took delight in showing off her prowess. I at least managed to keep up with her, once I learned to urge my horse directly from the walk—not having to suffer the jounces of trotting—into the easier-to-sit gait of the *galope*.

During those days, too, as our aches and pains diminished, I instructed Tiptoe in the charging and discharging of the arcabuz, letting her use one of those I had taken from the soldiers. Rather to my consternation, she proved to be better at *that*, as well, than I was. That is to say, she could make the lead ball hit whatever she was aiming at, even at a considerable distance, perhaps three times out of five, while I had long considered myself adept if I could do the same thing *one* time out of five. My masculine pride was salvaged, though, when I exchanged weapons with her, and our respective score of punctured targets changed accordingly. It was evident that the soldiers' arcabuces were for some reason more accurate than the copy that the artisan Pochotl had made for me. I carefully examined all three of the weapons now in our possession, and could see no difference among them to account for that. But of course I was no expert on such things, and neither had Pochotl been.

So, from then on, Tiptoe and I each carried one of the purloined arcabuces. I deemed it prudent to keep them hidden in our bedrolls, and we took one out only when we wished to kill game for fresh meat. Tiptoe liked to make that her task, and was inclined to flaunt her marksmanship by bringing down rabbits and pheasants. But I cautioned her that the pólvora was too precious to waste on such small creatures, especially because when the heavy ball did hit one, there was not much left of it to eat. Thereafter, she aimed at (and almost always hit) only deer and wild boars. I did not discard Pochotl's weapon, so painstakingly handcrafted, but kept it also hidden among our packs, in case it should sometime be needed.

On one of the nights of one of those days in the hinterlands, I again ventured to extend a caress to Tiptoe, in her blankets beside me, and again she fended me away, saying:

"No, Tenamáxtli. I feel unclean. You must have seen—I have grown a stubble of hair on my head and . . . and elsewhere. I feel that I am no longer a properly immaculate Purémpe. Until I am . . ." and she rolled over and went to sleep.

Exasperated and frustrated, I made sure, during the next day's ride, to seek out an amóli plant and dig up its root. That night, when I roasted a boar haunch over our fire, I also set my metal flask of water to boil. After we had eaten, I said:

"Pakápeti, here is hot water and here is a soap-root and here is a good steel knife, which I have whetted to utmost keenness. You can easily make yourself a properly immaculate Purémpe once more."

She said airily, "I think I will decline, Tenamáxtli. You have dressed me in man's clothing, so I have decided to let my hair grow out and make myself *look* like a man."

I naturally remonstrated with her, pointing out that the gods had put beautiful women on this earth for other and better purposes than to impersonate men. But she was adamant, and I had to conclude that her defilement back there at the outpost had simply made the copulative act hateful to

her—that she never again *would* couple with me or any other
man. There was no objection that I could, in conscience,
make to that. I could only respect her decision and, meanwhile, entertain two hopes. One was my hope that since Tiptoe now knew how to use an arcabuz, she would not take
the whim to use it on the nearest male, that being myself.
And I hoped that we would soon, in our journeying, come
upon a town or village where the women had not, for whatever reason, decided to repel the advances of every man of
mankind.

Instead, what we came upon, late one afternoon, was
something totally unexpected—a troop of mounted Spaniards, most of them armed and armored, riding through this
Tierra de Guerra—and we encountered them so suddenly
that we had no chance of evasion. They were not, as I might
have anticipated, a body of soldiers pursuing us to wreak
revenge for what we had done at the border outpost. I had
never ceased keeping a wary lookout to our rear. If I had
seen any sign of a patrol approaching from behind us, I could
have taken care to avoid capture. But this troop rode up upon
us from the farther side of a hill that we were ascending, and
obviously they were as surprised as we were when we met
at the top.

There was nothing I could do except tell Tiptoe in Poré,
"Keep silent!" then raise a comradely hand to the lead soldier—who was groping for the arcabuz slung across his saddle horn—and greet him cordially, as if he and we were
accustomed to meeting thus every day, *"Buenas tardes,
amigo. ¿Qué tal?"*

He stammered, "B-buenas tardes," and, with the hand that
had been reaching for the weapon, returned my salute. He
said nothing more, but deferred to two other riders—men in
officers' uniform—who shouldered their horses up beside
him.

One of them growled a vile blasphemy, *"¡Me cago en la
puta Virgen!"* then, eyeing my partial uniform and the army

brands on our horses, demanded impolitely, *"¿Quién eres, Don Mierda?"*

Disquieted though I was, I had wit enough to tell him the same thing I had told Padre Vasco, that I was Juan Británico, interpreter and assistant to the notarius who served the Bishop of Méxíco.

The officer sneered and exclaimed, *"¡Y un cojón!"* a vulgar expression of disbelief. "An indio on horseback? That is a thing forbidden!"

I was glad that our far-more-strictly-forbidden arcabuces were out of his sight, and said humbly, "You are riding in the direction of the City of Méxíco, Señor Capitán. If you like, I will accompany you thither, where Bishop Zumárraga and Notarius de Molina will assuredly vouch for me. It was they who provided these horses for this journey of mine."

I do not know if the officer had ever heard those two names before, but my speaking them seemed to mitigate his disbelief slightly. He was less gruff when he demanded, "And who is the other man?"

"My slave and attendant," I lied, grateful now for her having chosen to pose as a man, and gave her name in Spanish, *"Se llama de Puntas."*

The other officer laughed. "A *man* named *Tiptoe*! How stupid these indios!"

The first one laughed, too, then, derisively misspeaking my name, said, "And *you*, Don Zonzón, what are you doing here?"

More composed by now, I was able to say glibly, "A special mission, Señor Capitán. The bishop wishes to ascertain the temper of the savages here in the Tierra de Guerra. I was sent because I am of their race, and speak several of their languages, but also am manifestly vested with Spanish and Christian authority."

"¡Joder!" he rasped. "Everyone already knows the temper of these savages. Their temper is ugly. Murderous. Bloodthirsty. Why do you think *we* travel only in unassailable numbers?"

"Just so," I said blandly. "I intend to report to the bishop that he might palliate the savages' temper by sending Christian missionaries to do humanitarian works among them, in the manner of Padre Vasco de Quiroga."

Again, I do not know if the officer had ever heard of that priest, but my apparent familiarity with so many churchmen seemed finally to dispel his suspicions.

He said, "We too are on a humanitarian mission. Our Governor of New Galicia, Nuño de Guzmán, assembled this numerous company to escort four men to the City of Méxíco. They are three brave Christian Spaniards and a loyal Moro slave, long believed lost in the far-off colony called Florida. But, most miraculously, they fought their way hither—this close to civilization. Now they wish to tell the story of their wanderings to the Marqués Cortés himself."

"And I am sure you will safely deliver them, Señor Capitán," I said. "But this day latens. My own slave and I had intended to proceed farther, but we passed a good water hole not a league back, sufficient for your whole troop's camping. If you will allow, we will return there to lead you and, by your leave, camp there with you."

"By all means, Don Juan Británico," he said, companionably now. "Lead on."

Tiptoe and I turned our horses about, and as the company came clanking and shuffling and clattering behind us, I translated to her what had passed between me and the officer. She asked, her voice again trembly because she was speaking of white men:

"Why in the name of the war god Curicáuri do you wish to spend the night with them?"

"Because the officer mentioned that butcher Guzmán," I said. "The man who laid waste your land of Michihuácan and claimed it for his own. I had believed there were no Spaniards in these northern parts. I want to find out what Guzmán is doing, so distant from his New Galicia."

"If you must," she said resignedly.

"And you, Tiptoe, please just remain inconspicuous. Let

the white men hunt their own game for their night's meal. *Please* do not take out a thunder-stick to show them your mastery of it.''

The officer—his name was Tallabuena, and his rank was only *teniente*, but I kept on ingratiatingly addressing him as Capitán—sat beside me at the campfire. While the two of us gnawed on juicy roast deer meat, he confided quite freely what I wished to know about that Governor Guzmán:

"No, no, he has not come this far north. He is still safely resident in New Galicia. The canny Guzmán knows better than to risk his fat *culón* up here in the Tierra de Guerra. But he has established his capital right *on* the northern border of New Galicia, and hopes to make a fair city of it.''

"Why?'' I asked. "The old capital of Michihuácan was on the shore of the Lake of Rushes, far to the south.''

"Guzmán is no fisherman. His home province of Galicia back in Old Spain is silver-mining country. It follows that he expects to make his fortune here from silver. So he founded his capital in a region near the coast, where his prospectors have discovered rich veins of that and other ores. He has named it Compostela. So far, it consists just of himself and his favorite fawning *compinches* and his cadre of troops, but he will be rounding up native slaves to toil underground to mine the silver for him. I pity those poor wretches.''

"So do I,'' I murmured, while deciding that Tiptoe and I would set our direction more north of west when we moved on, not to stumble into that Compostela. Still, it troubled me that the butcher Guzmán had set his new city so close to my native Aztlan—no more than a hundred one-long-runs distant, as best I could estimate.

"But come, Don Juan,'' Tallabuena said now. "Come and meet the heroes of the hour.''

He led me to where the three heroes sat eating. They were being devotedly attended by a number of lesser-ranking soldiers, who plied them with the choicest portions of deer meat and poured for them wine from leather bags and jumped to fulfill their every least request. Also in attendance on them was a man in the traveling dress of a friar, who seemed even more servilely to seek their favor. The heroes, I could see, had originally been white-skinned, but they were now so sunburned that their complexion was darker than my own. The fourth man, who would also have been accounted a hero, I suppose, if he had been white, sat eating alone and apart and unattended. He was black and could not have been burned any blacker.

I would never see these several Spaniards again after this one night. But though I could not have known it then, the tonáli of every one of them was so linked with mine that our separate future lives—and numberless other lives, and even the destinies of nations—would inextricably be intertwined. So I will tell here of what I learned about them, and how I befriended one of them, in the brief time before we parted.

XVI

THE LEADER OF the heroes was respectfully addressed by everyone else by his Christian name of Don Álvar. But when he was introduced to me, I wondered why any Spaniards should have laughed at Tiptoe's name, because the surname of this man Álvar was Cabeza de Vaca, which means "Cow Head." Despite that inauspicious appellation, he and his fellows truly had done a heroic feat. I had to piece together their story from their converse with the soldiers attending them, and from what the Teniente Tallabuena told me—because the three heroes, after having greeted me politely enough, did not once thereafter speak directly to me. And when I knew their history, I could hardly blame them for wanting nothing to do with any indio.

I know that Florida means "flowery" in the Spanish tongue, but to this day I do not know where the land of that name is situated. Wherever it is, it must be a terrible sort of place. More than eight years before, this man Cow Head, his surviving companions and some hundreds of other white men, together with their horses and weapons and provisions, had sailed from the island colony of Cuba, intending to settle a new colony in that Florida.

From their first setting sail, they were beset by vicious springtime storms. Then, when they finally landed, they encountered other dismaying troubles. Where the countryside of Florida was not dense with nearly impenetrable forests, it was laced with swift rivers difficult to ford, or hot and stinking swamps, and in such wilderness their horses were next to useless. Rapacious woodland animals stalked the adventurers, and snakes and insects bit and stung them and lethal swamp fevers and illnesses assailed them. Meanwhile, the native inhabitants of Florida were not at all happy to receive these pale-skinned invaders, but picked them off, one after another, with arrows discharged from ambush among the concealing trees or, in open country, frontally attacked them in force. The travel-exhausted and fever-weakened Spaniards could fight back only feebly, and they were increasingly debilitated by hunger, because the indios also carried away their own domestic animals and burned their own crops of maize and other edibles, ahead of the white men's advance. (It seemed incredible to me, but the would-be colonists were evidently incapable of feeding themselves from the bounty of animals, birds, fish and plants that every wilderness offers to men of initiative and enterprise.) Anyway, the numbers of the Spaniards so alarmingly diminished that the remainder abandoned all hope of surviving in that place. They turned about and retreated to the coast, only to find that their ships' crews, doubtless having given them up for lost, had sailed away and left them marooned in that hostile land.

Discouraged, sick, fearful, besieged on every side, they determined on the desperate expedient of building new boats for themselves. And they did—five boats—of tree limbs and palm leaves, lashed together with ropes braided from the horses' manes and tails, caulked with pine pitch, rigged with sails made of their clothes sewn together. By this time, they had slaughtered their remaining horses for their meat, and had used their hides to make bags for carrying potable water. When the boats cast off, their five masters—Cow Head was one—took them not far out to sea, but kept within sight of the coastline, believing that if they followed it far enough westward they must eventually reach the shores of New Spain.

They found the sea and the land alike inimical, both earth and water frequently pounded by storms—cold winter storms now—of scouring winds and torrential rains. Even in calm weather there were rains—of arrows—from indios in war canoes that came out to harass them. Their scanty food supplies gave out, and their untanned leather water bags soon rotted, but every time the Spaniards tried to land to replenish their provisions, they were repelled by more swarms of arrows. Inevitably, the five boats were driven apart. Four of them were never seen or heard of again. The remaining boat, carrying Cow Head and some number of his comrades, after a long time did manage to get ashore.

The white men, now barely clothed, almost famished, cold to the bone, weakened to near decrepitude, found an occasional native tribe—a tribe as yet uninformed that it was being invaded—that was willing to shelter and feed strangers. But, as the white men dauntlessly forged westward in hope of finding New Spain, they were more often savaged than succored. As they crossed wooded lands, vast grasslands, unbelievably broad rivers, high mountains and parched deserts, they were captured by one tribe or roving band of indios after another. The captors would enslave them, put them to hard labor, mistreat and beat and starve them. ("The damned red *diablos*," I heard Cow Head remark, "even let their hellfry brats amuse themselves by yanking out tufts of our beards.") And from one after another of those captivities the Spaniards had to contrive to escape, each time losing one or more of their number to death or recapture. What became of those comrades they left behind, they never would know.

When at long last they reached the far outskirts of New Spain, there were only four of them left alive: three whites—Cabeza de Vaca, Andrés Dorantes and Alonso del Castillo—and Estebanico, the black slave belonging to Dorantes. Except for my overhearing Castillo's comment that "we have crossed an entire continent"—and I have only the vaguest idea of what a continent is—I have no way of estimating how many leagues and one-long-runs those men so painfully traversed. All that I—and they—know for certain is that it took them eight years to do it. They would have made the journey in less time, of course, if they had been able to keep to the shore of the Eastern Sea. But their various captors had passed them from hand to hand, among ever more inland-dwelling tribes—or their escapes from those captivities had impelled them ever farther inland—so that they were very nearly at the shore of the *Western* Sea when finally they encountered a group of Spanish soldiers patrolling daringly deep in the Tierra de Guerra.

Those soldiers—awed, admiring, almost incredulous of the strangers' story—escorted them to an army outpost, where they were clothed and fed, then brought them to Compostela. Governor Guzmán gave them horses and a more numerous escort and the friar, Marcos de Niza, to see to their spiritual needs, and set them on the cross-country trail toward the City of México. There, Guzmán had assured them, they would be feasted and honored and celebrated as they deserved. And, all along the way, the heroes had been telling and retelling their tale to every new-met and eager listener. I listened as avidly as any, and with unfeigned admiration.

There were many questions I would have liked to ask those three white men, if they had not been so sedulously ignoring me. But I could not help hearing that Fray Marcos was asking some of the very same questions I had in mind. He seemed frustrated—and so was I—when the heroes protested their inability to supply this or that piece of information the friar wanted. So I went over to where the black man, Estebanico, sat apart. Now, the *-ico* that the Spaniards appended to his name is a condescending diminutive such as is used when speaking to children, so I took care to address him properly, as an adult:

"*Buenas noches, Esteban.*"

"*Buenas . . . ,*" he mumbled, looking rather askance at an indio who spoke Spanish.

"May I talk with you, *amigo*?"

"Amigo?" he repeated, as if surprised to be addressed as an equal.

"Are we not both of us slaves to the white men?" I asked. "Here you sit, disdained, while your master preens and revels in the attention he is getting. I should like to know something of *your* adventures. Here, I have some picíetl. Let us smoke together, while I listen."

He still regarded me warily, but either I had established some comity between us or he was simply yearnful to be heard. He said, "What would you wish to know?"

"Just tell me what happened during the past eight years. I have listened to the Señor Cow Head's recollections. Now tell me yours."

And he did, from the expedition's first landing in that place called Florida, through all the disappointments and disasters that afflicted and decimated the fugitive survivors as they crossed the unknown lands from east to west. His account differed from the white men's only in two respects. Esteban clearly had suffered every hurt and hardship and humiliation that the other journeyers had endured, *but no more and no less.* He rather stressed this in his telling, as if to assert that those mutual sufferings had conferred on him an equality with his masters.

The other difference between his account and theirs was that Esteban had taken the trouble to learn at least some fragments of the various languages spoken by the peoples in whose communities they had spent any time. I had never heard the names of any of those tribes before. Esteban said they lived far to the northeast of this New Spain. The two last—or nearest—tribes that held the wanderers in captivity called themselves, he said, the Akimoél O'otam, or River People, and the To'ono O'otam, or Desert People. And of all the "damned red diablos" encountered, he said, they were the *most* devilishly *diabolico.* I tucked the two names into my memory. Whoever those people were, and wherever, they sounded like apt candidates for enlistment in my private rebel army.

By the time Esteban finished his story, everyone else around the fire had rolled himself in his blankets and gone to sleep. I was just about to ask the questions I had not been able to put to the white men, when I heard a stealthy footfall behind me. I spun about, and found it was only Tiptoe, asking in a whisper:

"Are you all right, Tenamáxtli?"

I answered in Poré, "Of course. Go back to sleep, Pakápeti." And I repeated that in Spanish, for Esteban to hear, "Go back to sleep, *my man.*"

"I was asleep. But I woke in sudden fear that the beasts might have harmed you or trussed you as a prisoner. And ayya! *This* beast is *black!*"

"No matter, my dear. A friendly beast, for all that. But thank you for your concern."

As she crept away, Esteban laughed without humor and said jeeringly, "My man!"

I shrugged, "Even a slave can own a slave."

"I do not give a ripe, fragrant *pedo* how many slaves you own. And a slave that one may be, and as short-haired as I am, but a *man* she is not."

"Hush, Esteban. A pretense, yes, but only to avoid any risk of her being molested by these *tunantón* bluecoats."

"I should not mind doing a bit of that molesting myself," he said, grinning whitely in the darkness. "A few times during our journey, I got a taste of the red women, and found them tasty indeed. And they found *me* no more distasteful than if I had been white."

Probably so. I supposed that, even among the people of my own race, a woman lewd enough to be tempted to sample a foreign flesh would hardly think black flesh any more freakish than white. But Esteban apparently took the women's unfastidiousness to be another token—however pathetic a token—that there in the unknown lands he had been the equal of any white man. I almost confided to him that I had once enjoyed a woman of *his* race—or half black, at any rate—and found her no different inside than any "red" woman. Instead, I said only:

"Amigo Esteban, I believe you would like to return to those far lands."

It was he who shrugged now. "Even in brute captivity there, I was not the slave of any one man."

"Then why not just go back? Go now. Steal a horse. I will not raise any outcry."

He shook his head. "I have been a fugitive these eight years. I do not want to have slave-catchers hunting me for the rest of my life. And they would, even into the savage lands."

"Perhaps . . ." I said, ruminating. "Perhaps we can concoct a reason for you to go there legitimately, and with the white men's blessing."

"Oh? How?"

"I overheard that Fray Marcos interrogating—"

Esteban laughed again, and again without humor. "Ah, *el galicoso.*"

"What?" I said. If I had understood the word, he had described the friar as suffering from an extremely shameful disease.

"I was jesting. A play of words. I should have said *el galicano.*"

"I still do not . . ."

"*El francés,* then. He comes from France. Marcos de Niza is only the Spanish rendering of his real name, Marc de Nice, and Nice is a place in France. The friar is as reptilian as any other Frenchman."

I said impatiently, "I do not care if he has scales. Will you listen, Esteban? He kept prodding your white comrades to tell him about the *seven cities.* What did he mean by that?"

"*¡Ay de mí!*" He spat disgustedly. "An old Spanish fable. I have heard it many times. The Seven Cities of Antilia. They are supposedly cities of gold and silver and gems and ivory and crystal, situated in some never-yet-seen land far beyond the Ocean Sea. That fable has been repeated since time before time. When this New World was discovered, the Spaniards hoped to find those seven cities here. Rumors reached us, even in Cuba, that you indios of New Spain could tell us, if you would, where they are. But I am not asking you, amigo, mistake me not."

"Ask if you like," I said. "I can answer honestly that I never heard of them until now. Did you or the others see any such things during your travels?"

"*¡Mierda!*" he grunted. "In all those lands we came through, any mud-brick-and-straw village is called a city. That is the *only* kind we saw. Ugly and wretched and squalid and verminous and odorous."

"The friar was being most insistent in his questioning. When the three heroes protested ignorance of any such fabulous cities, it seemed to me that Fray Marcos almost suspected them of keeping something secret from him."

"He would, the reptile! When we were at Compostela, I was told that all men who know him call him *El Monje Mentiroso.* Naturally, the Lying Monk suspects everyone else of lying."

"Well . . . did any of the indios you encountered even *hint* at the existence of—?"

"*¡Mierda más mierda!*" he exclaimed, so loudly that I had to hiss at him again, for fear that someone would awaken. "If you must know, yes, they did. One day, when we were among the River People—we were being used as pack animals when they moved from one unlovely riverbend to another—our slave-drivers pointed off to the northward and told us that in that direction lay six great cities of the Desert People."

"Six," I repeated. "Not seven?"

"Six, but they were *great* cities. Meaning that to those *estúpidos* the cities probably each had more than a handful of mud houses and perhaps a dependable water hole."

"Not the wealth of that fabled Antilia?"

"Oh, but yes!" he said sarcastically. "Our river indios said that they traded animal hides and river shells and bird feathers with the inhabitants of those elegant cities, and got in return *great riches*. What they called 'riches' being only those cheap blue and green stones that all you indios so revere."

"Nothing, then, that would arouse the avarice of a Spaniard?"

"Will you hear me, man? We are talking of a *desert*!"

"So your companions are not withholding anything from the friar?"

"Withholding *what?* I was the only one who comprehended the indios' languages. My master Dorantes knows only what I translated to him. And that was little enough, for there was little to tell."

"But suppose . . . *now* . . . you were to take Fray Marcos aside and whisper to him that the white men *are* being secretive? That you know the whereabouts of really rich cities."

Esteban gaped at me. "Lie to him? What profit in lying to a man known as the Lying Monk?"

"It is my experience that liars are the persons most ready to believe lies. He already seems to believe in that fable of the Antilia cities."

"So? I tell him they do exist? And that I know where? *Why* would I do that?"

"As I suggested a while ago, so that you can return to those lands where you were not a slave—where you found the native women to your taste—and return there not as a fugitive."

"Hm . . ." murmured Esteban, considering this.

"Convince the friar that you can lead him to those cities of immeasurable wealth. He will be the more easily persuaded if he thinks you are revealing to him something the white heroes will not. He will assume that they are waiting to tell their secret to the Marqués Cortés. He will rejoice in the delusion that he can get to those riches—with your help—ahead of Cortés or any treasure-seekers Cortés may send. *And* he will arrange for you to take him there.''

"But . . . when we get there and I have nothing to show him? Only laughable mud hutches and worthless blue pebbles and . . .''

"Now it is you, my friend, who are being estúpido. Lead him there and lose him. That should be easy enough. If he ever finds his way back here to New Spain, he can only report that you must have been slain by the vigilant guardians of those treasures.''

Esteban's face began almost to glow, if black can glow. "I would be free . . .''

"It is certainly worth the trying. You need not even lie, if that troubles you. The friar's own greedy and dishonest nature will supply to his mind any exaggerations necessary to convince him.''

"By God, I will do it! You, amigo, are a wise and clever man. *You* should be the Marqués of all New Spain!''

I made modest demurrers, but I must confess that I was fairly glowing myself, with pride in the intricate scheme I was setting in motion. Esteban, of course, did not know that I was using him to further my own secret plans, but that would not lessen his benefiting from the scheme. He would be free of any master, for the first time in his life, and free to take his chances of *staying* free among those far-off River People, and free to browse as much as he pleased—or dared—among their womenfolk.

I have recounted much of our night-long conversation in detail, because that will make clearer my explanation— which I will provide in its place—of *how* my meeting with the heroes and the friar did redound to the furtherance of my intended overthrow of the white men's dominion. And there was yet another encounter in store, to give me added encouragement. By the time Esteban and I finished talking, the morning was dawning, and with the morning came one more of those seeming coincidences that the gods, in their mischievous meddling with the doings of men, are forever contriving.

Four new Spanish soldiers on horseback came suddenly—from the direction Tiptoe and I had come—clattering into the camp and startling awake everyone else there. When I heard the news that they bawled at the Teniente Tallabuena, I was again heartily relieved; these men were not pursuing me and Tiptoe. Their horses were heavily lathered, so they had obviously been riding hard, and overnight. If they had passed that empty outpost away back yonder, they had not paused to pay it any attention.

"Teniente!" shouted one of the newcomers. "You are no longer under the command of that *zurullón* Guzmán!"

"Praise God for that," said Tallabuena, rubbing the sleep from his eyes. "But why am I not?"

The rider swung down from his horse, flung its reins to a sleepy soldier and demanded, "Is there anything to eat? Our belt buckles are rattling our backbones! Ay, there is news from the capital, Teniente. The king has finally appointed a *virrey* to head the Audiencia of New Spain. A good man, this Viceroy Mendoza. One of the first things he did was to hear the many complaints against Nuño de Guzmán—his countless atrocities against the slave indios and Moros here. And one of Mendoza's first decrees is that Guzmán be removed from the governorship of New Galicia. We are galloping to Compostela to take him in charge and fetch him to the city for his punishment."

I could have heard nothing that would have pleased me more. The news-bringer paused to take a massive munch at a cold chunk of deer meat before he went on:

"Guzmán will be replaced by a younger man, one who came from Spain with Mendoza, *un tal* Coronado, who is on his way hither as we speak."

"*¡Oye!*" exclaimed Fray Marcos. "Would that be Francisco Vásquez de Coronado?"

"It would," said the soldier, between bites.

"*¡Qué feliz fortuna!*" cried the friar. "I have heard of

him, and heard only praise of him. He is a close friend of
that Viceroy Mendoza, who is in turn a close friend of
Bishop Zumárraga, who is in turn a close friend of mine.
Also, this Coronado has recently made a most brilliant marriage to a cousin of *King Carlos himself.* Ay, but Coronado
will wield power and influence here!''

The other Spaniards were shaking their heads at this abundance of news coming all at once, but I sidled out of the
throng to where Esteban stood apart and said in a low voice:

''Things are looking better and better, amigo, for your
soon getting back among those River People.''

He nodded and said exactly what I was thinking. ''The
Lying Monk will persuade his friend, the bishop—and the
bishop's friend, the viceroy—to send him thither, ostensibly
as a missionary to the savages. Whether he tells the bishop
and the viceroy why he is really going does not matter. So
long as I go with him.''

''And this new Governor Coronado,'' I added, ''will be
eager to make his mark. If you bring Fray Marcos by way
of Compostela, I wager that Coronado will be most generous
in providing horses and equipment and weapons and provisions.''

''Yes,'' Esteban crowed. ''I owe you much, amigo. I will
not forget you. And if ever I *am* rich, be sure I shall share
with you.''

At that, he impulsively threw his arms around me and gave
me the crushing squeeze that is called in Spanish the *abrazo.*
A few of the Spaniards were watching, and I worried that
they might wonder why I was being so exuberantly thanked,
and for what. But then I had a more immediate worry. Over
Esteban's shoulder, I saw that Tiptoe was also watching. Her
eyes went wide, and abruptly she made a dash for our horses.
I realized what she was about to do, and wrenched myself
loose from the embrace and pelted after her. I got there just
in time to prevent her snatching one of our arcabuces from
the packs.

"No, Pakápeti! No need!"

"You are still unharmed?" she asked, her voice trembly. "I thought you were being assaulted by that black beast."

"No, no. You are a dear and caring girl, but overly impetuous. Please leave any rescuing to me. I will tell you later why I was being squeezed."

A good many of the Spaniards, now, were eyeing us curiously, but I smiled a reassuring smile in all directions, and they turned back to the news-bringers. One of those was telling his listeners:

"Another news, though not of such portentousness, is that Papa Paulo has established a new bishopric here in New Spain, the diocese of New Galicia. And he has elevated the Padre Vasco de Quiroga to a new and august station. Another of our couriers is riding to advise Padre Vasco that he is now to wear the miter, as Bishop Quiroga of New Galicia."

That announcement pleased me as much as any of the others I had heard here. But I did hope that Padre Vasco, now that he was such an important dignitary, would not forswear his good works and good intentions and good nature. No doubt Pope Paulo would expect his newest bishop to wring from those Utopía colonists yet more contributions to what Alonso de Molina had called the pope's "private King's Fifth." Be that as it may, this also augured well for my and Esteban's scheme. Probably Bishop Zumárraga would see Bishop Quiroga as a rival, and be even more ready to send Fray Marcos scouting either for new souls or new riches for Mother Church.

I purposely delayed departing from that place until the four newcome soldiers had gone galloping on toward Compostela. Then I bade farewell to Esteban and Teniente Tallabuena, and they and all their troop—except the three white heroes and the Lying Monk—cordially waved me off. When Tiptoe and I rode on, leading our two extra horses, I turned us slightly northward from the direction the soldiers had gone, in what I hoped was the direction of Aztlan.

XVII

NOT MANY DAYS later, we were among mountains that I recognized from the journey with my mother and uncle. It was still early in the rainy season, but on the day we reached the easternmost bounds of the lands ruled by Aztlan, the god Tlaloc and his attendant tlalóque spirits were amusing themselves by making a storm. They jabbed down from the skies their forked sticks of lightning and thunderously shattered their immense water jars to pour rain down on the earth. Through that curtain of rain, I espied the glow of a campfire on a hillside not far ahead of us. I halted our little train among some concealing trees and waited for a flare of lightning to show me more. When it did, I counted five men, standing or crouching around a fire sheltered by a lean-to made of leafy branches. The men all appeared to be wearing the quilted-cotton armor of Aztéca warriors, and seemed almost as if they had been put there to await our coming. If they were, I thought, this was a matter of some puzzlement, for how could anyone of Aztlan have known of our approach?

"Wait here, Tiptoe, with the horses," I said. "Let me make sure these *are* men of my people. Be prepared to turn and flee, if I signal that they are hostile."

I strode alone out into the downpour and up the hillside.

As I neared the group, I raised both hands to show that I was without any weapon, and called, "Mixpantzínco!"

"Ximopanólti!" came the reply, sociably enough, and in the familiar accent of old Aztlan, good to hear again.

Another few steps and I was close enough to see—by the next lightning flash—the man who had replied. A familiar face from old Aztlan, but not one very pleasing to encounter again, because I well remembered what he was like. I imagine my voice reflected that, when I greeted him without much enthusiasm, "Ayyo, Cousin Yeyac."

"Yéyac*tzin*," he haughtily reminded me. "Ayyo, Tenamáxtli. We have been expecting you."

"So it would seem," I said, glancing around at the four other warriors, all armed with obsidian-edged maquáhuime. I supposed they were his current cuilóntin lovers, but I did not remark on that. I said only, "How did you know I was coming?"

"I have my ways of knowing," said Yeyac, and a roll of thunder accompanying his words made them sound ominous. "Of course, I had no idea it was my own beloved cousin coming home, but the description was close enough, I see now."

I smiled, though I was not in a mood for smiling. "Has our great-grandfather again been exercising his talent for far-seeing, then?"

"Old Canaútli is long dead." To that announcement the tlalóque added another deafening smashing of water jars. When Yeyac could be heard, he demanded, "Now, where is the rest of your party? Your slave and the Spaniards' army horses?"

I was getting more and more disturbed. If Yeyac was not being advised by some Aztécatl far-seer, *who* was keeping him so well informed? I took note that he spoke of "Spaniards," not using the word Caxtiltéca that had formerly been Aztlan's name for the white men. And I remembered how, just recently, I had been made uneasy when I learned that the Governor Guzmán had set his province's capital city so close to ours.

"I am sorry to hear of great-grandfather's death," I said levelly. "And I am sorry, Cousin Yeyac, but I will report only to our Uey-Tecútli Mixtzin, not to you or any other lesser person. And I have much to report."

"Then report it here and now!" he barked. "I, Yéyactzin, *am* the Uey-Tecútli of Aztlan!"

"You? Impossible!" I blurted.

"My father and your mother never returned here, Tenamáxtli." I made some involuntary movement at that, and Yeyac added, "I regret having so many grievous tidings to impart"—but his eyes shifted away from mine. "Word came to us that Mixtzin and Cuicáni were found slain, apparently by bandits on the road."

This was desolating to hear. But if it was true that my uncle and mother were dead, I knew from Yeyac's manner that they had not died at the hands of any strangers. More lightning flashes and thunder roars and lashings of rain gave me time to compose myself, then I said:

"What of your sister and her husband—what was his name?—Káuri, yes. Mixtzin appointed *them* to rule in his stead."

"*Ayya*, the weakling Káuri," Yeyac sneered. "No warrior ruler, he. Not even a deft hunter. One day in these mountains he wounded a bear in the chase, and foolishly pursued it. The bear of course turned and dismembered him. The widow Améyatzin was content to retire to matronly pastimes and have me take on the burden of governing."

I knew that, too, to be untrue, because I knew Cousin Améyatl even better than I knew Yeyac. She would never willingly have yielded her position even to a real man, let alone this contemptible simulacrum whom she had always derided and despised.

"Enough of this dallying, Tenamáxtli!" Yeyac snarled. "You *will* obey me!"

"I will? Just as you obey the white Governor Guzmán?"

"No longer," he said, unthinking. "The new governor, Corona-do—"

He shut his mouth, but too late. I knew all I needed to know. Those four Spanish riders had arrived in Compostela to arrest Guzmán, and they had mentioned meeting me and Tiptoe on their way. Perhaps, by then, they had begun to wonder about the legitimacy of my churchly "mission," and made their suspicions known. Whether Yeyac had been there in Compostela, or had heard the word later, no matter. He was clearly in league with the white men. What else this might mean—whether all of Aztlan and its native Aztéca and resident Mexíca had similarly donned the Spanish yoke—I would find out in good time. Right now, I had to contend only with Yeyac. In the next lull of the storm's commotion, I said warningly:

"Take care, man of no manhood." And I reached for the steel knife at my waist. "I am no longer the untried younger cousin you remember. Since we parted, I have killed—"

"No manhood?" he bellowed. "I too have killed! Would you be my next?"

His face was contorted with rage as he raised high his heavy maquáhuitl and stepped toward me. His four companions did the same, right behind him, and I backed away, wishing I had brought with me some weapon more formidable than a knife. But suddenly, all those menacing black blades of obsidian turned to glittering silver, because Tlaloc's lightning forks began to jab and jab and jab in rapid sequence, close about the six of us. I was not expecting the thing that happened next, though I was gratified and not very much surprised when it did happen. Yeyac took another step, but backward this time, reeling, and his mouth opened wide in a cry that went unheard in the immediately succeeding tumult of thunder, and he dropped his sword and fell heavily on his back with a great splash of mud.

There was no need for me to fend off his four underlings. They all stood immobile, maquáhuime lifted and streaming rainwater, as if the lightning had petrified them in that position. Their mouths were as wide open as Yeyac's, but in astonishment, awe and fright. They could not have seen, as I had, the bright, wet, red hole that had opened in the cotton quilting of Yeyac's belly armor, and none of us had heard the sound of the arcabuz that had done that. The four cuilóntin could only have assumed that I had, by some magic, called down upon their leader the forked sticks of Tlaloc. I gave them no time to think otherwise, but bawled, *"Down weapons!"*

They instantly and meekly lowered their blades. Such creatures, I surmised, must be like the frailest of women— easily cowed when they hear a real man's voice of command.

"This vile pretender is dead," I told them, giving the body a disdainful kick—I did that only to heave Yeyac over onto his face, so that they should not see the hole in his front and the bloodstain spreading from it. "I regret that I had to invoke the gods' assistance so suddenly. There were questions I would have asked. But the wretch gave me no choice." The four stared glumly at the corpse, and took no heed when I made a beckoning gesture back toward the trees, to summon Tiptoe forward. "Now," I went on, "you warriors will take orders from me. I am Tenamáxtzin, nephew of the late Lord Mixtzin, hence, by right of succession, from this moment on, the Uey-Tecútli of Aztlan."

But I could think of no order to give them, except to say, "Wait here for me." Then I sloshed back through the rain to intercept Tiptoe, as she came leading all our horses. I intended to tell her, before she joined us, to hide the arcabuz that she had so timely and so accurately employed. But when I got close, I saw that she had already prudently stowed it away again, so I said only, "Well done, Pakápeti."

"I was not too impetuous, then?" She had regarded my approach with some anxiety in her face, but now she smiled. "I was afraid you might scold me. But I did think that this one, too, was a beast attacking you."

"This time you were right. And you did splendidly. At such a distance, in such poor light—your skill is enviable."

"Yes," she agreed, with what I thought rather unwomanly satisfaction. "I have killed a man."

"Well, not much of a man."

"I would have done my best to kill the others, too, if you had not waved to me."

"They are of even less account. Save your man-hatred, my dear, until you can start killing enemies really worth the killing."

The sky's tlalóque were lustily continuing their clamor and downpour as I commanded the four warriors to sling Yeyac's cadaver across one of my packhorses—thus he was still face-down, the wound in his front invisible. Next, I ordered the four to accompany me as I rode, two each on either side of my horse; Tiptoe brought up the rear of the train as we proceeded onward. When there came a pause in the thunder rumblings, I leaned down from my saddle and said to the man trudging alongside my left stirrup:

"Give me your maquáhuitl." He meekly handed it up to me and I said, "You heard what Yeyac told me—of the several convenient deaths that so fortuitously promoted him to Uey-Tecútli of Aztlan. How much of what he said was true?"

The man coughed and temporized, "Your great-grandfather, our Rememberer of History, died of old age, as all men must, if they live to be old."

"I accept that," I said, "but it has nothing to do with Yeyac's marvelous quick elevation to the status of Revered Governor. I accept also that all men must die, but—I warn you—some must die sooner than others. What of those other deaths? Of Mixtzin and Cuicántzin and Káuritzin?"

"It was just as Yeyac told you," the man said, but his eyes shifted just as Yeyac's had done. "Your uncle and mother were set upon by bandits—"

He got no further. With a backhanded swipe of his own obsidian sword, I took his head off his shoulders, and both pieces of him toppled into a rain-running ditch beside the trail. In the next interval between thunderings, I spoke to the warrior at the other side of my saddle, who was goggling fearfully up at me like a frog about to be stepped on.

"As I said, some men must die sooner than others. And I do dislike to invoke the aid of Tlaloc, who is presently being very busy with this storm, when I can kill as easily myself." As if Tlaloc had heard me, the storm began to abate. "Now, what have *you* to tell me?"

The man stuttered for a moment, but finally said, "Yeyac lied, and so did Quani." He gestured back at the pieces in the ditch behind us. "Yéyactzin posted lookouts around the far outskirts of Aztlan, there to wait patiently to espy the return of Mixtzin and his sister—and yourself—from that journey to Tenochtítlan. When the two did return . . . well . . . there was an ambush awaiting them."

"That ambush," I said, "of whom did it consist?"

"Yeyac, of course. And his most favored favorite, Quani. The warrior you just now have slain. You are fully avenged, Tenamáxtzin."

"I doubt that," I said. "No two men of this One World, even striking cowardly from ambush, could have overwhelmed my uncle Mixtzin." And I slashed again with the maquáhuitl. Separately, the man's head flew and his body slumped into the sodden brush on that side of the trail. I turned again, and spoke to the remaining warrior walking on my left.

"I am still waiting to hear the truth. As you must have noticed, I do not wait long."

This one, almost babbling in his terror, assured me, "The truth, my lord, I kiss the earth to it. We were all guilty. Yeyac and we four laid the ambush. It was all of us together who fell upon your uncle and mother."

"And what of Káuri, the co-regent?"

"Not he nor anyone else in Aztlan knew the fate of Mixtzin and Cuicántzin. We cajoled Káuritzin into joining us on a bear hunt in the mountains. He did indeed, by himself and most manfully, spear and slay a bear. But we, in turn, killed Káuri, then employed the dead animal's teeth and claws to maul and tear at him. When we took his body and the bear's carcass home, his widow, your cousin Améyatzin, could hardly dispute our story that the beast had been responsible for his death.''

''And then? Did you dastardly traitors kill her, as well?''

''No, no, my lord. She lives, I kiss the earth to that. But in seclusion now, no longer regent.''

''Why? She would still have been expecting her father to return and resume his proper place. Why would she have abdicated her regency?''

''Who can say, my lord? Out of grief at her widowhood, perhaps? Out of deep mourning?''

''Nonsense!'' I snapped. ''If the deeps of Míctlan's oblivion yawned before her, Améyatzin would never shirk her duty. How did you make her do it? Torture? Rape? *What?*''

''Only Yeyac could tell you that. It was he alone who persuaded her. And you have put him beyond the telling. One thing, though, I can tell you.'' He said most haughtily, and with a fastidious sniff, ''My lord Yéyactzin would never have sullied himself by raping or otherwise toying with the body of a mere female.''

That remark infuriated me more than had all his comrades' lies, and my third slash of the obsidian sword cleft him from shoulder to belly.

On my other side, the sole surviving warrior had prudently sidled out of reach of my weapon, but he was also prudently eyeing the no-longer-raining but still ominously dark sky.

''You are wise not to run,'' I told him. ''Tlaloc's forks are much longer than my arm. But be at ease. I am sparing you, for a time, at least. And for a reason.''

''Reason?'' he croaked. ''What reason, my lord?''

''I wish you to tell me of everything that has occurred in Aztlan in the years since I left there.''

''Ayyo, every least thing, my lord!'' he said eagerly. ''I kiss the earth to it. How shall I begin?''

''I already know that Yeyac befriended and colluded with

the white men. So tell me first: are there any Spaniards in our city or its outer domains?''

''None, my lord, not anywhere in the Aztlan lands. Yeyac and we of his personal guard have frequently visited Compostela, true, but no white men have come north from there. The Spanish governor gave oath that Yeyac could continue his rule of Aztlan, undisputed, on only one single condition. That Yeyac bar any native marauders from making forays into the *governor's* lands.''

''In other words,'' I said, ''Yeyac was prepared to fight his own people of The One World on behalf of the white men. Did that ever come to pass?''

''Yes,'' said the warrior, trying to look unhappy about it. ''On two or three occasions, Yeyac led troops whose loyalty to him personally was unwavering, and they . . . well . . . discouraged this or that small band of malcontents marching southward to make trouble for the Spaniards.''

''When you say loyal troops, it sounds as if not *all* the warriors and inhabitants of Aztlan have been overjoyed to have Yeyac as their Uey-Tecútli.''

''That is so. Most of the Aztéca—and Mexíca, too—much preferred to be ruled by Améyatzin and her consort. They were dismayed when the Lady Améyatl was deposed from her regency. They would, of course, be even better pleased to have Mixtzin back again. And they still expect his return, even after these many years.''

''Do the people know of Yeyac's treacherous pact with the Spanish governor?''

''Very few know of it. Not even the elders of the Speaking Council. It is known only to us of Yeyac's personal guard, and those loyal troops of whom I spoke. And his closest, best-trusted adviser, a certain person newcome to these parts. But the people have accepted Yeyac's rule, if only grudgingly, because he claimed that he, and he only, could prevent an invasion of the white men. That, he has done. No resident of Aztlan has yet seen a Spaniard. Or a horse,'' the man added, glancing at mine.

"Meaning," I mused, "that Yeyac's keeping the Spanish free of molestation gives them time to increase their forces and weaponry unimpeded, until they are *ready* to come. Which they will. But wait—you spoke of a certain person giving advice to Yeyac. Who would that be?"

"Did I say a person, my lord? I should have said a woman."

"A *woman?!* Your late companion just now made it plain that Yeyac had no use for women in any capacity, even as victims."

"And this one has no use for *men*, I gather, though a man who favors women would probably find her most comely and personable. But she is truly sagacious in the arts of governing and strategy and expediency. That is why Yeyac willingly gave ear to her every counsel. It was at her urging that he originally made embassy to the Spanish governor. When we got word of your approach, I daresay she would have come with us to intercept you, except that she has charge of keeping your cousin Améyatl in close confinement."

"Let me hazard a conjecture," I said grimly. "This clever female's name is G'nda Ké."

"It is," said the man, surprised. "You have heard of her, my lord? Is the lady's reputation for sagacity as well known abroad as it now is in Aztlan?"

I growled, "She has a reputation, I will say that much."

The storm was gone, and most of the clouds, so the day was lightened by Tonatíu's serenely settling into the west, and I recognized where we were. The first scattered habitations and tilled lands of Aztlan's outskirts would soon be in sight. I beckoned for Pakápeti to bring her horse alongside mine.

"Before dark, my dear, you will be in the last remaining bastion of what was once the Aztéca dominion. A lesser but still proud and flourishing Tenochtítlan. I hope you will find it to your liking."

Curiously, she said nothing, only looked not at all anticipatory. I asked, "Why so downcast, dear Tiptoe?"

She said, sounding extremely peeved, "You could have let *me* kill at least one of those three men."

I sighed. It seemed that Pakápeti was becoming as unwomanly a woman as that terrible G'nda Ké. I turned again to the warrior at my right stirrup and asked, "What is your name, man?"

"I am called Nochéztli, my lord."

"Very well, Nochéztli. I want you to walk ahead of this train as we enter the city. I expect the populace will be coming out-of-doors to gaze upon us. You are to announce, loudly, over and over, that Yeyac has—deservedly—been struck dead by the gods who finally wearied of his treacheries. And that I, Tenamáxtzin, the legitimate successor, am arriving to take residence in the city palace as Aztlan's new Uey-Tecútli."

"I will do that, Tenamáxtzin. I have a voice that can bawl almost as loudly as Tlaloc's."

"Another thing, Nochéztli. As soon as I get to the palace, I shall doff this alien costume and don the proper regalia. While I am doing that, I want you to assemble Aztlan's entire army in the city's central square."

"My lord, I am only a tequíua in rank. I have not enough authority to order—"

"I here and now endow you with that authority. In any case, your fellows will probably assemble simply out of curiosity. I want *every* warrior there in the square, Aztéca and Mexíca, not only those who are professional men at arms, but also every able-bodied male of every other trade and profession who has been trained for combat and is subject to conscription in time of war. See to it, Nochéztli!"

"Er . . . excuse me, Tenamáxtzin, but some of those warriors lately loyal to Yeyac may well take to the hills at the news of their master's demise."

"We will hunt them down at our leisure. Just be sure *you* do not disappear, Nochéztli, or you will be the first hunted, and the manner of your execution will be a subject for legend forever after. I have learned things from the Spaniards that would horrify even the most vicious gods of punishment. I kiss the earth to that.''

The man gulped audibly and said, ''I am and will be yours to command, Tenamáxtzin.''

''Good. Remain so, and you may yet live to die of old age. Once the army is assembled, you will go among the men and mark for me every one, of highest rank or lowest, who joined Yeyac in his groveling to the Spaniards. Later, we shall do the same with the rest of Aztlan's citizenry. You will mark for me every man and woman—respected elder or priest or meanest slave—who has ever in the least collaborated with Yeyac or been the beneficiary of his patronage.''

''Excuse me again, my lord, but chief among those would be the woman G'nda Ké, who is right now in residence at the palace you intend to occupy. She guards the chamber allotted to the captive Lady Améyatl.''

''I know well enough how to deal with that creature,'' I said. ''You find the others for me. But now—here are the first huts of outer Aztlan, and the people are emerging to get a look at us. Move to the fore, Nochéztli, and do as I bade you.''

Somewhat to my surprise—he being a cuilóntli and presumably effeminate in nature—Nochéztli could bellow like the male animal the Spanish call a *toro*. And he bellowed what I had told him to say, and he did so again and again, and the eyes and mouths of the watching people gaped wide. Many of those folk fell in behind our little train, so Nochéztli and I and Pakápeti were leading quite a procession by the time we got to the paved streets of the city proper at nightfall—and we had a veritable throng behind us as we crossed the torch-lit central square to the wall-enclosed palace.

At either side of the wall's broad, open portal stood a warrior guardsman, wearing full quilted armor and the fanged fur helmet of the knightly Jaguar order, each man armed with maquáhuitl sword, belt knife and long spear. According to custom, they should have crossed those spears to bar our entry until our business was made known. But these two men merely gawked at us curiously garbed strangers, our strange animals and the hordes of people filling the square. They were understandably uncertain what to do in these circumstances.

I leaned around my horse's neck to inquire of Nochéztli, "These two, were they Yeyac's men?"

"Yes, my lord."

"Kill them."

The two knights stood unresisting, but bravely unflinching, as Nochéztli wielded his own obsidian sword—slashing left, then right—and felled them like so much peskily obstructive underbrush. The crowd behind us gave a concerted gasp, and moved back a step or two.

"Now, Nochéztli," I said, "summon a few strong men from this mob and dispose of these carrion." I indicated the fallen guards and Yeyac's body, still draped across one of the packhorses. "Next, bid the crowd disperse, on pain of my displeasure. Then do as I commanded—assemble the army in this square to await my inspection, as soon as I am formally attired in gold and gems and plumage as their chief commander."

When the cadavers had been removed, I beckoned for Pakápeti to follow, and without dismounting—our other two horses at trail—we rode like conquerors, arrogantly, into the courtyard of the splendid palace of the Revered Governor of Aztlan, henceforward the palace of the Uey-Tecútli Téotl-Tenamáxtzin. Myself.

XVIII

UNDER TORCHES BRACKETED around the courtyard wall's interior, a number of field slaves were still at work at that late hour, tending the many flowering shrubs set in immense stone urns all about. As Pakápeti and I dismounted, we gave the reins of our four horses to a couple of those men. Their eyes bulging, the slaves accepted the reins gingerly and fearfully, and held them at arm's length.

"Be not afraid," I told the men. "The beasts are gentle. Only bring them ample water and shelled maize, then stay with them until I give you further instructions in their care."

Tiptoe and I went to the palace building's main door, but it opened before we got there. The Yaki woman G'nda Ké flung it wide and gestured for us to enter, as brazenly as if she had been the palace's official mistress or hostess, welcoming guests who had come at her invitation. She no longer wore rough garments suited to the outdoors and her wandering way of life, but was splendidly arrayed. She had also lavished cosmetics on her face, possibly to conceal the freckles that marred her complexion. Anyway, she was handsome to behold. Even the cuilóntli Nochéztli, no admirer of womankind, had rightly referred to this specimen of it as "comely and personable"—but I mainly took note that she still had the lizard eyes and lizard smile. Also, she still referred to herself always by name—or as "she" or "her"—as if speaking of some entirely separate entity.

"We meet again, Tenamáxtli," she said cheerfully. "Of course G'nda Ké knew of your journey hither, and she was sure you would destroy the usurper Yeyac on the way. Ah, and dear Pakápeti! How truly lovely you will be when your hair grows longer! G'nda Ké is so pleased to see you both, and most eager to—"

"Be silent!" I snapped. "Take me to Améyatl."

The woman shrugged and led me, Tiptoe following, to the palace's upstairs chambers, but not to the one Améyatl had formerly occupied. G'nda Ké lifted a heavy bar from a heavy door and disclosed a room not much bigger than a steam hut, windowless and smelly from being long closed, without so much as a fish-oil lamp to relieve its darkness. I reached out and took the bar from the woman—lest she try to lock me in there, too—and told her:

"Bring me a torch. Then take Tiptoe to a decent chamber, where she can cleanse herself and don proper feminine clothing. Then return here immediately, you reptile woman, so I can keep you in my sight."

Torch alight, I stepped into the little room, nearly retching at the stench of it. The only furniture it contained was a single axixcáli pot, reeking of its contents. There was a stir in one corner, and Améyatl stood up from the stone floor there, though I would scarcely have recognized her. She was clad in filthy rags, her body was gaunt, her hair was matted, her face was ashen, hollow-cheeked, and there were dark circles about her eyes. And this was the woman who had been the most beautiful in all Aztlan. But her voice was still nobly firm, not feeble, when she said:

"I thank all the gods that you have come, cousin. For these many months I have been praying—"

"Hush, cousin," I said. "Conserve what strength you still have. We will talk later. Let me take you to your quarters and see that you are attended and bathed and fed and given rest. Then we will have much to discuss."

In her chambers, there were several female servants waiting—a few of whom I recalled from former days—all nervously wringing their hands and avoiding my eye. I curtly
dismissed them, and Améyatl and I waited until G'nda Ké
returned with Tiptoe, who had been as richly garbed as if
she were a princess herself—no doubt the Yaki woman's
notion of ironic japery.

She said, "All of G'nda Ké's own new apparel fitted Pakápeti, except the sandals. We had to search for a pair small
enough for her." She went on, conversationally, "Having
been afoot and frequently barefoot during so much of her
earlier life, G'nda Ké is now most insistent on being luxuriously shod. And she is grateful to have had Yeyac as her
patron—however odious she found him in other ways—
because he could indulge G'nda Ké's fondness for footwear.
She has whole closets full. She can wear a different pair of
sandals every—"

"Cease your witless prattle," I told her, and then presented Améyatl to Tiptoe. "This much abused lady is my
dear cousin. Since I trust no one else in this palace, Pakápeti,
I will ask you to attend her, and tenderly. She will show you
where to find her steam room and her wardrobe and so on.
From the kitchens downstairs, fetch for her nourishing food
and good chocólatl. Then help her to her pallet, and pile it
high with many soft quilts. When Améyatl sleeps, you join
me downstairs."

"I am honored," said Tiptoe, "to be of service to the
Lady Améyatl."

My cousin leaned to kiss me on the cheek, but only briefly
and lightly, not to repel me with the prisoner-smell of her
body or breath, and went away with Tiptoe. I turned again
to G'nda Ké.

"I have already slain two of the palace guards. I assume
that everyone else currently employed here likewise served
Yeyac without demur during his false reign."

"True. There were a number who disdainfully refused to
do so, but they left long ago to seek employment elsewhere."

"I charge you, then, have those loyal servants found and brought back here. I charge you also, dispose of the present retinue. All of them. I cannot be bothered with the slaughtering of so many menials. I am sure that you, being a serpent yourself, must know of some venom that can poison them all, and expeditiously."

"But of course," she said, as tranquilly as if I had asked for a soothing syrup.

"Very well. Wait until Améyatl has been well fed—doubtless the first decent meal she will have had during her captivity. Then, when the domestics gather for *their* evening repast, see to it that their atóli has been well dosed with your poison. After they are dead, Pakápeti will take charge of the kitchens until we can find reliable servants and slaves."

"As you command. Now, would you have these menials die in agony or with ease, quickly or lingeringly?"

"I do not give a putrid pochéoa how they die. Just see that they do."

"Then G'nda Ké chooses to do it mercifully, for kindness comes naturally to her. She will dose their meal with the tlapatl weed that makes its victims die in madness. In their delirium, they will see glorious colors and wondrous hallucinations, until they see no longer. But now, Tenamáxtli—tell G'nda Ké—is she also to partake of this final, fatal repast?"

"No. I still have use for you. Unless Améyatzin overrules me, when she regains her strength. She may demand that I dispose of you, and in some highly imaginative, not kindly manner."

"Do not blame G'nda Ké for your cousin's mistreatment," said the woman as she followed me to the royal chambers that had once been Mixtzin's and then Yeyac's. "It was her own brother who decreed that she be so inhumanly confined. G'nda Ké was merely ordered to keep barred the door. Even G'nda Ké could hardly overrule *him*."

"You lie, woman! You lie more often and more easily than you change your precious footwear." To one of the hovering manservants I gave orders to place hot coals and water buckets in the royal steam room, and to do it instantly. To the Yaki woman, as I began to discard my Spanish apparel, I went on, "With your poisons and your magics—ayya, even with your reptilian eye—you could have slain Yeyac at any time. I *know* you worked your evil charm to aid him in his alliance with the Spaniards."

"Mere mischief, dear Tenamáxtli," she said airily. "G'nda Ké's usual mischief. Delightedly setting men against men. Merely to while away the time until you and she were together again, and could *really* ravage and rampage."

"Together!" I snorted. "I had rather be yoked with the terrible underworld goddess Mictlancíuatl."

"Now *you* are telling an untruth. Look at yourself." I was nude by now, waiting impatiently for the servant to report that my steam room was ready. "You *are* pleased to be again with G'nda Ké. You are wantonly, seductively showing your naked body—and a superb one it is. You are deliberately tempting her."

"I am deliberately regarding her as inconsequential, of no account. Whatever you see and whatever you think concerns me no more than if you were a slave or a woodworm in the wall's paneling."

Her face went so dark at the insult that her cold eyes glittered out from it like chips of ice. The servant returned and I followed him to the steam room, saying to the Yaki woman, "Remain here."

After a prolonged and thorough and voluptuous steaming and sweating and scraping and toweling, I emerged, still nude, to find that G'nda Ké had been joined in the main room by the warrior Nochéztli. They stood apart and eyed one another, he warily, she sneeringly. Before he could speak, she did, and with malice:

"So, Tenamáxtli, this is why you cared not if G'nda Ké saw you naked. Nochéztli I know to have been one of the late Yeyac's favorite cuilóntin, and he tells me now that he stands henceforth at *your* right hand. *Ayya*, so you keep sweet Tiptoe in your company merely as a disguise. G'nda Ké would never have suspected it of you.''

"Ignore the woodworm," I told Nochéztli. "Have you something to report?"

"The assembled army awaits your inspection, my lord. They have been waiting for quite some time."

"Let them wait," I said, as I began rummaging through the Uey-Tecútli's wardrobe of formal cloaks, headdresses and other regalia. "It is what is expected of an army, and what an army expects—long tediums and boredoms only occasionally briskened by killings and dyings. Go and make *sure* they wait."

While I dressed—now and then commanding the sullen G'nda Ké to assist me in affixing some jeweled ornament or fluffing up a feathered crest—I told her:

"I may have to throw away half that army. When you and I parted at the Lake of Rushes, you said you would be traveling in furtherance of my cause. Instead, you came here to Aztlan, just as did your bitch ancestress of the same name, sheaves of sheaves of years ago. And you did exactly as she did—fomented dissension among the populace, set comradely warriors at odds, turned brother against—"

"Hold now, Tenamáxtli," she interrupted. "G'nda Ké is not guilty of *every* wrong done hereabouts in your absence. It must have been years ago that your uncle and mother returned from the City of Mexíco, and were ambushed by Yeyac, a crime still unknown to almost everybody else in Aztlan. How long he waited to dispatch the co-regent Káuri, G'nda Ké does not know, or how much more time went by before he so cruelly banished his own sister and claimed the mantle of Revered Governor. G'nda Ké knows only that all those things had occurred before she arrived here."

"At which time you goaded Yeyac into collaboration with the Spaniards at Compostela. *The white men I have sworn to exterminate!* And you lightly dismiss your meddling as 'mere mischief.' ''

"*Ayyo*, entertaining, to be sure. G'nda Ké enjoys meddling

in men's affairs. But think, Tenamáxtli. She has in fact done you a valuable favor. As soon as your new cuilóntli—''

"Damn you, woman, to nethermost Míctlan! I do not consort in intimacy with cuilóntin. I spared Nochéztli from the sword only so he could expose all of Yeyac's other followers and fellow conspirators.''

"And when he does, you will weed them out—warriors and civil folk alike—the traitors, the unreliables, the weaklings, the fools—*everyone* who would rather obey a Spanish overlord than risk spilling his own blood. You will be left with a smaller but better army, and with a populace wholeheartedly committed to supporting your cause, the cause for which that army will wholeheartedly fight.''

"Yes," I had to concede, "there is that aspect to appreciate.''

"And all because G'nda Ké came to Aztlan and made mischief.''

I said dryly, "I should have preferred to manage all those ruses and intrigues on my own. Because, when I have, as you put it, plucked Aztlan clean of weeds—ayya!—*you* will be the one person remaining whom I dare not trust.''

"Believe me or do not, as you will. But insofar as she *can* be to any male person, G'nda Ké is your friend.''

"May all the gods be with me," I muttered, "whenever you become otherwise.''

"Come, set G'nda Ké a task of trust. See if she performs it to your satisfaction.''

"I have already set you two. Dispose of every domestic now serving in this palace. Seek and summon those loyal ones who departed. Here is another. Send swift-messengers to the homes of all the members of the Speaking Council— Aztlan, Tépiz, Yakóreke, and elsewhere—bidding them convene in the throne room here at midday tomorrow.''

"It shall be done.''

"In the meantime, while I do my winnowing of that army outside, you stay indoors and out of their sight. There will

be many men in that square who will wonder why I did not
kill you first of all.''

Downstairs, Pakápeti was waiting to inform me that Améyatl
was clean, fresh and perfumed, that she had eaten ravenously
and finally was sleeping the sleep of the long-exhausted.

"Thank you, Tiptoe," I said. "Now, I would like you to
stand with me while I review all those warriors out yonder.
Nochéztli is supposed to mark for me the ones I should get
rid of. But I do not know how well I can depend on *him*.
He may take this chance to settle old grudges of his own—
superiors who denied him promotion, perhaps, or former cuilóntin lovers who discarded him. Before I make pronounce-
ment in each case, I may ask you for a woman's
softer-hearted opinion."

We crossed the courtyard, where those field slaves were
still minding the horses but not looking much more comfortable in that job, and stopped at the open portal of the
wall, where Nochéztli waited for us. Some ten paces distant
from the wall, the rest of the square was packed with the
ranks and files of the warriors, all in fighting garb but unarmed, and every fifth man holding a torch so that I could
see every individual face. Here and there, one held aloft the
banner of a particular knight's company, or the smaller gui-
don of a lesser troop led by a cuachic, an "old eagle." I
believe the city's army there before me totaled about one
thousand men.

"*Warriors—stand tall!*" Nochéztli roared, as if he had
been commanding troops all his life. The few men who had
been slumping or fidgeting instantly stiffened erect. Nochéztli boomed again, "*Hark to the words of your Uey-Tecútli
Tenamáxtzin!*"

Whether obediently or apprehensively, the crowd of men
was so silent that I did not have to shout. "You were summoned to assembly by my order. Also by my order, the Tequíua Nochéztli here will now go up and down your lines
and touch the shoulder of certain men. Each of those will

step forward from the ranks and stand against this wall. There will be no dawdling, no remonstrance, no questions, no *sound* until I speak again.''

Nochéztli's process of selection took such a long while that I will not recount it step by step and man by man. But when he had finished with the last, farthermost line of warriors, I counted one hundred thirty and eight standing along the wall, looking variously unhappy, ashamed or defiant. They ranged from rankless yaoquízquin recruits upward through the ranks of íyactin and tequíuatin to the cuáchictin under-officers. I myself was ashamed to see that all the accused miscreants were Aztéca. Among them was not a one of the old Mexíca warriors who had long ago come from Tenochtítlan to *train* this army, nor were there any younger Mexíca who might have been the sons of those proud men.

The highest-ranking officer against the wall was a single Aztécatl knight, but he was only of the Arrow order. The Jaguar and Eagle orders confer their knighthood on true heroes, warriors who have distinguished themselves in many battles and have slain *enemy* knights. The Arrow Knights are honored merely because they have become skilled at wielding the notoriously inaccurate bow and arrow, whether or not they have felled many enemies with those weapons.

''All of you know why you stand here,'' I said to the men at the wall, and loudly enough for the rest of the troops to hear. ''You are accused of having sided with the unrightfully Revered Governor Yeyac, though all of you knew that he seized that false title by assassinating his own father and affinal brother. You followed Yeyac when he made alliance with the white men, our One World's conquerors and oppressors. Pandering to those Spaniards, you fought with Yeyac against brave men of your own race, to stop their resisting the oppressors. Do any of you deny these allegations?''

To their credit, none of them did. That was to Nochéztli's credit, as well; obviously he had acted honestly in singling out the collaborators. I asked another question:

"Do any of you plead any circumstance that might mitigate your guilt?"

Five or six of them did step forward, at that, but each of them could say only words to this effect: "When I took the army oath, my lord, I swore to obey the orders of my superiors, and that is what I did."

"You swore oath to the *army*," I said, "not to any individuals whom you knew to be acting against the army's interests. Yonder stand some nine hundred other warriors, your comrades, who did *not* let themselves be led into treachery." I turned to Tiptoe, and quietly asked her, "Does your heart feel compassion toward any of these deluded wretches?"

"Toward none," she said firmly. "Back in Michihuácan, when we Purémpecha had the rule of it, such men would have been staked out on the ground—and left there until they became so weak that the scavenger vultures did not even have to wait for them to die before beginning to eat them. I would suggest you do the same to all of these, Tenamáxtli."

By Huitzli, I thought, Pakápeti *had* become as bloodthirsty as G'nda Ké. I spoke again aloud, to be heard by all, though I addressed the men accused:

"I have known two *women* who were more manly warriors than any of you. Here beside me stands one of them, who would merit knighthood if she were not a female. The other brave woman died in the act of destroying an entire fortress full of Spanish soldiers. You, by contrast, are a disgrace to your comrades, to your battle flags, to your oath, to us Aztéca and every other people of The One World. I condemn you, without exception, to death. But I will, in mercy, let you each decide on the manner of your dying."

Tiptoe made a murmur of indignant protest.

"You may choose one of three endings to your lives. One would be your sacrifice tomorrow on the altar of Aztlan's patron goddess, Coyolxaúqui. Since you would be going not of your own free will, that public execution would shame all your family and descendants to the end of time. Your houses, property and possessions will be confiscated, leaving those families in destitution as well as shame.''

I paused, to let them think about that.

''Or I will accept your word of honor—what little honor you may have retained—that each of you will go from here to your home, prop the point of your javelin against your chest and lean onto it, thus dying at the hand of a warrior, though it be your own hand.''

Most of the men nodded at that, if somberly, but a few still waited to hear my third suggestion.

''Or you may choose another, even more honorable means of self-sacrifice to the gods. You may volunteer for a mission I have planned. And''—I said with scorn—''it will mean your turning against your *friends*, the Spaniards. Not a man of you will survive this mission, I kiss the earth to that. But you will die in battle, as every warrior hopes to do. And to the gratification of all our gods, you will have spilled enemy blood as well as your own. I doubt that the gods will be mollified enough to grant you the warriors' happy afterlife in Tonatíucan. But even in the drear nothingness of Míctlan, you can spend eternity remembering that, at least once in your days, you behaved like *men*. How many of you will volunteer?''

They all did, to a man, stooping in the tlalqualíztli gesture to touch the earth, signifying that they kissed it in fealty to me.

''So be it,'' I said. ''And you, Arrow Knight, I appoint to lead that mission when the time comes. Until then, all of you will be imprisoned in the temple of Coyolxaúqui, under guard. For now, speak your names to the Tequíua Nochéztli, that a scribe may record them for me.''

To the men still in the square, I called out, ''I thank the rest of you—not least, for your unswerving loyalty to Aztlan. You are dismissed until I again call assembly.''

As Tiptoe and I reentered the palace courtyard, she chided me, ''Tenamáxtli, until this very evening, you slew men as abruptly and uncaringly as I would do. But then you put on that headdress and cloak and bangles—and, with them, an unbecoming mood of leniency. A Revered Governor should be *more* fierce than ordinary men, not less. These traitors deserved to die.''

''And they will,'' I assured her. ''But in a way that furthers my cause.''

''Executing them here, and publicly, would help your cause, too. It would deter all other men from trying any future duplicity. If Butterfly and her troop of women were here to do the executing by, say, slitting open those men's bellies—carefully, not fatally—and then pouring fire ants inside, certainly no onlooker would ever risk incurring your wrath again.''

I sighed. ''Have you not looked upon enough dying already, Pakápeti? Then look yonder.'' And I pointed. At the distant rear of the palace's main building, in the area of the kitchens, a line of slaves was emerging from a lighted doorway, each bent under the weight of a body he was carrying off into the darkness. ''On my order, and at one stroke, so to speak, the Yaki woman has slain every servant employed in this palace.''

''And you did not even allow me to assist in that!'' Tiptoe said angrily.

I sighed again. ''Tomorrow, my dear, Nochéztli will be listing for me the local citizens who—like the warriors— abetted Yeyac's crimes or benefited from them. If you promise to cease nagging at me, I promise to let you practice your delicate feminine arts on two or three of those.''

She smiled. ''Now, that is more like the old Tenamáxtli. However, it will not satisfy me entirely. I want you also to promise that I may go along with the Arrow Knight and the others on that mission you propose, whatever it is.''

''Girl, have you gone tlahuéle? That will be a suicidal mission! I know you enjoy killing men. But *dying* with them . . . ?''

She said loftily, "A woman is not obliged to explain her every whim and fancy."

"I am not asking that you explain this one. I am *commanding* that you *forget* it!" And I strode away from her, into the palace and up the stairs.

I was seated at Améyatl's bedside—I had been keeping vigil there all night—when finally in late morning she opened her eyes.

"Ayyo!" she exclaimed. "It *is* you, cousin! I feared I had only dreamed that I had been rescued."

"You have been. And happy I am that I came in time, before you wasted entirely away in that fetid cell."

"Ayya!" she said now. "Turn aside your gaze, Tenamáxtli. I must look like the skeletal Weeping Woman of the old legends."

"To me, beloved cousin, you look as you ever did, even when you were a girl-child all knees and elbows. Pleasing to my eye and to my heart. You will soon be your former self again, beautiful and strong. You need only nourishment and rest."

She said urgently, "My father, your mother, did they come with you? Why were you all so long away?"

"I regret being the one to tell you, Améyatl. They are not with me. They will never be with us again."

She gave a small cry of dismay.

"I also regret having to tell you that it was your brother's doing. He secretly slew them both—and later slew your husband Káuri as well—long before he imprisoned you and supplanted you as ruler of Aztlan."

She pondered this for a while in silence, and wept a little, and at last said, "He did such horrible deeds . . . and for only a paltry little eminence . . . in a negligible little corner of The One World. Poor Yeyac."

"Poor *Yeyac?!*"

"You and I both knew, from our childhood, that Yeyac

was born with an inauspicious tonáli. It has made him suffer unhappiness and dissatisfaction all his life.''

"You are far more tolerant and forgiving than I, Améyatl. I do *not* regret telling you that Yeyac suffers no longer. He is dead, and I am responsible for his death. I hope you will not hold me hateful on that account.''

"No . . . no, of course not.'' She reached for my hand and squeezed it affectionately. "It must have been ordained by the gods who cursed him with that tonáli. But now''—she visibly braced herself—"have you imparted *all* the bad news?''

"You must judge of that yourself. I am in the process of ridding Aztlan of all Yeyac's confederates and confidants.''

"Banishing them?''

"Far, far away. To Míctlan, I trust.''

"Oh. I understand.''

"All of them, anyway, except the woman G'nda Ké, who was warder of your prison cell.''

"I know not what to make of that one,'' said Améyatl, sounding perplexed. "I can hardly hate her. She had to obey Yeyac's orders, but sometimes she would contrive to bring me bits of food more tasty than atóli, or a perfumed cloth with which I could wash myself a little. But something . . . her name . . .''

"Yes. You and I are probably the only two who would even dimly recognize that name, now that my great-grandfather is dead. It was he, Canaútli, who told us about the long-ago Yaki woman. Do you recall? We were children then.''

"*Yes!*'' said Améyatl. "The evil woman who sundered the Aztéca—and led half of them away to become the all-conquering Mexíca! But, Tenamáxtli, that was back at the beginning of time. This cannot be the same G'nda Ké!''

"If not,'' I growled, "she has certainly inherited all the base instincts and motives of her namesake ancestress.''

"I wonder,'' said Améyatl, "did Yeyac realize this? He heard Canaútli's account at the same time we did.''

"We will never know. And I have not yet inquired whether Canaútli has been succeeded by another Rememberer of History—or whether Canaútli passed on that story to his successor. I am inclined to think not. Surely that new Rememberer would have incited the people of Aztlan to rise up in outrage, once the woman joined Yeyac's court. Especially when she inveigled Yeyac into offering his friendship to the Spaniards."

"Yeyac did *that*?" gasped Améyatl, appalled. "But . . . then . . . why are *you* sparing the woman?"

"I have need of her. I will tell you why, but it is a long story. And—ah!—here is Pakápeti, my faithful companion on the long way hither, and now your handmaiden."

Tiptoe had arrived with a platter of light viands—fruits and such—for Améyatl's breaking of her fast. The two young women greeted one another amiably, but then Tiptoe, realizing that my cousin and I were in serious converse, left us to it.

"Tiptoe is more than your personal servant," I said. "She is chamberlain of this whole palace. She is also the cook, the laundress, the housekeeper, everything. She and you and I and the Yaki woman are the only persons still resident here. All the domestics who served under Yeyac have joined him in Míctlan. G'nda Ké is at present seeking replacements."

"You were about to tell me why G'nda Ké still lives, when so many others do not."

So, while Améyatl dined, with good appetite and obvious pleasure, I recounted all—or most—of my doings and adventurings since our parting. I touched only lightly on some of the occurrences. For instance, I did not describe in all its gruesome detail the burning of the man who I later learned had been my father—and whose death had impelled me to do so many of the things I did afterward. Also I condensed the telling of my education in the Spanish language and the Christian superstitions and my learning how to make a working thunder-stick. Also I did not dwell on my brief carnal connection with the mulata girl Rebeca, or the deep devotion that the late Citláli and I had shared, or the various Purémpe women (and one boy) I had sampled before I met Pakápeti, and I made it clear that *she* and I had for quite a long time now been no more than fellow travelers.

But I did tell Améyatl, in painstaking detail, the plans— and the so-far few preparations—I had made for leading an insurrection against the white men that would drive them utterly out of The One World. When I had done, she said pensively:

"You were ever valiant and ambitious, cousin. But this sounds like a vainglorious dream. The entire mighty Mexíca nation collapsed at the onslaught of the Caxtiltéca—or the Spaniards, as you call them. Yet you believe that you alone—"

"Your own august father Mixtzin said that very thing, among the last words he ever spoke to me. But I am not alone. Not every nation succumbed as did the Mexíca. Or as Yeyac would have had Aztlan do. The Purémpecha fought so nearly to the last man that the land of Michihuácan is now almost entirely populated by women. And even they will fight. Pakápeti rallied a goodly troop of them before she and I left there. And the Spaniards have not yet dared engage the fierce nations of the north. All that is required is someone to lead those disparate diehard peoples in a concerted effort. I know of no one else vainglorious enough to do that. So—if not I—*who*?"

"Well . . ." said Améyatl. "If sheer determination counts for anything in such an enterprise . . . But you still have not explained why the alien G'nda Ké has any part in this."

"I want her to help me recruit those nations and tribes as yet unconquered but not yet organized into a cohesive force. That long-ago Yaki woman undeniably did inspire a ragtag rabble of outcast Aztéca to a belligerence that led, in time, to the most splendid civilization in The One World. If she could do that, so, I think, might her many-times-great-granddaughter—or whoever our G'nda Ké is. I will be satisfied if she can recruit for me only her own native Yaki nation. They are said to be the most savage fighters of all.''

"As you deem best, cousin. You are the Uey-Tecútli.''

"I meant to speak of that, too. I assumed the mantle only because you, being a female, cannot. But I have not yet Yeyac's itch for title and authority and sublimity. I shall reign only until you are well enough to resume your position as regent. Then I will be on my way, resuming my campaign of recruitment."

She said, shyly for her, "We could reign together, you know. You as Uey-Tecútli and I as your Cecihuatl."

I asked teasingly, "You have so short a memory of your marriage to the late Káuritzin?''

"Ayyo, he was a good husband to me, considering that ours was a marriage arranged for others' convenience. But we were never so close as you and I once were, Tenamáxtli. Káuri was—how do I put it?—shy of experimentation.''

"I do admit," I said, smiling in recollection, "I have never yet known a woman who could outdo you in that respect.''

"And there is no traditional or priestly stricture against marriage between cousins. Of course, you may regard a widow woman as used goods, hand-me-down, not worthy of you." She added, roguishly, "But at least, on our wedding night, I would not have to deceive you with a pigeon egg and an astringent ointment.''

Astringent, almost acid, came another voice, that of G'nda Ké: "How touching—the long-parted lovers reminiscing of the 'oc ye nechca,' the once-upon-a-time.''

"You viper," I said through clenched teeth. "How long have you been lurking in this room?''

She ignored me and spoke to Améyatl, whose prison-pale face had blushed very pink. "Why should Tenamáxtli marry *anyone*, my dear? He is master here, the one man among three delectable women whom he can bed at random and without commitment. A onetime mistress, a current mistress and a mistress yet untasted.''

"Fork-tongued woman," I said, seething, "you are inconstant even in your malignant taunts. Last night you called me a cuilóntli.''

''And G'nda Ké is so glad to learn she was mistaken. Though she cannot *really* be sure, can she, until you and *she*—?''

''Never in my life have I struck a woman,'' I said. ''I am now about to do exactly that.''

She prudently stepped back from me, her lizard smile both apologetic and insolent. ''Forgive this one, my lord, my lady. G'nda Ké would not have intruded had she realized . . . Well, she came only to tell you, Tenamáxtzin, that a group of prospective new servants awaits your approval in the downstairs hall. Some of those say they, too, knew you in the oc ye nechca. More important, the members of your Speaking Council await you in the throne room.''

''The servants can wait. I will see the Council in a moment. Now slither out of here.''

Even after she had left, my cousin and I remained as embarrassed and flustered as two adolescents surprised in undressed and indecent proximity. I stammered foolishly when I asked Améyatl's leave to depart and, when she gave it, so did she. No one would have believed that we were mature adults, and we the two of highest rank in Aztlan.

XIX

JUST SO, THE elders of the Speaking Council seemed disinclined to regard me as a grown man, worthy of my rank and of their respect. They and I greeted each other politely, with exchanges of "Mixpantzínco," but one of the old men—I recognized him as Tototl, tlatocapíli of the village of Tépiz—immediately and angrily demanded of me:

"Have we been unceremoniously rushed hither at the presumptuous bidding of an upstart? Several of us remember you, Tenamáxtli, from the days when you were only a snotnosed bantling, creeping into this room to gawk and eavesdrop on our councils with your uncle, the Revered Governor Mixtzin. Even when we last saw you, when you left with Mixtzin for Tenochtítlan, you were still no more than a callow stripling. It appears that you have risen in stature unaccountably high and fast. We require to know—"

"Be silent, Tototl!" I said sharply, and all the men gasped. "You must also remember the Council protocol—that no man speaks until the Uey-Tecútli speaks the subject to be discussed. I am not meekly hoping for your acceptance or approval of me. I know who I am and what I am—legitimately your Uey-Tecútli. That is all *you* need to know."

There was some muttering around the room, but no further challenge to my authority. I may not have captivated their affection, but I definitely had seized their attention.

"I called you together because I have demands to make of you, and—out of simple courtesy and my esteem for you, my elders—I would wish to have your unanimous agreement to these demands. But I tell you also, and I kiss the earth to this, my demands *will* be met, whether you agree or not."

While they goggled at me and muttered some more, I stepped back to open the throne room's door and beckoned in Nochéztli and two of the Aztlan warriors he had pronounced trustworthy. I made no introduction of them, but went on addressing the Council members:

"By now, all of you certainly have heard of the incidents that have lately occurred and the revelations that have lately transpired hereabouts. How the abominable Yeyac assumed the mantle of Uey-Tecútli through the murder of his own father and"—here I spoke directly to Kévari, tlatocapíli of Yakóreke—"the murder of your son Káuri, then the atrocious overthrow and imprisonment of your son's widow Améyatzin. All of you certainly have heard that Yeyac was secretly conspiring with the Spaniards to help them maintain their oppression of all our peoples of The One World. You certainly have heard—with pleasure, I trust—that Yeyac is no more. You certainly have heard that I, as the sole surviving male relative of Mixtzin—hence rightful successor to the mantle—have ruthlessly been ridding Aztlan of Yeyac's confederates. Last night I decimated Aztlan's army. Today I shall deal with Yeyac's lickspittles among the civil population."

I reached my hand behind me, and Nochéztli put into it a number of bark papers. I scanned the columns of word-pictures on them, then announced to the room at large:

"This is a list of those citizens who abetted Yeyac in his nefarious activities—from marketplace stallkeepers to respectable merchants to prominent pochtéca traders. I am pleased to find that only one man of this Speaking Council is named in the list. Tlamacázqui Colótic-Acatl, step forward."

Of this man I have spoken earlier in this narrative. He was the priest of the god Huitzilopóchtli, who, at the first news of the white men's arrival in The One World, had been so fearful of being deposed from his priesthood. Like all our tlamacázque, he had been unwashed all his life, and wore black robes that had never been cleaned. But now, even under its grimy crust, his face went pale and he trembled as he came forward.

I said, "Why a priest of a Mexícatl god should turn traitor to that god's worshipers is beyond my understanding. Did you intend to convert to the white men's religion of Crixtanóyotl? Or did you simply hope to wheedle them into leaving you secure in your old priesthood? No, do not tell me. I pick my teeth at such as you." I turned to the two warriors. "Take this creature to the central square, not to any temple— he deserves not the honor of being a sacrifice, or of having an afterlife—and strangle him to death with the flower garland."

They seized him and the priest went whimpering away with them, while the rest of the Council stood stunned.

"Hand these papers around among yourselves," I told them. "You tlatocapíltin of other communities will find names of persons in your own neighborhoods who either gave aid to Yeyac or received favors from him. My first demand is that you exterminate those persons. My second demand is that you comb the ranks of your own warriors and personal guards—Nochéztli here will assist you in that—and exterminate also any traitors among them."

"It shall be done," said Tototl, sounding rather more respectful of me now. "I think I speak for the entire Council in saying that we concur unanimously in this action."

Kévari asked, "Have you any further demand, Tenamáxtzin?"

"Yes, one more. I want each of you tlatocapíltin to send to Aztlan every true and untainted warrior you have, and every able-bodied man who has been trained to be conscripted if necessary. I intend to integrate them into my own army."

"Again, agreed," said Teciúapil, tlatocapíli of Tecuéxe. "But may we ask why?"

"Before I answer that," I said, "let me ask a question of my own. Who among you is now the Council's Rememberer of History?"

They all looked slightly uncomfortable at that, and there was a short silence. Then spoke a man who had not spoken before. He was also elderly—a prosperous merchant, to judge from his garb—but new to the Council since my time.

He said, "When old Canaútli, the previous Rememberer, died—I am told he was your great-grandfather, Tenámax-tzin—none other was appointed to take his place. Yeyac insisted that there was no need for a Rememberer because, he said, with the arrival of the white men, The One World's history had come to an end. Furthermore, said Yeyac, we would no longer count the passing years by sheaves of fifty-two, nor any longer observe the ceremony of lighting the New Fire to mark the start of each new sheaf. We would, he said, count our years as the white men do, in an unbroken sequence that began with a year numbered simply One—but began we know not how long ago."

"Yeyac was wrong," I said. "There is still much history—and I intend to make more—for our historians to remember and record. That, to answer your earlier question, councillors, is why I want your warriors for my army."

And I went on to tell them—as I had just told Améyatl and, before her, Pakápeti and G'nda Ké and the late Citláli and the thunder-stick artisan Pochotl—of my plans to mount a rebellion against New Spain and take back all of The One World for our own. Like those others who had listened to me, these members of the Speaking Council looked impressed but incredulous, and one of them began to say:

"But, Tenamáxtzin, if even the mighty—"

I interrupted, with a snarl, "The first man among you who tells me that I cannot succeed where *even the mighty Mexíca failed'*—that man, however aged and wise and dignified, even decrepit though he may be—that man will be ordered to lead my first assault against the Spanish army. He will go at the front of my forces, at the very point, and he will go unarmed and unarmored!''

There was dead silence in the room.

''Then does the Speaking Council agree to support my proposed campaign?'' Several of the members heaved a sigh, but they all nodded assent. ''Good,'' I said.

I turned to that merchant who had informed me that there was no longer a Rememberer of History on the Council. ''Canaútli no doubt left many books of word-pictures telling what occurred in all the sheaves of sheaves of years up to his own time. Study and memorize them. And I bid you do this, too. Commence a new book—with these words: 'On this day of Nine-Flower, in the month of the Sweeping of the Road, in the year Seven-House, the Uey-Tecútli Tenamáxtzin of Aztlan declared The One World's independence of Old Spain and began preparations for an insurrection against the unwelcome white overlords, in both New Spain and New Galicia, this plan having the consent and endorsement of his Speaking Council in assembly agreed.' ''

The man promised, ''Your every word, Tenamáxtzin,'' and he and the other councillors went their way.

Nochéztli, still in the room, said, ''Excuse me, my lord, but what shall be done with those warriors imprisoned in the goddess's temple? They are so crowded in there that they must take turns sitting down, and cannot lie down at all. They are also getting very hungry and thirsty.''

''They deserve worse than discomfort,'' I said. ''But tell the guards to feed them—only atóli and water—and only a minimum of each. I want those men, when I am ready to put them to use, hungry for battle and thirsty for blood. Meanwhile, Nochéztli, I believe you said you have visited Compostela in Yeyac's company?''

''Yes, Tenamáxtzin.''

''Then I want you to visit there again, this time being a

quimíchi for me." That word properly means "mouse," but we use it also to mean what the Spanish call an *espión*. "Can I trust you to do that? To go there, secretly get information, and return here with it?"

"You can, my lord. I am alive only because of your sufferance, therefore my life is yours to command."

"Then that is my command. The Spanish cannot yet have heard that they have lost their ally Yeyac. And since they already know you by sight, they will suppose you to be Yeyac's emissary, come on some errand."

"I will carry gourds of our fermented coconut milk to sell. All the white men, high and low, are fond of getting drunk on it. That will be sufficient excuse for my visit. And what information would you wish me to gather?"

"Anything. Keep your eyes and ears open, and linger there as long as necessary. Find out for me, if you can, what the new Governor Coronado is like, and how many troops he now has stationed there, and how many other people—both Spanish and indio—now inhabit Compostela. Also be alert for any news or rumor or gossip of what is happening elsewhere in the Spanish lands. I will await your return before I send Yeyac's pack of disloyal warriors on their suicidal mission, and the outcome of that mission will largely depend on what information you bring back to me."

"I go at once, my lord," he said, and he did.

Next, I gave quick and desultory approval to all the would-be servants that G'nda Ké had gathered in the hall. I recognized a number of them from the old days, and I was sure that if any of the others had ever been in league with Yeyac, they would not now have dared to apply for service under my eye. From then on, we pípiltin of the palace—Améyatl, Pakápeti, G'nda Ké and myself—were most assiduously attended and most sumptuously fed, and we never had to lift a finger to do anything that could be done *for* us. Though Améyatzin now had a bevy of women to wait upon her, she and I both were pleased that Tiptoe insisted on continuing to be her closest personal handmaiden.

What time Tiptoe was not attending Améyatl, she gladly passed in accompanying the warriors I sent to arrest and execute the Aztlan townsmen whose names had been on Nochéztli's bark papers. I gave no orders except "execute them!" and I never bothered to find out what means the warriors employed—whether the flower-garland garrote or the sword or arrows or the knife that tears out the heart—or whether Tiptoe personally dispatched some of those men with one or another of the horrid methods she had mentioned to me. I simply did not care. Sufficient for me that all the property and possessions and wealth of those who died came to Aztlan's treasury. I may seem callous in having said that, but I could have been even more callous. By ancient tradition, I *could* have slain those traitors' wives, children, grandchildren, relatives of even more remote degree, and from that I refrained. I did not wish to depopulate Aztlan entirely.

I had never been a Uey-Tecútli before, and the only other one I had ever observed in the exercise of that office had been my Uncle Mixtli. It had seemed to me—then—that to accomplish anything whatsoever that required accomplishing, all Mixtzin had to do was smile or scowl or wave a hand or put his name-sign to some document. I soon learned—now—that being a Revered Governor was no easy occupation. I was being continually petitioned—I could say pestered—for decisions, judgments, pronouncements, intercessions, advice, verdicts, consents or denials, acceptances or rejections . . .

The other officials of my court, charged with various governing responsibilities, regularly came to see me with their various problems. A dike restraining the swamp waters needed crucial repairs, or the swamp would soon be in our streets; would the Uey-Tecútli authorize the cost of materials and the rounding-up of workmen? The fishers of our ocean fleet were complaining that the long-ago draining of that same swamp had resulted in the gradual silting up of their accustomed seaside harbors; would the Uey-Tecútli authorize the dredging of those harbors deep again? Our warehouses were bulging with sea-otter pelts, sponges, shark skins and other unsold goods, because, for years now, Aztlan had been trading only with lands to the north of us, none to the south; could the Uey-Tecútli devise a plan to get rid of that glut, and at a profit? . . .

I had to contend with not just my court officials and major matters of policy, but also with the most trivial doings of the common folk. Here a quarrel between two neighbors over the boundary between their plots of land; there a family squabbling over the division of their recently dead father's meager estate; here a debtor asking relief from an usurious and harassing moneylender; there a creditor asking permission to oust a widow and her orphans from their home, to satisfy some obligation her late husband had failed to meet . . .

It was exceedingly difficult for me to find time to attend to matters that were—to me—of much more urgency. But somehow I managed. I instructed all the loyal knights and cuáchictin of my army to put their forces (and every available conscript) to intensified training, and to make place in their ranks for the additional warriors levied and daily arriving from the other communities subordinate to Aztlan.

I even found time to take out of hiding the three arcabuces Pakápeti and I had brought, and to give personal training in the use of them. Needless to remark, every warrior was, at first, timorous of handling these alien weapons. But I selected only those who could overcome their trepidation, and who showed an aptitude for using the thunder-stick efficiently. Those eventually numbered about twenty, and when one of them asked, diffidently, "My lord, when we go to war, are we to take turns employing the thunder-sticks?" I told him, "No, young iyac. I expect you to wrest from the white men *their* arcabuces with which to arm yourselves. Furthermore, we will also be confiscating the white men's horses. When we do, you will be trained in the handling of them, as well."

My being continuously busy had at least one gratifying aspect: it kept me from having anything to do with the Yaki woman G'nda Ké. While I was occupied with affairs of state, she occupied herself with overseeing the palace household and its domestics. She may have been a nuisance to those servants, but she had little opportunity to be a nuisance to me. Oh, occasionally we might meet in a palace corridor, and she would utter some taunting or teasing remark:

"I weary of waiting, Tenamáxtli. When do you and I go forth together and commence our war?"

Or "I weary of waiting, Tenamáxtli. When do you and I go to bed together, so that you may kiss every one of the freckles that sprinkle my most intimate parts?"

Even if I had not been kept too busy to bed *anybody,* and even if she had been the last human female in existence, I would not have been tempted. Indeed, during my tenure as Uey-Tecútli—when by custom I could have had any Aztlan woman I wanted—I was having none at all. Pakápeti seemed staunch in her determination never again to couple with any man. And I would not have dreamed of intruding myself into Améyatl's sickbed, even though she was getting healthier and stronger and more beautiful every day.

I did visit my cousin's bedside whenever I had a free moment, simply to converse with her. I would apprise her of all my activities as Uey-Tecútli, and of all happenings in and about Aztlan—so that she could the more easily resume her regency when the time came. (And, frankly, I was yearning for that time to come, so I could be off to war.) We talked of many other things, too, of course, and one day Améyatl, looking vaguely troubled, said to me:

"Pakápeti has taken loving care of me. And she *looks* lovely, now that her hair is nearly as long as my own. But the dear girl might as well be repellently ugly, because the anger in her is so very nearly *visible.*"

"She is angry toward men, and she has reason. I told you of her encounter with those two Spanish soldiers."

"White men, then, I could understand. But—excepting only you—I think she would gladly slay *every* man alive."

I said, "So would the venomous G'nda Ké. Perhaps her

propinquity has influenced Pakápeti to an even deeper hatred
of men.''

Améyatl asked, ''Including the one inside her?''

I blinked. ''What are you saying?''

''Then you have not noticed. It is just beginning to show,
and she is carrying it high. Tiptoe is pregnant.''

''*Not by me,*'' I blurted. ''I have not touched her in—''

''Ayyo, cousin, be at ease,'' said Améyatl, laughing despite her evident concern. ''Tiptoe blames that encounter of
which you spoke.''

''Well, she could reasonably be bitter about carrying the
mongrel child of a—''

''Not because it is a child. Or a mongrel. Because it is a
male. Because she detests all males.''

''Oh, come now, cousin. How could Pakápeti possibly
know it will be a boy?''

''She does not even refer to it as a *boy*. She speaks sav-
agely of 'this *tepúli* growing inside me.' Or 'this kurú'—the
Poré word for that same male organ. Tenamáxtli, is it possible that Tiptoe's distress is causing her to lose her mind?''

''I am no authority,'' I said with a sigh, ''on madness *or*
women. I will consult a tícitl of my acquaintance. Perhaps
he can prescribe some palliative for her distress. In the meantime, let us both—you and I—be watchful that Tiptoe does
not try to do some hurt to herself.''

But it was a while before I got around to summoning that
physician, because I had other distractions. One was a visit
from one of the guards at the Cóyolxaúqui temple, come to
report that the imprisoned warriors were most miserable,
having to sleep on their feet, eating nothing but mush, being
so long unbathed, and so forth.

''Have any of them yet suffocated or starved?'' I demanded.

''No, my lord. They may be near dead, but one hundred
thirty and eight were confined in there, and that number still
remain. However, even we guards outside the temple can
hardly endure their stink and their clamor.''

"Then change the guard more frequently. Unless those traitors begin to die, do not trouble me again. *Near* dead is not punishment enough for them."

And then Nochéztli returned from his mission as a qui-míchi in Compostela. He had been gone for about two months—and I had begun to worry that he had again defected to the enemy—but he came back, as promised, and came brimming with things to tell.

"Compostela is a much more thriving and populous town, my lord, than when I last saw it. Most numerous of the male white inhabitants are the Spanish soldiers, whom I estimate to number about a thousand, half of those horse-mounted. But many of the higher-ranking soldiers have brought their families, and other Spanish families have come as colonists, all of those families having built houses for themselves. The governor's palace and the town church are of well-worked stone; the other residences are of dried-mud brick. There is a marketplace, but all the goods and produce for sale there have been brought by trains of traders from the south. The whites of Compostela do no farming or raising of herds— they all prosper on the output of the many silver mines now being worked in the vicinity. And evidently they prosper sufficiently to afford the expense of importing all their co-mestibles and other necessities."

I asked, "And how many of our own people are resident there?"

"The indio population is about equal to that of the whites. I speak only of those who serve as domestic slaves in the households of the Spanish—and there are numerous black slaves as well, those creatures called Moros. If the slaves are not domiciled with their masters, they have derelict huts and shacks on the town's outskirts. There is another considerable population of our men working the mines under the earth, and in surrounding buildings atop the earth, called mills. I fear I could not estimate the number of those men, because so many of them work underground, turn about, half of them daylong, the other half during the night. Also, they and their

families, if they have any, live penned in locked and guarded
compounds where I could not enter. The Spanish call these
places obrajes."

"Ayya, yes," I said. "I know about the infamous obrajes."

"The word is that those laborers—since our people never
before had to slave underground or in such wretched conditions—keep dying off, several every day. And the mine
owners cannot replace them as fast as they die, because, of
course, all the indios in New Galicia not already enslaved
have made haste to move and hide themselves far beyond
the reach of the slave-catchers. So Governor Coronado has
asked the Virrey Mendoza in the City of México to send to
Compostela quantities of Moro slaves from—from wherever
those Moros are brought from."

"Some land called Africa, I have been told."

Nochéztli grimaced and said, "It must be a place akin to
our fearsome Hot Lands in the far south. Because I hear that
the Moros can easily endure the terrific heat and closeness
and clangor of the mines and mills. Also the Moros must be
more like the Spaniards' beasts of burden than like human
beings, for it is also said that they can labor unceasingly,
under crushing loads, without dying or even complaining. It
may be that if enough Moros are imported into New Galicia,
Coronado will cease trying to capture and enslave our own
people."

"This Governor Coronado," I said. "Tell me about him."

"I glimpsed him only twice, when he was reviewing his
troops, elegantly costumed and astride a prancing white
horse. He is no older than yourself, my lord, but his rank, of
course, is inferior to yours of *Revered* Governor, for he is
answerable to superiors in the City of México, and you are
answerable to no one. Nevertheless, he is clearly determined
to make a more lordly name for himself. He is remorseless
in demanding that the slaves extract every pinch of silver
ore—not just for the enrichment of himself and his New
Galicia subjects, but for all of New Spain and that ruler

called Carlos in distant Old Spain. On the whole, though, Coronado seems less of a tyrant than his predecessor. He does not allow his subjects to torment or torture or execute our people at whim, as the Governor Guzmán used to do.''

''Tell me of the governor's arms and fortifications for the defense of Compostela.''

''That is a curious thing, my lord. I can only assume that the late Yeyac must have persuaded Compostela that it need never fear attack from our people. In addition to the usual thunder-sticks carried by the Spanish soldiers, they have also those much more immense thunder-tubes mounted on wheeled carriages. But the soldiers do not defensively ring the town; they are chiefly employed in keeping the mine slaves submissively at work or in guarding the obrajes where they are confined. And the massive thunder-tubes positioned around the town are not pointed outward, but *inward,* obviously to turn back any slaves' attempt to revolt or escape.''

''Interesting,'' I murmured. I rolled and lighted and smoked a poquíetl while I meditated on what I had learned. ''Have you anything else of moment to report?''

''Much else, my lord. Though Guzmán claimed to have conquered Michihuácan and sent its few surviving warriors into slavery abroad, it seems he did not subdue *all* of them. The new Governor Coronado hears regularly of uprisings in the south of his domain, mostly in the area around Lake Pátzcuaro. Bands of warriors, armed only with blades made of the famous Purémpe metal, and with torches, have been assaulting Spanish army outposts and the estancias of Spanish settlers. They attack always by night, slay the armed guards and steal their thunder-sticks, and set afire the estancia buildings, thereby killing many white families—men, women, children, all. Those whites who have survived swear that the attackers were *women*—though how they could tell, considering the darkness and the fact that all the Purémpecha are bald, I know not. When the remaining Spanish soldiers comb the countryside by daylight, they find the Purémpe women doing nothing but what they have always done—

peaceably weaving baskets, making pottery and the like."

"Ayyo," I said to myself, with satisfaction. "Pakápeti's troops are indeed proving their worth."

"The result has been that additional troops have been sent out from New Spain to try—so far, in vain—to quell those disturbances. And the Spaniards in the City of Méxíco are vociferously lamenting that this diversion of troops leaves *them* vulnerable to indio invasions or insurrections. If the attacks in Michihuácan have done damage that is really only trifling, they have undoubtedly made all the Spaniards—everywhere—uneasy and uncertain of their security."

I muttered, "I must find some way to send my personal commendation to that frightful cóyotl-woman Butterfly."

"As I say," Nochéztli went on, "the Governor Coronado receives these reports, but he refuses to send southward any of his own troops from Compostela. I heard that he insists on keeping his men ready for some grandiose plan he has conceived to further his own ambitions. I heard also that he was eagerly awaiting the arrival of a certain emissary of the Virrey Mendoza, from the City of Méxíco. Well, that person arrived, just before I left Compostela, my lord, and a very peculiar emissary he turned out to be. A common Christian friar—and I recognized him, for he had been a resident in Compostela before, and I had seen him there. I know not his name, but at that earlier time he was disparagingly called the Lying Monk by all his fellows. And I know not why he has returned, or why the viceroy sent him, or how he could possibly assist in the ambitions of Governor Coronado. The only other thing I can tell you in this respect is that the friar arrived accompanied by a single attendant, a mere Moro slave. Both of them, friar and slave, went immediately into private conference with the governor. I was tempted to stay and try to learn more about this mystery. However, by this time, I was beginning to get suspicious looks from the townspeople. I feared also that you, my lord, might have had suspicions about my being so long away."

"I confess that I did have, Nochéztli, and I apologize. You

have done well—very well indeed. From what you have discovered, I can divine much more.'' I chuckled heartily. ''The
Moro is leading the Lying Monk in search of the fabulous
Cities of Antilia, and Coronado expects to share the credit
when they are discovered.''

''My lord . . . ?'' said Nochéztli, puzzled.

''No matter. What it means is that Coronado *will* be de-
taching some of his troops to aid in that search, leaving the
complacent town of Compostela even more defenseless. The
time approaches for the late Yeyac's pet warriors to expiate
their crimes. Go you, Nochéztli, and tell the guards at that
temple prison to start feeding those men on good meat and
fish and fats and oils. They are to be made strong again. And
have the guards let them out of the temple occasionally, to
bathe and exercise and drill and get themselves fit for vigorous action. See to this, Nochéztli, and when you deem the
men ready, come and tell me so.''

I went to Améyatl's chambers—where she was no longer
bedridden, but seated on an icpáli chair—and told her everything I had heard, and what I had deduced from that information, and what I intended to do about it. My cousin
seemed still dubious about my plans, but did not withhold
her approval of them. Then she said, ''Meanwhile, cousin,
you have done nothing yet about Pakápeti's precarious condition. I worry more about her each day.''

''Ayya, you are right. I have been remiss.'' To one of her
other servants, presently in attendance, I ordered, ''Go and
fetch the Tícitl Ualíztli. He is surgeon to the army. You will
find him at the knights' barracks. Tell him I require him
immediately.''

Améyatl and I chatted of various matters—for one thing,
she said she felt quite her former self again, and if I would
allow it, she would begin to help me with some of the routine
details of my office—until Ualíztli arrived, bearing the pouch
of instruments and medicaments that all tíciltin carry everywhere. Being a rather elderly, stout man, and having hurried

at my summons, he was slightly out of breath, so I had the servant bring a cup of chocólatl to refresh him, and told her to bring Tiptoe at the same time.

"Esteemed Ualíztli," I said, "this young woman is my good friend Pakápeti of the Purémpe people. Tiptoe, this gentleman is the highest-regarded physician of Aztlan. Améyatzin and I would like you to let him examine your physical condition."

She looked a little wary, but made no demur.

I told the tícitl, "From all indications, Pakápeti is with child, but apparently having something of a difficult pregnancy. All of us here would value your opinion and advice."

Immediately Tiptoe exclaimed, "I am *not* with *child!*" but she obediently lay supine on Améyatl's pallet when the physician bade her do so.

"Ayyo, but you *are,* my dear," he said, after only briefly kneading her through her clothes. "Please to raise your blouse and lower your skirt band, so I may make a thorough examination."

Tiptoe seemed not embarrassed to expose her breasts and now-bloated belly in the presence of Améyatl and myself—and she seemed equally indifferent to the tícitl's frowns and sighs and mutters as he pressed and poked her here and there. When at last he sat back away from her, she spoke before he could:

"I am not pregnant! And I do not wish to be this way, either!"

"Be easy, child. There are certain potions I could have administered, early on, to induce a premature birth, but you are too far—"

"I will not give birth, early or late or ever!" Tiptoe insisted vehemently. "I want this thing inside me *killed!*"

"Well, to be sure, the fetus would not have survived a premature birth. But now—"

"It is not a fetus. It is a—a male *thing.*".

The tícitl smiled tolerantly. "Did some meddlesome

midwife tell you it would be a boy because you are carrying it high? That is only an old superstition.''

"No midwife told me anything!" Tiptoe declared, getting more and more agitated. "I did not say a boy—I said a male *thing*. The thing that only a male person . . ." She paused, shamefaced, then said, "A kurú. A tepúli."

Ualíztl gave her a searching look. "Let me have a word with your eminent friend here." He drew me out of the women's hearing and whispered, "My lord, does this perhaps involve an unsuspecting husband? Has the young woman been unfaith—?"

"No, no," I hastened to defend her. "There is no husband at all. Several months ago, Pakápeti was raped by a Spanish soldier. I fear that her dread of bearing an enemy's child has somewhat addled her faculties."

"Unless Purémpe women are built differently than ours—which I doubt—something has addled her insides, as well. If she is carrying a child, it is growing more in the area of her stomach than her womb, and that is a thing impossible."

"Can you do *anything* to give her relief?"

He made a face of uncertainty, then went back to lean over Tiptoe again. "You could be right, my dear, that it is not a viable fetus. Sometimes a woman can develop a fibrous growth that only mimics pregnancy."

"I *told* you it is growing! I *told* you it is not a fetus! I *told* you it is a tepúli!"

"Please, my dear, that is an unbecoming word for a well-bred young lady to utter. Why do you persist in speaking so immodestly?"

"Because I know what it is! Because I *swallowed* it! *Take it out!*"

"Poor girl, you are distraught." He began searching for something in his pouch.

But I was staring agape at Pakápeti. I was remembering . . . and I was wondering . . .

"Here, drink this," said Ualíztli, holding out a small cup to her.

"Will that rid me of the thing?" she asked hopefully, almost pleadingly.

"It will calm you."

"I do not want to be calm!" She dashed the cup from his hand. "I want to be free of this hideous—"

"Tiptoe," I said sternly, "do as the tícitl tells you. Remember, we should shortly be on the road again. You cannot come with me unless you get well. For now, just drink the potion. Then the good physician will consult with his fellow tíciltin as to what measures will next be taken. Is that not right, Ualíztli?"

"Exactly so, my lord," he said, concurring in my lie.

Though still looking obstinate and defiant, Tiptoe obeyed me, and drank down the cup he had refilled. Ualíztli gave her permission to rearrange her clothing and take her leave. When she was gone, he said to me and Améyatl:

"She is worse than distraught. She is demented. I gave her a tincture of the nanácatl mushroom. That will at least alleviate her mental turmoil. I know nothing else that can be done, except to cut into her with an obsidian lancet, and few patients survive such a drastic exploration. I will leave you a supply of the tincture, to be administered whenever she gets delusional again. I am sorry, my lord, my lady, but the signs prognostic are not at all promising."

In the ensuing days, Améyatzin occupied a throne slightly smaller than my own, and slightly below and on the left side of my own, and she joined in my conferences with the Speaking Council when there was occasion for those elders to convene, and helped me with many of the decisions that my other officials came to ask for, and relieved me of much of the wearisome burden of dealing with petitions from the common folk. Améyatl kept always at *her* left side our dear Pakápeti, mainly as a precaution against the girl's doing something harmful to herself, but partly also in the hope that Tiptoe's mind might be diverted from its dark obsession by the activities in the throne room.

We three were there on the day that an army messenger came to tell me, "The Tequíua Nochéztli sends word, my lord, that the warriors of Yeyac are as fit as they ever were."

"Then bid Nochéztli to come hither and to bring that Arrow Knight with him."

When they came, the knight, whose name was Tapachíni, humbly stooped to make the tlalqualíztli touching of the throne-room floor. I let him remain in that subservient posture while I said:

"I offered you and your comrades in treachery three ways of dying. All of you chose the same, and this day you will lead those men marching to that death. As I promised, it will be a death in battle, good in the eyes of the gods. And this I tell you for the first time: You will have had the honor of waging the opening battle of what will be a total and unconditional war to oust the white men from The One World."

Tapachíni said, his head still bowed, "An honor we could hardly have hoped to merit, my lord. We are grateful. Only command us."

"Your arms and armor will be returned to all of you. Then you will march southward and attack the Spaniards' town of Compostela. You will do your best to *obliterate* it and its white inhabitants. You will not succeed, of course. You will be outnumbered ten to one, and your weapons will be no match for the white men's. However, you will find the town fatuously believing itself safeguarded because of the pact it made with the late Yeyac. Compostela will be unprepared for your assault. So the gods—and I—will be desolated if you each do not dispatch at least five of the enemy before you fall yourselves."

"Rely on it, my lord."

"I expect to *hear* of it. The news of such an unprecedented slaughter will not be long in reaching my ear. Meanwhile, dismiss any delusion that you and your men will elude my *eye* as soon as you leave Aztlan."

I turned to Nochéztli. "Pick sturdy and loyal warriors to serve as escort. Have them accompany Knight Tapachíni and

his contingent along the southbound trails—it should be a
march of no more than five days—until they get within striking range of Compostela. When the Knight Tapachíni leads
the charge against the town—and not until then—the escorts
are to return here and report. Along the way south, they are
continuously to keep count of their wards. The knight and
his men number one hundred thirty and eight as of this moment. That same number is to attack Compostela. Is that
understood, Tequíua Nochéztli?''

"Yes, my lord."

"And you, Knight Tapachíni," I said with heavy sarcasm.
"Are those conditions satisfactory to you?"

"I can scarcely blame you, my lord, for having found us
less than deserving of your trust."

"Then be gone. Much may be forgiven you when you
have spilled a whole river of the white men's blood. And
your own."

Nochéztli himself went along with Tapachíni's men and their
escorts during their first day's march, then turned back at
nightfall, and early the next morning reported to me:

"No one of the condemned men tried to escape, my lord,
and there were no untoward incidents, and there were still
one hundred thirty and eight of them when I left them."

I not only commended Nochéztli for his assiduous and
continued attention to every aspect of this mission, I promoted him on the spot.

"From this day, you are a cuáchic, an 'old eagle.' Further,
I give you permission to select for yourself the warriors who
will serve under your command. If any of the haughty
knights or the other cuáchictin have any complaints about
that, tell them to complain to me."

Nochéztli so hastily and happily stooped to make the gesture of kissing the earth that he very nearly fell asprawl at
my feet. When he scrambled erect, he left my presence even
more respectfully, walking *backward* all the way out of the
throne room.

But he had barely gone when he was succeeded by another warrior requesting audience, and this one had brought with him a rather frightened-looking woman of the common folk. They both touched the floor in the tlalqualíztli gesture, and the man said:

"Forgive my urgency, my lord, but this woman came to our barracks to report having found, when she first opened her door this morning, a dead body in the alley outside."

"Why are you telling me this, iyac? Likely some drunkard who drank beyond his capacity."

"Forgive my correcting you, my lord. This was a warrior, and he had been stabbed in the back. Furthermore, he had been stripped of his battle armor, left wearing only his loin-cloth, and he bore no weapons."

"Then how do you know he *was* a warrior?" I snapped, rather peeved at having my day start this way.

Before he answered me, the iyac stooped again to touch the floor, and I turned to see that Améyatl had entered the room.

"Because, my lord," he continued, "I have served as guard of the prisoners in the Coyolxaúqui temple, so I recognized this dead warrior. He was one of the late Yeyac's detestable accomplices."

"But ... but ..." I stammered, confounded. "They all were to have left the city last night. They *did* leave. All one hundred thirty and eight of them ..."

Améyatl interrupted, her voice unsteady, "Tenamáxtzin, have you seen anything of Tiptoe?"

"What?" I said, even more confounded.

"She was not at my bedside this morning, as she always has been. I do not recall having seen her since we three were in this room yesterday."

Améyatl and I must both have realized, on the instant. But we and every remaining servant and even G'nda Ké went searching the palace, every corner of it, and all the palace grounds. No one found Pakápeti, and the only significant discovery was made by me—to wit, that one of the three hidden thunder-sticks also was missing. Tiptoe had deliberately gone forth to kill—and to have whatever was inside her killed—and to be killed herself.

XX

I HAD CALCULATED that the Knight Tapachíni's troop and its escorts should take about five days to get to Compostela, and that the escorts should take rather less time to return and report—or, if there was a good runner among them, he might race ahead and arrive even sooner. Anyway, I had some days to wait to hear the outcome of that mission, and rather than stew in impatience and anxiety, I put the days to profitable use. I left *all* the boring and exasperating routine of government to Améyatl and the Speaking Council—I was consulted only on major matters—and betook myself to outdoor pursuits.

My four horses had been well fed and groomed, as I had instructed the handler slaves, and were now handsomely sleek and obviously eager to stretch their legs. So I sought volunteers to learn the riding of them. The first I asked was G'nda Ké, for I expected that she and I would soon be traveling far and fast, in advance of my army, gathering recruits for that army. But she disdainfully spurned the idea of riding. In her inimitable way, she said:

"G'nda Ké already knows everything worth the knowing. What point in learning something new? Besides, G'nda Ké has crossed and recrossed the whole of The One World, and many times, and always on foot, as best becomes a stalwart

Yaki. You ride, if you prefer, Tenamáxtli, like a weakling white man. G'nda Ké warrants that she will keep up with you.''

I said dryly, ''You will wear out a lot of those precious sandals of yours,'' but did not press her further.

I next offered the opportunity to the army knights, in deference to their rank, and was not too surprised when they also declined—though of course not so insultingly as G'nda Ké had done. They said only, ''My lord, eagles and jaguars would be ashamed to depend on lesser beasts for their mobility.''

So I turned to the ranks of cuáchictin, and two of those did volunteer. As I might have expected, the new Cuáchic Nochéztli hardly waited to be asked. The other was a middleaged Mexícatl named Comitl, who had, in his youth, been among those warriors brought from Tenochtítlan to train ours. He had more recently been one of the men who learned from me how to wield an arcabuz. My third volunteer was, to my astonishment, the army's surgeon, that Tícitl Ualíztli of whom I have spoken.

''If you seek only men who can *fight* on horseback, my lord, naturally I will understand your refusing me. But, as you can easily see, I am considerably overaged and oversized for marching with the army, and carrying my heavy sack while I do so.''

''I do not refuse you, Ualíztli. I think a tícitl *should* be enabled to move quickly about a battlefield, the more easily to administer his services. And I have seen many mounted Spaniards much older and heavier than yourself; if they could ride, surely you can learn.''

So, during those days of waiting, I taught the three men as much as I myself knew about handling a horse—devoutly wishing that the far more adroit Tiptoe were there to oversee their training. We did our practices alternately on the paved central square and on grassier grounds elsewhere, and wherever we did, crowds of city folk came to stare—from a discreet distance—in awe and admiration. I let Tícitl Ualíztli

use the other saddle on his horse, and Comitl and Nochéztli
manfully refrained from complaining at having to jounce
about on the ridgepole-steep bare backs of the other two
mounts.

"It will toughen you," I assured them, "so that when
eventually we confiscate other horses and their saddles from
the white soldiers, you will find riding to be easeful indeed."

However, by the time my three students had become at
least as adept at riding as I was, our activities had ceased to
distract me from anxiety. Seven days had passed since the
departure of Tapachíni and his men, time enough for a swift-
messenger to have returned to Aztlan, and none had. An
eighth day passed, and then a ninth, time enough for *all* the
escort guards to have returned.

"Something has gone terribly wrong," I growled, on the
tenth day, as I moodily paced the throne room. For the moment, I was confiding my consternation only to Améyatl and
G'nda Ké. "And I have no way of knowing *what!*"

My cousin suggested, "The condemned men may have
decided to evade their doom. But they could not have slipped
away from the line of march by ones and twos, or the escorts
would have reported to you. So they must have risen up in
mass—they were many and the escorts few—then, after slaying their guards, fled together or separately beyond your
reach."

"I have naturally thought of that," I grumbled. "But they
had kissed the earth in oath. And they had once been honorable men."

"So was Yeyac—once," Améyatl said bitterly. "While
our father was present to keep him loyal and manly and
trustworthy."

"Still," I objected, "I find it hard to believe that not *one*
of those men would have kept his oath—at least to come
and tell me that the others had not. And remember, it is
virtually certain that Pakápeti was among them in man's disguise. *She* would never desert."

"Perhaps it was she," said G'nda Ké, with her distinctive gloating grin, "who slew them all."

I did not dignify that crass remark with any comment of my own. Améyatl said, "If Yeyac's men did kill their escorts, they would scarcely have balked at killing Tiptoe—or any others of their own—who stood firm against them."

"But they were *warriors*," I continued to object. "They still *are* warriors, unless the earth opened and swallowed them. They know no other way of life. Together or separately, what will they do with their lives now? Resort to vulgar skulking banditry? That would be unthinkable for a warrior, however dishonorably he had behaved otherwise. No, I can think of only one thing they must have done."

I turned to the Yaki woman and said, "In a time before time, a certain G'nda Ké turned good men into bad, so *you* must be well versed in the matter of betrayal. Do you think those men treacherously resumed their alliance with the Spaniards?"

She shrugged indifferently, "To what end? As long as they were Yeyac's men, they could expect favor and preferment. Without Yeyac to lead them, they are nobodies. The Spanish might accept them into their ranks, but would utterly despise them—rightly reckoning that men who had turned against their own people could easily turn again."

I had to admit, "You speak with logic."

"Those deserters would find themselves the lowliest of the low. Even that Arrow Knight would be degraded to yaoquíz-qui in rank. Certainly he and all the others would have known that, even before they deserted. So why should they? No warrior, however desperate to escape your wrath, could have accepted so much worse a fate."

"Well, whatever they did," said Améyatl, "they did it between here and Compostela. Why not send another quimíchi scurrying to find out?"

"No!" snapped G'nda Ké. "Even if that troop never got near Compostela, the news *will* inevitably have got there. Any rustic woodcutter or herb-gatherer taking his wares to the town's market must by now have mentioned having seen an armed and menacing force of Aztéca in the vicinity. That Governor Coronado may already be bringing his soldiers hither to forestall your planned insurgency by laying waste to Aztlan. You can no longer afford, Tenamáxtli, merely to afflict the Spaniards with random engagements—like this failed one and those of the Michihuácan women. Whether you are ready or not, whether you like it or not, *you are now at war.* Committed to wage war. Total war. You have no alternative but to lead your army into it.''

I said, ''It galls me to admit again that you are right, witch-woman. I wish I could deny you your greatest pleasure, that of seeing blood spilled and destruction widespread. However, what must be, must be. Go you, then, since you are the most war-eager of all in my court. Send word to every knight of Aztlan, to have our army assembled in the central square at tomorrow's dawn, armed and provisioned and ready to march.''

G'nda Ké smiled her vile smile and left the room in a hurry.

To Améyatl I said, ''I am not going to wait for the Speaking Council's assent to this deployment. You can summon them at your leisure, cousin, and inform them that a state of war now exists between the Aztéca and the Spaniards. The councillors can hardly countermand an action already taken.''

Améyatl nodded, but not joyfully.

''I will detach a number of good men to remain here as your palace guard,'' I went on. ''Not enough to repel an assault upon the city, but enough to rush *you* to safety in case danger threatens. Meanwhile, as regent, you again wield the authority of Uey-Tecútli—the Council knows that—until such time as I return.''

She said wistfully, ''The last time you left, you were gone for years.''

I said cheerfully—trying to cheer *her*—''Ayyo, Améyatl! On my return this time, whenever that may be, I hope it will

be to tell you that our Aztlan is the new Tenochtítlan, capital
of a One World rewon, restored, renewed, unshared by aliens. And that we two cousins are the absolute rulers of it.''

"Cousins . . .'' she murmured. "Time was, oc ye nechca,
we were more like brother and sister.''

I said lightly, "Rather more than *that,* if I may remind
you.''

"I need no reminding. I held you very dear, then, when
you were only a boy. Now you are a man, and a most manly
man. What will you be when you return again?''

"Not an *old* man, I trust. I should hope to be still capable
of . . . well . . . worthy of your holding me very dear.''

"I did and I do and I will. When that boy Tenamáxtli
departed from Aztlan, I gave him only a wave of farewell.
The man Tenamáxtzin deserves a more heartfelt and memorable leavetaking.'' She held out her arms. "Come . . . my
very dear . . .''

As in her youth, Améyatl still so gushingly personified the
meaning of her name—Fountain—that we repeatedly enjoyed our mutual surges, all the night long, and finally fell
asleep only when our juices were totally exhausted. I might
have overslept the appointed assembly of my army, except
that the uncouth G'nda Ké, never a respecter of privacy,
strode unbidden into my chambers and roughly shook me
awake.

Curling her lip at the sight of myself and Améyatl intertwined, she brayed loudly, "Behold! Behold the alert and
keen and vigilant and warlike leader of his people—wallow-
ing in lechery and sloth! *Can* you lead, my lord? Can you
even stand? It is time.''

"Go away,'' I grunted. "Go and sneer elsewhere. I will
steam and bathe and dress and be with the army when I am
ready. Go away.''

But the Yaki woman had to fling a rude insult at Améyatl
before departing:

"If you have drained Tenamáxtli of all his manhood, my

lustful lady, it will be your fault should we lose this war.''

Améyatl—having the grace and wit that G'nda Ké did not—only smiled with drowsy, happy satisfaction and said, ''I bear witness that Tenamáxtzin's manhood will stand *any* test.''

The Yaki gnashed her teeth and dashed angrily out of the room. I did my ablutions, donned my quilted armor and the quetzal-feather-fan headdress of command, then leaned to give a final kiss to Améyatl, still abed and still smiling.

''This time I will not wave good-bye,'' she said softly. ''I know you will return—and victorious. Only do try, for my sake, to hasten the day.''

To the gathered army, I announced, ''Comrades, it appears that Yeyac's despicable warriors have again betrayed us. They have either failed or disobeyed my order to sacrifice themselves in an attack on the Spaniards' stronghold. So we will make an assault in full force. However, it is likely that Compostela now is expecting us. For that reason, you knights and cuáchictin, pay heed to my instructions. During our first three days of going southward, we will march in standard column formation, to advance as rapidly as possible. On the fourth day, I will issue different orders. Now . . . *we go!*''

I rode, of course, at the head of the train, with the three other mounted men abreast behind me and, behind them, the warriors in a column of fours, all of us proceeding at a brisk walking pace. G'nda Ké trudged along at the tail of the procession, without arms or armor, for she was to do no fighting, but merely accompany us on our expedition—after the fighting—to recruit other warriors from other nations.

There exists a certain small tree-dwelling animal that we call the huitzlaiuáchi, the ''prickly little boar''—it is the *puerco espín* in Spanish—which is bristled all over with sharp spines instead of fur. No one knows why Mixcoatl, the god of hunters, created that particular animal, because its meat is distasteful to humans, and other predators sensibly stay clear of its unassailable coat of innumerable spikes. I mention it only because I imagine our marching army must have resembled the prickly little boar, but an immensely large and long one. Each warrior carried on one shoulder his long spear and, on the other, his shorter javelin and its atlatl throwing-stick, so the entire column was as bristly as the animal. But ours was much more brilliant and gaudy, for the sunlight glinted from the obsidian points of those weapons, and the column also flaunted the severally colored flags and standards and guidons of its separate contingents—and my own flamboyant headdress at the front. To any distant observer, we must indeed have looked impressive; I could only wish that there had been more of us.

Truth to tell, I *was* rather sleepy, after my night of frolicking with Améyatl, so, to keep myself awake by talking to somebody, I beckoned for Tícitl Ualíztli to move his horse forward and ride alongside me. He and I conversed on various topics, including the manner by which my cousin Yeyac had been slain.

"So the arcabuz kills by hurling a metal ball," he said, reflectively. "What sort of wound does that inflict, Tenamáxtzin? A blow? A penetration?"

"Oh, a penetration, I assure you. Much like that made by an arrow, but more forcefully and deeply."

The tícitl said, "I have known men to live, and even go on fighting, with an arrow in them. Or more than one arrow, providing that none has pierced a vital organ. And an arrow, of course, by its very nature, plugs its own puncture and stanches the bleeding to a considerable degree."

"The lead ball does not," I said. "Also, if an arrow-wounded man is quickly attended, a tícitl can pluck out the arrow in order to treat the injury. A ball would be almost impossible to extract."

"Still," said Ualíztli, "if that ball had not irreparably damaged some internal organ, the victim's only real danger would be of bleeding to death."

I said grimly, "I made sure of Yeyac's doing just that. As soon as his belly was punctured, I turned him facedown—

and kept him that way—so his life's blood would the more
quickly pour out.''

''Hmm,'' said the tícitl, and rode in silence for a bit, then
commented, ''I wish I had been called, when you brought
him to Aztlan, so I could have examined that wound. I daresay I shall have to attend many such in the days to come.''

Our column continued the three-day march always in formation, as I had commanded, for I wanted my warriors all
compact in case we should meet an enemy force coming
north from Compostela. But we encountered none, and never
even espied any enemy soldiers scouting the route. So, during that time, I had no cause to try concealing or dispersing
my men. And, when we camped each night, we made no
attempt to hide the light of the fires over which we cooked
our meals. Very good and nourishing and strengthening
meals they were, too, of game killed along the way by warriors assigned to that duty.

But I had estimated that, by the fourth morning, we *would*
be within sight of any sentinels Coronado might have posted
around his town. At dawn of that day, I summoned my
knights and cuáchictin to tell them:

''I expect us to be in charging distance of Compostela by
nightfall. But I do not intend to make a charge from this
direction, which the Spaniards would be most likely to anticipate. Nor do I intend to make our assault immediately.
We will circle around the town and assemble again on the
far southern side of it. So, from here onward, your forces are
to be divided in twain, one half to move well to the west of
this main trail, the other half well to the east. And each of
those halves is to be divided even further—into separate,
individual warriors, each making his way most cautiously
and silently southward. All standards are to be furled, spears
to be carried at the level, every man to take advantage of
trees, underbrush, cactus, whatever other cover serves to
make him as invisible as possible.''

I took off my own ostentatious headdress, folded it carefully and tucked it behind my saddle.

"Without the flags, my lord," said one knight, "how do we men afoot maintain contact with each other?"

I said, "I and these three other mounted men will continue openly, in full sight, along this trail. Atop these horses we will be guides conspicuous enough for the men to follow. And tell them this: The foremost among them is to stay at least a hundred paces behind me. Meanwhile, they need no contact with each other. The farther apart they are, the better. If one man comes upon a lurking Spanish scout, he is of course to kill that enemy, but quietly and unnoticeably. I want all of us to get close to Compostela without detection. However, if any of your men should encounter an enemy patrol or outpost that he cannot vanquish single-handed, *then* let him raise the war cry, and let the guidons be unfurled and let all your men—but *only* on that side of the trail—rally to that signal. The men on the other side are to go on silently and furtively, as before."

"But, scattered as we will be," said another knight, "is it not equally possible that Spaniards waiting in hiding can pick *us* off, one by one?"

"No," I said flatly. "No white man will ever be able to move as noiselessly and invisibly as can we who were born to this land. And no Spanish soldier, encumbered with metal and leather, can even patiently sit *still* without making some inadvertent sound or movement."

"The Uey-Tecútli speaks truly," said G'nda Ké, who had elbowed her way into the group and, as usual, had to interpose a comment, however unnecessary. "G'nda Ké is acquainted with Spanish soldiers. Even a shuffling, stumbling cripple could steal upon them unawares."

"Now," I went on, "assuming that we are *not* interrupted by any hand-to-hand fighting or discovered by any uproar or impeded by any superior force, both halves of the troop are to keep going southward, guiding on me. When I judge that the time is right, I will turn my horse westward, toward where the sun will then be setting—because I would like to have Tonatíu's favor shining upon me as long as possible.

The warriors on that western side of the trail will continue to follow me—a hundred paces behind—and trust me to lead them safely around the outside of the town.''

''G'nda Ké will be right behind them,'' she said complacently.

I threw her a glance of exasperation. ''At the same time, the Cúachic Comitl will turn his horse eastward, and the men on that side of the trail are to follow *him*. Sometime late in the night, both halves of our forces should be south of the city. I will send messengers to make contact between the two and arrange for our reassembly. Am I understood?''

The officers all made the gesture of tlalqualíztli, then went to pass on my orders to their men. In a very little while, the warriors had almost magically—like the morning's dew—vanished into the brush and trees, and the trail behind was empty. Only Ualíztli, Nochéztli, the Mexícatl Comitl and I still sat our mounts there in full view.

''Nochéztli,'' I said, ''you will take the point. Ride on ahead, still at the walk. We three will not follow until you are out of sight. Keep going until you espy *any* sign of the enemy. Even if they have put out guards or barricades far to this side of the town and they see you before you can avoid them, they will not be expecting just *one* attacker. Also, they may well recognize you and be perplexed by your approach—especially since you come like a Spaniard, astride a horse. Their hesitation should give you chance enough to get away unharmed. Anyway, if and when you do sight the enemy—in force or otherwise—turn straight about and hurry back to me with the report.''

He asked, ''And if I see nothing at all, my lord?''

''Should you be gone too long, and I decide the time has come for division of our men, I will loudly give the owl-hoot call. If you hear that—and are not dead or captured—race back to join us.''

''Yes, my lord. I am gone.'' And he was.

When he was no longer visible, the tícitl, Comitl and I put our own horses to the walk. The sun crossed the sky at about the same slow pace, and the three of us passed that long, anxious day in desultory conversation. It was late in the afternoon when at last we saw Nochéztli coming back toward us, and he was hardly hurrying—moving only at an easy trot, though I doubt that it felt very easy to his backside.

"What is this?" I demanded, as soon as he was within hearing. "Nothing *whatever* to report?"

"Ayya, yes, my lord, but most curious news. I rode all the way to the town's outlying slave quarter, without ever being challenged. And there I found the defenses I long ago told you about—the gigantic thunder-tubes on wheels, and with soldiers all about them. But those thunder-tubes are still aimed *inward*, toward the town itself! And the soldiers gave me only a casual wave of greeting. So I made gestures to indicate that I had found this unsaddled horse wandering loose in the vicinity, and that I was trying to find its proper owner, and then I turned and came back this way—not in haste, for I had heard no owl hoot."

The Cuáchic Comitl frowned and asked me, "What do you make of this, Tenamáxtzin? Is this man's report to be believed? Remember, he was once in league with that enemy."

Nochéztli protested, "I kiss the earth to the truth of it!" and made the tlalqualíztli—as well as he could, sitting atop a horse.

"I believe you," I said to him, and then to Comitl, "Nochéztli has several times before now proved himself loyal to me. However, the situation is curious indeed. It is possible that the Arrow Knight Tapachíni and his men never came to warn Compostela at all. But it is just as possible that the Spaniards are laying some cunning trap. If so, we are still clear of it. Let us proceed as planned. I and Ualíztli will now turn westward. You and Nochéztli go east. The men afoot will separately follow us. We will circle wide around the town and meet again well south of it, sometime after dark."

At this place on the trail, there was fairly thick forest to either side, and when the tícitl and I rode into it, we found

ourselves in a gradually deepening twilight. I was hoping that
the warriors a hundred paces behind us could still see us,
and worrying that I might outdistance them when the dark
really came down. But that worry was suddenly, shockingly
driven from my mind—when I heard a loud and familiar
noise from somewhere back of us.

"That was an arcabuz!" I gasped, and Ualíztli and I both
reined our horses to a halt.

The words were scarcely spoken when there came a pos-
itive clamor of arcabuces being discharged—singly, severally, randomly, or a good number of them simultaneously—
and all of them somewhere to our rear. But not far to our
rear; the evening breeze brought me the acrid smell of their
pólvora smoke.

"But how could we all have missed seeing—?" I started
to say. Then I remembered something, and I realized what
was happening. I remembered that Spanish soldier-fowler on
the shore of Lake Texcóco, and how he discharged a whole
battery of his arcabuces by yanking on a string.

These I was hearing now did not even have Spaniards
holding them. They had been fastened to the ground or to
trees, and a string tautly stretched from each of their gatillos
through the underbrush. My horse and Ualíztli's had not so
far touched any string, but the warriors behind us were trip-
ping against them, thus raking their own ranks with lethal
flying lead balls.

"Do not move!" I said to the tícitl.

But he objected, "There will be wounded to attend!" and
started to rein his horse around.

Well, it would eventually turn out that I had miscalculated
regarding more things than just the ingenuity of the defenders
of Compostela. But I had been right about one thing: The
people of my own race could move as soundlessly as shad-
ows and as invisibly as wind. The next moment, a terrific
blow to my ribs knocked me clear off my saddle. As I thud-
ded to the ground, I barely glimpsed a man in Aztéca armor,
wielding a maquáhuitl, before he struck me again—using the

wooden flat of the sword, not the obsidian edge—in the head, this time, and all the world around me went black.

When I came awake, I was seated on the ground, my back propped against a tree. My head was throbbing abominably and my vision was fogged. I blinked to clear it, and when I saw the man standing before me—leaning on his maquáhuitl, waiting patiently for me to regain consciousness—I involuntarily moaned:

"By all the gods! I have died and gone to Míctlan!"

"Not yet, cousin," said Yeyac. "But be assured that you will."

XXI

Wʜᴇɴ ɪ ᴛʀɪᴇᴅ to move, I discovered that I was securely roped to the tree, and so was Ualíztli, beside me. Evidently he had not been so emphatically unhorsed, for he was well awake and cursing under his breath. Still dazed, slurring my words, I asked him:

"Tícitl, tell me. Is it possible that this man, once killed, could have come back to life?"

"In this case, clearly, yes," the physician said morosely. "The possibility had earlier occurred to me, when you told me that you had kept him lying facedown, so his blood would the more copiously drain out of him. What that in fact accomplished was to allow the blood to *clot* at the entry site of the wound. If no vital organs had been mangled, and if the seeming corpse was whisked away by his friends, quickly enough, any competent tícitl could have healed him. Believe me, Tenamáxtzin, it was not I who did it. But, yya ayya ouíya, you should have kept him face *up*."

Yeyac, who had listened to this exchange with wry amusement, now said, "I was worried, cousin, that *you* might have caught one of those lead balls from the ambuscade that my good Spanish allies so craftily arranged. When one of my íyactin came to tell me that he had taken you alive, I was so very pleased that I knighted the man on the spot."

As my addled wits began to clear somewhat, I growled, "You have no authority to knight anyone at all."

"Have I not? Why, cousin, you even brought me the quetzal-feather headdress. I am again the Uey-Tecútli of Aztlan."

"Then why would you want me alive, able to contest that gross assumption?"

"I am merely obliging my confederate, the Governor Coronado. It is he who wants you alive. For a short time, at least, so he can ask you certain questions. After that . . . well . . . he has promised you to me. I leave the rest to your imagination."

Not being overeager to dwell on that, I asked, "How many of my men *are* dead?"

"I have no idea. I do not care. All those who survived certainly scattered in a hurry. They are no longer a fighting force. Now, apart and in the darkness, they are doubtless wandering far and wide—lost, unnerved, disconsolate—like the Weeping Woman Chicocíuatl and the other aimless ghosts of the night. Come daylight, the Spanish soldiers should have little difficulty subduing them, one by one. Coronado will be pleased to have such strong men to slave in his silver mines. And, ayyo, here comes a squad to escort *you* to the governor's palace."

The soldiers loosed me from the tree, but kept my arms tightly bound as they led me out of the woods and down the trail to Compostela. Yeyac followed, with Ualíztli, and where they went I did not see. I was penned overnight in a cell room of the palace, unfed and unwatered but well guarded, and not brought before the governor until sometime the next morning.

Francisco Vásquez de Coronado was, as I had been told, a man no older than myself, and he was—for a white man— of goodly appearance, neatly bearded, even clean-looking. My guards untied me, but stayed in the room. And there was another soldier present, who, it became apparent, spoke Náhuatl and was to serve as interpreter.

Coronado addressed him at length—of course I understood every word—and the soldier repeated to me, in my native tongue:

"His Excellency says that you and another warrior were carrying thunder-sticks when you were captured and the other was killed. One of the weapons was obviously the property of the Royal Spanish Army. The other was obviously a handmade imitation. His Excellency wants to know who made that copy, and where, and how many have been made and how many *are* being made. Tell also whence came the pólvora for them."

I said, "Nino ixnéntla yanquic in tláui pocuíahuíme. Ayquic."

"The indio says, Your Excellency, that he knows nothing about arcabuces. And never has."

Coronado drew the sword sheathed at his waist, and said calmly, "Tell him that you will ask again. Each time he pleads ignorance, he will lose a finger. Ask him how many fingers he can spare before he gives a satisfactory answer."

The interpreter repeated that in Náhuatl, and asked the same questions again.

I tried to look properly intimidated, and spoke haltingly, "Ce nechca . . ." but I was temporizing, of course. "One time . . . I was traveling in the Disputed Lands . . . and I came upon a guard post. The sentinel was fast asleep. I stole his thunder-stick. I have saved it ever since."

The interpreter sneered. "Did that sleeping soldier teach you how to use it?"

Now I tried to look stupid. "No, he did not. He could not. Because he was sleeping, you see. I know one squeezes the little thing called a gatillo. But I never had the chance. I was captured before—"

"Did that sleeping soldier also show you all the inner parts and workings of his thunder-stick, so that even you primitive savages could make a replica of it?"

I insisted, "Of that I know nothing. The replica you speak of—you must ask the warrior who carried it."

The interpreter snapped, "You have already been told! That man was killed. Struck by one of the balls of the trip-string trap. But he must have thought he was facing actual soldiers. As he fell, he discharged his own thunder-stick at them. *He* knew well enough how to use one!"

What I had said, and what he had said, the interpreter again relayed in Spanish to the governor. I was thinking: *Good man, Comitl, a true Mexícatl "old eagle" to the last. You are by now enjoying the bliss of Tonatíucan.* But then I had to start thinking about my own predicament, for Coronado was glaring at me and saying:

"If his comrade was so dexterous with an arcabuz, so must he be. Tell the damned redskin this. If he does not instantly confess to me everything he—"

But the governor was interrupted. Three other people had just entered the room, and one of them said, in some astonishment:

"Your Excellency, why do you bother employing an interpreter? That indio is as fluent in Castilian as I am myself."

"What?" said Coronado, confounded. "How do you know that? How could you *possibly* know?"

Fray Marcos de Niza simpered smugly. "We white men like to say that we cannot tell the damned redskins apart. But that one—I noticed when I first saw him—is exceptionally tall for his race. Also, at that time, he was wearing Spanish attire and riding an army horse, so I had further reason to remember him. It happened while I was accompanying Cabeza de Vaca to the City of Mexíco. The teniente in charge of the escort let this man pass the night in our camp, because—"

Now it was Coronado who interrupted. "This is all exceedingly puzzling, but save your explanation for later, Fray Marcos. Right now, there is more urgent information I require. And by the time I have whittled it out of this prisoner, I think he will no longer be so tall."

The interpreter was again required, because now spoke up the other man who had entered with the Lying Monk, my loathsome cousin Yeyac. He had few words of Spanish, but evidently he had caught the tenor of Coronado's remark. Yeyac protested in Náhuatl, and the interpreter translated:

"Your Excellency holds a naked sword and speaks of paring pieces off this person. I can tell you that a flake of obsidian is keener than steel, and can pare even more artfully. I may not have told Your Excellency that I carry inside me a thunder-stick ball put there by this person. But I remind Your Excellency that you promised the chipping and mincing of him to *me*."

"Yes, yes, very well," Coronado said testily, and slammed his sword back into its scabbard. "Produce your damned obsidian. I will ask the questions and *you* can hack away at him when his answers are unsatisfactory."

But now it was Fray Marcos who protested. "Your Excellency, when first I met this man he claimed to be an emissary of Bishop Zumárraga. Furthermore, he introduced himself as Juan Británico. Whether or not he has ever been anywhere near the bishop, he has incontrovertibly been baptized at some time, and given a Christian name. Ergo, he is at the least an apostate and more likely a heretic. It follows that he is primarily subject to ecclesiastic jurisdiction. I myself would be happy to try him, convict him and condemn him to the stake."

I was already beginning to sweat, and I had yet to hear anything from the third person who had entered with Yeyac and the Lying Monk. That was the Yaki woman, G'nda Ké, and I was not surprised to see her in that company. It was inevitable that having survived the ambush—or having known of it in advance—she would now have given her allegiance to the victors.

The soldier-interpreter was looking quite giddy from having to turn from person to person while he translated all the foregoing conversations to the various participants. What G'nda Ké now said, and said most oilily, he translated into Spanish:

"Good friar, this Juan Británico may be a traitor to your

Holy Mother Church. But, Your Excellency Coronado, he
has been much more a traitor to *your* domain. I can aver that
he is responsible for the numerous attacks—by persons unknown and so far unapprehended—all over New Galicia.
Were this man to be tortured properly and lingeringly, he
could enable Your Excellency to end those attacks. That
would seem, to me, to take precedence over the friar's intent
to send him straight to the Christian hell. And in that inter-
rogation I would be pleased to assist your loyal ally, Yéyactzin, for I have had much practice in the art.''

''¡*Perdición!*'' shouted Coronado, irritated beyond measure. ''This prisoner has so many claimants on his flesh and
his life and even his soul that I almost feel sorry for the
wretch!'' He turned his glare again on me and demanded, in
Spanish, ''Wretch, you are the only one in this room who
has not yet suggested how I should deal with you. Surely
you have some ideas on the subject. Speak!''

''Señor Gobernador,'' I said—I would not concede him
any excellency—''I am a prisoner of war, and a noble of the
Aztéca nation that is at war with yours. Exactly as were the
Mexíca nobles dethroned and overthrown by your Marqués
Cortés so many years ago. The marqués was and is no weak
man, but he found it compatible with his conscience to treat
those earlier defeated nobles in a civilized manner. I would
ask no more than that.''

''There!'' Coronado said to the three latest arrivals. ''That
is the first reasonable speech I have heard during all this
turbulent confabulation.'' He came back to me to ask, but
not menacingly, ''Will you tell me the source and the number
of the replica arcabuces? Will you tell me who are the in-
surgents beleaguering our settlements south of here?''

''No, Señor Gobernador. In all the conflicts among our
nations of this One World—and I believe in all that your
own Spain has fought with other peoples—no prisoner of
war was ever expected by his captors to betray his comrades.
Certainly *I* will not, even if I am interrogated by that hen-
vulture yonder, so boastful of her scavenger skills.''

The scathing glance that Coronado gave G'nda Ké indicated, I was sure, that he shared my opinion of her. Perhaps he really *had* begun to feel some sympathy for me, because when G'nda Ké, the friar and Yeyac all began indignantly speaking at once, he silenced them with a peremptory slash of his hand, then said:

"Guards, take the prisoner back to his cell, unbound. Give him food and water to keep him alive. I will ponder on this matter before I question him again. The rest of you, begone! Now!"

My cell had a stout door, barred on the outside, where my two guards were posted. In the opposite wall was a single window, unbarred, but too small for anything larger than a rabbit to wriggle through. It was not, however, too small for communication with a person outdoors. And, sometime after nightfall, there did come someone to that window.

"¡Oye!" said a voice, barely loud enough for me to hear, and I arose from the straw that was my bedding.

I looked out, and at first could see nothing but darkness. Then the visitor grinned and I saw white teeth, and realized that I was being visited by a man as black as the night outside, the Moro slave Estebanico. I greeted him warmly, but also in a low murmur.

He said, "I told you, Juan Británico, that I would be always in your debt. You must know by now that I *am*—as you foretold—appointed to guide the Lying Monk to those nonexistent cities of riches. So I owe you whatever help or comfort I can give."

"Thank you, Esteban," I said. "I would be most comfortable if I were at liberty. Could you somehow draw off the guards and unbar my door?"

"That, I fear, is beyond my ability. Spanish soldiers do not pay much heed to a black man. Also—forgive me for sounding selfish—I value my *own* liberty. I will try to think of some means of effecting your escape that would not put me in your place. In the meantime, word has just come from a Spanish patrol that may be cheering to you. It assuredly is not cheering to the Spaniards."

"Good. Tell me."

"Well, some of your slain or wounded warriors were found immediately after the ambush that cut them down last night. But the governor waited until this morning to send a full patrol combing that entire area. Of additional dead or incapacitated warriors, they came upon comparatively few. Clearly, most of your men survived and got away. And one of those fugitives—a man on a horse—boldly let himself be seen by the patrol. When they returned here, they described him. The two indios now in league with Coronado—Yeyac and that awful woman G'nda Ké—seemed to recognize the man described. They spoke a name. Nochéztli. Does that mean anything to you?"

"Yes," I said. "One of my best warriors."

"Yeyac seemed oddly disturbed to learn that this Nochéztli is one of yours, but he made little comment, because we were all in the presence of the governor and his interpreter. However, the woman laughed scornfully and called Nochéztli an unmanly cuilóntli. What does that word mean, amigo?"

"Never mind. Go on, Esteban."

"She told Coronado that such an unmanly man, even armed and at large, would be no danger. But later news proved her wrong."

"How so?"

"Your Nochéztli not only escaped the ambush, he apparently was among the few not terrified and panicked and sent fleeing. One of your wounded who was brought here has proudly related what happened next. The man Nochéztli, sitting his horse alone in the darkness and smoke, shouted curses at the others for running away, and insulted them as weakling cowards, and bellowed for them to regroup on his position."

"He does have a compelling voice," I said.

"Evidently he rallied all your remaining warriors, and has removed them somewhere into hiding. Yeyac told the governor they would number high in the hundreds.''

"About nine hundred, originally," I said. "There must be nearly that many still with Nochéztli."

"Coronado is reluctant to try chasing them down. His whole force here amounts to not many more than a thousand men, even including those Yeyac contributed. The governor would have to send them all, and leave Compostela undefended. For the moment, he has only taken the precaution of turning all the town's *artillería*—what you call the thunder-tubes—outward again."

I said, "I do not think Nochéztli would mount another assault without instructions from me. And I doubt that he knows what has become of me."

"He is a resourceful man," said Esteban. "He removed more than your army from the reach of the Spaniards."

"What do you mean?"

"The patrol that went out this morning—one of their tasks was to fetch back all the arcabuces that had been fixed in place and strung to be tripped by your warriors. The patrol returned without them. Before he disappeared, it seems, your Nochéztli had them all collected and carried with him. From what I hear, between thirty and forty of those weapons."

I could not help exclaiming jubilantly, "*Yyo ayyo!* We are armed! Praise be to the war god Huitzilopóchtli!"

I should not have done that. Next instant, there was a grating sound as my cell door was unbarred. The door swung open and one of the guards peered suspiciously into the gloom—by which time I was again sprawled on my straw and Esteban had gone.

"What was that noise?" demanded the guard. "Fool, are you shouting for help? You will get none."

I said loftily, "I was singing, señor. Chanting to the glory of my gods."

"God help your gods," he growled. "You have a damnably disagreeable singing voice," and he slammed the door on me again.

I sat there in the dark and pondered. I was now aware of

another misjudgment I had made, not recently but a long while ago. Influenced by my distaste for the odious Yeyac and his male intimates, I had deemed all cuilóntin to be malevolently rancorous and spiteful until—when challenged by a real man—they turned as servile and cowering as the meekest of women. Nochéztli had cured me of that misapprehension. Obviously, cuilóntin were as various in nature as any other men, for the cuilóntli Nochéztli had acted with manliness and valor and capability worthy of a true hero. If I ever saw him again, I would make plain my respect and my admiration of him.

"I *must* see him again," I muttered to myself.

Nochéztli had, in one swift and daring swoop, armed a good portion of my forces with weapons equal to the white men's. But those arcabuces were useless without ample supplies of pólvora and lead. Unless my army could storm and plunder Compostela's own armory—not a very likely prospect—the lead would have to be found and the pólvora would have to be made. I was the only man of us who knew how to compound the powder, and I now cursed myself for never having imparted that knowledge to Nochéztli or some other of my under-officers.

"I *have* to get away from here," I muttered.

I had one friend here in the town, and he had said he would *try* to conceive some plan for my escape. But besides the understandably inimical Spaniards, I had also many foes in this town—the vindictive Yeyac, the sanctimonious Lying Monk, the ever-evil G'nda Ké. Surely it would not be long before the governor again had me brought to face him—or to face them all—and I could hardly hope for rescue by Esteban in so short a time.

Still, I reminded myself, a summons from Coronado would at least get me out of this cell. Could I perhaps, on my way to him, elude my guards and make a dash for freedom? My own palace at Aztlan had so many rooms and alcoves and niches that the dodging of pursuers and slipping into concealment would not be impossible for a fugitive as desperate as myself. But Coronado's palace was not nearly so big nor so grand as mine. I mentally reviewed the route along which the guards had twice now led me between this cell and the throne room—if that was what it was called—where the governor had questioned me. My cell was one of four at this far end of the building; I knew not whether the others were occupied. And beyond, there was a long corridor . . . then a flight of stairs . . . another corridor . . .

I could recall no place where I might break away, no accessible window through which I might lunge. And once in the governor's presence, I would be quite surrounded. Afterward, if I was not summarily executed right in front of him, there was every probability that I would not be led back to this cell, but to some kind of torture chamber or even the burning stake. Well, I thought dolefully, I would have to be burned *outdoors*. Conceivably, on the way there . . .

But that thought provided wan hope, indeed. I was trying to fend off black despair, and reconcile myself to the worst, when suddenly I heard: "Oye."

It was Esteban's murmur again at my tiny window. I bounded to my feet and peered again at darkness that was again split by a white-toothed grin, as he said, softly but jauntily, "I have an idea, Juan Británico."

When he told it to me, I realized that he had been thinking much as I had been, only—I must say—with a great deal more optimism. What he proposed was so reckless as to verge on madness, but he *had* had an idea, and I had not.

The guards bound my arms before they escorted me to my next confrontation with the governor, the following morning, but at his dismissive gesture, they untied me and stood aside. Besides several other soldiers, G'nda Ké and Fray Marcos and his guide Esteban were also in the room, and they ambled about it as freely as if they were Coronado's equals.

To me, the governor said, "I have excused Yeyac from attendance at this conference because, frankly, I detest the duplicitous *hijoputa*. However, from our previous interview,

Juan Británico, I take you to be an honorable and forthright
man. Therefore, I here and now offer you the same pact that
my predecessor, Governor Guzmán, made with that Yeyac.
You will be set free, as will also the other horseman captured
alive with you.''

He gestured again, and a soldier brought in from some
other room Ualíztli the tícitl, looking grumpy and disheveled,
but not impaired in any way. This put a small complication
into the projected plan of escape, but not, I thought, an in-
superable one, and I was pleased that I might be able to take
Ualíztli with me. I motioned for him to come and stand beside me, and I waited to hear the rest of the governor's so-
called offer.

He said, ''You will be allowed to return to that place
called Aztlan, and resume your rule there. I guarantee that
not Yeyac nor any of his cohort will contest your suprem-
acy—if I have to kill the damned *maricón* to make sure of
it. You and your people will retain your traditional domains
and live there in peace, untroubled by invasion or conquest
by mine. In time, you Aztecs and we Spaniards may find it
profitable to engage in trade and other intercourse, but nothing of that sort will be forced upon you.''

He paused and waited, but I stood silent, so he went on:

''In reciprocation, *you* will guarantee not to lead or incite
any further rebellion against New Galicia, New Spain or any
other of His Majesty's lands and subjects here in the New
World. You will send word to those insurgent bands in the
south to cease their depredations. And you will swear to ward
off, as Yeyac did, any incursions of those pestiferous indios
to the north, in the Tierra de Guerra. So, what say you, Juan
Británico? Agreed?''

I said, ''I thank you, Señor Gobernador, for your flattering
estimate of my character and for your trust that I would keep
my given word. I take you, too, to be an honorable man. For
that reason, I would not disrespect you and disgrace myself
by giving my word and then breaking it. You must be fully
aware that what you offer me and my people is nothing but

what we have always had, and will fight to keep. We *Aztecs* have declared war against you and every other white man. Strike me dead this moment, señor, and some other Aztec will arise to lead our warriors in that war. I respectfully decline the pact you offer.''

Coronado's face had been darkening during my speech, and I am sure he was about to reply in wrath and malediction. But just then, Esteban, who had all this while been sauntering idly about the room, came within my reach.

I flung an arm around his neck, hauled him tight against me and, with my free hand, plucked from his waist belt the steel knife sheathed there. Esteban made an apparently strenuous effort to struggle loose, but desisted when I laid the knife blade across his bare throat. Ualíztli, at my side, regarded me with astonishment.

''Soldiers!'' screeched G'nda Ké from across the room. ''Take aim! Slay that man!'' She was ranting in Náhuatl, but no one could have mistaken what she meant. *''Slay them both!''*

''No!'' cried Fray Marcos and *''Hold!''* bellowed Coronado, exactly as Esteban had predicted they would. The soldiers, already having raised their arcabuces or drawn their swords, stood perplexed, making no other move.

''No?'' bawled G'nda Ké in disbelief. ''Not kill them? What kind of timid women *are* you white fools?'' She would have gone on with her incomprehensible tirade, but the friar desperately outshouted her:

''Please, Your Excellency! The guards must not take the risk of—''

''I know it, you imbecile! Shut your mouth! And strangle that howling bitch!''

I was slowly backing toward the door, seemingly dragging the helpless black man, and Ualíztli was right with us. Esteban was turning his head from side to side, as if looking for help, his eyes fearfully bulging so that they showed white all around. The movement of his head was deliberate, to cause my blade to cut his throat skin slightly, so that everyone could see a trickle of blood run down his neck.

"Ground your arms, men!" Coronado commanded the soldiers, who were alternately gaping at him and at our slow, wary progress. "Stand as you are. No firing, no swordplay. I had rather lose both the prisoners than that single miserable Moro."

I called to him, "Tell one of them, señor, to run outside before us, and loudly to inform every soldier in the vicinity. We are not to be molested or impeded. When we are safely gone beyond the town, I will release your precious Moro unharmed. You *do* have my word on that."

"Yes," said Coronado, through gritted teeth. He motioned to a soldier near the door. "Go, *Sargento*. Do as he says."

Circling well clear of us, the soldier scuttled out the door. Ualíztli and I and the limp, goggle-eyed Esteban were not far behind. No one pursued us as we followed that soldier along a short hall I had not been in before, and down a flight of stairs, and out through the palace's street door. The soldier was already shouting as we three emerged. And there, at a hitching rack, as Esteban had arranged, a saddled horse was waiting for us.

I said, "Tícitl Ualíztli, you will have to run alongside. I am sorry, but I had not counted on your company. I will hold the horse to a walk."

"No, by Huitztli, go at a gallop!" the physician exclaimed. "Old and stout though I am, I am eager enough to be out of here that I will move like the wind!"

"In the name of God," growled Esteban, under his breath. "Cease your gibbering and *move!* Fling me across the saddle and leap up behind and *go!*"

As I heaved him atop the horse—actually, he bounded and I only seemed to impel him—our herald-soldier was crying commands to everyone within hearing, "Make way! Safe passage!" All the other people in the street, soldiers and citizens alike, were gawking numbly at this remarkable spectacle. Not until I was seated behind the saddle's cantle, now holding Esteban's knife ostentatiously pointed at his kidneys, did I realize that I had neglected to unhitch the horse from the rail. So Ualíztli had to do that, and handed the reins up to me. Then, true to his word, the tícitl waddled off at a speed commendable in one of his age and girth, enabling me to put the horse to a trot beside him.

When we were out of sight of the palace, and out of hearing of that soldier's shouts, Esteban—though being jounced while hanging uncomfortably head down—began giving me directions. Turn right at the next street, left at the next and so on, until we were beyond the city's center and out in one of the mean quarters where the slaves lived. Not many of those were about—most were doing slave work somewhere at this hour—and the few we saw took care to avert their eyes. They probably supposed us—two indios and a Moro— to be slaves also, employing a truly unique mode of escape, and wanted to be able to say, should they be questioned, that they had seen nothing of us.

When we reached Compostela's outskirts, where even the slave shacks were few and far apart and no one at all was in sight, Esteban said, "Stop here." He and I clambered down from the horse and the tícitl collapsed full length on the ground, panting and sweating. While Esteban and I rubbed the sore places on our bodies—he his stomach and I my rump—he said:

"This is as far as I can play hostage to your safety, Juan Británico. There will be Spanish outposts beyond, and they will not have got the word to let us pass. So you and your companion will somehow have to make your own way, on foot, and stealthily. I can only wish you good fortune."

"Which we have had thus far, thanks to you, amigo. I trust that fortune will not desert us now, when we are so near to freedom."

"Coronado will not order a pursuit until he has me back in one piece. As I told you, and as events have proved, the ambitious governor and the avaricious friar *dare* not endanger my black hide. So—" He climbed stiffly back onto the saddle, right side up this time. "Hand me the knife." I did, and he used it to rip his clothes in several places, and even to nick his skin here and there, just enough to draw blood, then gave the knife back to me.

"Now," he said, "use the reins to tie my hands tight to the saddle pommel here. To give you as much of a running start as I can, I will plod only slowly back to the palace. I can plead weakness from having been cruelly cut and beaten by you savages. Be glad that I am black; no one will notice that I am *not* bruised all over. More than that I cannot do for you, Juan Británico. As soon as I get to the palace, Coronado will fan out his whole army to look for you, turning over every least pebble. You *must* be far, far from here by then."

"We will be," I said. "Either safely deep in our native forests or securely deep in that dark place you Christians call hell. We thank you for your kind help, for your bold imagination and for your putting yourself at hazard on our behalf. Go you, amigo Esteban, and I wish you joy in your own freedom soon to be realized."

XXII

"**W**HAT DO WE do now, Tenamáxtzin?" asked Ual-íztli, who had recovered his breath and was sitting up.

"As the Moro said, there has not been time for the governor to have sent word to his guard posts, to let us—if we still held our hostage—pass unhindered. Therefore, neither will they have been alerted to expect us at all. They will, as usual, be looking outward, for enemies trying to enter the town, not leave it. Just follow me, and do as I do."

We walked upright until we were past the last shanties of the slave quarter, then we stooped over and went very, very cautiously farther out from the town until I espied, at a distance, a shack with soldiers around it, none of them looking our way. We went no nearer to that, but turned left and kept on until we saw another such shack and soldiers, these standing around one of those thunder-tubes, the kind called a culebrina. So we turned back and retraced our path until we were about midway between those guard posts. Happily for us, at that spot a dense underbrush stretched away toward a tree line on the horizon. Still stooping, duck-walking, I led the way into those bushes, staying below the tops of them, trying not to shake any of them, and the tícitl—though again panting heavily—did likewise. It seemed to me that we had to endure that awkward, cramped, excruciating, slow progress for countless one-long-runs—and I know it was far more fatiguing and painful for Ualíztli—but we did, at long last, reach the line of trees. Once within them, I gratefully stretched erect—all my joints creaking—and the tícitl again sprawled full length on the ground, groaning.

I lay down nearby and we both rested for a luxurious while. When Ualíztli had regained breath enough to speak, but not yet strength enough to stand, he said:

"Would you tell me, Tenamáxtzin, *why* did the white men let us leave? Surely not just because we took with us one of their black slaves. A slave of any color is as expendable as spittle."

"They believe that particular slave holds the secret to a fabulous treasure. They are foolish to think so—but I will explain all that another time. Right now, I am trying to think of some way to find the Cúachic Nochéztli and the rest of our army."

Ualíztli sat up and gave me a worried look. "You must be still unsettled of mind, from that blow to your head. If all our men were not slain by the thunder-sticks, they are bound to have scattered and fled far from this place by now."

"They were not and they did not. And I am not deranged. Please stop talking physician's talk, and let me think." I glanced upward; Tonatíu was already slipping down the sky. "We are again north of Compostela, so we cannot be too far from where we were ambushed. Would Nochéztli have kept the warriors assembled hereabouts? Or led them south of the town, as originally intended? Or even started them back to Aztlan? What *would* he have done, not knowing what had become of me?"

The tícitl considerately refrained from comment.

"We cannot simply go wandering about in search of them," I went on. "Nochéztli must find *us*. I can think of nothing but to make a signal of some sort, and hope it attracts him hither."

The tícitl could not keep silent for long. "Best hope it

does *not* attract the Spanish patrols that are certain to be looking for us very soon.''

''It would be the last thing they would expect,'' I said. ''That we would deliberately call attention to our hiding place. But if our own men *are* anywhere about, they must be near frenzied for some news of their leader. Anything out of the ordinary ought to draw at least a scout. A big fire should do it. Thanks be to the earth goddess Coatlícue, there are many pines among these trees, and the ground is thick with dry needles.''

''Now call on the god Tlaloc to strike the needles alight with a fork of his lightning,'' Ualíztli said wryly. ''I see no usable embers glowing anywhere here. I had combustible liquids in my physician's sack that could be easily ignited, but that sack was taken from me. It will take us all night to find and fashion and use a drill and block.''

''No need for that, nor for Tlaloc,'' I said. ''Tonatíu will help us before he sets.'' I felt around inside the quilted armor I still wore. ''My weapons were taken, too, but the Spaniards evidently did not think this worth confiscating.'' I brought out the lente, the crystal given me so long ago by Alonso de Molina.

''Neither would I think it worth anything,'' said Ualíztli. ''What earthly use is a little blob of quartz?''

I said only, ''Watch,'' and got up and moved to where a stray sunbeam came down through the trees to the ground's litter of brown needles. Ualíztli's eyes widened when, after only a moment, a wisp of smoke rose from there, then a flicker of flame. A moment more, and I had to jump back away from what was becoming a very respectable blaze indeed.

''How did you do that?'' the tícitl asked, marveling. ''Where did you get such a sorcerous thing?''

''A gift from father to son,'' I said, smiling in reminiscence. ''Blessed with the help of Tonatíu and of a father in Tonatíucan, I believe I can do just about anything. Except sing, I suppose.''

"What?"

"The guard of my cell at the palace disparaged my singing voice."

Ualíztli again gave me the probing look of a physician. "Are you *sure*, my lord, that you are not still affected by that blow to your head?"

I laughed at him, and turned to admire my fire. As it spread among the ground needles, it was not very visible, but now it was igniting the resin-full green needles of the pines above, and so was sending up a plume of smoke that rapidly got higher, denser and darker.

"That should fetch *somebody*," I said with satisfaction.

"I suggest that we move back among the bushes we came through," said the tícitl. "We can perhaps get an early warning glimpse of *who* comes. And whoever it is will not find us just a pair of roasted cadavers."

We did that, and crouched out there, and watched the fire eat through the grove, sending up a smoke to rival that which always hangs above the great volcano Popocatépetl outside Tenochtítlan. Time passed, and the lowering sun turned the high smoke cloud a ruddy gold in color, an even more conspicuous signal against the sky's deepening blue. More time passed, before finally we heard a rustling in the bushes around us. We had not been talking, but when Ualíztli gave me a questioning look, I held a cautionary finger to my lips, then raised slowly up to see over the bushes' tops.

Well, they were not Spaniards, but I could almost have wished they were. The men surrounding our hiding place were armor-clad Aztéca, prominent among them the Arrow Knight Tapachíni—these were Yeyac's warriors. One of them, cursedly keen-eyed, saw me before I could crouch down again, and gave the owl-hoot cry. The circle of them closed in upon us, and Ualíztli and I resignedly stood erect. The warriors stopped at a distance from us, but ringed us completely about, so that we were the center and aim of all their leveled spears and javelins.

Yeyac himself now elbowed through the circle and came

closer to us. He was not alone; G'nda Ké came with him; both were smirking triumphantly.

"So, cousin, we are face-to-face again," he said. "But this will be the last time. Coronado may have been reluctant to raise the alarm at your escape, but the good G'nda Ké was not. She ran immediately to tell me. Then I and my men had only to wait and watch. Now, cousin, let us escort you well away from here, before the Spaniards do come. I want privacy and ample leisure in which to do the slow slaying of you."

He motioned for the warriors to close in upon us. But before they could converge, a single one of them stepped forward from the circle, the only warrior bearing an arcabuz.

"I killed you once before, Yeyac," said Tiptoe, "when you menaced my Tenamáxtli. As you say, this will be the last time."

The other warriors on either side of her recoiled as the thunder-stick thundered. The lead ball took Yeyac in his left temple and for an instant, his head blurred in a spray of red blood and pink-gray brain substance. Then he toppled, and no back-alley tícitl would be able to revive him ever again.

Every other one of us stood frozen, stunned, for the space of several heartbeats. Obviously, in her bulky quilted armor, Pakápeti—even with something of a belly now—had been able, all this while, to pass as a man of the company, and to keep her arcabuz concealed somewhere until it was really needed.

Now she had just time enough to send me a brief, affectionate, sad smile. Then there was a bellow of outrage from all of Yeyac's men, and those nearest Tiptoe surged to get at her, and the first one who did gave a mighty overhand slash of his obsidian sword. It opened Tiptoe's armor, her skin, her body, from breastbone to groin. Before she fell, there spilled out of her a great gush of blood, all her organs and guts . . . and something else. The men about her reeled back away from her, staring aghast and uttering exclamations loud enough to be heard above the noise of all the other

angry shouts—"tequáni!" and "tzipitl!" and "palanquí!"—
meaning "monstrosity" and "deformity" and "putridity."

In that tumult, none of us had paid heed to other rustlings
in the brush roundabout, but now we heard a wild, concerted
war cry combining eagle shrieks, jaguar grunts, owl hoots
and parrot ululations. There came crashing through the
bushes innumerable men of my own army, and they flung
themselves upon Yeyac's warriors, hacking and thrusting
with maquáhuime and spears and javelins. Before joining the
affray myself, I pointed to what was left of Pakápeti and
commanded Ualíztli, *"See to her, tícitl!"*

It was a battle fought by profile shapes, not full-rounded
figures, just the outlines of us warriors, black against the
sheet of fire still consuming the grove. So every man soon
dropped his heavier weapons, lest he find himself stabbing
or slicing one of his own comrades. All resorted to knives—
most of them obsidian; a few, like mine, of steel—and fought
hand to hand, sometimes the opponents grappling on the
ground. I personally slew the Arrow Knight Tapachíni. And
the battle was a short one, because my men far outnumbered
Yeyac's. As the last of those fell, the great blaze also began
to die down, as if its accompaniment was no longer required,
and we all found ourselves in the near darkness of early
night.

Doubtless through god-arranged coincidence, I found myself standing next to the perfidious G'nda Ké, still alive and
entire, evidently spared from the slaughter only because she
wore woman's garb.

"I should have known," I said, panting. "Even in furious
battle, you remain unscathed. I am glad. As your friend
Yeyac said just now, I shall have privacy and leisure in
which to slay you slowly."

"How you talk!" she chided me, with maddening composure. "G'nda Ké lured Yeyac and his men into this trap,
and what thanks does she get?"

"You lying bitch!" I snarled, then told two warriors
nearby, "Take this female and hold her tight between you

and march her with us when we leave here. If she disappears, so will you two, and in fragments.''

Next moment, I was being tightly embraced by the Cuáchic Nochéztli, as he exclaimed, ''I *knew* the white men could not long hold captive so valiant a warrior as my lord Tenamáxtzin!''

''And you have proved a more than capable substitute in the meantime,'' I said. ''As of tonight, you are my second in command, and I will see that our Order of Eagle Knights bestows on you its accolade. You have my congratulations, my gratitude and my esteem, Knight Nochéztli.''

''You are most gracious, my lord, and I am most honored. But now—let us make haste away from this place. If the Spaniards are not already on their way, their thunder-tubes could fling their missiles as far as here.''

''Yes. When our men have retrieved all their weapons, rally them and start a withdrawal northward. I will catch up to you as soon as I have attended to one final matter.''

I sought among the throng until I found Ualíztli, and asked him:

''What of that dear, brave girl, Pakápeti? She saved both our lives, tícitl. Was there anything you could do for her at the last?''

''Nothing. She was dead and at peace before she hit the ground.''

''But that other—whatever caused her assailants such horror. What was—?''

''Hush, my lord. Do not ask. You would not wish to know. I wish *I* did not.'' He gestured toward where the trees had been, now only charred poles amid a bed of smoldering embers. ''I gave over everything into the hands of the kindly hearth goddess Chántico. Fire cleanses the earth of even unearthly things.''

Nochéztli had recovered from the site of the Spaniards' ambush, besides the numerous arcabuces, the slain warrior Comitl's horse. So he and I were both mounted as we led our men off into the night—though I soon wished fervently that I had a saddle between me and the horse.

I again praised the new knight for having shown so much initiative during my absence, but added, "To make any use of those weapons you acquired for us, we must mix the powder for them and somehow find a source of lead."

"Well, my lord," he said, almost apologetically, "as to the first necessity, I know nothing whatever of making the powder. However, lacking any orders to the contrary, I decided, while we waited for news of you, to put the time to profitable employment. So we do have the lead, a good supply of it."

"You astound me, Knight Nochéztli. How ever did you contrive that?"

"One of our older Mexíca warriors told me he was the son of a silversmith, therefore he knew that lead is often found in the same mines from which come the more precious silver, and the lead also is used in the process by which the mills refine that silver."

"By Huitztli! You actually went to the Spaniards' mines and mills?"

"Remember, my lord, I once before acted as your quimíchi among the white men. I and others of our troop stripped down to our loincloths and sandals, and dirtied our faces and bodies, and, one by one, slipped past the mine guards and in among the laboring slaves. That was easy enough. The guards were hardly expecting anyone to sneak *into* slavery. The getting out again was rather more difficult, especially because lead is so heavy. But, thanks to my experience as a quimíchi, we managed that as well. At least two twenties of the men behind us are carrying a lead ingot apiece in their provisions bags. And that Mexícatl son of a silversmith says he can easily melt the metal and cast it into balls with simple molds made of wood and wet sand."

"Yyo ouiyo ayyo!" I exclaimed, delighted. "We are much nearer to being equal in armament to the white men than I could have hoped. The compounding of the powder will be far less of a problem than the one you have already solved. Listen, now, and memorize this and share it with any under-officers whom you trust, in case something should happen to both you and myself. What the Spaniards call pólvora was thought by our elders to be truly thunder and lightning, captured and confined, to be let loose when it suited the bearer. And those Spaniards still would not wish any of our race to know the secret of its making. It took me a long and weary while to discover it, but that process is simplicity indeed.'' I went on to explain about the three substances, how they were to be ground fine, and the proportions in which they were to be mixed.

Then, when I judged we were sufficiently distant from Compostela to stop for a night's rest, I went among the men and selected two twenties of those well muscled and with long legs, and told them:

''Tomorrow, when you have slept and refreshed yourselves, prepare to leave us and do some swift traveling. Give your arms and armor to your comrades and take only your mantles.''

The first twenty I ordered to journey to the volcano Tzebóruko, which few of us had ever seen but all of us knew by reputation, from its so frequently erupting and causing great devastation in the villages around it. I was sure Tzebóruko's slopes would be thickly crusted with that mineral called azufre. The volcano is in the Nauyar Ixú region of what was now New Galicia, meaning that those twenty men would have to traverse Spanish-held territory.

''So I suggest that you go straight west from where we are now, to the coast of the Western Sea, and there commandeer boatmen to carry you south to the volcano, then back north again, bearing your mantle-loads of that yellow substance. You are not likely to encounter any enemy patrols on the sea.''

To the other twenty I said, ''You will betake yourselves directly to Aztlan. Since our fishermen there are accustomed to making salt to preserve some of their catch, they are certain to know of the bitter kind of salt that is called first-harvest. You are to load your mantles with that.''

I added, to all those men, ''You are to rejoin the army at Chicomóztotl—you know it, 'the place of the seven caverns'—in the mountains east of Aztlan, in the land where the Chichiméca tribe called the Huichol lives. The army will be there waiting for you. I urge you to get there, with your burdens, as soon as you can.''

To Nochéztli I said, ''You heard. Now give all our warriors leave to sleep, but widely dispersed among the trees, and with sentries staying awake by turns. Tomorrow you will march the army toward that Chicomóztotl, because I have other places to go. While you wait there for my return, put the men to work at forging lead balls and burning charcoal. Those mountains are amply forested. When the bearers bring you the azufre and salitre, start making supplies of the pólvora. Then let the warriors already familiar with the arcabuz start training all others who show any aptitude in its use. In the meantime, send recruiters around among the Huichol and every other Chichiméca people farther afield, to persuade their men—with the promise of much killing and looting—to join our army of insurrection. The doing of those several preparations should keep everyone well occupied until I get back, and I hope to be bringing many more warriors with me. Right now, Nochéztli, have the two men holding that witch-woman G'nda Ké fetch her here. They need not do it tenderly.''

They did not. They roughly hauled her before me, and they continued to grip her upper arms tight, even when she addressed me with an immodest request that she obviously intended to scandalize the most hardened and worldly of men.

''If you are about to offer G'nda Ké a choice of ways to die, Tenamáxtli, she would like to be *raped* to death. You and these two stalwarts employing her three orifices for the purpose.''

But nothing she could say or do would surprise me in the

least. I only said stonily, "I have other employment for you, before I cram your three orifices full of fire ants and scorpions. That is to say, you will go on living just *exactly* as long as you obey my orders. Tomorrow you and I will start for your Yaki country."

"Ah, it has been a long time since G'nda Ké last visited her homeland."

"It is well known that the Yaki detest outlanders even more than they detest each other, and that they prove it by ripping off the scalp of any imprudent stranger, before doing worse things to him. I shall rely on your presence to prevent any such misadventure, but we will take along the Tícitl Ualíztli, should it happen that his ministrations are required. These two stalwarts will also come with you—to guard you—and whatever else they do with or to you along the way, I do not care."

XXIII

T HE DISTANCE FROM our starting place to the Yaki
lands is three times the distance between Aztlan and the City
of Méxíco, so my going there and my returning constituted
the longest journey I ever made in my life.

I let G'nda Ké do the guiding of us, because she had come
that way at least once before. For all I knew, generations of
G'nda Kés had made the journey back and forth innumerable
times during the sheaves of sheaves of years since that infamous first G'nda Ké had arrived among my ancestors in
Aztlan. Those G'nda Kés' collective memory of this whole
western part of The One World might well have been in-
scribed on *this* G'nda Ké's brain at birth, as plainly as a
word-picture map.

It seemed that she might truly be eager to see her homeland
again, because she did not—as certainly could be expected—
try to make the journey as tiresome or uncomfortable or hazardous or endless as she could. Except when she directed us
to veer around a tar pit ahead, or a quaking sand, or some
other obstacle, I could tell by the sun that she was keeping
to a course as directly northwestward as was possible,
through the valleys of the coastal mountain ranges. The distance would have been shorter if we had followed the coastline west of the mountains or the flat Dead-Bone Lands to

the east—but either way would have taken more time and been far more arduous for us, sweltering in the seaside swamps or shriveling in the mercilessly hot desert sands.

Nevertheless, and even without G'nda Ké's attempting to add hardships to it, the journey was rigorous and tiresome enough. Climbing a steep mountainside, of course, strains and cramps a body's muscles, seemingly all of them. You reach the crest with a sigh of heartfelt relief. But then you discover, going down the steep other side, that your body has countless *other* muscles to get strained and cramped. G'nda Ké and I and the two warriors—they were named Machíhuiz and Acocótli—endured those travails well enough, but we frequently had to stop and let the Tícitl Ualíztli regain his breath and strength. None of those mountains is high enough to wear a perpetual crown of snow, as does Popocatépetl, but many of them rise as far as the chill regions of the sky where Tlaloc reigns, and many were the nights that we five shivered sleepless, even wrapped in our heavy tlamáitin mantles.

Often and often, at night, we would hear a bear or jaguar or cuguar or océlotl snuffling inquisitively about our camp site, but they kept their distance, for wild animals have a natural abhorrence of humans—of live ones, anyway. Other game was plentiful by day, however: deer, rabbits, the masked mapáche, the pouch-bellied tlecuáchi. And there were abundant growing things: camótin tubers, ahuácatin fruits, mexíxin cress. When Ualíztli found some of the herb called camopalxíhuitl, he mixed that with the fat of our slain animals and made an ointment with which to soothe our sore muscles.

G'nda Ké asked him for some of the herb, to squeeze juice from it into her eyes, "because it makes them more dark and lustrous and beautiful." But the tícitl refused her because, he said, "Anyone fed a bit of that herb can soon be dead, and I would not trust you, my lady, to have it in your possession."

There were many waters in those mountains, both ponds and streams, all of them cold and sweet and delicious. We were not equipped for netting their fish or waterfowl, but the axólotl lizards and frogs were easily caught. We also dug amóli root and, cold though the waters were, bathed almost every day. In short, we never lacked for good food and drink and the pleasure of being clean. I can also say—now that I am no longer having to climb them—that those mountains are surpassingly lovely to look at.

During most of our journey, we were hospitably welcomed by the villages we came to. We slept under roofs, and the local women cooked for us many delicacies that were new to us. At every village, Ualíztli immediately sought out its tícitl, and begged various medicaments and implements from his colleague's stores. Though Ualíztli muttered that most of those backwoods tíciltin had pathetically antiquated notions of the physician's art, he was soon again carrying a well-stocked sack.

The person I sought to befriend in every community was its headman, or chief, or lord, or whatever he called himself. During most of our journey, we were traversing the lands of the peoples called the Cora, the Tepehuáne, the Sobaípuri and the Rarámuri, which is why they were amicable toward us, all those nations and tribes having long had dealings with Aztéca traveling traders and, before the downfall of Tenochtítlan, with Mexíca traders as well. They all spoke different languages, and some of their words and phrases I had learned—as I have earlier told—from their scouts sent to get a look at the white men, when those scouts and I resided at the Mesón de San José in the City of Mexíco. But G'nda Ké, because of her many and extensive travels, was much more fluent than I in all those languages. So, untrustworthy though she was at *any* responsible task, I employed her as my interpreter.

The message I wished to convey to every headman was the same: that I was collecting an army to overthrow the alien whites, and would he lend me as many strong, brave, truculent men as he could spare? Evidently G'nda Ké did not spitefully mistranslate my words, because almost all the headmen responded eagerly and generously to my request.

Those who had sent scouts south into the Spanish-held lands had already heard vivid firsthand reports of the white men's brutal oppression and mistreatment of those of our people who had survived the Conquest. They knew of the enslavements in obrajes, the killings, the whippings, the brandings, the humiliation of once-proud men and women, the imposition of an incomprehensible but cruel new religion. Those reports had naturally circulated among all the other tribes and communities and nations nearby, and, even at secondhand, had fired every manly and able-bodied man with an ardor to do *something* in retaliation. Now, here was their opportunity.

The headmen hardly had to call for volunteers. As soon as they relayed my words to their subjects, I would be surrounded by men—some of them mere adolescents, some old and rickety—enthusiastically shouting war cries and waving their weapons of obsidian or bone. I could take my choice, and those I picked I sent southward, with directions—as precise as I could make them—to enable their finding Chicomóztotl and joining Nochéztli there. Even to those too old or too young, I assigned an important errand:

"Go and spread my message to every other community, as far abroad as you can take it. And to every man who volunteers, give those same directions I have just given."

I should remark that I was not collecting men who merely *wanted* to be warriors. All of these were well accustomed to battle, because their tribes so often fought with neighboring ones, over territorial boundaries or hunting grounds or even to abduct each other's women for wives. However, none of these rustics had any experience of mass warfare, of being a component in an *army*, of serving in organized contingents that would act in disciplined concert. I was relying on Nochéztli and my other knights to teach them all they would need to know.

I suppose it was only to be expected that as we five travelers made our way farther and farther to the northwest, I would find my message received with more incredulity than enthusiasm. The communities in those distant reaches of The One World were smaller and more isolated, one from another. They apparently had little wish or need for mutual intercourse or trade or even communication. The few contacts between or among them occurred only when two or more had occasion to fight each other—as did those communities we had previously visited—usually for causes that more civilized people would have thought trifling.

Even the numerous tribes of the Rarámuri country—the name means the Runner People—seemed seldom to have done their running very far from their home villages. Most of their headmen had heard only vague rumors of strangers from beyond the Eastern Sea having invaded The One World. Some of those men felt that if any such thing really had happened, it was a disaster so distant that it was of no concern to them. Others flatly refused to believe the rumors at all. And eventually our little group arrived in regions where the resident Rarámuri had heard nothing whatever of the white men, and several of them laughed uproariously at the notion that whole hordes of uniformly white-skinned persons could *exist*.

The prevailing attitudes of indifference or skepticism or outright disbelief notwithstanding, I continued to reap harvests of new recruits for my army. I do not know whether to credit that to my urgent and persuasive argument, or to the men's having got tired of fighting their neighbors and desiring new enemies to vanquish, or to their simply wanting to journey far from their old familiar and unexciting haunts. The reason did not matter; what mattered was that they took up their arms and went south toward Chicomóztotl.

The Rarámuri lands were the northernmost in which the names Aztéca and Mexíca were even remotely recognized, and the last in which we travelers could expect to be received with hospitality or even with toleration. When we passed around the rim of a magnificent waterfall, admiring its grandeur as we did so, G'nda Ké said:

"The cascade is called Basa-séachic. It marks the boundary of the Rarámuri country, and indeed the farthest limit to which the Mexíca, at the very peak of their power, claimed to hold dominion. When we follow the riverside below the falls, we will be venturing into the Yaki lands, and we must go cautiously and watchfully. G'nda Ké does not much care what a wandering party of Yaki hunters would do to the rest of you. But she does not want them slaughtering *her* before she has a chance to hail them in their own tongue."

So, from there on, we went almost as stealthily as Ualíztli and I had crept through the underbrush while escaping from Compostela. But the wariness proved to have been unnecessary. For the space of three or four days, we met no one, and by the end of that time our course had brought us down from the thickly forested mountains into a region of low-growth rolling hills. On one of those we saw our first Yaki— a hunting party of six men—and they saw us at the same moment, and G'nda Ké called to them some greeting that stopped them from charging upon us. They stayed where they were, and regarded her icily as she went ahead of us to introduce herself.

She was still earnestly talking to them in the unlovely Yaki language—all grunts and clicks and mumbles—as we other four approached. The hunters were not speaking at all, and gave us men only the same icy stare. But neither did they make any threatening moves, so while G'nda Ké yammered on, I took the opportunity to look them over.

They had good hawklike faces and strong-muscled bodies, but they were about as unclean as are our priests, and wore their hair just as long and greasy and tangled. They were bare to the waist, and at first, I thought they were wearing skirts made of animal pelts. Then I made out that the skirts were of hair hanging loose all around, hair as long as their own and much longer than grows on any wild animal. It was human hair, the dried scalps still attached and tied about the men's waists with belt ropes. Several of them had added to the skirts the game they had slain this day—all small animals, carried by their tails tucked into those scalp belts. I might mention here that all kinds of game are abundant in those lands, and are eaten by the Yaki. But their *men* like best the meat of the pouch-bellied tlecuáchi, because it is so heavily larded with fat, which they believe gives them endurance in their hunting or fighting forays.

Their weapons were primitive, but hardly less lethal for that. Their bows and spears were of cane, their arrows of stiff reed and the spears were similar to those used by some fisher people, having three pointed prongs at the striking end. The arrows and spears were tipped with flint, a sure sign that the Yaki never had dealings with any of the nations to the south, where obsidian comes from. They had no swords like our maquáhuime, but two or three of them carried—dangling from thongs about their wrists—clubs of the quauxelolóni wood that is as hard and heavy as Spanish iron.

One of the six men now grunted a brief remark to G'nda Ké, jerked his head backward in the direction from which they had come, and they all turned and went that way. We five followed, though I wondered if G'nda Ké had merely urged her countrymen to take us to some larger gathering of hunters, where we could more easily be overpowered, scalped and slain.

Either she had not, or if that had been her intent, she had failed to persuade them. They led us, without ever once turning their heads to see if we came along, through the hills and through the rest of that day until, at evening, we came to their village. It was situated on the north bank of a river called, unsurprisingly, the Yaki, and the village was named, unimaginatively, Bakúm, which means only "water place." To *me* it was a village, and a meager and exceptionally squalid one, but G'nda Ké insisted on calling it a *town*, explaining:

"Bakúm is one of the Uonáiki—that is, one of the Eight

Sacred Towns—founded by the revered prophets who begot the whole race of us Yaki in the Batna'atóka—that is, in the Ancient Time.''

In the matter of living conditions and amenities, Bakúm appeared to have made very little progress since that Ancient Time, however long ago that had been. The people dwelt in dome-shaped huts crudely made of split cane crisscrossed into mats, and the mats laid overlapping. The entire village— every Yaki village I visited—was enclosed by a high fence of cane stalks held together and upright by intertwined vines. I had never before, anywhere in The One World, seen any community so seclusive and unsociable that it fenced itself off from everybody and everything beyond. None of the huts was a steam hut, and despite the village's name of ''water place,'' it was unpleasantly evident that the villagers took from the river only drinking water, never washing water.

The river's plentiful canes and reeds were employed for every conceivable purpose, not just for weapons and building mats and fencing material, but also for all the utensils of daily life. The people slept on woven-reed pallets, the women used split-cane knives and scooped-out cane spoons in their cooking, the men wore cane-and-reed headdresses and too-tled on cane whistles in their ceremonial dances. The only other evidences of artisanry that I saw among the Yaki were ugly brownware clay pots, carved and painted wooden masks and the cotton blankets woven on back-strap looms.

The land all about Bakúm was as fertile as I had seen anywhere, but the Yaki did only perfunctory farming—the Yaki *women* did, I should say—of maize, beans, amaranth, squash and just enough cotton to provide them with blankets and the women's apparel. Their every other vegetable need was supplied by wild-growing things—fruits of trees and cactus, various roots and grass seeds, bean pods of the miz-quitl tree. Because the Yaki preferred to eat the fat of game animals, rather than render it into oil, they used for their cooking an oil laboriously pressed—by the women—from certain seeds. They knew nothing of making octli or any other such drink; they grew no picíetl for smoking; their only intoxicant was the cactus bud called peyotl. They neither planted nor gathered any medicinal herbs, or even collected wild bees' honey for an alleviative balm. As Ualíztli observed, early on, with disgust:

"The Yaki tíciltin, such as they are, rely on fearsome masks and chants and wooden rattles and pictures drawn in trays of sand to cure any and every indisposition. Except for women's complaints—and most of those are *only* complaints, not genuine illnesses—the tíciltin have precious few cures to their credit. These people, Tenamáxtzin, are truly savages."

I entirely agreed. The one and only aspect of the Yaki that a civilized person could find worthy of approbation was the ferocity of their warriors, whom they called yoem'sontáom. But that ferocity was, after all, exactly what I had come looking for.

When, in time, and with G'nda Ké translating, I was allowed to converse with Bakúm's yo'otuí—its five elders; there was no single chief in any community—I discovered that the word *Yaki* is really an all-inclusive name for three different branches of the same people. They are the Ópata, the Mayo and the Káhita, each inhabiting one, two or three of the Eight Sacred Towns and the country roundabout, each staying strictly segregated from the others. Bakúm was Mayo. I discovered also that I had been misinformed about the Yaki's detesting and slaughtering each other. At least, they did not *quite*. No man of the Ópata would kill another of the Ópata, unless he had very good reason for the act. But he *would* cheerfully slay any of his neighbor Mayo or Káhita who gave the slightest offense.

And all the three branches of the Yaki, I learned, were closely related to the To'ono O'otam, or Desert People, of whom I had first heard from the much-traveled slave Esteban. The To'ono O'otam lived far away to the northeast of the Yaki lands. To do some enjoyable killing of them required a long, long march and an organized onslaught. So, about once a year, *all* the Yaki yoem'sontáom would put aside their mutual animosities and would companionably combine to make that march against their Desert People cousins. And *those* would almost rejoicingly welcome the incursions, as giving them good excuse for butchering some of their Ópata, Mayo and Káhita cousins.

About one thing, however, I had not been misinformed, and that was the Yaki's abominable attitude toward their womenfolk. I had always referred to G'nda Ké simply as Yaki, and it was not until we got to Bakúm that I learned she was of the Mayo branch. I would have thought it her good fortune that the hunting party we had encountered were also Mayo, bringing her to a Mayo community. Not so. I soon realized that Yaki women were not regarded as being Mayo or Káhita or Ópata or anything else except *women*, the lowest form of life. When we entered Bakúm, G'nda Ké was not embraced as a long-lost sister blessedly returned to her people. All the villagers, including the females and children, watched her arrival as icily as the hunters had done, and as icily as they regarded us male outlanders.

That very first evening, G'nda Ké was put to work with the other women, preparing the night's meal—lardy tlecu-áchi meat, maize cakes, roasted locusts, unidentifiable beans and roots. Then the women, including G'nda Ké, served the fare to the village men and boys. When those had eaten their fill, before they went off to chew peyotl, they indicated off-handedly that I, Ualíztli, Machíhuiz and Acocótli could scav-enge among their leftovers. And not until we four had eaten most of what was left did the women, including G'nda Ké, dare to come and pick through the scraps and crumbs.

The men of whatever Yaki breed, when they were not fighting one cousin or another, did nothing but hunt all the day long—except in the Káhita village called Be'ene, on the shore of the Western Sea, where later I saw the men do some lackadaisical fishing with their three-pronged spears and some lazy digging for shellfish. Everywhere, the women did *all* the work and lived only on remainders, including what little remainder of—I cannot say "affection"—what little remainder of forbearance their men might come home with, after a hard day afield.

If a man returned home in a fairly benign mood, he might greet his woman with a mere passing snarl instead of a blow. If he had had a really successful hunt or fight, and came home in a really good frame of mind, he might even condescend to fling his woman to the ground, lift her cotton skirt and his skirt of scalps, and engage her in a less than loving act of ahuilnéma, uncaring of how many onlookers might be present. That, of course, was why the village populations were so scant; the couplings occurred so seldom. More often, the men came home disgruntled, muttering curses and would beat their women as bloody as they would *like* to have bloodied the deer or bear or enemy that had got away.

"By Huitztli, I wish I could treat *my* woman so," said Acocótli, because, he confided, back in Aztlan he had a wife almost as mean-spirited as G'nda Ké, who bullied and nagged him unmercifully. "By Huitztli, I *will*, from now on, if I ever get home again!"

Our G'nda Ké found few opportunities in Bakúm to exercise her mean spirit. Being worked like a slave, being regarded as otherwise worthless, she endured those humiliations not apathetically like the other women, but in sullen and smoldering anger, because even the other *women* looked down on her—for her having no man to do the beating of her. (I and my companions refused to oblige her in that respect.) I know she would mightily have liked to command some awed and admiring adulation from her people, by boasting of her far travels and her evil exploits and the turmoils she had caused among *men*. But the women scorned to respect her in the least, and the men glared her to silence whenever she tried to speak to them. Perhaps G'nda Ké had been so long away from her people that she had forgotten how miserably insignificant she would be even in such coarse and ignorant company—that she would be accounted something less than vermin. Vermin at any rate could make themselves an annoyance. She no longer could.

No one beat her, but she was subject to orders from everyone, including the women, because they performed or assigned all the work of the village. They may have been envious of G'nda Ké's having seen something of the world outside the dreary Bakúm, or of her having once ordered men around. They may have despised her simply for her being not of their village. Whatever the reason, they behaved as maliciously as only small-minded women of petty authority can behave. They worked G'nda Ké unceasingly, taking special delight in giving her the dirtiest and hardest of tasks. It gladdened my heart to see it.

The only injury she received was a small one. While gathering firewood, she was bitten by a spider on the ankle, and it made her slightly ill. I personally would have thought it impossible for one tiny venomous creature to sicken a much larger and far more venomous one. Anyway, since no woman was allowed to shirk her work for any indisposition short of giving birth or visibly dying, G'nda Ké—screeching and protesting in mortification—was forced to stretch out on the ground for the ministrations of the village tícitl. As Ualíztli had said, that old fraud did nothing but don a mask designed to frighten off evil spirits, and bellow a nonsensical chant, and make nonsensical pictures on the ground with varicolored sands and shake a wooden rattle full of dried beans. Then he pronounced G'nda Ké hale and whole and ready for work again, and to work she was put.

The single small distinction G'nda Ké was accorded in Bakúm was the permission, when she was not at some other labor, to sit as interpreter between me and the five old yo'otuí. There she could speak, at least, and—since I never learned more than a few words of the language—she almost certainly must have tried to make herself a heroine by denouncing me as a quimíchi, or an agitator of dubious motives, or anything else that might have made the elders order us outlanders ousted or executed. But this much I know:

There is no word for *heroine* in the Yaki tongue, no concept of any such kind of woman in the Yaki mind. If G'nda Ké *did* desperately try that tactic, I am sure the yo'otuí heard her rantings as nothing but woman-wind to be ignored. If she did insist that we Aztéca be exterminated, and if the old men took any notice at all, they would perversely have done just the opposite. So it may have been thanks to another of G'nda Ké's attempts at perfidy that the yo'otuí not only let me stay and speak my message but also listened attentively to me.

I should explain how those yo'otuí governed—if governed is the word—for the Yaki system was unique in The One World. Each of the old men was responsible for one ya'úra, meaning "function," of the five ya'úram of his village: religion, warfare, work, customs and dance. Necessarily, some of their duties overlapped, while others were scarcely required at all. The elder in charge of work, for example, had little to do but punish any female malingerer, and such a woman simply did not exist in Yaki society. The elder in charge of warfare had only to give his blessing whenever the yoem'sontáom of his village decided to make a raid on some other, or whenever the yoem'sontáom of all the three Yaki branches combined to make their almost-ritual raids on the Desert People.

The other three old men more or less governed in concert: the Keeper of Religion, the Keeper of the Customs and the Leader of the Dances. The Yaki religion could rightly be called no religion at all, for they worship only their own ancestors, and of course anyone among them who dies becomes, that moment, an ancestor. Since the anniversary of any ancestor's death is a cause for ceremonies honoring it, hardly a night goes by in the Yaki lands without a ceremony, major or minor, depending on how important that person had been in life. The only "gods" recognized by the Yaki are their two longest-ago ancestors, scarcely real gods, but more like the Lord and Lady Pair whom we Aztéca have always believed were the first begetters of our race. We do not actively worship ours, but the Yaki call theirs Old Man and Our Mother, and venerate them most deeply.

Also, the Yaki believe that their deserving dead go to a happy and eternal afterlife, like our Tonatíucan or Tlálocan, or the Christians' heaven. They call theirs The Land Beneath the Dawn, and rather foolishly insist that it is not immeasurably far away but nearby, just east of a notched mountain peak called Takalá'im, which sits in the very middle of the Yaki lands. Where their *undeserving* dead go, the Yaki do not know and do not seem to care, for they can conceive of no place like our Míctlan or the Christians' hell.

They do, however, believe that they, the living, must be constantly on their guard against a whole host of invisible evil godlings or spirits called the chapáyekám. Those are the pestiferous fomenters of illness, accidents, drought, flood, defeat in battle and every other misfortune that besets the Yaki race. So, while the Keeper of Religion sees to it that his people properly honor their ancestors, all the way back to Old Man and Our Mother, the Keeper of the Customs is charged with warding off the chapáyekám. It is he who carves and colors the wooden masks intended to frighten them away, and he is continually trying to devise ever more hideous visages.

It follows that the Leader of the Dances is the busiest of the five yo'otuí, for the communal dances are considered essential to the affairs of all the other four. The village work will not get properly done, the battles will not be won, the ancestors will not be sufficiently honored and the malignant spirits will not be adequately propitiated or dispelled unless the dances are done—and done *just so*. The Leader himself is too old to dance, and I found it somewhat comical that all the other men, who devoted their days to rough and bloody pursuits, should spend their every night in dancing solemnly, formally, even daintily, around celebratory bonfires. (It is hardly necessary to remark that the women never took part.)

The Leader dispensed to the dancers enough peyotl to give them unflagging energy, but not enough to fuddle or frenzy

them so that they missed the precise steps and figures that
had been prescribed through all the ages since the Ancient
Times. The Leader hovered close to keep his hawk eye on
the dancers, and to yank from among them any man who
made a misstep or had the impudence to introduce a new
one. They danced to what they called music, made by the
men too old or crippled to dance. But since they lacked the
variety of instruments invented by more civilized people,
what they made was, to my ears, sheer noise. They blew on
cane whistles, blew through water-filled gourds, rasped
notched cane stalks together, shook wooden rattles and
pounded on double-headed drums. (Though there was no
paucity of animal hides, those drumheads were of human
skin.) And the dancers themselves added to the noise, wearing anklets of cocoons, the dead insects inside clattering at
every step.

For the dances honoring Old Man and Our Mother, or
more recently departed ancestors, the men wore fanlike headdresses, but fashioned either of stiff cane strips or fluttering
reeds, rather than feathers. For the dances intended to repel
the wicked chapáyekám, every man wore one of those gruesome carved and daubed masks, no two alike. For the dances
danced to celebrate a battle victory—or to anticipate one—
the men wore cóyotin skins with the dead animals' toothy
heads capping their own.

Then there was a dance done by one man alone, he the
acknowledged best dancer in the village. This was the per-
formance done to attract game for the hunters, in seasons
when a drought or a disease had diminished the local population of wild animals. It truly was a graceful and exciting
dance, and the more enjoyable because it was done without
any "music." The man wore atop his head, secured by
thongs, a buck deer's head—the handsomest procurable, with
an impressive rack of antlers—and he was otherwise naked,
except for bracelets and anklets of cocoons and he held in
either hand an intricately carved wooden rattle. These provided the only accompanying noise as he various bounded

like a startled buck, capered like a carefree fawn, shuffled bent over and wary, jerking his head about, like a hunter on the prowl. He might have to do this dance to exhaustion, many nights in a row, before some scout came to report that the game *had* returned to their usual habitats.

The Leader of the Dances confided to me, through G'nda Ké, that the game-attracting dance was much more efficacious in accomplishing its purpose when the dancer could dance around a sacrificial "doe." That would be a human female, tightly bound inside a doeskin. After she had been danced around for the ritual length of time, she would be butchered—just as was done to a real doe—dismembered, cooked and eaten by the men, they doing much slobbering and lip-smacking, so the wild game would sense their gratitude. Unfortunately, said the Leader, the Mayo men had not recently made any female-abducting raids on any alien village, so that part of the ceremony could not be demonstrated for my admiration. There were plenty of expendable Mayo females, he conceded, but they were too tough and stale and stringy to be lip-smackingly eaten. G'nda Ké managed to look affronted and sulky even at being slighted in *that* regard.

It mattered not to me that the Yaki men spent half their lives in dancing for reasons that I deemed absurd. What mattered was that the other half of their lives they dedicated to pure savagery, and that was what I wanted from them. When G'nda Ké translated my words to the five yo'otuí, they very pleasantly surprised me by being more receptive to my message than some of the Rarámuri chiefs had been.

"White men . . ." murmured one of the elders. "Yes, we have heard of white men. Our cousins, the To'ono O'otam, claimed to have had some of those wandering through their country. They even mentioned a *black* man."

Another grumbled, "What is the world coming to? Men should all be one color. Our color."

And another cautioned, "How can we know if the degenerate Desert People spoke truly? Had they been Yaki, now, they would have taken *scalps* to prove the existence of such beings."

And he was reminded by another, "We have never seen scalps of the evil chapáyekám, but we know they exist. And they are of no color at all."

And the fifth, the elder in charge of warfare, said, "I believe it would do our yoem'sontáom good to fight someone besides their own relatives for a change. I vote that we lend them to this outlander."

"I concur," said the elder in charge of the village work. "If this outlander speaks truly about the rapacity of the white men, we may someday not have any relatives to fight, anyway."

"I agree," said the Leader of the Dances. "Let us keep here only the Deer Dancer and enough other dancers to satisfy Old Man and Our Mother."

"And to repulse the chapáyekám," said the Keeper of the Customs.

"Surely all others of our color," said the elder who governed religion, "will wish to join in annihilating those of different color. I vote that we invite our cousins the Ópata and Káhita to participate."

The warfare elder spoke up again. "And why not our cousins the To'ono O'otam as well? This would be the grandest-ever alliance of relatives. Yes, that is what we will do."

So it was arranged. Bakúm would send a warrior "bearing the staff of truce" to relay my message to all the others of the Eight Sacred Towns, and a second messenger to the far-off Desert People. I promised two things in return for such generous cooperation. I would appoint one of my own warriors to lead all the Yaki men south to our gathering place at Chicomóztotl, and the other to wait here in Bakúm to guide the Desert People's warriors when they came. I would also, when all those yoem'sontáom got to Chicomóztotl, equip them with obsidian weapons far superior to theirs of flint. The elders accepted my offer of guides, but indignantly rejected the offer of weapons. What had been good enough for Old Man, and for their every male ancestor since, was good enough for modern warfare, they said, and I prudently did not argue the matter.

I was glad we had reached agreement when we did, for thereafter I was deprived of my means of communicating with the Yaki. G'nda Ké claimed to be feeling ever more ill, and incapable of even the exertion of interpreting. Indeed, she *looked* ill, her complexion having faded almost to the pallor of a white woman, so that her freckles were her most visible feature. When even the elder in charge of work, and the women who had worked her so hard, allotted her a domed hut of her own in which to lie and rest, it seemed they had decided—since she was not about to give birth—that she must be about to die. But I, knowing G'nda Ké, dismissed that notion. I was sure that her prostration was just another of her ruses, doubtless her way of expressing her vexation at my having been more cordially accepted by her own people than she had been.

XXIV

WHILE WE WAITED for the men of the other Yaki branches to assemble, Machíhuiz, Acocótli and I occupied our time in doing a sort of training of the Mayo warriors of Bakúm. That is to say, we mock-fought against them with our swords and javelins of obsidian edges and points, so that they would learn to parry such assaults with their primitive weapons. It was not that I expected the Yaki ever to be battling against the men of my own army. But I was fairly certain that when my army fully engaged the Spaniards, *they* would add to their ranks many of their native allies, such as the Texcaltéca who had helped the white men in their long-ago overthrow of Tenochtítlan. And those allies would not be carrying arcabuces, but obsidian-bladed maquáhuime and spears and javelins and arrows.

It was rather a slow and awkward process, training these yoem'sontáom without someone to translate my commands and instructions and advice. But warriors of every race and nation, probably even the white ones, share an instinctive understanding of each other's movements and gestures. So the Mayo men had not too much trouble learning our Aztéca arts of thrusts and slashes and feints and withdrawals. They learned so well, in fact, that I and my two companions frequently got bruised by their dense-wood war clubs and pricked or scratched by their triple-flint spears. Well, of course, we three gave as good as we got, so I kept the Tícitl Ualíztli always in attendance at our training sessions, to apply *his* arts when necessary. And I gave no thought whatever to the absent G'nda Ké until, one day, a Bakúm woman came and timidly tugged at my arm.

She led me—and Ualíztli came along—to the little cane hut that had been lent to G'nda Ké. I went in first, but what I saw made me instantly back out and motion for the tícitl to enter instead. Clearly, G'nda Ké had not been pretending; she appeared to be as near dying as the villagers had earlier supposed.

She lay stretched out naked on a reed pallet, and she was copiously sweating, and she had somehow got extremely *fat*, not just in the places where well-fed women often do, but *all over*—nose, lips, fingers, toes. Even her eyelids had become so fat that they practically closed her eyes. As she once had told me, G'nda Ké was freckled over her whole body, and now, with that body so bloated, her countless freckles were so large and distinct that she might have grown a jaguar's skin. In my one brief glance, I had seen the Mayo tícitl squatting beside her. I never yet had glimpsed that man's face, but even the grim-visaged mask he wore seemed now to have a puzzled and helpless expression, and he was only listlessly shaking his curative wooden rattle.

Ualíztli emerged from the hut, looking rather perplexed himself, and I asked him, "What could they possibly have been feeding her, to make her so grossly fat? In this Yaki land, I have never seen a woman more than meagerly fed."

"She has not grown fat, Tenamáxtzin," he said. "She is swollen with putrid fluids."

I exclaimed, "A simple spider bite could have done that?"

He gave me a sidelong look. "She says it was you, my lord, who bit her."

"What?!"

"She is in excruciating agony. And much as we all have loathed the woman, I am sure you would wish to be a little merciful. If you will tell me what kind of poison you applied to your teeth, I might be able to give her a more easeful death.''

"By all the gods!" I raged. "I have long known that G'nda Ké is criminally insane, but are *you*?''

He quailed away from me, stammering, "Th-there is a horribly gaping and suppurating sore on her ankle . . .''

Through gritted teeth I said, "I grant you, I have often contemplated how I might most ingeniously slay G'nda Ké, when she was of no more use to me. But *bite* her to death? In your wildest imaginings, man, can you credit that I would put my *mouth* to that reptile? If ever I did that, *I* would be the one poisoned and suffering and suppurating and dying! It was a spider that bit her. While she was gathering wood. Ask any of the drabs who first attended her.''

I started to reach for the Mayo woman who had fetched us, and who was goggling at us in fright. But I desisted, realizing that she could neither comprehend nor answer a question. I simply flailed my arms in futile disgust, while Ualíztli said placatively:

"Yes, yes, Tenamáxtzin. A spider. I believe you. I should have known that the witch-woman would lie most atrociously, even on her deathbed.''

I took several deep breaths to calm myself, then said, "She doubtless hopes that the accusation will reach the ears of the yo'otuí. Worthless though they hold every woman, this one *is* a Mayo. If they give heed to her perjury, they might vengefully refuse me the support they have promised. Let her die.''

"Best she die quickly, too,'' he said, and went again into the hut. I suppressed several different kinds of repulsion, and followed him inside, only to be further repulsed by the sight of her and—I noticed now—the rotting-meat stench of her.

Ualíztli knelt beside the pallet and asked, "The spider that bit you—was it one of the huge, hairy sort?''

She shook her fat and mottled head, pointed a fat finger at me, and croaked, "Him.'' Even the Mayo tícitl's wooden mask wagged skeptically at that.

"Then tell me where you hurt," said Ualíztli.

"All of G'nda Ké," she mumbled.

"And where do you hurt *worst*?"

"Belly," she mumbled and, just then, a spasm of pain must have stricken her there. She grimaced, shrieked, flung herself onto her side and doubled over—or as far as she could, her distended stomach folding into fat rolls.

Ualíztli waited until the spasm passed, then said, "This is very important, my lady. Do the *soles of your feet* hurt?"

She had not recovered sufficiently to speak, but her bulbous head nodded most emphatically.

"Ah," said Ualíztli with satisfaction, and stood up.

I said, marveling, "That told you something? The soles of her *feet*?"

"Yes. That pain is the distinctive sign diagnostic of the bite of one particular spider. We seldom encounter the creature in our lands to the south. We are more familiar with the big, hairy one that looks more fearsome than it really is. But in these northerly climes there is found a truly lethal spider that is not large and does not look especially dangerous. It is black, with a red mark on its underside."

"Your breadth of knowledge astounds me, Ualíztli."

"One tries to keep well informed in one's trade," he said modestly, "by exchanging bits of lore with other tíciltin. I am told that the venom of this black northern spider actually *melts* the flesh of its prey, to make it the more easily eaten. Hence that ghastly open sore on the woman's leg. But, in this case, the process has spread within her whole body. She is literally *liquefying* inside. Curious. I would not have expected such extensive putrefaction except in an infant or a person old and infirm."

"And what will you do about it?"

"Hasten the process," Ualíztli murmured, so that only I might hear.

G'nda Ké's eyes, from between their puffed lids, were anxiously asking also: What is to be done for me? So Ualíztli

said aloud, "I shall bring special medicaments," and left the
hut.

I stood gazing down at the woman, not pityingly. She had
regained breath enough to speak, but her words were dis-
jointed, her voice only croaks and rasps:

"G'nda Ké must not . . . die here."

"Here as well as anywhere," I said coldly. "It appears
that your tonáli has brought you to the end of your roads and
your days, right here. The gods are far more inventive than
I could possibly be, in devising the proper disposal of one
who has lived ever evilly, and already lived too long."

She said again, but stressing one word, "G'nda Ké must
not . . . die *here*. Among these louts."

I shrugged. "They are your own louts. This is your own
land. It was a spider native to this land that poisoned you. I
think it fitting that you should have been felled not by an
angry human's hand, but by one of the tiniest creatures inhabiting the earth."

"G'nda Ké must not . . . die here," she said yet again,
though it seemed she spoke more to herself than to me.
"G'nda Ké will not . . . be remembered here. G'nda Ké was
meant . . . to be remembered. G'nda Ké was meant . . . somewhere . . . to be royalty. With the *-tzin* to her name . . ."

"You are mistaken. You forget that I have known women
who *deserved* the *-tzin*. But you—to the very last, you have
striven to make your mark on the world only by doing harm.
And for all your grandiose ideas of your own importance,
for all your lies and duplicities and iniquities, you were destined by your tonáli to be nothing more than what you were
and what you are now. As venomous as the spider and, inside, just as small."

Ualíztli returned then, and knelt to sprinkle plain picíetl
into her leg's open sore. "This will numb the local pain, my
lady. And here, drink this." He held a gourd dipper to her
protuberant lips. "It will stop your feeling the other pains
within."

When he rose again to stand beside me, I growled, "I did

not give you permission to relieve her agony. She inflicted enough on other people.''

"I did not ask your permission, Tenamáxtzin, and I will not ask your pardon. I am a tícitl. My allegiance to my calling takes precedence even over my loyalty to your lordship. No tícitl can prevent death, but he can refuse to prolong it. The woman will sleep and, sleeping, die.''

So I held my tongue, and we watched as G'nda Ké's swollen eyelids closed. What happened next I know surprised Ualíztli as much as it did myself and the other tícitl.

From the hole in G'nda Ké's leg began to trickle a liquid—not blood—a liquid as clear and thin as water. Then came fluids more viscous but still colorless, as malodorous as the sore. The trickle became a flow, ever more fetid, and those same noxious substances started issuing from her mouth, too; and from her ears and from the orifices between her legs.

The bloat of her body slowly but visibly diminished, and as the taut-stretched skin subsided, so did the jaguar spots of it shrink to a profusion of ordinary freckles. Then even they commenced to disappear as the skin slackened into furrows and creases and puckers. The flow of fluids increased to a gush, some of it soaking into the earthen floor, some of it remaining as a thick slime from which we three watchers stepped warily well away.

G'nda Ké's face collapsed until it was just a featureless, wrinkled skin shrouding her skull, and then all her hair wisped away from it. The leakage of fluids lessened to an ooze, and finally the whole bag of skin that had been a woman was empty. When that bag began to split and shred and slip downward and dissolve into the slime on the ground, the masked tícitl gave a howl of pure horror and bolted from the hut.

Ualíztli and I continued to stare until there was nothing to be seen but G'nda Ké's slime-glistening, gray-white skeleton, some hanks of hair, a scatter of fingernails and toenails. Then we stared at one another.

"She wanted to be remembered," I said, trying to keep my voice steady. "She will certainly be remembered by that Mayo in the mask. What in the name of Huitztli was that potion you gave her to drink?"

In a voice about as shaky as mine, Ualíztli said, "This was not my doing. Or the spider's. It is a thing even more prodigious than what happened to that girl Pakápeti. I daresay no other tícitl has ever seen anything like this."

Stepping cautiously through the stinking and slippery puddle, he reached over and down to touch a rib of the skeleton. It instantly broke loose of its attachment there. He gingerly picked it up and regarded it, then came to show it to me.

"But something like this," he said, "I *have* seen before. Look." Without any effort, he broke it between his fingers. "When the Mexíca warriors and workers came with your Uncle Mixtzin from Tenochtítlan, you may remember, they drained and dried the nastier swamps around Aztlan. In doing so, they dug up the fragments of numerous skeletons—of both humans and animals. The wisest tícitl of Aztlan was summoned. He examined the bones and declared them to be old, incredibly old, sheaves and sheaves of years old. He surmised that they were the remains of persons and animals sucked down in a quaking sand that had, at some time long forgotten, existed in that place. I got to know that tícitl before he died, and he still had some of the bones. They were as brittle and crumbly as this rib."

We both turned to look again at G'nda Ké's skeleton, now quietly falling apart as it lay there, and Ualíztli said, in a voice of awe, "Neither I nor the spider put that woman to death. She had been dead, Tenamáxtzin, for sheaves of sheaves of years before you or I were born."

We emerged from the hut to see that Mayo tícitl dashing about the village and jabbering at the top of his voice. In his immense and supposed-to-be-dignified mask, he looked very foolish and the other Mayo were regarding him with incredulity. It occurred to me that if the whole village should get excited about the uncommon manner of G'nda Ké's dissolution, the elders might still have reason for suspicion of me. I decided to remove all traces of the woman's death. Let it be even more of a mystery, so the tícitl's fantastic account would be unprovable. To Ualíztli I said:

"You told me you carry something combustible in that sack." He nodded and took out a leather pouch of liquid. "Splash it all on the hut." Then, rather than go and take a brand from the cooking fire that stayed always alight in the middle of the village, I surreptitiously employed my burning-glass, and in moments the cane-and-reed hut was blazing. The people all stared in amazement at that—and Ualíztli and I pretended to do the same—as it and its contents burned to ashes.

I may have ruined forever the local tícitl's reputation for truthfulness, but the elders never summoned me to demand an explanation of those strange occurrences. And, during the next days, the warriors from other villages came straggling in from various directions, all well armed and appearing eager to get on with my war. When I was informed, by gestures, that I had collected every available man, I sent them south with Machíhuiz, and Acocótli went off northward with another Yaki, to spread the word among the Desert People.

I had already decided that Ualíztli and I would not make the arduous mountain journey to Chicomóztotl, but would take an easier and quicker course. We left Bakúm and went west, along the river, through the villages of Torím, Vikám, Potám and so on—those names, in the unimaginative Yaki manner, meaning the "places of," respectively, wood rats, arrow points, gophers and so on—until we came to the sea-side village of Be'ene, "sloping place." Under other circumstances, it would have been suicidal for two strangers to essay such a journey, but of course all the Yaki by now had been told who we were, and what we were doing in these lands, and that we had the sanction of the yo'otuí of Bakúm.

As I have said, the Káhita men of Be'ene do some fishing off that Western Sea shore. Since most of the men had gone off to enlist in my war, leaving only enough fishers to keep the village fed, there were a number of their seaworthy acáltin not being used. I was able, with gestures, to "borrow" one of those dugout canoes and two paddles for it. (I did not expect ever to return those things, and I did not.) Ualíztli and I stocked our craft with ample supplies of atóli, dried meats and fish, leather bags of fresh water, even one of the fishermen's three-pronged cane spears, so we could procure fresh fish during our voyage, and a brownware pot full of charcoal over which to cook them.

It was my intent that we would paddle to Aztlan—rather more than two hundred one-long-runs distant, I calculated, if one can speak of "runs" on water. I was eager to see how Améyatl was faring, and Ualíztli was eager to tell his fellow tícitltin about the medically marvelous two deaths he had witnessed while in my company. From Aztlan, we would go inland to rejoin the Knight Nochéztli and our army at Chicomóztotl, and I expected we would reach there at about the same time the Yaki and To'ono O'otam warriors did.

I was unacquainted with the Western Sea that far north, where it borders the Yaki lands, except that I knew—Alonso de Molina had told me—that the Spaniards called it Mar de Cortés, because the Marqués del Valle had "discovered" it during his idle wanderings about The One World after he was deposed from his rulership of New Spain. How anyone could presumptuously claim to *discover* something that had existed since time began, I do not know. Anyway, the Be'ene fishermen informed me, with unmistakable gestures, that they fished only close inshore, because farther out the sea was dangerous, having strong and unpredictable tidal currents and vagarious winds. That information did not much dismay me, for I certainly intended to keep just outside the surf line the whole way.

And, for many days and nights, that is what Ualíztli and I did, paddling in unison, then taking turns at sleeping while the other paddled. The weather stayed clement and the sea stayed calm, and the voyage during those many days was more than pleasant. We frequently speared fish, some of them new to both of us, but delicious when broiled over the charcoal fired by my lente. We saw other fish—those giants called yeyemíchtin—which, even if we had somehow speared one, we could not have cooked over any pot smaller than the crater of Popocatépetl. And sometimes we would knot our mantles in such a way that they could be dragged through the water behind us to scoop up shrimp and crayfish. And there were the flying fish, which did not have to be caught at all, because one of them would leap into our acáli almost every other day. And there were turtles, large and small, but of course too hard-shelled to be speared. Now and then, when we saw no people on shore to whom we would have to explain ourselves, we put in just long enough to gather whatever fruits, nuts and greens were in season, and to replenish our water bags. For a long while, we lived well and enjoyed ourselves immensely.

To this day, I *almost* wish the voyage had continued so. But, as I have remarked, Ualíztli was not young, and I will not blame that good old man for what happened to interfere with our serene progress southward. I woke from one of my stints of sleep, in the middle of the night, feeling that I had somehow *over*slept my allotted time, and wondering why Ualíztli had not waked me to take my turn at paddling. The moon and stars were thickly clouded over, the night so very black that I could see nothing whatever. When I spoke to Ualíztli, then shouted, and he made no answer, I had to grope my way all along the acáli to ascertain that he and his paddle were gone.

I will never know what became of him. Perhaps some monster sea creature rose from the night waters to snatch him from where he sat, and did it so silently that I never woke. Perhaps he was stricken with some one of the seizures not uncommon in old men—for even tíciltin die—and, flailing in its grip, inadvertently threw himself over the acáli's side. But it is more likely that Ualíztli simply fell asleep and toppled over, paddle in hand, and got a mouthful of water before he could call for help, and so drowned—how long ago and how far away I had no idea.

There was nothing I could do but sit and wait for the day's first light. I could not even use the remaining paddle, because I did not know how long the acáli had been adrift or in which direction the land lay. Usually, at night, there was an onshore wind, and we had so far kept our course in the dark by keeping that wind always on the paddler's right cheek. But the wind god Ehécatl seemed to have chosen this worst possible night to be whimsical; the breeze was only light, and puffed at my face first on one side, then the other. In air so gently moving, I should have been able to hear the sea's surf, but I heard nothing. And the canoe was rocking more than was usual—that was probably what had waked me—so I feared that I had been carried some distance away from the solid, safe shore.

The first glimmer of day showed me that that was what had happened, and had happened to a distressing degree. *The land was nowhere in sight.* The glimmer at least enabled me to know which way was east, and I seized up my paddle and began stroking furiously, frantically, in that direction. But I could not hold a steady course; I had been caught in one of those tidal currents the fishermen had told of. Even when I could keep the prow of the acáli pointed east toward land, that current moved me sideways. I tried to take some comfort from the fact that it was carrying me south, not back northward again or—horrible to contemplate—carrying me *west* and farther out to sea, out where *nobody* had ever gone and returned from.

All that day I paddled, struggling mightily to keep moving east of south, and all the next day, and the next, until I lost count of the days. I paused only to take an occasional drink of water and bite of food, and ceased for longer spells when I got absolutely fatigued or knotted with cramp or desperate for sleep. Still, however often I awoke and resumed paddling, no land appeared on the eastern horizon . . . and never did. Eventually my store of food and water ran out. I had been improvident. I should earlier have speared fish that I could have eaten, even raw, and from which I could have wrung drinkable juices. By the time my provisions were gone, I was too weak to waste any energy in fishing; I put what strength I had left into my futile paddling. And now my mind began to wander, and I found that I was mumbling aloud to myself:

"That vicious woman G'nda Ké did not really die. Why should she have done, after living unkillable all those sheaves and sheaves of years?"

And, "She once threatened that I would never be rid of her. Since she lived only to do evil, she might easily live as long as evil does, and that must be until the end of time."

And, "Now she has taken her revenge on us who watched her *seeming* to die—a quick revenge on Ualíztli, a lingering revenge on me. I wonder what appalling thing she has done to that poor innocent tícitl back in Bakúm . . ."

And at last, "Somewhere she is gloating at my plight, at my pitifully trying to stay alive. May she be damned to Míctlan, and may I never meet her there. I shall entrust my fate to the gods of wind and water, and hope I shall have merited Tonatíucan when I die . . ."

At that, I threw away my paddle and stretched out in the acáli to sleep while I waited for the inevitable.

I said that, to this day, I *almost* wish the voyage had continued as uneventfully as it had begun. The good Tícitl Ualíztli would not have been lost, I would soon have seen Aztlan and dear Améyatl again, and then Nochéztli and my army, and then have got on with my war. But if things *had* happened so, I would not have been impelled into the most extraordinary of all my life's adventures, and I would not have met the extraordinary young woman I have most loved in all my life.

XXV

❚ DID NOT exactly sleep. The combination of my being unutterably weary, weakened by hunger, blistered by the sun, parched with thirst—and withal, too dispirited to care—simply sank me into an insensibility that was relieved only by an occasional bout of delirium. During one of those, I raised my head and thought I saw a distant smudge of land, off where the sea met the sky. But I knew that could not be, because it lay on the southern horizon, and there is no land mass in the southern stretches of the Western Sea. It had to be only a taunting apparition born of my delirium, so I was grateful when I subsided again into insensibility.

The next unlikely occurrence was that I felt water splashing on my face. My dull mind did not respond with alarm, but dully accepted that my acáli had been swamped by a wave, and that I would shortly be entirely underwater, and drowned, and dead. But the water continued just to splash my face, stopping my nostrils so that I involuntarily opened my dry, cracked, gummed-together lips. It took a moment for my dulled senses to register that the water was sweet, not salt. At that realization, my dull mind began to fight its way upward through the layers of insensibility. With an effort, I opened my gummed-together eyelids.

Even my dulled, dimmed eyes could descry that they were

seeing two human hands squeezing a sponge, and behind the hands was the extremely beautiful face of a young woman. The water was as fresh, cool and sweet as her face. Dully, I supposed that I *had* attained Tonatíucan or Tlálocan or some other of the gods' blissful afterworlds, and that this was one of that god's attendant spirits waking me to welcome me. If so, I was exceedingly glad to be dead.

Anyway, dead or not, I was slowly recovering my vision, and also the ability to move my head slightly, to see the spirit the better. She was kneeling close beside me and she wore nothing but her long black hair and a maxtlatl, a man's loincloth. She was not alone; other spirits had convened to help welcome me. Behind her, I could now see, stood several other female spirits of various sizes and apparently various ages, all wearing the same costume—or lack of it.

But, I dully wondered, *was* I being welcomed? Though the lovely spirit was gently rousing and refreshing me with water, she regarded me with a not very kindly look and addressed me in a tone of mild vexation. Curiously, the spirit spoke not my Náhuatl tongue, as I would have expected in an afterlife arranged by one of the Aztéca gods. She spoke the Poré of the Purémpe people, but a dialect new to me, and it took a while for my dull brain to comprehend what she was repeating over and over:

"You have come too soon. You must go back."

I laughed, or intended a laugh. I probably squawked like a seagull. And my voice was raw and raspy when I summoned up enough Poré to say, "Surely you can see . . . I came not by choice. But where . . . so providentially . . . have I come *to*?"

"You truly do not know?" she asked, less severely.

I shook my head, only feebly, but I should not have done that, for it rocked me back into insensibility. As my mind went reeling and fading away into darkness, though, I heard her say:

"Iyá omekuácheni uarichéhuari."

It means, "These are The Islands of the Women."

* * *

A long while back, when I described what Aztlan was like in the days of my childhood, I remarked that our fishermen took from the Western Sea every sort of edible and useful and valuable thing except those things that are called, in all the languages of The One World, "the hearts of oysters." By ancient tradition, and by agreement throughout the Aztéca dominions, the collection of the Western Sea's oyster-heart pearls has always been done exclusively by the fishermen of Yakóreke, the seaside community situated twelve one-long-runs south of Aztlan.

Oh, now and again, an Aztécatl fisherman elsewhere, dredging up shellfish just to sell as food, would have the good fortune to find in one of his oysters that lovely little pebble of a heart. No one bade him throw it back into the sea, or forbade him to keep or sell it, for a perfect pearl is as precious as a solid gold bead of equal size. But it was the Yakóreke men who knew how to find those oyster-hearts in quantity, and they kept that knowledge a secret, handing it down from fisher fathers to fisher sons, none ever confiding it to any outsider.

Nevertheless, over the sheaves of years, outsiders *had* learned a few tantalizing things about that pearl-gathering process. One thing everyone knew was that just once each year all the sea-fishers of Yakóreke set out in their several acáltin, each canoe heavily laden with some kind of freight, the nature of which was hidden by coverings of mats and blankets. The natural presumption would have been that the men carried some secret sort of oyster bait. Whatever it was, they carried it *out of sight of land*. That, in itself, was a feat so bold that no envious fisherman from any other place, in all the sheaves of years, had ever dared to try to follow them to their secret oyster ground.

This much else was known: the Yakóreke men would *stay* out there, wherever they went, for the space of nine days. On the ninth day, their waiting families—and pochtéca traders gathering there from all over The One World—would

sight the fleet of acáltin coming landward from the horizon.
And the canoes came no longer heaped with shrouded
freight, nor even laden with oysters. Each man brought home
only a leather pouch full of the oysters' hearts. The merchants waiting to buy those pearls knew better than to ask
where the men had got them, or how. And so did the fishermen's womenfolk.

So much was known; outsiders had to conjecture the rest,
and they made up various legends to fit the circumstances.
The most credible supposition was that there *had* to be some
land out there west of Yakóreke—islands, maybe, surrounded by shoal waters—because it would be impossible
for any fishermen to dredge up oysters from the great depths
of the open sea. But why did the men go out only once a
year? Perhaps they kept slaves on those islands, collecting
oyster-hearts all year round, and saving them until their masters came at an appointed time, bearing goods to trade for
the pearls.

And the fact that the fishermen told their secret only to
their sons, not to the females of Yakóreke, inspired another
touch to the legend. Those supposed slaves on those supposed islands must be females themselves, and the Yakóreke
women must never know, lest they jealously prevent their
menfolk from going there. Thus grew the legend of The Islands of the Women. All my young life I had heard that
legend and variants of it—but, like everyone else of good
sense, I had always dismissed the tales as mythical and absurd. For one reason, it was foolish to believe that an isolated
populace all female could have perpetuated itself over so
many lifetimes. But now, by pure chance, I had found that
those islands did and do exist in fact. I would not have survived if they did not.

The islands are four, in a line, but only the middle two, the
largest, have sufficient fresh water to allow of population,
and they *are* populated entirely by women. I counted at that
time one hundred and twelve of them. I should more accu-

rately say females instead of women, since they included infants under a year old, small children, nubile girls, young women, mature women and old women. The most ancient was the one they called Kukú, or Grandmother, she whom they all obeyed as if she had been their Revered Speaker. I made a point of looking at all the children—they wore not even a maxtlatl—and the very youngest of them, the very newest born, were of the female sex.

Once I had convinced the women that I had indeed come to their islands inadvertently, unknowing of their existence— not even believing in them—their Kukú gave me leave to stay awhile, long enough to regain my strength and to carve for myself a new canoe paddle, both of which I would need to get back to the mainland. The young woman who had first succored me with a spongeful of water was commanded to see to my sustenance, and to see that I behaved myself, and she seldom let me out of her sight during the first days of my stay.

Her name was Ixínatsi, which is the Poré word for that tiny chirping insect called a cricket. The name was apt, for she was as perky and sprightly and good-humored as is that little cricket creature. To the casual eye, Ixínatsi would have seemed just another Purémpe woman, though of a countenance unusually gorgeous to look at and a demeanor never less than vivacious. Any observer could admire her sparkling eyes, glossy hair, luminous complexion, beautifully rounded, firm breasts and buttocks, shapely legs and arms, dainty hands. But only I and the gods who made her would ever know that Cricket was in fact very different—darlingly and deliciously different—from all other women. However, I am getting ahead of my chronicle.

As old Kukú had bidden her, Cricket cooked for me—all kinds of fish, and garnished the dishes with a yellow flower called tirípetsi; the flower, she said, possesses curative properties. Between meals she plied me with raw oysters and mussels and scallops—in much the same way that some of our mainland peoples forcibly feed their techíchi dogs before slaughtering them for food. When the comparison occurred to me, it made me uneasy. I wondered if the women were manless because they were man-eaters, and I inquired, which made Ixínatsi laugh.

"We have no men, for eating or for anything else," she said, in that dialect of Poré which I was hurrying to learn. "I feed you, Tenamáxtli, to make you healthy again. The more quickly you get strong, the more quickly you can go away."

Before I went away, though, I wished to know more about those legendary islands, besides the obvious fact that they were no baseless legend. I could surmise for myself that the women had had Purémpe ancestors, but that those ancestors had departed from their native Michihuácan long, long ago. The women's altered language was evidence of that. So was the fact that they did not follow the very old Purémpe fashion of shaving their heads bald. When Cricket was not busy gorging me with food, she had no qualms about answering my many questions. The first thing I asked was about the women's houses, which were not houses at all.

The islands, in addition to their being fringed with coconut palms, are heavily forested with hardwood trees on their upper slopes. But the women live all day in the open and at night, to sleep, they crawl into crude shelters underneath the many fallen trees. They had dug small caves under them or, where a trunk leaned at an angle, they had walled in the space with palm leaves or slabs of bark. I was lent one of those makeshift nooks for my own, next to the one occupied by Ixínatsi and her four-year-old daughter (named Tirípetsi, after that yellow flower).

I asked, "Why, with all these trees, do you not cut them into boards for building decent houses? Or at least use the saplings, which do not require slicing?"

She said, "It would be of no use, Tenamáxtli. Too often, the rainy season brings such terrible storms that they scour these islands bare of anything movable. Even the strong trees, many of them are blown down each year. So we make our shelters under the fallen ones, that *we* may not be blown away. We build nothing that cannot easily be rebuilt. That is also why we do not try to grow crops of any sort. But the sea gives us abundant food, we have good streams for drink, coconuts for sweets. Our only harvest is of the kinúcha, and we trade them for the other things we need. Which are few,'' she concluded and, as if to illustrate, swept her hand down her all but naked body.

The word *kinúcha* of course means "pearls." And there was good reason why the island women needed little from the world across the sea. All except the youngest girls spent every day hard at work, which tired them so that they passed their nights in deep slumber. Barring the brief intervals they allowed themselves for eating and obligatory functions, they worked or they slept, and they could imagine no other activities. They were as indifferent to the ideas of diversion and leisure as they were to the lack of male mates and boy children.

Their work is certainly demanding—and unique among feminine occupations. As soon as the day is light enough, most of the girls and women either swim out into the sea or push out on rafts made of vine-lashed tree limbs. Each woman carries looped to her arm a basket made of loosely woven withes. From then until the light fades at dusk, those women dive repeatedly to the bottom of the sea, to pry loose the oysters that abound there. They surface with a basket full of the things, empty them onto the beach or their raft, then dive to fill it again. Meanwhile, the girls too young and the women too old to dive do the drudgery of opening the oysters—and throwing away almost all of them.

The women do not want the oysters, except for the comparatively few they eat. What they seek are the oysters' kinúcha, the hearts, the pearls. During my stay in the islands, I saw pearls enough to have paid for raising an entire modern city there, if a city had been wanted. Most of the pearls were perfectly round and smooth, some were irregularly bulbous; some were as small as a fly's eye, some as large as my thumb end; most were of sizes varying between those extremes. Most, also, were a softly glowing white, but there were pinks and pale blues and even an occasional kinú the silver-gray color of a thundercloud. What makes pearls so esteemed and so valuable are their rarity and difficulty of acquisition, though one would suppose that if any oyster has a heart, they all should.

"They all do," said Cricket. "But only a very few have the right sort." She tilted her pretty head, gazing at me. "Your own heart, Tenamáxtli, it is for feeling emotions, yes? Like love?"

"So it seems," I said, and laughed. "It thumps more noticeably when I love somebody."

She nodded. "As does mine, when I look at my little Tirípetsi and feel love for her. But oysters do not all have hearts that know emotion as human hearts do. Most oysters just lie inert, and wait for the water currents to bring them nourishment, and aspire to nothing more than oyster-bed placidity, and do nothing but exist as long as they can."

I started to remark that she might be describing her own island sisters or, for that matter, the majority of humankind, but she went on:

"Only one oyster in many—perhaps one in a hundred hundreds—has a heart that can feel, that can want to be something more than a slime in a shell. That one oyster among so many, that one with a feeling heart, well, his is the heart that becomes a kinú, visible and beautiful and precious."

Surely that nonsense could be believed nowhere except in The Islands of the Women, but it was such a sweet fancy that my own heart would not let me dispute it. And, now that I think back, that must have been the moment when I fell in love with Ixínatsi.

At any rate, her belief in questing for unoysterlike oysters seemed to console her on those days when she might dive a hundred hundreds of times between first and last light, and bring up whole nations of oysters without a kinú among them. So she never once—as I would have done—cursed the oysters or the gods or even spat angrily into the sea when a whole day's work was done in vain.

And cursedly hard work that is, too. I know, for I tried it one day, in secret, in waters the women were not then working—staying underwater long enough to pry just *one* oyster off a rock down there. That was as long as I *could* stay. But the women begin their diving when they are mere children. By the time they are grown, they have so developed in the upper body that they can hold their breath and remain submerged for an astonishingly long time. Indeed, those women of the islands have bosoms more remarkable than I have ever seen elsewhere.

"Look at them," said Cricket, holding one of her magnificent breasts in either hand. "It is because of these that the islands have come to be the domain of women only. You see, we worship the big-bosomed goddess Xarátanga. Her name means New Moon, and in the arc of every new moon you can see the curve of *her* ample breast."

The similarity had never occurred to me before, but it is so.

Cricket continued, "New Moon long ago ordained that these islands should be inhabited only by females, and all men have respected that commandment, for they fear that Xarátanga would take away the oysters—or at least their valuable kinúcha—if any but women tried to harvest them. Anyway, the men could not do that. As you confessed to me, Tenamáxtli, you proved your own ineptitude at it. We women are fitted by New Moon to be superior divers." She jiggled her breasts again. "These help our lungs to be capable of holding much more air than any man's can."

I could not divine any connection between milk-giving and air-breathing organs, but I was no tícitl, so I did not argue the matter. I could only admire. Whatever extra function the women's breasts might or might not serve, their superb development and ageless firmness indubitably add to the women's handsomeness. And there is another thing that makes the islanders differ from mainland women, and makes them attractive in a striking way, but to explain that aspect I must digress slightly.

There are on those islands many other inhabitants besides the women. Various kinds of sea turtles lumber from shore to sea and back, and there are crabs everywhere, and of course there is a multitude of birds, raucous of voice and promiscuous of droppings. But the most distinctive creature is the animal the women call the pukiitsí, which is to say a sea-dwelling version of the beast called cuguar in Náhuatl. The name must have come down to them from their Michi-huácan ancestors, for none of the islanders could ever have seen a cuguar.

The pukiitsí does vaguely resemble the mountain-dwelling cuguar, though its expression is not fierce, rather winningly mild and inquisitive. A pukiitsí is similarly whiskered about the muzzle, but its teeth are blunt, its ears tiny and its finlike paws are not killer-clawed. We of Aztlan saw these sea animals only rarely—when an injured or dead one washed up on our shores—because they do not care for sandy or swampy places, but prefer rocky ones. And we called them sea-does, simply because of their big, warm, brown doe eyes.

There might be hundreds of the sea-cuguars about The Islands of the Women at any one time, but they live on fish and are not at all to be feared, as real cuguars are. They would gambol in the waters right alongside the diving women, or lazily sun themselves on the offshore rocks, or even sleep floating on their backs in the sea. The women never killed them for food—the meat is not very tasty—but occasionally a sea-cuguar would die of some other cause, and the women would hasten to skin it. The glossy brown pelt is valued as a garment, both for its beauty and for its water-shedding properties. (Ixínatsi made me an elegant overmantle from one of the skins.) That coat of hair is dense enough that the sea-cuguars can live in the sea without their bodies ever getting cold or waterlogged, and the sleekness of the coat enables them to arrow through the water as swiftly as any fish.

The perpetually diving women have developed a trace of a similar coat. Now, I long ago made the point that our peoples of The One World are usually devoid of body hair, but I should amend that assertion. Every human being, even the newest and apparently hairless baby, wears an almost invisibly fine *down* over most of his or her body. Stand a naked man or woman between you and the sun and you will see. But the down of those island women has grown longer— encouraged, I imagine, by their having been sea divers for so many generations.

I do not mean that they are furred with coarse hair like that of white men's beards. The down is as fine and delicate and colorless as milkweed floss, but it covers their coppery bodies with a sheen like that of the sea-cuguars and serves the same purpose of making them more agile in the water. When an island woman stands with the sunlight falling from behind her, she is edged and outlined in shining gold. In moonlight she glistens silver. Even when she is long out of the sea and completely dry, she looks delightfully dewy, and more supple than other women are, and as if she could slip easily from the embrace of the strongest man . . .

Which brings me to the subject that had, all this while, been uppermost in my mind. I have mentioned the many generations of the women divers. But how did one generation beget the next?

The answer is so simple as to be ridiculous, even vulgar, even somewhat revolting. But I did not summon up enough nerve to ask the question until the night of my seventh day in the islands, on which day old Kukú had decreed that I must depart the next morning.

XXVI

HAD FINISHED cutting and shaping my paddle, and Ixí-natsi had stocked my acáli with dried fish and coconut meat, plus a line and a bone hook with which I could catch fresh fish. She added five or six green coconuts from which she had sliced the stem end of each, so it remained closed only by a thin membrane. The heavy shell would keep the contents cool even in the sun; I had only to puncture the membrane to drink the sweet and refreshing coconut milk.

She gave me the directions which all the women had memorized, though none of them had ever had reason or wish to visit The One World. Between the islands and the mainland, she said, the tidal currents were always southerly, mild and stable. I was to paddle directly east each day at a steady but not overstrenuous pace. She rightly presumed that I knew how to maintain an eastward course, and she said that what southward drifting my acáli would do—while I slept at night—was allowed for in the instructions. On the fourth day I would sight a seaside village. Cricket did not know its name, but I did; it had to be Yakóreke.

So, on the night that Kukú had said would be my last there, Cricket and I sat side by side, leaning against the fallen tree trunk that roofed our two shelters, and I asked her, "Ixí-natsi, who was your father?"

She said simply, "We have no fathers. Only mothers and daughters. My mother is dead. You are acquainted with my daughter."

"But your mother could not have created you all by herself. Nor you your Tirípetsi. Sometime, somehow, in each case, there had to have been a man involved."

"Oh, that," she said negligently. "Akuáreni. Yes, the men come to do that once a year."

I said, "So that is what you meant when you first spoke to me. You told me I had come too soon."

"Yes. The men come from that mainland village to which you are going. They come for just one day in the eighteen months of the year. They come with loaded freight canoes, and we select what we need, and we trade our kinúcha for them. One kinú for a good comb made of bone or tortoise-shell, two kinúcha for an obsidian knife or a braided fishing line—"

"Ayya!" I interrupted. "You are being outrageously cheated! Those men exchange those pearls for countless times that value, and the next buyers trade them for another profit, and the next and the next. By the time the pearls have passed through all the hands between here and some city market . . ."

Cricket shrugged her moon-radiant bare shoulders. "The men could have the kinúcha for no payment at all, if Xará-tanga should choose to let them learn to dive. But the trading brings us what we need and want, and what more could we ask? Then, when the trading is all done, Kukú gathers those women who want to have a daughter—even those who may not be so eager, if Kukú says it is their turn—and Kukú selects the more robust of the men. The women lie in a row on the beach, and the men do that akuáreni we must endure if we are to have daughters."

"You keep saying daughters. There must be *some* boys born."

"Yes, some. But the goddess New Moon ordained that these be The Islands of the Women, and there is only one way to keep them so. Any male children, being forbidden by the goddess, are drowned at birth.''

Even in the dark, she must have seen the expression on my face, but she misinterpreted it, hastening to add:

''That is not a waste, as you may think. They become nourishment for the oysters, and that is a very worthwhile use for them.''

Well, as a male myself, I could hardly applaud that merciless weeding out of the newborn. On the other hand, like most god-commanded doings, it had the purity of stark simplicity. Keep the islands a female preserve by feeding the oysters on whose hearts the islanders depend.

Cricket went on, ''My daughter is almost of an age to commence diving. So I expect Kukú will order me to do akuáreni with one of the men when they come next time.''

At that I did speak up. ''You make it sound as enjoyable as being attacked by a sea monster. Does none of you ever lie with a man just for the pleasure of it?''

''Pleasure?!'' she exclaimed. ''What pleasure can there be in having a pole of flesh painfully stuck inside you and painfully moved back and forth a few times and then painfully pulled out? During that while, it is like being constipated in the wrong place.''

I muttered, ''Gallant and gracious men you women invite for consorts,'' then said aloud, ''My dear Ixínatsi, what you describe is rape, not the loving act it should be. When it is done with love—and you yourself have spoken of the loving heart—it can be an exquisite pleasure.''

''Done how with love?'' she asked, sounding interested.

''Well . . . the loving can start long before a pole of flesh is involved. You know that *you* have a loving heart, but you may not know that you also have a kinú. It is infinitely more capable of being loved than that of the most emotional oyster. It is there.''

I pointed to the place, and she seemed immediately to lose interest.

''Oh, that,'' she said again. She unwound her single garment and shifted to move her abdomen into a moonbeam, and with her fingers she parted the petals of her tipíli, and looked incuriously at her pearl-like xacapíli, and said, "A child's plaything."

"What?"

"A girl learns very young that that little part of her is sensitive and excitable, and she makes much use of it. Yes— as you are doing now with your fingertip, Tenamáxtli. But, as a girl matures, she grows bored with that childish practice and finds it unwomanly. Also, our Kukú has taught us that such activity depletes one's strength and endurance. Oh, a grown woman does it once in a while. I do it myself— exactly as you are doing it to me this moment—but only for relief when I feel tense or ill-humored. It is like scratching an itch."

I sighed. "Itching and push-pull and constipation. What awful words you use to speak of the feeling that can be the most sublime of feelings. And your aged Kukú is wrong. Lovemaking can invigorate you to much greater strength and satisfaction in *every* other thing you do. But never mind that. Just tell me. When *I* fondle you there, is it like your own scratching of an itch?"

"N-no," she admitted, with a break in her voice. "I feel . . . whatever I feel . . . it is very different . . ."

Trying to suppress my own arousal, so I could speak as soberly as an examining tícitl, I asked, "But it feels good?"

She said softly, "Yes."

When I kissed her nipples, she whispered, "Yes."

As I kissed farther down the sleek-pelted, moon-glistening length of her body, she said almost inaudibly, "Yes."

I kissed to where my hand was, then moved my hand out of the way. She started and gasped, "*No!* You cannot . . . that is not how . . . oh, yes, it is! Yes, you can! And I . . . oh, *I* can!"

It took a while for Cricket to recover, and she breathed as if she had just come up from the sea depths when she said,

''Uiikíiki! Never . . . when I myself . . . it has never been like that!''

"Let us make up for the long neglect," I suggested, and I did things that took her to those depths—or heights—twice again before I even let her know that I had a pole of flesh available when it should be wanted. And when it was, I was embraced and enfolded and engulfed by a creature as lithe and sinuous and pliant and nimble as any sea-cuguar cavorting in its own element.

Then it was that I discovered something absolutely novel about Ixínatsi—and I would have sworn that no woman could ever again surprise me in any way. It was not until we lay together that I discovered it, because her delightful difference from all other women resided in her most intimate parts. Manifestly, when the unborn Cricket was being fashioned by the gods, while she was still within her mother's womb, the kindly goddess of love and flowers and connubial happiness must have said:

"Let me endow this girl-child Ixínatsi with one small uniqueness in her female organs, so that when she grows to womanhood she can perform akuáreni with mortal men as joyously and voluptuously as I myself might do." It was indeed only a small alteration that the goddess effected in Cricket's body, but *ayyo!*—I can attest that it added an incredible piquancy and exuberance when she and I joined in the conjugal act.

The love goddess is called Xochiquétzal by us Aztéca, but is known as Petsíkuri by the Purémpecha, including these island women. Whatever her name, what she had done was this. She had set Cricket's tipíli opening just a *little* farther back between her thighs than is the case in ordinary women. Thus her tipíli's inner recess did not simply extend straight upward inside her body, but upward and *forward.* When she and I coupled face-to-face, and I slid my tepúli into her, it gently flexed to fit that curve. So, when it was fully sheathed inside her, my tepúli's crown was pointing back toward me, or, rather, toward the back of her belly's navel button.

In our Náhuatl language, a woman's body is often respect-fully referred to as a xochitl, a "flower," and her navel as the yoloxóchitl, or "bud center" of that flower. When I was inside Ixínatsi, then, my tepúli literally became the "stalk" of that bud, that flower. Just to realize, in my mind, that she and I were so *very* intimately conjoined—not to mention the vivid sensations involved—heightened my ardor to a degree I could never have believed possible.

And, in her arranging of Ixínatsi's feminine parts, the god-dess had provided, for both Cricket and myself, yet a further enhancement of the joy that comes in the act of love. The slightly rearward placement of her tipíli orifice meant that when my tepúli penetrated her to its hilt, my pubic bone was necessarily close and hard against her sensitive xacapíli pearl, much more tightly than it would be with an ordinary woman. So, as Ixínatsi and I clasped and rocked and writhed together, her little pink kinú accordingly got caressed, rubbed, kneaded—to excited erection, then to urgent throbbing, then to paroxysms of rapture. And Cricket's increasingly heated response naturally heated me as well, so that we were equally, gleefully, dizzily, almost swooningly exultant when together we came to climax.

When it was over, she of the prodigious lungs, of course, got her breath back before I did. While I still lay limp, Ixí-natsi slipped into her den under the tree and emerged to press something into my hand. It glowed in the moonlight like a piece of the moon itself.

"A kinú means a loving heart," she said, and kissed me.

"This single pearl," I said weakly, "would buy you much. A proper house, for instance. A very good one."

"I would not know what to do with a house. I *do* know—now—how to enjoy akuáreni. The kinú is to thank you for showing me."

Before I could gather breath to speak again, she had bounded upright and called across the tree trunk, "Marú-uani!" to the young woman who lived in the shelter on the other side. I thought Cricket was going to apologize for the doubtlessly unfamiliar noises we had been making. Instead she said urgently, "Come over here! I have discovered a thing most marvelous!"

Marúuani came around the root end of the tree, idly combing her long hair, pretending to be not at all curious, but her eyebrows went up when she saw us both unclothed. She said to Ixínatsi, but with her eyes on me, "It sounded—as if you were enjoying yourselves."

"Exactly that," Cricket said with relish. "Our . . . selves. Listen!" She moved close, to whisper to the other woman, who continued to regard me, her eyes widening more each moment. Lying there, being described and discussed, I felt rather like some hitherto unknown sea creature just washed ashore and causing a sensation. I heard Marúuani say, in a hushed voice, "He *did?*" and after some more whispering, "*Would* he?"

"Of course he will," said Ixínatsi. "Will you not, Tenamáxtli? Will you not do akuáreni with my friend Marúuani?"

I cleared my throat and said, "One thing you must realize about men, my dearest. It takes them at least a little resting— between times—for the pole to stiffen again."

"It does? Oh, what a pity. Marúuani is eager to learn."

I considered, then said, "Well, I have shown you some things, Cricket, that do not require my participation. While I regather my faculties, you could demonstrate the preliminaries to your friend."

"You are right," she said brightly. "After all, we will not always have men with poles at our bidding. Marúuani, take off your loincloth and lie down here."

Somewhat guardedly, Marúuani obeyed, and Ixínatsi stretched out beside her, both of them just a little way from me. Marúuani flinched and gave a small shriek at the first intimate touch.

"Be still," said Cricket, with the confidence of experience. "This is how it is done. In a moment you will know."

And it was not long before I was watching *two* supple, shining sea-cuguars doing the contortions of coupling—

much as the real animals do it—except that these were much
more graceful, since they had long, shapely arms and legs to
intertwine. And the watching of it hastened my own availa-
bility, so I was ready for Marúuani when she was ready for
me.

I repeat, I was in love with Ixínatsi even before we did
the *act* of love. I had already, that very night, determined to
take her and her little girl with me when I left the island. I
would do it by persuasion, if possible. If not, I would—like
a brute Yaki—abduct them by force. And now, having found
out how uniquely and wonderfully Cricket was constructed
for the act of love, I was more determined than before.

But I am human. And I am male. Therefore I am incura-
bly, insatiably curious. I could not help wondering if *all* these
island women possessed the same physical properties that
Cricket did. Although the young woman Marúuani was
comely and appealing, I had never felt any desire for her,
certainly not what I had felt and still felt for Ixínatsi. However, after watching what had just occurred, and being
aroused by it to an indiscriminate lustfulness, and with Ixínatsi unselfishly urging me on . . .

Well, that is how my stay in the islands came to be indefi-
nitely prolonged. Ixínatsi and Marúuani spread the word that
there *was* something more to life than just working and
sleeping and occasionally playing with one's self—and the
other island women clamored to be introduced to it. Grandmother's scandalized objections were shouted down, probably for the first time in her reign, but she became resigned
to the new state of affairs when it effected a noticeable increase in the workers' good spirits and productivity. Kukú
enforced only one condition: that all akuáreni be confined to
the nighttimes—which I did not mind, because it gave me
the days for sleeping and regaining my stamina.

Let me say here that I would not have obliged any of the
other women if Cricket had evinced the least jealousy or
possessiveness. I did it mainly because she seemed so happy

to have her sisters thus enlightened, and seemed to take pride in that being done by "her man." In truth, I would rather have restricted my attentions to her alone, for she was the one that I deeply loved—the only one, then or ever—and I know she loved me, too. Even Tirípetsi, who at first had been shy and uneasy about having a man in residence, came to regard me fondly, as other little girls elsewhere regard their fathers.

Also, and this is important, the other island women were *not* physically constructed as was Ixínatsi. They were as ordinary in that respect as every other woman I have coupled with in my lifetime. In short, I was so infatuated with Cricket that *no* other woman would ever measure up to the standards she had set. It was only because she wished it that I lent my services to the women at large. I did that more dutifully than avidly, and even instituted a sort of program—a petitioning woman every other night, the nights between being devoted to Cricket alone—and those were nights of love, not just loving.

It may be that because I had seldom lacked for women— and certainly did not now—I had become somewhat jaded with the commonplace, and the very *newness* of Ixínatsi was what vitalized me so. I only know that the sensations shared by her and myself kindled in me fires that I had never felt, even in my lustiest youth. As for dear Cricket, I am sure she had no idea that she was physically superior to ordinary women. Nothing could ever have made her suspect that she had been so god-blessed at birth. And, of course, it may be that she was not the *only* female in human history to have been thus endowed by a goddess. Possibly some aged midwife, after numberless years of attending a numberless multitude of females, could have told of having *sometime* found some other young woman similarly constructed.

But I cared not. From this time forward, I would not ever need or seek or want any other lover—however extraordinary—now that I possessed this most exceptional one of all. And whether or not Ixínatsi realized that in our frequent and fervent embraces she was enjoying ecstasies surpassing those that the love goddess grants to every other woman in the world . . . well, she *did* enjoy them. And so did I, so did I. *Yyo ayyo*, how we did *enjoy* them!

Meanwhile, I lay at least once with every island woman and girl who was physically mature enough to appreciate the experience. Though our akuáreni was always done in the darkness, I know I also coupled with some who were rather *beyond* mature—but none of the really old ones, like Kukú, for which I was thankful. I might well have lost count of the women I obliged with my teachings, if I had not been recompensed for my services. Eventually, I owned exactly sixty-five pearls, the largest and most perfect of that year's harvest. That was Cricket's doing; she insisted that it was only fair exchange that my students pay me one pearl apiece.

In the beginning, there was such mass enthusiasm that there was a constant traffic of females rafting every night back and forth between the two inhabited islands. But there was only one of me, and the other women had to alternate with Ixínatsi, so during that time many of them earnestly essayed to learn by imitation, as Ixínatsi had taught Marú-uani. Sometimes I would be lying with a woman, going through the ceremony from first fondlings to final consummation, and two other females—her sister and her daughter, it might be—would lie right next to us, alternately eyeing our doings and then doing them to one another, insofar as possible.

After I had personally served every eligible girl and woman at least once, and the demand for me was not so imperative, the women continued, on their own, to discover the numerous ways they could pleasure one another, and freely traded partners, and even learned to do it in threes and fours—all this with blithe disregard for any consanguinity among them. Ixínatsi and I, in our intervals of rest at night, would often hear, among the other forest sounds, the sound of those women's wonderful breasts slapping rhythmically together.

All this while, I was ardently wooing Ixínatsi—not to make her love me; we knew we loved one another. I was trying to persuade her to come with me, and bring the daughter I now thought of as my own, to The One World. I besieged her with every argument I could muster. I told her, with honesty, that I was the equivalent of Kukú in my own domain, that she and Tirípetsi would live in a genuine palace, with servants at their command, lacking nothing they could possibly need or want, never again having to dive for oysters, or skin sea-cuguars for their hides, or fear the storms that might ravage the islands, or lie down to mate with strangers.

"Ah, Tenamáxtli," she would say with an endearing smile, "but *this* is palace enough"—indicating the tree-trunk shelter—"as long as you share it with us."

Not quite so honestly, I omitted all mention of the Spaniards' having occupied most of The One World. These island women did not yet know that such things as white men existed. Evidently the men from Yakóreke had likewise refrained from speaking of the Spaniards, possibly out of concern that the women might withhold their kinúcha, hoping to start a new commerce with richer traders. For that matter, I reminded myself, I could not be sure that the Spaniards had not already overwhelmed Aztlan, in which case I had no Kukúdom, so to speak, with which to tempt Cricket. But I firmly believed that she and Tirípetsi and I could make a new life for ourselves *somewhere*, and I regaled her with tales of the many lovely, lush, serene places I had found in my travels, where we three might settle down together.

"But this place, Tenamáxtli, these islands, they are *home*. Make them your home, too. Grandmother is accustomed to having you here now. She will no longer be demanding that you depart. Is this not as pleasant a life as we could find anywhere else? We need not fear the storms and strangers. Tirípetsi and I have survived all the storms, and so will you. As for the strangers, you know I will never again lie with one of those. I am yours."

In vain, I tried to make her envision the more *varied* life that could be lived on the mainland—the abundance of food and drink and diversion, of travel, of education for our daughter, the opportunities of meeting new people quite different from those she was used to.

"Why, Cricket," I said, "you and I can have other children there, to be company for little Tirípetsi. Even *brothers* for her. She can never have any here."

Ixínatsi sighed, as if she was wearying of my importunities, and said, "She can never miss what she has never had."

I asked anxiously, "Have I made you angry?"

"Yes, I am angry," she said, but with a laugh, in her cricket-merry way. "Here—take back all your kisses." And she began kissing me, and kept on kissing me every time I tried to say anything more.

But always, with sweet stubbornness, she dismissed or countered my every argument—and one day she did it by alluding to my own enviable current situation:

"Do you not see, Tenamáxtli, that any mainland man would absolutely *pounce* to trade places with you? Here you have not only me to love you and lie with you—and you will have Tirípetsi, too, when she is of age—you have, when you so desire, any *other* woman of these islands. Every woman. And, in time, *their* daughters."

I was hardly qualified to start preaching morality. I could only protest, and with utmost sincerity, "But *you* are all I want!"

And now I must confess something shameful. That same day, I went off into the woods to think, and I said to myself, "She *is* all I want. I am captivated by her, obsessed, besotted. If I dragged her away from here against her will, she would never love me again. Anyway, what would I be dragging her to? What awaits *me* yonder? Only a bloody war—killing or being killed. Why should I not do what she says? *Stay* here in these fair islands."

Here I had peace, love, happiness. The other women were making ever fewer demands on me, now that the novelty had worn off. Ixínatsi and Tirípetsi and I could be a self-

contained and self-sufficient family. Since I had broken one
of the islands' sacred traditions—by living here as no man
had ever done before—I believed that I could break others.
Old Grandmother had gone unheeded in that instance, and,
anyway, she would not live forever. I had every expectation
that I could wean the women away from their man-hating
goddess New Moon, and turn them instead to worship of the
kindlier Coyolxaúqui, goddess of the full-hearted *full* moon.
No longer would boy infants be fed to the oysters. Cricket
and I and all the others could have *sons*. I would eventually
be the patriarch of an island domain, and its benevolent ruler.

For all I knew, the Spaniards had by now overrun the
entire One World, and I could hope to accomplish nothing
by going back there. Here, I would have my own One World,
and it might be sheaves of years before any farther-reaching
Spanish explorers should stumble upon it. Even if the white
men had subjugated so much of the mainland—or later
would—that the Yakóreke fishermen could no longer visit
the islands, I was sure that *they* would not reveal the location.
If they came no more, well, *I* now knew the course back and
forth. I and, in time, my sons could paddle stealthily to that
shore to procure the necessities of life—knives and combs
and such—that had to be bought with pearls . . .

Thus shamefully did I contemplate abandoning the quest
that I had pursued during all the years since I watched my
father burn to death, the quest that had led me along so many
roads, into so many hazards, through so many adventures.
Thus shamefully did I seek to justify discarding my plans to
avenge my father and all others of my people who had suffered at the hands of the white men. Thus shamefully did I
try to concoct excuses for forgetting those many—Citláli and
the child Ehécatl, dauntless Pakápeti, the Cuáchic Comitl, the
Tícitl Ualíztli, the others—who had perished in helping me
toward my aim of vengeance. Thus shamefully did I seek
plausible reasons for my deserting the Knight Nochéztli and
my hard-gathered army and, indeed, all the peoples of The
One World . . .

I have been ashamed, ever since that day, that I even *thought* of so disgracing myself. I would have lost the race I never ran. Had I actually done that—succumbed to Ixínatsi's love and the islands' easefulness—I doubt that I could long have lived with my shame. I would have come to hate myself, and then have turned the hate on Cricket for her causing me to hate myself. What I might have done for love would have destroyed that love.

Further to my shame, I cannot even claim with conviction that I would *not* have chosen to surrender my quest—and my honor—because it so happened that the gods made the choice for me.

Toward twilight, I returned to the seaside, where the divers were wading ashore with their last baskets of the day. Ixínatsi was among them, and when she saw me waiting for her, she called cheerily, mischievously, with a meaningful grin:

"I think by now, darling Tenamáxtli, I must owe you at least one more kinú. I shall dive this moment and bring you the Kukú of all kinúcha." She turned and swam to the nearest rock outcrop, where some indolent sea-cuguars were basking and gleaming in the last low rays of sunlight.

I called to her, "Come back, Cricket. I wish to talk."

She must not have heard me. Glistening as golden as the animals about her, radiant and beautiful, she stood poised on one of the rocks, gave me a jaunty wave of her hand, dove into the sea and never came out again.

When finally I realized that not even the strongest-lunged woman could have stayed underwater so long, I raised an outcry. All the other divers still in the shallows came splashing ashore in fright, probably thinking I had espied a shark's fin. Then, after some hesitation, the more intrepid of them swam back to the area I pointed to—where I had seen Ixínatsi plunge under—and they dove again and again, until they were exhausted, without finding her or any indication of what had happened to her.

"Our women," said a creaky old voice beside me, "do not all live to my great age."

It was Kukú, who had naturally hastened to the scene. Although she might have berated me for having disturbed the complacency of her realm, or for having been partly to blame for Cricket's loss, the old woman sounded as if she wished to solace me.

"Kinú-diving is more than rigorous work," she said. "It is perilous work. Down there lurk savage fish with tearing teeth, others with poisonous stings, others with clutching tentacles. I do not think, however, that Ixínatsi fell prey to any such fish. When there are predators in the vicinity, the sea-cuguars bark a warning. More likely she has been swallowed."

"Swallowed?" I echoed, thunderstruck. "Kukú, how could a woman be swallowed by the sea in which she has lived for half her life?"

"Not by the sea. By the kuchúnda."

"What is the kuchúnda?"

"A giant mollusk, like an oyster or clam or scallop, only unbelievably bigger. As big as that rock islet yonder where the sea-cuguars are dozing. Big enough to swallow one of those sea-cuguars. There are several of the kuchúndacha hereabouts, and we do not always know where, for they have the ability, like a snail, to creep from place to place. But they are visible and recognizable—each kuchúnda keeps its massive upper shell agape, to clamp down on any unwary prey— so our women know to stay well clear of them. Ixínatsi must have been unusually intent on her oyster-gathering. Perhaps she saw a prize kinú—it happens sometimes, when an oyster lies open—and she must have relaxed her vigilance."

I said miserably, "She went promising to fetch just such a kinú for me."

The old woman shrugged and sighed. "The kuchúnda would have slammed its shell shut, with her—or most of her—inside. And since it cannot chew, it is now slowly digesting her with its corrosive juices."

I shuddered at the picture she evoked, and I went sorrowfully away from the place where I had last seen my beloved

Cricket. The women all looked sad, too, but they did no keening or weeping. They appeared to regard this as no uncommon event in a day's work. Little Tirípetsi had already been told, and she was not weeping, either. So I did not. I grieved only silently, and silently cursed the meddling gods. If they *had* to intervene in my life—sternly pointing me to my destined future roads and days—they could have done it without so gruesomely ending the life of the innocent, vivacious, marvelous little Cricket.

I said good-bye only to Tirípetsi and Grandmother, not to any of the other women, lest they try to detain me. I could not now take the child with me, because of where I was going, and I knew she would be lovingly cared for by all her aunts and cousins of the islands. At dawn, I put on the elegant skin mantle Ixínatsi had made for me, and I took my sack of pearls, and I went to the southern end of the island, where my acáli had waited all this time, stocked with the provisions put into it by Ixínatsi, and I pushed off and paddled eastward.

So The Islands of the Women are still The Islands of the Women, though I trust they are now a more convivial place by night. And any Yakóreke fishermen who visited after my time could have had no cause to resent my having been there. Those who may have come *immediately* after me could hardly have sired any children—surely every possible mother-to-be was already on her way to being one—but the men must have been so riotously welcomed and overwhelmingly entertained that they would have been ingrates indeed if they complained about a mysterious outlander's having preceded them.

But I thought, and I hoped, as I went away, that perhaps I would not be gone forever. Someday, when I had finished doing what I must do, and if I survived the doing of it . . . someday, when Tirípetsi had grown to be the image of her mother, the only woman I ever truly loved . . . someday toward the end of my days . . .

XXVII

MY HEART WAS so heavy and my thoughts so melancholy that I felt no alarm, scarcely even noticed, when the islands sank out of sight behind me and I was again alone on the fearsomely empty open sea. What I was thinking was this:

"It seems that I somehow confer a curse upon all the women toward whom I feel love or even affection. The gods cruelly take them away, and cruelly leave me alive, to live with regret and grief."

And this: "But ayya, when I bemoan my bereavement, I am being callously selfish, because what happened to Ixínatsi and Pakápeti and Citláli was so much worse. *They* lost the whole world and all their tomorrows."

And this: "Ever since childhood, my cousin Améyatl and I have been merely *fond* of one another, yet she nearly died of imprisonment and degradation."

And this: "The little mulata girl Rebeca and I considered one another only an *experiment*. But, when she went from my arms into a convent's suffocating confinement, she too could be said to have lost the world and all her tomorrows."

Thus it was that, then and there, I made a decision. I would live the kind of life, from now on, that would be most prudent—and most considerate of every woman remaining in

The One World. I would never again let myself be lured into love of any of them, or let any of them love me. For myself, the remembrances of the idyll I had shared with Cricket would sustain me for the rest of my days. For the women, I would be doing a mercy, not endangering them with whatever was the curse I carried with me.

If, when I got ashore at Yakóreke and walked north to Aztlan, I should find the city still intact and Améyatl still ruling there, I would decline her suggestion that we wed and reign side by side. Henceforth, I would devote myself entirely to the war I had instigated, and to the extermination or expulsion of the white men. I would let no woman, ever again, into my heart, my life. If and when my physical needs got overwhelmingly urgent, I could always find some female to use, but that would be all she would mean to me—a handy yet disposable receptacle. I would never love again; I would never be loved again.

And in all the time since I swore that vow to myself in the vast expanses of the Western Sea, I have kept steadfast to that oath. Or I did until I found you, querida Verónica. But again I get ahead of my chronicle.

While I thought those thoughts, I was occupied with something else as well. I cut small slits in the inner skin of the sea-cuguar mantle Cricket had made for me—sixty-five slits—and in each of them secreted one of the pearls I carried, and sewed them invisibly there, using the bone hook and fishing line Cricket had provided. What with my preoccupation of mind and hands, I was often neglecting to paddle as steadily as I had been instructed, and forgetful of the fact that the sea's current was carrying my acáli farther southward than I should have let it do.

In consequence, when at last the mainland came into view on the eastern horizon, I saw there no Yakóreke or any other village. Well, small matter. At least I was back on the solid ground of The One World, and I did not much mind having a longer journey to make along the coast to Aztlan. As I neared the shore, I saw a beach on which several rough-clad men of my own complexion were busily engaged at some employment I could not make out, so I steered my craft toward them. When I got closer, I could see that they were fishermen, mending their nets. They all dropped their work to watch me wade and drag my acáli up onto the sand among their own acáltin, but they did not seem overly surprised at seeing a rather luxuriously mantled stranger suddenly appear out of nowhere.

When I called "Mixpantzínco!" to them and they replied with "Ximopanólti!" I was relieved to hear them speak Náhuatl. It meant that I was still somewhere in the Aztéca regions, and had not drifted into totally unfamiliar lands.

I introduced myself only as "Tenamáxtli," without elaboration, but one of the men was uncommonly acute and well informed for a mere fisherman. He asked:

"Would you be that same Tenamáxtli who is cousin to Améyatzin, the lady of Aztlan who once was wed to the late lord Káuritzin of our own Yakóreke?"

"I am he," I admitted. "So you are men of Yakóreke?"

"Yes, and rumor reached us long ago that you are traveling over all The One World on some mission in behalf of that lady and our late lord."

"In behalf of *all* our peoples," I said. "You will soon hear more than rumors. But tell me. What are you doing here? I know not where I have landed, exactly, but I know it is south of the Yakóreke fishing grounds."

"Ayya, there were too many of us crowding the waters there. So we few wandered hither to try our fortunes and— ayyo!—found abundant nettings *and* a new market for them. We supply the white residents of the town they call Compostela, and they pay handsomely. It is yonder"—he pointed due east—"only a few one-long-runs."

I realized that I had veered farther off course than I had supposed. I was uncomfortably close to those same Spaniards from whom I had escaped. But all I said to the fishermen was, "Do you not worry that you will be snatched into slavery when you go there?"

"For a wonder, no, Tenamáxtli. The soldiers have lately ceased to exert themselves to impound slaves. And the man called the gobernador seems even to have lost interest in grubbing silver from the earth. He is busy equipping his soldiers—and gathering others from other places—in preparation for some grand expedition to the northward. As best we can discover, he is not marching against Yakóreke or Tépiz or Aztlan or any other of our communities still free of subjugation. It will not be an expedition of raiding or conquering or occupying. But whatever he is planning, it has caused a fever of excitement in the town. The gobernador has even relinquished the governing of Compostela to a man called an *obispo*, and that one seems leniently disposed toward us unwhite persons. We are let freely to come and go and peddle our fish and set our own prices."

Well, this was interesting news. The expedition certainly must have something to do with those mythical rich Cities of Antilia. And the bishop had to be my old acquaintance Vasco de Quiroga. I was meditating on how to turn these matters to my advantage, when the fisherman spoke again:

"We shall be sorry to leave here."

"Leave?" I asked. "Why leave?"

"We must return to Yakóreke. The time approaches for all us sea-fishers to embark upon our annual oyster-harvesting."

I smiled reminiscently, and more than a little sadly, thinking, "Ayyo, happy men!" But what I said was, "If you are going north again, friends, would one of you do a favor for me—and for the widow of your late Káuritzin?"

"Assuredly. What would that be?"

"Go the twelve one-long-runs farther north—to Aztlan. It has been a very long time since I was last there, and my cousin Améyatl may be thinking that I have died. Simply tell her that you saw me, that I am in good health and still pursuing my mission. That I hope shortly to be bringing it to fruition, and once I have accomplished that, I will report to her in Aztlan.''

"Very well. Anything else?''

"Yes. Give her this fur mantle. Tell her that—just in case my mission should fail somehow, and she should find herself imperiled by the white men or any other enemy—this mantle will afford her lifelong sustenance and protection.''

The man looked puzzled. "A simple sea-doe skin? How?''

"A very special sea-doe skin. There is magic in it. Améyatl will discover that magic when and if she needs it.''

The man shrugged. "As you say. Consider it done, Tenamáxtli.''

I thanked them all, said good-bye and set off inland, toward Compostela.

I was not particularly apprehensive of danger in so boldly returning to the town from which I had made my rather memorable escape. Of those who might recognize and denounce me, Yeyac and G'nda Ké were dead. Coronado was apparently being too busy to be paying much heed to stray indios in his streets. And so, presumably, was that Fray Marcos, if he was in residence. Nevertheless, I remembered the piece of advice I had been given long ago—carry something and look purposeful. In the slave-quarter outskirts of the town I found a balk of timber, roughly square-hewn, lying unattended on the ground. I hefted it to my shoulder and pretended it was heavy, so I could walk hunched over a bit, to disguise my tallness.

Then I made for the center of the town, where stand its only two stone-built structures, the palace and the church. The palace had its usual guards at the entrance, but they paid me no notice as I slouched past. At the church's unguarded door, I dropped the timber, went inside and accosted the first shaven-pated Spaniard I saw. I told him, in Spanish, that I brought a message from his superior's fellow bishop, Zumárraga. The monk eyed me somewhat askance, but he went away somewhere, came back and beckoned, and led me to the bishop's chambers.

"Ah, Juan Británico!" cried that good and trusting old man. "It has been a long time, but I would have known you on sight. Be seated, dear fellow, be seated. What a pleasure to see you again!" He called to a servant to bring refreshments, then went on, not a whit suspiciously, "Still doing Bishop Zumárraga's evangel work among the unconverted, eh? And how *is* my old friend and colleague Juanito? You say you bring a message from him?"

"Er, he thrives and prospers, Your Excellency." Padre Vasco was the only white man to whom I would ever accord that title of respect. "And his message—er, well ..." I glanced around; this church was far inferior to Zumárraga's in the City of Mexíco. "He expresses the hope, Your Excellency, that you will soon have a house of worship befitting your high station."

"How kind of Juanito! But surely His Excellency knows that a grand cathedral is already being planned for New Galicia."

"Perhaps he does, by now," I said lamely. "But I, what with my constant traveling ..."

"Ah, then rejoice with me, my son! Yes, it will be built in the province your people call Xalíscan. There is a fine new town rising there, currently called by the native name of Tonalá, but I think that name will be changed to Guadalajara, to honor the city in Old Spain whence originated the house of Mendoza. Our viceroy's family, you know."

I asked, "And how fare your Utopía communities around the Lake of Rushes?"

"Better than I might have expected," he said. "All about that area have occurred uprisings of disaffected Purémpecha. Of Purémpe *women*, can you imagine that? *Amazonas*, they are—vicious and vindictive. They have caused many deaths and much damage and every sort of pilferage among the Spanish settlements. But, for what reason I know not, they have spared our little Eden."

"They probably recognize and esteem you, padre, as an

exemplary Christian," I lied, but with no irony intended. "Why did you leave there?"

"His Excellency the Governor Coronado had need of me here. He will shortly be undertaking a venturesome journey that could greatly increase the wealth of all New Spain. And he asked me to administer the governing of Compostela in his absence."

"Excuse me, my lord," I said, "but you sound not entirely approving of that venture."

"Well . . . mere wealth . . ." said the bishop with a sigh. "Don Francisco aspires to the stature of the earlier conquistadores. And with the same rallying cry: 'Glory, God and gold.' I only wish he would put God first. He will be journeying—not as you do, Juan Británico, to evangelize for Holy Mother Church—but to find and plunder some far-off and reputedly treasure-filled cities."

Feeling a twinge of shame at my imposture, I murmured, "I have traveled far and wide, but I know of no such cities."

"It seems that they do exist, though. A certain friar was led to them by a Moro slave who had been there before. The good Fray Marcos has but recently returned, with his soldier escorts but without the slave. Fray Marcos affirms that he saw the cities—they are called the Cities of Cíbola, he says—but he saw them only from a distance, because they are of course vigilantly guarded against discovery. He had to turn back when that poor loyal slave guide was slain by the guardian savages. But the staunch and valiant friar is now about to lead Coronado there, this time with an invincible host of armed soldiers."

It was the first time I had ever heard any human being say a commendatory word for the Lying Monk. And I was willing to wager that Esteban was still alive, at liberty now, and that he would likely spend the rest of his life—when he was not enjoying the desert women—laughing at his greedily gullible former masters.

"If the friar saw the cities only from a distance," I said, "how can he be sure they are full of treasures?"

"Oh, he saw the house walls gleaming, sheathed in gold, studded with sparkling gems. And he was close enough to descry the inhabitants walking about, clad in silks and velvets. These things he swears to. And Fray Marcos is; after all, bound by the vows of his order never to tell an untruth. It seems certain that Don Francisco will return from Cíbola in triumph, laden with riches, to be rewarded with fame and adulation and the favor of His Majesty. Still . . ."

"You would prefer that he brought souls instead," I suggested. "Converts to the Church."

"Well, yes. But I am not a pragmatic man of the world." He gave a little laugh of self-deprecation. "I am only an ingenuous old cleric, piously and unfashionably believing that our true fortunes await us in another world altogether."

I said, and sincerely, "All of Spain's vaunted conquistadores combined would not equal the worth of one Vasco de Quiroga."

He laughed again, and waved away the compliment. "Still, I am not the only one who questions the wisdom of the governor's hastening headlong toward that Cíbola. Many think it a rash and reckless venture—that it may work more harm than good to New Spain."

"How so?" I asked.

"He is collecting every soldier he can muster from the farthest corners of the land. And he needs not to conscript them. Everywhere, officers and rankers alike are pleading to be detached from their customary duties, in order to join Coronado. Even nonsoldiers, city merchants and country planters, are mounting and arming themselves to join. Every would-be hero and fortune hunter sees this as the opportunity of a lifetime. Also, Coronado is collecting remount horses for his troopers, packhorses and mules, extra arms and ammunition, every other kind of supplies, indio and Moro slaves to be bearers and drovers, even herds of cattle to be provisions along the way. He is seriously weakening the defenses of New Spain, and the people are worried about this. The depredations of those Purémpe Amazonas here in New

Galicia are well known, and the frequent sallies of savages
across our northern frontiers, and there have been distress-
ingly bloody incidents of unrest even among the prisoners
and slaves in our mines and mills and obrajes. The people
fear, with good reason, that Coronado is leaving all of New
Spain uncomfortably vulnerable to despoliation, both from
without and within.''

"I can see that," I said, trying not to sound pleased,
though nothing could have pleased me more to hear. "But
the viceroy in the City of Méxíco—that Señor Mendoza—
does he also regard Coronado's project as folly?"

The bishop looked troubled. "As I said, I am not a pragmatic man. But I can recognize expediency when I see it.
Coronado and Don Antonio de Mendoza are old friends. Coronado is married to a cousin of King Carlos. Mendoza is
also a friend of Bishop Zumárraga, and *he*, I fear, is ever too
ready to endorse any venture calculated to please and enrich
King Carlos—and endear *himself* to the king and the pope,
may God forgive me for saying so. Marshal all those facts,
Juan Británico. Is it likely that anyone, high or low, will
speak to Coronado a discouraging word?"

"Certainly not I," I said lightly, "and I am lowest of the
low." *The worm in the coyacapúli fruit*, I thought, *long
having eaten from within, now about to burst the fruit asunder.* "I thank you for your graciousness in receiving me,
Your Excellency, and for the refreshing cakes and wine, and
I ask your leave to be on my way."

Still being more decent to a lowly indio than any other
white man I ever met, Padre Vasco cordially urged me to
remain awhile—to reside under his roof, to attend services,
to make confession, to take communion, to converse at
greater length—but I lied some more, telling him that I had
instructions to hurry and "bear the message" to a still un-
regenerate pagan tribe some distance away.

Well, it was not entirely a lie. I did have a message to
deliver, and at a considerable distance. I left Compostela, not

having to sneak this time, no one paying any attention to me at all, and went briskly toward Chicomóztotl.

"Thanks be to Huitzilopóchtli and every other god!" exclaimed Nochéztli. "You have come at last, Tenamáxtzin, not a moment too soon. I have here the most numerous army ever assembled in The One World, every man of it impatiently stamping his feet to be on the march, and I have been barely able to hold them in check, awaiting your orders."

"You have done well, faithful knight. I have just come through the Spanish lands, and clearly no one there has any inkling of this gathering storm."

"That is good. But, among our own people, the word must have been passed from mouth to ear to mouth. We have acquired far more recruits than the many we enlisted from the lands hereabout, and the *very* many who came from the north, wave after wave of them, saying you had sent them. For example, all those women warriors from Michihuácan have made their way hither. They say they are tired of inflicting merely skirmish attacks on Spanish properties; they want to be with us when we march in force. Also there are countless runaway slaves—indios and Moros and mixtures of breeds—escaped from mines and plantations and obrajes, who have managed to find this place. They are even more avid than the rest of us to wreak havoc on their masters, but I have had to put them to special training, because few have ever even *held* a weapon before."

"Every man counts," I said, "and every woman. Can you tell me how many we have, in total?"

"As best I can estimate, a hundred of hundreds. A formidable host, in truth. They long ago overflowed the seven caverns here and are camped all over these mountains. Since they hail from so many different nations and perhaps a hundred different tribes within those nations, I thought it best to assign and segregate their camping places according to their origins. Many of them, as you doubtless know, have been

for ages inimical to one another—or to *every* other. I did not
want an intestine war erupting *here.*"

"Very astute management, Knight Nochéztli."

"However, the very variety of our forces makes the management of them most complicated. I have delegated my best
fellow knights and under-officers, each to be responsible for
one or another mass of warriors. But their orders, instructions, reprimands, whatever, given in the Náhuatl tongue, can
be given only to those tribal chief warriors who can understand Náhuatl. Those, in turn, must relay the words to their
men in *their* language. And then the words must be passed
along to the next tribe, who may speak a different dialect of
the same language, but can at least be made to understand.
And then *they* somehow transmit the words to yet another
tribe. Probably one man in every hundred of all these hundreds spends a good part of his time acting as interpreter.
And of course the commands frequently get contorted down
the course of that long process, which has made for some
marvelous misunderstandings. It has not *quite* happened yet,
but one of these days, when I form a contingent of our men
into ranks and give the command to the first rank, 'Stand to
arms!' and the command is passed along, the men in the last
rank are going to hear it as 'Lie down and go to sleep!' As
for those Yaki you sent, *none* of us can communicate with
them. They would not understand if I *did* order them to go
to sleep."

I had to stifle a smile at Nochéztli's overflow of exasperation. But I was proud and admiring of the way he had handled the vast army under those difficult conditions, and told
him so.

"Well, so far," he said, "I have been able to keep all the
men from getting too restive, and from quarreling among
themselves, by giving them orders that can be conveyed—
even to the Yaki—with gestures and demonstrations instead
of words, and thus keeping them all occupied with various
labors. Appointing certain groups to do the hunting and fishing and gathering of food, for instance, others to do the burn-

ing of charcoal, the mixing of pólvora, the casting of lead balls and so on. Those couriers you sent to Tzebóruko and to Aztlan did return with ample supplies of the yellow azufre and the bitter salitre. So we now have as much powder and as many balls as we can carry when we leave here. I am pleased to report, too, that we have many more of the thunder-sticks than before. The Purémpe women brought many that they captured from the Spaniards in New Galicia, and so did numerous warriors of the northern tribes who stole them from Spanish army outposts as they came hither through the Disputed Lands. We now have nearly a hundred of those weapons, and about twice that many men who have become expert at using them. We have also acquired a goodly armory of steel knives and swords.''

"This is all most gratifying to hear,'' I said. "Have you anything *not* so gratifying to report?''

"Only that we are better supplied with armament than with food. Given a hundred of hundreds of mouths to be fed, well, you can imagine. Our hunters and foragers have by now killed every last animal and bird and plucked every fruit, nut and edible green from all these mountains, and emptied the waters of every last fish. I had to set a limit to their foraging, you see, not let them go too far abroad, lest word of their activity reach the wrong ears. But you may wish to countermand that order, Tenamáxtzin, for we are now reduced to scant rations indeed—roots and tubers and frogs and insects. Such deprivation is of course beneficial for warriors. It makes them lean and hard and eager to reap from the fat lands we will be invading. However, besides the Purémpe women now among us, a good number of those runaway slaves who fled here are women and children. I hate to sound like a woman myself, but I do feel sorry for those weaker ones who came trusting that we would care for them. I hope, my lord, that you will give instant order for us all to march from here into more bounteous lands.''

"No,'' I said. "That order I will not give yet, and I will not countermand any of yours, even if we all must live for a time by chewing the leather of our own sandals. And I will tell you why.''

Thereupon, I repeated to Nochéztli everything the Bishop Quiroga had confided to me, and added:

"This, then, is my first order. Send sharp-eyed and fleet-footed men west from here. One is to be posted, well hidden, beside every road, every trail, every deer path that wends northward from Compostela. When Governor Coronado passes with his train, I want a count of his men, his arms, his horses, mules, bearers, packs—everything he is taking with him. We will not attack that train, because the foolish man is doing us a favor immeasurable. When I have the report that he and his fellows have passed, and when I judge they have gone far enough north, then—but not until then— will *we* move. You concur, Knight Nochéztli?''

"But of course, my lord,'' he said, wagging his head in wonderment. "What astonishingly good fortune for us, and what astonishingly imbecilic behavior on the part of Coronado. He leaves the field wide open for us.''

It was immodest of me, but I could not help saying, "I flatter myself that I had some small part, a long while ago, in arranging both the good fortune and the imbecility. I sought for years to find the one pregnable gap in the white men's seeming invulnerability. It is greed.''

"That reminds me,'' said Nochéztli. "I almost forgot to mention another astonishing thing. Among those fugitives who came seeking sanctuary with us are *two white men.*''

"What?'' I said, incredulous. "Spaniards fleeing their own kind? Turning against their own kind?''

Nochéztli shrugged. "I do not know. They seem very peculiar Spaniards. Even those few of us Aztéca who have some words of Spanish cannot understand the Spanish they try to speak to us. But the two of them jabber between themselves with noises like geese honking and hissing.'' He paused, then added, "I have heard that the Spanish are forbidden by their religion to do away with any children born deficient of brain. Perhaps these are two of those defectives, grown to man-size, not knowing *what* they are doing.''

"If so, *we* will do away with them rather than feed them. I will have a look at them later. In the meantime, speaking of feeding, may *I* request a meal—of whatever grubs and thorns may be the fare today?''

Nochéztli grinned. "We would be as foolish as the white men if we starved and weakened our lord commander. I have some smoked deer parts put by.''

"I thank you. And while I feast on those viands, send me whichever officer you have appointed leader of those Purémpe women.''

"They have their own—a woman. They refused to be ordered about by any man.''

I should have known. The leader was that same cóyotl-faced woman with the inappropriate name of Butterfly. To forestall her trying to bully me, I congratulated her on being still alive, and on the many successful forays she had led against the whites in New Galicia, and thanked her for having spared the Utopía communities, as I had asked. Butterfly preened at being so fulsomely praised, and looked even more appreciative when I said:

"I want to arm your gallant contingent of women warriors with a special weapon all your own. Also, it is a weapon that can best be made by women, whose fingers are more delicate and nimble and precise than any man's.''

"Only command us, Tenamáxtzin.''

"It is a weapon that I invented myself, though the Spaniards have something similar, and call it a *granada*.''

I explained how to wrap clay tightly around a packing of pólvora, and insert into it a thin poquíetl for a wick, and bake the thing to hardness in the sun.

"Then, when we go into battle, my lady Butterfly, have each of your women go smoking a poquíetl herself and carrying several of those granadas. Whenever opportunity offers, ignite the wick of a granada and throw it at the enemy or— better yet—inside their houses or guard posts or fortresses. You will see some spectacular damage done.''

"It sounds delightful, my lord. We will get to work on them straightaway."

When I had done gnawing on the deer meat, drinking some octli and smoking a poquíetl myself, I called for those two "peculiar" white men to be brought before me.

Well, they turned out to be neither Spanish nor defective, though it took me a confusing while to figure that out. One of the men was considerably older than myself, the other a little younger. Both were as white and hairy as Spaniards, but, like all the other slaves now in our encampment, barefooted and dressed in tatters. They had evidently, somehow, been made aware that I was chief of all the people assembled here, so they approached me respectfully. As Nochéztli had said, they spoke very imperfect Spanish, but we managed *mostly* to understand each other. However, they sprinkled their converse with words that I can hope only to approximate here, for they *did* sound like goose talk.

I introduced myself in Spanish simple enough for even a defective to comprehend. "I am called by you Spanish folk Juan Británico. What are you—?"

But the older one interrupted, *"John British?!"* and both of them stared at me, wide-eyed, then quacked excitedly at one another. I could catch only repetitions of that word *British*.

"Please," I said, "speak Spanish, if you can."

So they did, mostly, from then on. But in my recounting of that conversation, I am making them sound much more fluent than they were, and also I am doing my best to pronounce the frequent goose words.

"Your pardon, John British," said the elder of the two. "I was saying to Miles here that, by the blood, we are finally having a run of—a run of what we call luck—a run of *buena suerte.* You must be a castaway, same as us. But Miles said, and so do I—begod, Cap'n, you do not *appear* to be British."

"Whatever that is, I am not," I said. "I am Aztécatl— you would say indio—and my name is properly Téotl-

Tenamáxtli.'' Both men looked at me with faces as blank as only white faces can be. ''None but the Spanish call me by the Christian name of Juan Británico.''

Some more honking and hissing went on between them, the word *Christian* occurring several times. The elder turned again to me.

''At least you are a Christian indio, then, Cap'n. But would you be one of these damned crossback Papists? Or would you be good Bishop's-Book Church of England?''

''I am not any kind of Christian!'' I snapped. ''And I am asking the questions here. *Who are you?*''

He told me, and it was my turn to look blank. The names could as well have been Yaki as goose. They certainly were not Spanish.

''Here,'' he said. ''I can write.'' He looked about for a sharp stone, while saying, ''I am a ship's sea-artist, I am. What the Spaniards call a *navegador*. Miles is only fo'c'sle, and ignorant.'' With the stone, he scratched in the earth at my feet, which is why I can accurately render the names here, JOB HORTOP—''That is me''—and MILES PHILIPS— ''That is him.''

He had mentioned ships and sea, so I asked, ''Are you in the sea service of King Carlos?''

''*King Carlos?!*'' they bellowed together, and the younger one added indignantly, ''We serves good King Henry of England, bless his brass ballocks. And that, God damn it, is why we are here where we are at!''

''Pardon him, John British,'' said the elder. ''Common seamen got no manners.''

''I have heard of England,'' I said, remembering what Padre Vasco had once told me. ''Are you perhaps acquainted with Don Tomás Moro?'' Blank looks again. ''Or his book about Utopía?''

The sea-artist sighed and said, ''Your pardon again, Cap'n. I can read and write, some. But I never read no books.''

I sighed, too, and said, ''Please just tell me how you come to be here.''

"Aye aye, sir. What happened, see, we shipped on a Haw-kins merchantman out of Bristol, sailing under Genoese pat-ent to take a cargo of ebony—you know what I mean—the middle passage from Guinea to Hispaniola. Well, we got as far as Tortoise Island. A storm wrecked us on them reefs, and me and Miles was the only ones of the white crew that washed ashore alive, along with numerous of the ebony. The damned piratical Jack Napeses there took *us* slaves, same as they did the blacks. We been passed from hand to hand ever since—Hispaniola, Cuba—wound up picking oakum in a Vera Cruz dockyard. When a bunch of the blackamoor slaves busted loose, we come with them. No place to aim for, but the blacks got word that some rebels was mustering in these mountains. So here we are, Cap'n. Rebels against them firk-ing Spanish *we* be, by damn, if you will have us. And happy we will be, me and Miles, to kill every whoreson Jack Napes you can point us at. Just give us a cutlass apiece."

Not much of that made any sense to me, except the last part, at which I said:

"If you mean you wish to fight beside us, very well, you will be given weapons. Now, since I am the only person in this army who can—even toilsomely—understand and be understood by you . . ."

"Your pardon again, John British. A good many of them slaves yonder—blacks and indios and mongrels too—speaks the Spanish better than we does. One little half-breed wench, she can even read and write it."

"Thank you for telling me. That one may be useful when I want to send some Spanish city a declaration of siege, or dictate terms of its surrender. Meanwhile, I being the only *commander* in this army who can speak to you, I suggest that, when we go into battle, you both stay close to me. Also, since your names come hard to my tongue—and in battle I may have to speak them with urgency—I shall call you Uno and Dos."

"We been called worse names," said Dos. "And please, sir, can we call you Cap'n John? Make us feel at home, like."

XXVIII

"THE MAN CORONADO ... passed me ... six days ago ..." the runner gasped, as he sank wearily to his knees and elbows on the ground before me, his body heaving for breath and streaming with sweat.

"Then why," I demanded angrily, "has it taken you so long to report here?"

"You wanted ... a count ... my lord," he panted. "Four days counting ... two days running ..."

"By Huitztli," I murmured, now sympathetically, and I patted the man's wet, trembling shoulder. "Rest, man, before you speak more. Nochéztli, send for water and some kind of food for this warrior. He has been hard at his duty for six days and nights."

The man drank gratefully but, being an experienced swift-runner, drank only sparingly at first, then tore voraciously at the stringy deer meat. As soon as he could speak coherently and uninterrupted by gasps, he said:

"First came the man Coronado and beside him a man in priest-black garb, both mounted on fine white horses. Behind them came many mounted soldiers, four by four where the path was wide enough, more often two by two, because Coronado chose a trail not much traveled, hence not much cleared. Every horseman, except that one in black, wore the metal helmet and full metal and leather armor, every man carrying a thunder-stick and steel sword. Every mounted man led behind him one or two more horses besides. Then there came more soldiers, similarly armored, but these on foot, carrying thunder-sticks and long, wide-bladed spears. Here, my lord—the count of all those soldiers.''

He handed me three or four grape leaves from a bunch he had brought, and on them were white marks scratched by a sharp twig. I was pleased to see that the runner knew how to count properly—the dots for ones, the little flags for twenties, the little trees for hundreds. I handed the leaves to Nochéztli and said, ''Sum up the total for me.''

The runner went on to tell that the column was so long and populous, and moving only at a walking pace, that it was four days in passing his hiding place. Though it stopped each night and made rough camp, he dared not sleep himself, for fear of missing anyone or anything that Coronado might have ordered to proceed secretly in the dark. At intervals during his story, the runner handed me more leaves—''the count of the horses for riding, my lord'' and ''the count of the horses and other beasts bearing packs'' and ''the count of the unarmored men—some white, some black, some indio—herding the animals or bearing packs themselves'' and finally ''the count of the horned beasts called cattle, which brought up the end of the column.''

I handed each leaf tally in turn to Nochéztli, then said, ''Swift-runner, you have done exceedingly well. What is your name and rank?''

''I am Pozonáli, my lord, and I am only a yaoquízqui recruit.''

''No longer. Henceforth you are an iyac. Go you now, Iyac Pozonáli, and eat and drink and sleep your fill. Then take you a woman—any Purémpe or any slave, your choice, and tell her it is by my command. You deserve the best refreshment we can accord you.''

Nochéztli had been shuffling the grape leaves and muttering to himself. Now he said:

"If the count is correct, Tenamáxtzin, and I can vouch for Pozonáli's reputation for reliability, this defies belief. Here is what I make the totals. Besides Coronado and the friar, two hundreds plus fifty of mounted soldiers, with *six* hundreds plus twenty of riding horses. Another seventy and four of soldiers afoot. Fully *ten* hundreds of pack animals. *Another* ten hundreds of those unarmored men—slaves, bearers, drovers, cooks, whatever they are. And four hundreds plus forty of cattle." He concluded, a little wistfully, "I envy the Spaniards all that fresh meat on the hoof."

I said, "We can assume that Coronado took with him only the most experienced officers and best-trained men available, and the best horses, and even the strongest and most loyal slaves. Also the newest and best-made arcabuces, the swords and spears of stoutest and sharpest steel. And many of those packs would have been full of pólvora and lead. It means that he has left New Galicia—perhaps all this western end of New Spain—garrisoned only with discards and dregs of the soldiery, all of them probably ill-supplied with weapons and the charges for them, all of them also probably ill at ease, since they are under the command of officers Coronado thought unfit for his expedition." Half to myself, I added, "The fruit is ripe."

Still wistfully, Nochéztli said, "Even a fruit would taste good, about now."

I laughed and said, "I agree. I am as hungry as you are. We shall delay no longer. If the tail of that long procession is already two days north of us, and we go south, there is not much likelihood that Coronado will get news of our move. Spread the word throughout the camps. We will march at tomorrow's dawn. Right now, send your hunters and foragers out ahead of us, so we can hope to have a decent meal tomorrow night. Also have all your knights and other leading officers attend me for their instructions."

When those men—and the one female officer, Butterfly—were assembled, I told them:

"Our first objective will be a town called Tonalá,

southeast of here. I have information that it is growing fast, attracting many Spanish settlers, and that a cathedral is planned to be built there."

"Excuse me, Tenamáxtzin," said one of the officers. "What is a cathedral?"

"A tremendous temple of the white men's religion. Such great temples are erected only in places that are expected to become great cities. Thus I believe that the town of Tonalá is intended to replace Compostela as the Spaniards' capital city of New Galicia. We will do our utmost to discourage that intention—by destroying, leveling, obliterating that Tonalá."

The officers all nodded and grinned at each other in gleeful anticipation.

"When we approach that place," I went on, "our army will halt while scouts steal out around the town. When they report back to me, I will decide the disposition of our forces for the assault. Meanwhile, I also want scouts preceding us on the way there. Ten of them, alert Aztéca men, fanned out well ahead of our column. If they espy any kind of settlement or habitation in our path, even a hermit's hut, I am to be told immediately. If they encounter anyone at all, of whatever color, even a child out picking mushrooms, I want that person brought immediately to me. Go now. Make sure those orders are understood by all."

I do not know—once our column was on the march and strung out behind me—how many days it would have been in passing any given point. We numbered nearly eight times as many people as Coronado was leading, but we did not have his herds of horses, mules and cattle. We possessed only the same two unsaddled horses that Nochéztli had retrieved from the long-ago ambush outside Compostela. He and I rode those as we left the Chicomóztotl encampment and took a southeastward winding trail that brought us gradually down from the mountains to the lower lands. And I have to say that whenever I looked back at the long, coiling, weapon-

bristled train that followed us, I could not help feeling pridefully rather like a conquistador myself.

To everyone's great relief and greater joy, the vanguard
hunters and foragers did provide us all with a fairly substantial meal from our first night on the march, and increasingly
tasty and nourishing victuals during the subsequent days.
Also, to the great relief of my rump and Nochéztli's, we
eventually acquired two saddles. One of our advance scouts
came running, one day, to report that there was a Spanish
army outpost just one-long-run farther along the trail. It was,
like the one Tiptoe and I had once encountered, a shack
containing two soldiers and a pen containing four horses, two
of them saddled.

I halted the train and Nochéztli summoned to us six warriors armed with maquáhuime. To them I said:

"I will not waste powder and lead on such a trivial obstacle. If you six cannot sneak up to that post and dispatch
those white men on the instant, you do not deserve to be
carrying swords. Go and do exactly that. One caution, however: try not to tear or bloody the clothes they wear."

The men did the gesture of kissing the earth, and dashed
off through the underbrush. In a very short time they came
back, all of them beaming happily and two of them holding
high, by the hair, the heads of the two Spanish soldiers, drip-
ping blood from their bearded neck stumps.

"We did it ever so neatly, my lord," said one of them.
"Only the ground got bloody."

So we proceeded on to the guard shack, where we scav-
enged, besides the four horses, two more arcabuces, pólvora
and balls for them, two steel knives and two steel swords. I
set some men to stripping the soldiers' bodies of their armor
and other garb, which was indeed unblemished except for
the ingrained dirt and crusted sweat to be expected of un-
cleanly Spaniards. I congratulated the six warriors who had
slain the soldiers, and the scouts who had found them, and
told those scouts to go on ahead of us as before. Then I called
for *our* two white men, Uno and Dos, to report to me.

"I have gifts for you," I told them. "Not only better clothes than those rags you are wearing, but also steel helmets and armor and stout boots."

"By the blood, Cap'n John, but we are grateful to you," said Uno. "Traveling shanks's-nag is hard enough on our old sea legs, let alone doing it baldfooted."

I took that goose language to be a complaint about their having to walk, and said, "You will not need to walk any farther, if you can ride horseback."

"If we could ride a shipwreck over the Tortoise reefs," said Dos, "I would reckon we can ride anything."

"Might I ask, Cap'n," said Uno. "How come *we* gets kitted out so fancy, and not some of your chief mates?"

"Because, when we get to Tonalá, you two are going to be my mice."

"*Mice*, Cap'n?"

"I will explain when the time comes. Now, while the rest of us move on, you get into those uniforms, strap on the swords, get onto the two horses I am leaving for you and catch up to us as soon as you can."

"Aye aye, sir."

So Nochéztli and I had comfortable saddles again, and the two spare horses I put to use as pack animals, relieving several of my warriors of the heavy lead they were carrying.

The next event of any note occurred some days later, and this time I was not forewarned by my Aztéca scouts. Nochéztli and I rode over a low ridge and found ourselves looking down on some mud huts clustered on the bank of a large pond. Four of our scouts were there, drinking water given them by the villagers and sociably smoking poquíetin with them. I raised a hand to halt the column behind me and said to Nochéztli, "Collect all your knights and leading officers and join me yonder." He saw the look on my face and wordlessly went back to the train as I rode down to the little settlement.

I leaned from my horse and asked one of the scouts, "Who are these people?"

My look and my tone of voice made him stammer slightly. "Only—only simple fisher folk, Tenamáxtzin." And he beckoned to the oldest of the men present.

The old rustic sidled closer to me, fearful of my horse, and addressed me as respectfully as if I had been a mounted Spaniard. He spoke the tongue of the Kuanáhuata, which is a language sufficiently similar to Náhuatl that I was able to understand him.

"My lord, as I was telling your warrior here, we live by fishing this pond. Only we few families, as our ancestors have done since time before time."

"Why you? Why here?"

"There lives in this pond a small and delectable whitefish that can be found in no other waters. Until lately, they have been our commodity of trade with other Kuanáhuata settlements." He waved vaguely eastward. "But now there are white men—south, in Tonalá. They also esteem these unique fish, and we can trade for rich goods such as we have never before—"

He broke off, looking past me as Nochéztli and his officers came to stand, maquáhuime in hand, in a menacing ring about the cluster of huts. All the other folk huddled together, the men protectively putting their arms about the women and children. I spoke over my shoulder:

"Knight Nochéztli, give the order to kill the scouts."

"What? Tenamáxtzin, they are four of our best—" But he also broke off, when I turned my look on him, and obediently nodded to his nearest officers. Before the stunned and unbelieving scouts could move or make a sound of protest, they had been beheaded. The old man and his villagers stared in horror at the bodies lying twitching on the ground, and at the heads, apart, which were blinking their eyes as if still in disbelief of their fate.

I told the old man, "There will be no more white men for you to trade with. We are marching on Tonalá to make sure of that. Any of you who wish to come with us—and help us slaughter those white men—may do so, and welcome. Any who do not will be put to death right here where you stand."

"My lord," pleaded the old man. "We have no quarrel with the white men. They have traded fairly with us. Since they came, we have prospered more than—"

"I have heard that argument too often before," I interrupted him. "I will say this just once again. There will *be* no white men, fair traders or otherwise. You saw what I have done to men of my own who took my words too lightly. Those of you who are coming, come now."

The old man turned to his people and spread his arms helplessly. Several of the men and boys, and two or three of the sturdier women, one of them leading her boy-child, stepped forward and made the kissing-the-earth gesture to me.

The old man sadly shook his head and said, "Even were I not too aged to fight and even to march, my lord, I would not leave this place of my fathers and my fathers' fathers. Do what you will."

What I did was take off his head with my own steel sword. At that, all the remaining men and boys of the village hastened to step forward and make the tlalqualíztli gesture. So did most of the women and young girls. Only three or four other females, holding babies in their arms or with infants clutching to their skirts, remained where they were.

"Tenamáxtzin," said the cóyotl-faced officer Butterfly, with a solicitude I would not have expected of her, "those are innocent women and tiny children."

"You have killed others just like them," I said.

"But those were *Spaniards!*"

"These women can talk. These children can point. I want no witnesses left alive." I tossed her my spare sword, an obsidian-edged maquáhuitl that hung by a thong from my pommel, because she was carrying only an arcabuz. "Here. Pretend they are Spaniards."

And so she did, but clumsily, because she was obviously reluctant to do it. Hence her victims suffered more than the several men had done, cowering under her blows and having to be hacked at more often than should have been necessary. By the time Butterfly was done, their copiously spilled blood had trickled down the bank and was staining the water red at the pond's margin. The villagers who had surrendered themselves to me—all of them wailing and tearing their hair and mantles—were herded back among our slave contingent, and I ordered that they be closely watched, lest they try to flee.

We had gone a considerable distance from that place before Nochéztli worked up courage enough to speak to me again. He nervously cleared his throat and said:

"Those were people of our own race, Tenamáxtzin. The scouts were men of our own *city*."

"I would have slain those if they were my brothers born. I grant you that I have cost us four good warriors, but I promise you that, from this day on, not a single other of our army will ever be negligent of my commands, as were those four."

"That is certain," Nochéztli admitted. "But those Kuanáhuata you ordered slain—they had neither opposed nor angered you . . ."

"They were, at heart, as much in league with and dependent on the Spaniards as Yeyac was. So I gave them the same choice I gave Yeyac's warriors. Join us or die. They chose. See here, Nochéztli, you have not had the benefit of Christian teaching, as I did in my younger days. The priests were fond of telling us stories from the annals of their religion. They particularly rejoiced in recounting the exploits and sayings of their godling called Jesucristo. I well remember one of that godling's sayings. 'He that is not with me is against me.' "

"And you wished to leave no witnesses to our passage, I realize that, Tenamáxtzin. But you *must* know that eventually, inevitably, the Spanish are going to hear of our army and our intent."

"*Ayyo,* indeed they will. I want them to. I am planning to threaten and taunt them with it. But I want the white men to know only enough to keep them in uncertainty, in apprehension, in terror. I do *not* wish them to know our number, our strength of armament, our position at any given time, or our course of march. I want the white men starting in fright at every unexpected noise, recoiling from every unfamiliar sight, becoming distrustful of every stranger they see, getting neck cramps from forever looking over their shoulders. Let them think us evil spirits, and countless, impossible to find, and likely to strike here, there, anywhere. There must be no witnesses who can tell them anything different.''

Some days later, one of our scouts came trotting from the southern horizon to tell me that the town of Tonalá was within easy reach, about four one-long-runs distant. His fellow scouts, he said, were at the moment making their cautious way around the town's outskirts, to determine the extent of it. All he could tell me, from his own brief observation, was that Tonalá seemed to be mostly of new-built structures, and there were no visible thunder-tubes guarding its perimeter.

I halted the column and gave orders for all contingents to spread out into separate camps, as they had done at Chicomóztotl, and to prepare to stay encamped for longer than just overnight. I also called for Uno and Dos and told them:

''Another gift for you, señores. Nochéztli and I are going to lend you our *saddled* horses for a time.''

''Bless ye, Cap'n John,'' said Dos with a heartfelt sigh. ''From Hell, Hull and Halifax, Good Lord deliver us.''

Uno said, ''Miles bragged that we could ride anything, but, begod, we did not reckon on riding the German Chair. Our blindcheeks are hurting like we been catted and keelhauled the whole way here.''

I did not ask for explanation of this goose gabble, but only gave them their instructions.

''The town of Tonalá is yonder. This scout will lead you there. You will be my mice on horseback. Other scouts are circling the town, but I want you to probe the interior. Do

not ride in until after dark, but then try to look like haughty
Spanish soldiers and prowl around as much as possible.
Bring me, as best you can, a description of the place—an
estimate of its population, both white and otherwise—and,
most important, a fair count of the soldiers stationed there.''

"But what if we are challenged, John British?'' asked
Uno. "We can hardly speak any response, let alone a pass-
word. Do we give them a taste of our steel?'' He touched
the sheathed sword at his belt.

"No. If anyone addresses you, simply wink lewdly and
put a finger to your lips. Since you will be moving quietly
and in the dark, they will assume that you are skulking off
to visit your maátime.''

"Our what?''

"A soldiers' brothel. A house of cheap whores.''

"Aye aye, sir!'' Dos said enthusiastically. "And *can* we
tickle the little coneys while we are there?''

"No. You are to do no fighting and no whoring. Only get
inside the town, get around in it and get yourselves back
here. You can wield your steel when we assail the place, and
when we have taken it, you will have plenty of females to
frolic with.''

From the information brought back by the scouts—including
Uno and Dos, who said that their presence and prowling had
excited no comment whatever—I was able to picture Tonalá
in my mind. It was about the same size as Compostela, and
about equally populated. Unlike Compostela, though, it had
not grown up around an already existing native settlement,
but apparently had been founded by Spaniards newly come
there. So, except for the usual outlying shacks to house their
servants and slaves, they had built substantial residences of
adobe and wood. There were also, as in Compostela, two
sturdy stone structures: a small church—not yet expanded to
be the bishop's cathedral—and a modest palace for the of-
fices of government and barracks for the soldiers.

"Only enough soldiers to keep the peace,'' said Uno.

"Roundsmen and beadles and catchpoles and the like. They carry harquebuses and halberds, aye, but they are not real fighting men. Me and Miles only saw three besides us that even rode horses. No artillery nowhere. I would say the town thinks it is far enough deep inside New Spain that it runs no risk of besiegement."

"Maybe four thousand people all together," said Dos. "Half of them Spanish, looking firking fat and oily and lay-about, like."

"The other half are their slaves and drudges," said Uno. "Pretty much mixed—indios and blacks and breeds."

"Thank you, señores," I said. "I will take back the two saddled horses now. When we assault the town, I trust you will have the initiative to procure saddles of your own."

Then I sat and ruminated for a time, before I sent for Nochéztli, to tell him:

"We shall need only a small part of our forces for this taking of Tonalá. First, I think, our Yaki warriors, because their sheer savagery will be most terrifying to the whites. In addition, we will employ all our men equipped with arca-buces, and all those Purémpe women armed with granadas, and a contingent of our best Aztéca warriors. The rest of our forces, the greater part, will remain encamped here, invisible to the townsfolk."

"And those of us attacking, Tenamáxtzin, do we attack all together?"

"No, no. In advance of any attack whatever, send the women, carrying their granadas and smoking their poquíetin, sneaking at a prudent distance around the town, to lurk on the far side of it, well concealed. The assault will commence when I give the word, and then only the Yaki will attack—from *this* side of the town—rushing openly upon it and mak-ing as much bloodcurdling noise as they can. That will bring all the Spanish soldiers also to this edge of the town, thinking they are being raided only by some bare-breasted, cane-wielding small tribe that can be easily repelled. When the soldiers come running, our Yaki are to withdraw, as if fleeing in fright and consternation. Meanwhile, have every one of our thunder-stick warriors spread in a line, also on this side of the town, crouched in concealment. As soon as the Yaki have fled past them, and they have clear sight of the Spaniards, they are to rise and aim and discharge their weapons. That should strike down so many of the soldiers that the Yaki can turn again and finish off the survivors. At the same time, when the Purémpe women hear the thunder sounds, they are to run into the town from that far side and start hurling their granadas into every abode and building. Our force of Aztéca warriors—led by you and myself and our own two mounted white men—will follow the Yaki into the town, slaying the resident white men at will. How does that plan sound to you, Knight Nochéztli?"

"Ingenious, my lord. Eminently workable. And enjoyable."

"Do you think that you and your under-officers can communicate those instructions so that everyone understands his and her part? Even the inarticulate Yaki?"

"I believe so, Tenamáxtzin. The plan is not overly complicated. But it may take us some while to do all the necessary gesticulation and drawing of diagrams in the earth."

"There is no hurry. The town seems complacently snug in its security. So, to give you time to impart those various instructions, we will not make our assault until the dawn of the day after tomorrow. Now, two further instructions, Nochéztli—or, rather, restrictions. Some random and needless slaughter will be of course inevitable. However, insofar as possible, I want our warriors to kill only white *men*, to spare the white females *and* all the slaves, male or female, of whatever color."

Nochéztli looked slightly surprised. "You would leave living witnesses this time, my lord?"

"The white women are to be left alive only long enough for our warriors to make free use of them. The customary reward for the victors. Those women probably will not survive that ordeal, but any that do will then be mercifully slain.

As for the slaves, those who choose to join our ranks may do so. The others can remain and inherit the ruins of Tonalá, for all I care.''

"But, Tenamáxtzin, as soon as we are gone again, they could scatter all over New Spain—any of them still loyal to their late masters—crying warning to all other Spaniards.''

"Let them. They can give no accurate report of our number and strength. I had to slay those Kuanáhuata fisher people because—through the carelessness of our own scouts—they had glimpsed our full force. No one here in Tonalá will have seen more than a few of us.''

"That is true. Have you anything else to command, my lord?''

"Yes, one more thing. Tell the Purémpe women not to waste their granadas on the town's two stone buildings, the church and the palace. Granadas could not cause much damage there. Besides, I have a reason for wanting to do the taking of those two structures myself. Now go. Begin the preparations.''

The initial assault on Tonalá went as I had planned it, except for one brief balk, which I myself should have foreseen and made provision against. I and Nochéztli, Uno and Dos, sat our mounts on a small hillock with a good view of the town, and watched as the Yaki warriors swarmed into the slave-quarter outskirts at first dawn, shrieking inhuman war cries and ferociously flailing their war clubs and three-pronged spears. As I had commanded, they made more noise than ruination, killing only (as I would later learn) a few slave men who started up from sleep and, bravely but foolhardily trying to defend their families, threw themselves deliberately in the path of the Yaki.

As I had expected, the Spanish soldiers came running—some galloping on horseback—from their garrison palace and their various posts, to converge at the scene of action. Some of them were still awkwardly putting on their armor as they came, but they all came armed. And, still doing as I had commanded, the Yaki melted away before them, withdrawing onto the open ground this side of the town. But they pranced backward as they fled, facing the soldiers, yelling defiance, waving their weapons menacingly. That brash display cost some of them their lives, because the Spaniards, though taken unawares and unprepared, *were* soldiers, after all. They formed lines, knelt, took careful aim with their arcabuces and discharged them accurately enough to bring down several of the Yaki before the rest ceased their posturing and turned and ran to safety at a distance. That left a clear field for my own arcabuz men, and we saw them all—there were ninety and four of them—rise up from their concealment, take their several aims and at a word from their commanding knight, all discharge their weapons simultaneously.

That was effective, indeed. A good number of the soldiers afoot went down, and a few others toppled from their saddles. Even at our distance, I could see the confused milling about of the astonished Spaniards who had survived that storm of lead. However, there now occurred the balk that I have mentioned. My arcabuz men had employed their weapons as efficiently as any Spanish soldiers could have done—but they had done so *all together*. And now, all together, they had to recharge those weapons. As I well knew, and should have taken into account, that process requires some time, even for the most adept and practiced man.

The Spaniards had discharged their arcabuces *not* all together, but sporadically, as targets and opportunities afforded, hence most of them had weapons still charged. While my own arcabuz men stood unarmed—ramming the pólvora and wads and lead balls down the thunder-sticks' tubes, priming the pans, rewinding the wheels' locks, cocking the cat's-paws—the Spaniards regained enough composure and discipline to resume their sporadic but deadly discharging. Many of my arcabuz men were struck, and almost all the others crouched low or flopped flat on the ground, in which positions their recharging of their weapons was further impeded and delayed.

I cursed aloud in several languages and barked at Nochéztli, "Send the Yaki in again!"

He made a sweeping gesture with his arm and the Yaki, who had been watching for that, swept anew past our line of now disconcerted arcabuz men. Having seen their fellows fall during the earlier foray, the Yaki went really vengefully this time, not even wasting their breath to shout war cries. More of them fell to the Spanish lead as they went, but there were still many of them to plunge in among the Spaniards, viciously stabbing and clubbing.

I was just about to give the order for us four mounted men to charge, with our Aztéca behind us, when Uno reached from his horse to clutch my shoulder and say, "Your pardon, John British, if I presume to give you a bit of advice."

"By Huitztli, man!" I snarled. "This is no time to—"

He overrode me, "Best I do it now, Cap'n, while I have life to speak and you to hear."

"Get on, then! Say it!"

"Me, I would not know one end of a harquebus from the other, but I *have* shipped along of His Majesty's marine soldiers a time or two, and seen them in action. What I mean, they do not all fire at once, as your men did. They form up in three ranks, parallel. The first rank fires, then falls back while the second rank aims. The second rank fires and falls back while the third rank aims. By the time the third rank has fired, the first has reloaded and is ready to fire again."

There were goose words in that speech, but I readily comprehended the sense of it, and said:

"I humbly ask *your* pardon, Señor Uno. Forgive my having snapped at you. The advice is sound—and welcome— and I will heed it ever after this day. I kiss the earth to that. Now, señores, Nochéztli . . ." I swept my sword arm to start the Aztéca running. "If you fall, *fall forward!*"

XXIX

THE MOST MEMORABLE aspect of any battle—and, having now experienced many of them, I can say this with authority—is its dizzying commotion and confusion. But of this one, my first major engagement with the enemy, I do retain a few memories more distinct.

As we four mounted men pounded across the open ground and into the affray, only a few stray lead balls flew harmlessly past us, because the Spanish soldiers were very much occupied with the Yaki among them. Then, as we new assailants also closed with them, I vividly remember the sounds of that encounter—not so much the clashing of arms, but the clamor of voices. I and Nochéztli and all the Aztéca who followed us were uttering the traditional cries of various wild animals. But the Spaniards were shouting the name of their war santo—"*¡Por Santiago!*"—and, to my surprise, our own two white men, Uno and Dos, were apparently doing the same. They roared what sounded to me like this: "*For Harry and Saint George!*" though I had never, even in my Christian-schooling days, heard of any santos named Harry and George.

There were other noises from the distance, from inside the town—some sharp as thunderclaps, others mere muted thumps—the burstings of the clay-ball granadas being

employed by our women warriors. Doubtless the Spanish
officers would have liked to detach some of their men from
the struggle here at the town's edge, and send them to deal
with those inexplicable thunders. But they had no hope of
doing that, because, right here, their men were by now outnumbered and fighting for their lives. Neither their fighting
nor their lives lasted very long.

If there *are* such beings as Saints Harry and George, they
lent their followers greater strength of arm than Santiago did
to his. Uno and Dos, though unsteadied by saddles and stir-
rups, slashed left and right from atop their mounts, as tire-
lessly, mercilessly and killingly as did I and Nochéztli. We
four struck at the soldiers' throats and faces, the only vulnerable places between their steel helmets and steel breastplates, and so did our Aztéca warriors wielding obsidian
maquáhuime. The Yaki warriors, however, did not have to
be so precise in their aim. In these close quarters, they had
dropped their unwieldy long spears and were almost indis-
criminately swinging their ironwood war clubs. A blow to
an opponent's head would dent his helmet deeply enough
that his skull would cave in beneath it. A blow to an opponent's body would so dent his breastplate that he would either die of crushed bones and organs or—more agonizingly—
suffocate, his chest unable to expand to breathe.

During all that turmoil, other people were dodging among
us or scampering around us, in a panic to get out of the
contested area, and many others could be seen, farther off,
likewise fleeing from the town into the open country. None
wore armor or uniform, and most were barely dressed,
having leapt straight from their night's pallets. They were
the slave inhabitants of this quarter where we had chosen to
strike—or most of them were. The tumult had of course wak-
ened all of Tonalá, so more than a few Spanish men, women
and children, equally ill-clothed, were among the fugitives,
obviously and unashamedly hoping to be mistaken for slaves
themselves, and let to go free. But not many of those got
away. We marauders allowed the passage of everyone of our

own color, or darker, but every white-skinned person of whatever sex or age who came within our reach we instantly skewered or hacked or clubbed to death. To my regret, two of the Spaniards' horses also got killed, inadvertently, and four or five others wandered skittishly about, riderless, wild-eyed, wide-nostriled, trying to snort away the smells of blood and pólvora smoke.

When every last Spanish officer and soldier and pretended slave lay dead or dying, my three mounted comrades rode off into the streets of the town, the Aztéca warriors hooting and howling behind them. I stayed at the scene of this first combat for a brief while, partly to count our own fallen people. They were very few, compared to the Spanish losses. And the male slaves of our company who had been detailed as Swaddlers and Swallowers would shortly be arriving, either to bind up the wounds of any warriors who might be revived or to slip an easeful blade into those who were beyond the help of any tíciltin.

But what mainly detained me at the scene was the fact that all the Yaki also were staying, every man of them vigorously sawing at the head of a Spanish corpse, usually using the belt knife that the soldier had worn when he was alive. After a warrior had cut a circle in the skin around the head, from nape of neck, above the ears and eyebrows, back to the nape, he had only to give a sudden, forceful tug, and the hair and scalp and forehead skin came ripping away, leaving the cadaver crowned with only a pulp of raw flesh that oozed blood. Then the Yaki would dash away to another and do the same. However, some of the fallen Spaniards were not yet *quite* corpses. Those could and did shriek or moan or convulse when the tug was given, and their heads' exposed pulp bled profusely.

Cursing vehemently, I edged my horse here and there among that carnage, swatting at the Yaki warriors with the flat of my sword and pointing townward with it, shouting orders. They flinched and grumbled in their unlovely language—I gathered that they were accustomed to collect enemy scalps while they were fresh and easy to cut loose. But I did my best to convey, with gestures, that there would be many more scalps, far more than enough to adorn every Yaki's skirt, and I cursed some more, and urgently waved them onward. They went, still grumbling, and only slowly at first, but then running, as if it had suddenly occurred to them that others of our army might already be harvesting the finest-quality scalps of the townsfolk.

It was not difficult for me to follow my men who had preceded me, for they seemed to have gone spreading havoc everywhere. Whatever street I took, whatever cross street I turned into, there lay corpses everywhere—half-clad, bloody, pierced or slashed or thoroughly mangled—sprawled on the street cobblestones or across their own homes' thresholds. From some houses, the residents had not had time to flee, but I could tell that there were bodies inside, for much blood had flowed out the open doors. Only once in those ravaged streets did I come upon a living white person. A man wearing nothing but his underclothes, bleeding from a gash in his neck that had failed to kill him, came running up to me, ranting insanely. In his hands he held, by their hair, three severed heads: one a woman's, the other two smaller. He could not have expected me to understand his Spanish, but what he shouted—over and over—was:

"These things were my wife and my sons!"

I said nothing in reply, but kindly used my sword to send him to join them in whatever Christian afterworld they had gone to.

In time, I caught up to my foot warriors, Yaki and Aztéca intermingled, scuttling in and out of houses or chasing runaways through streets and alleys. I was pleased to see that they were obeying my instructions, or at least as well as I could have expected. Every Tonalá inhabitant of our own complexion, or darker, was being left unmolested. The Yaki were no longer wasting time in scalping, but were letting the dead bodies lie while they went to kill more. My instructions were being only slightly disregarded in one respect, and that

was a matter of no great concern to me. I had ordered that
the white females be let to live for a while, but the warriors
were keeping—and herding before them—only the more
comely women and young girls. Those, of course, were easy
to discern, for few of them had been wearing much clothing
at all, and now had been stripped naked. So the flabby or
skinny or obese or wrinkled old women, and the children so
young as to be indeterminate of sex, were being slaughtered
along with their fathers and husbands and brothers and sons.

My men no longer had breath to spare in uttering war
cries, but were doing their selecting and butchering in silence. Of course, the victims were not silent. Every living
white female loudly pleaded or prayed or screamed or cursed
or wept; and so did the men and the old women and the
children, as long as they could. Those same despairing noises
came from every direction—and other noises, too: the splin-
terings of doors being forced; the occasional blast of an arcabuz owned by some householder, discharging its single
futile pellet, the continuing random thunders and thuds, not
far off now, of our Purémpe women's granadas. And some
heroically foolish person was even ringing a frantic, pathetic,
far-too-late alarm on the town's church bell.

I turned my horse toward the sound of that bell, knowing
it must come from the town's center. Along the way there,
I saw—besides my energetically working warriors and their
victims—many houses and merchants' shops and artisans'
workshops that had formerly been well-built and perhaps
even handsome structures, but were now mere ruins, irreparably shattered or totally leveled, clearly the doing of our
women's granadas. There were yet more corpses visible
within the rubble of those places, but they were so dismembered and shredded that they could hardly provide even intact
scalps for the Yaki. I was eyeing one particularly fine house
just ahead of me—certainly the abode of some high Spanish
dignitary—and wondering why *it* had not been demolished,
when I heard an urgent cautionary cry in the Poré tongue:
"Take care, my lord!" and I yanked my horse to a halt.

Next instant, that house before me *bulged*—like the cheeks of a musician playing one of those jug flutes called "the warbling waters"—but it made no such sweet sound. The noise it uttered was more like that of the drum called "the drum that tears out the heart." I gave a violent start and my horse shied in fright, and the two of us nearly parted company. The house was enveloped in a thundercloud of smoke, and though it was too solidly constructed to fly asunder, its doors and shutters and bits of furniture and unidentifiable other contents came darting in shards like lightning out of that thundercloud. As chance would have it, I and my horse were struck by only a single fragment apiece, and those did us no harm, being only gobbets of some person's flesh. When things stopped falling roundabout, the woman emerged from the nearby alley where she had taken cover. It was Butterfly, and she came carrying a floppy leather bag and smoking a poquíetl.

"You do excellent work," I said. "I thank you for the warning."

"Those were my last two granadas," she said, shaking the bag to show me. Only a handful of thin reed-rolled poquíetin fell out. She gave me one, I took a light from hers, and we smoked companionably as she fell in beside my horse and we went leisurely on together.

She said, "We did as you ordered, Tenamáxtzin. Employed our granadas only on buildings, and we tried to choose the most imposing ones to destroy. Only twice did we have to squander the weapons just to slay individuals. Two mounted soldiers. There was not much left of them."

"That is a pity," I said. "I want to collect all the horses we can."

"Then I am sorry, Tenamáxtzin. But it was unavoidable. They came upon us suddenly, just as two of my warriors were about to toss their lighted granadas through a house window, and the soldiers were waving swords and shouting—for us to surrender, I suppose. Of course we did no such thing."

"Of course," I said. "I was not chiding you, Butterfly."

The church bell continued its useless pealing until she and

I reached the open square fronting that church and the ad-
joining palace—and just then the ringing ceased abruptly.
My arcabuz men had followed the rest of us into the town,
to pick off any runaways that might outdistance our foot
warriors, and one of those men very neatly put a ball into
the bell-ringer up in the little tower that sat atop the church.
The Spaniard, a black-clad priest or friar, pitched out of the
bell tower, bounced off the slanted roof and was dead when
he thumped onto the cobblestones of the square.

"As well as I can tell," said Knight Nochéztli, bringing
his blood-spattered horse alongside mine, "there very soon
will be only three white men still alive in Tonalá. They are
in the church yonder—three men, unarmed. I glanced inside
and saw them, but left them for you, my lord, as you commanded."

His knights and officers began grouping about us, waiting
for further orders, and the square was rapidly filling with
other people, as well. Every warrior not otherwise and elsewhere occupied was herding the captive white women and
girls into that open space, and hurrying to claim the favor
that is the common soldier's traditional celebration of a victory. That is to say, the men were violently raping the females. Since there were considerably more men than women
and girls, and since many of the men were disinclined to wait
their turn, in some cases two or three warriors would be simultaneously using the various orifices of a single female.

Needless to say, those women and girls capable of screaming or pleading or protesting were doing so, and vociferously.
But I am sure that these victims were making a noise even
more horrified and horrible than has ever been heard at any
other such scene of celebration. That was because the white
females, all having abundant and long and lustrous hair,
made the Yaki warriors more lustful of having their scalps
than of possessing any other part of them. Each of those Yaki
who had dragged hither a Spanish female threw her down
and tore off the top of her head before he threw himself on
top of her bare body. Several other Yaki, who had brought

no captives of their own, were scurrying about the square and sawing the scalps off supine women and girls *while* they were being violated by another man—or two or three.

I myself found those females, however comely and shapely and desirable in other respects, almost impossible even to look at, with their heads peeled nakedly round and red and pulpy. I could not have brought myself to couple with one—not even with my eyes shut, because there would have been no way to shut out the equally repellent stench of them. The smell of their torn heads' blood was rank enough, but many of the creatures also were voiding their bladders and bowels from sheer terror, and others were vomiting because of what had been put down their throats.

"I thank the war god Cuticáuri," said Butterfly, at my stirrup, "that we Purémpecha do not let our hair grow."

"I wish you did," growled Nochéztli, "so I could snatch all *you* stupid bitches bald of head!"

"What is this?" I asked, surprised, because he was ordinarily so amiable of nature. "Why do you revile our meritorious warrior women?"

"That one has not told you, Tenamáxtzin? Of the two they so incompetently killed?"

Butterfly and I regarded him with puzzlement, and I said, "Two white soldiers, yes, who surprised them while they were very capably doing their duty."

"*Our* two white soldiers, Tenamáxtzin. The men you called Señor Uno and Señor Dos."

"Yya ayya," I murmured, really sadly.

"They were our allies?" asked Butterfly. "How should we have known? They were mounted. They were armored and bearded. They waved swords. They shouted."

"They would have been shouting *encouragement*, you blundering woman!" said Nochéztli. "Could you not see that their horses were without saddles?"

Butterfly looked chagrined, but shrugged. "Ours was a dawn attack. Not many *people* were dressed."

To me, Nochéztli said ruefully, "They had been riding

before me, so I came upon their remains right after they were
blown to pieces. I could not even tell which man was which.
Indeed, it would have been hard to tell their fragments from
those of their horses.''

"Be easy, Nochéztli," I said with a sigh. "We shall miss
them, but there are bound to be such casualties in any war.
Let us just hope that Uno and Dos are now in their Christian
heaven, if that is where they would wish to be, with their
Harry and George. Now, back to the business of our war.
Give orders that the men, as soon as each has had his satisfaction with the captured women, are to fan out through
the town and loot it. Salvage everything that might be of use
to us—weapons, pólvora, lead, armor, horses, clothes, blankets, any portable provisions. When every ruin and every
surviving building has been emptied, it is to be set afire.
Nothing is to be left of Tonalá except the church and palace
here.''

Nochéztli dismounted and went among his under-officers,
passing along those orders, then returned to me and asked:

"Why, my lord, are you sparing these two buildings?"

"For one thing, they will not easily burn," I said, dismounting also. "And we could not possibly make enough
granadas to tear them down. But chiefly I am leaving those
for a certain Spanish friend—a truly *good* Christian white
man. If *he* outlives this war, he will have something around
which to build anew. He has already told me that this place
will have a new name. Now, come, let us have a look inside
the palace.''

The lower floor of that stone building had been the soldiers' barracks, and it was expectably in disorder, since its
inhabitants had so wildly scrambled out a little while before.
We climbed the stairs and found ourselves in a warren of
small rooms, all furnished with chairs and tables, some
rooms full of books, others full of shelved maps or stacked
documents. In one was a table on which lay a thick sheaf of
fine Spanish paper, an inkhorn, a penknife and a jar full of
goose quills. Beside them lay an ink-stained quill and a paper

only half written over, by whatever scribe had been at work there the day before. I stood looking at those things for a moment, then said to Nochéztli:

"I was told that there is, among our slave contingent, a certain girl who can read and write the Spanish language. A Moro or a mongrel, I forget. Ride back to our encampment, right now, at a gallop, find that girl and bring her here, as quickly as you can. Also send in some of our men to scavenge whatever is useful from the soldiers' quarters downstairs. I will wait here for you and the girl, after I have visited the church next door."

The Tonalá church was as modest in size and appointments as was the church Bishop Quiroga currently occupied in Compostela. One of the three men in there was a priest, decently dressed in the usual black, the other two were pudgy, merchant-looking men, ridiculously clad in nightwear and whatever other clothes they had had time to fling over them. They both quailed back from me, against the altar rail, but the priest boldly came forward, thrusting a carved wooden cross at me and babbling in that Church language that I had heard at the few Masses I had once attended.

"Not even other Spaniards can understand that nonsensical *guirigay*, padre," I said sharply. "Speak to me in some sensible tongue."

"Very well, you heathen renegade!" he snapped. "I was adjuring you, in the name and language of the Lord, to depart from these sacred precincts."

"Renegade?" I repeated. "You seem to assume that I am some white man's runaway slave. I am not. And these precincts are *mine*, built on the land of my people. I am here to reclaim them."

"This is the property of Holy Mother Church! Who do you think you are?"

"I *know* who I am. But your Holy Mother Church gave me the name of Juan Británico."

"Dear God!" he exclaimed, appalled. "Then you are apostate! A heretic! *Worse* than a heathen!"

"Far worse," I said pleasantly. "Who are those two men?"

"The *alcalde* of Tonalá, Don José Osado Algarve de Sierra. And the *corregidor*, Don Manuel Adolfo del Monte."

"The town's two foremost citizens, then. What are they doing here?"

"God's house is sanctuary. Holy refuge. Inviolable. It would be sacrilege were they to be harmed here."

"So they cringe cowardly behind your skirts, padre, and abandon their people to the storm and the strangers? Including their own loved ones, perhaps? Anyway, I do not share your superstitions."

I stepped around him and, with my sword, stabbed each of the men to the heart.

The priest cried, "Those señores were high and valued functionaries of His Majesty King Carlos!"

"I do not believe that. Anyone of any majesty could hardly have been proud of them."

"I adjure you again, you monster! Begone from this church of God! Remove *all* your savages from this parish of God!"

"I will," I said equably, turning to look out the door. "As soon as they tire of it."

The priest joined me at the door and said, beseechingly now, "In God's name, man, some of those poor females yonder are *children*. Many were virgins. Some of them are virgin *nuns*. The brides of Christ."

"They will shortly be with their husband, then. I hope he proves tolerant of his wives' impairments. Come with me, padre. I wish you to see something, probably less distressing than this sight."

I ushered him out of the church, and there I found, among others of my men not busy at the moment, the trustworthy Iyac Pozonáli, to whom I said, "I am putting this white priest in your charge, Iyac. I do not think you need expect him to make mischief. Only stay by him to keep *him* from harm by any of our people."

Then I led them both into the palace and upstairs to that writing room, and pointed to the partly done document, and told the priest, "Read that to me, if you can."

"Of course I can. It is merely a respectful salutation. It says, 'To the very illustrious Señor Don Antonio de Mendoza, viceroy and governor for His Majesty in this New Spain, president of the Audiencia and the Royal Chancellery . . .' That is all. Evidently the alcalde was about to dictate to the scribe some report or request to be sent to the viceroy."

"Thank you. That will do."

"Now you kill me, too?"

"No. And for that, be thankful to another padre whom I once knew. I have already instructed this warrior to be your companion and protector."

"Then may I take my leave? There are last rites to be bestowed on my many, many unfortunate parishioners, and short shrift it is that I can give them."

"Vaya con Dios, padre," I said, meaning no irony, and gestured for Pozonáli to go with him. Then I simply stood and looked out the window of that room, at what was still going on in the square below, and at the fires beginning to spring up at more distant places in the town, and I waited for Nochéztli to return with the reading-and-writing girl slave.

She was a mere child, and certainly not a Moro, for her complexion was only a slightly darker copper color than my own, and she was too pretty to have had much black blood in her. But she obviously was *some* kind of mongrel female, for those have bodies maturely developed at a very young age, and so did she. I supposed she must be one of the more complex breeds that Alonso de Molina had once told me about—pardo, cuarterón, whatever—and that fact might account for her having been given some education. My first test of that was to speak to her in Spanish:

"I am told that you can read the writing of the Spaniards."
She understood, and said respectfully, "Yes, my lord."

"Read this to me, then." I pointed to the document on the table.

Without having to study it or laboriously puzzle it out, she immediately and fluently read, "*Al muy ilustrísimo Señor Don Antonio de Mendoza, visorrey é gobernador por Su Majestad en esta Nueva España, presidente de la Audiencia y la Chancellería Real . . .* It stops there, my lord. If I might say so, the scribe is not highly accomplished in his spelling."

"I am told that you also can write in that language."

"Yes, my lord."

"I wish you to write something for me. Use a different piece of paper."

"Certainly, my lord. Only give me a moment to prepare. The materials are dry."

"While we wait, Nochéztli," I said to him, "go and find that church's priest. He is somewhere in the crowd outside, in company with our Iyac Pozonáli. Fetch the priest here to me."

In the meantime, the girl had laid the scribe's stained quill to one side, plucked a fresh one from the jar, expertly used the penknife to whittle a point to it, spat delicately into the inkhorn, stirred it with the new quill and finally said, "I am ready, my lord. What shall I write?"

I looked out the window, briefly meditating. The day was darkening now, the fires were more numerous and blazing higher; the whole of Tonalá would soon be aflame. I turned back to the girl and spoke just a few words, slowly enough that she had finished her scribbling almost as soon as I stopped speaking. I went and reached over her shoulder, laying the scribe's paper and hers side by side. Of course, I could make nothing of either of them, but I could tell that the girl's writing was, to the eye, more bold and forthright than the spidery lines of the scribe.

She asked timidly, "Shall I read it back to you, my lord?"

"No. Here is the priest. Let him do it." I pointed. "Padre, can you read that writing, too?"

"Of course I can," he said again, this time impatiently.

"But it makes little sense. All it says is, 'I can still see him burning.' "

"Thank you, padre. That is what I meant it to say. Very good, girl. Now take that unfinished document and append these words to it. *I have only just begun.* Then write my name, Juan Británico. Then add my real name. Can you also make the word-pictures of Náhuatl?"

"I am sorry, no, my lord."

"Then put it in that Spanish writing, as best you can. Téotl-Tenamáxtzin."

That she did, though not so swiftly, being very careful to make it as correct and comprehensible as she could. When she was done, she blew on the paper to dry it before she gave it to me. I handed it to the priest and asked, "Can you still read it?"

The paper shook in his fingers and his voice was quavery. "To the very illustrious . . . et cetera, et cetera. I have only just begun. Signed Juan Británico. Then that fearsome other name. I can make it out, yes, but I cannot well pronounce it."

He started to give it back to me, but I said, "Keep the paper, padre. It was intended for the viceroy. It still is. If and when you can find a living white man, who can serve as your messenger, have him deliver that to the very illustrious Mendoza in the City of Méxíco. Until then, simply show it to every other Spaniard who comes this way."

He went out, the paper still shaking in his hand, and Pozonáli went with him. To Nochéztli I said:

"Help the girl gather and bundle together all this paper and the writing materials, for safekeeping. I shall have other use for them. And for you, child. You are bright and obedient and you did exceedingly well here today. What is your name?"

"Verónica," you said.

XXX

WE LEFT TONALÁ a smoldering, smoking desert of a town, unpeopled except for the priest and what few slaves had elected to stay, only the two stone buildings still upright and entire. We left it, too, with our warriors looking rather flamboyant, not to say ridiculous. The Yaki were so heavily festooned with skirts of scalps that every man seemed to be walking waist-deep through a hillock of bloody human hair. The Purémpe women had appropriated the finest gowns of the late Spanish ladies—silks and velvets and brocades—so (although some had ignorantly donned the dresses backward) they made a gaudily colorful throng. Many of the arcabuz men and Aztéca warriors now wore steel breastplates over their quilted cotton armor. They disdained to avail themselves of the enemies' high boots or steel helmets, but they had pillaged from the Spanish women's wardrobes also, and now wore on their heads fancy feathered bonnets and ornate lace *mantillas*. All our men and women were carrying bales and bundles of plunder besides—every sort of thing from hams and cheeses and bags of coins to those weapons that Uno had called halberds, which combine spear, hook, and ax. Our Swaddlers and Swallowers followed, supporting our less severely wounded men, and twelve or fourteen led the

captured horses, bridled and saddled, on which rode or were
draped the wounded who could not walk.

When we got back to our camping place, those wounded
warriors were turned over to our various tíciltin, for most of
the tribes composing the army had brought along at least one
native physician. Even the Yaki had done so, but since their
tícitl could have administered little more than masked chant-
ings and prancings and rattlings, I ordered that the Yaki casualties be also attended by the more enlightened physicians
of other tribes. As they had done before and would always
do, the Yaki grumbled angrily at my disrespect for their sacred traditions, but I firmly insisted and they had to comply.

That was not the only dissension I would discover when
my forces were regathered. The men and women who had
participated in the taking of Tonalá wanted to keep for themselves all the booty they had collected there, and were much
disgruntled when I ordered that the goods be distributed, as
equitably as was possible, among the entire army and the
slaves as well. But that enforced apportionment did not satisfy the many bands who had *not* participated. Though they
had known, from the start, my reasons for using in this battle
only a fraction of my available forces, the very success of
our mission seemed now to have made them begrudge us
that success. They muttered sullenly that I had been unjust
to leave them behind, that I had shown undue preferment to
my "favorites." I swear, they even evinced envy of the
wounds the "favored" warriors had brought back, and there
was no way I could order *those* shared around. I did my best
to appease the malcontents by promising that there would be
many more such battles and victories, that every contingent
would eventually get its chance at acquiring glory, loot and
wounds—and even god-pleasing deaths. But just as I had
long ago learned that being a Uey-Tecútli was no easy occupation, so I was now learning that being the leader of a
vast and conglomerate army was no easier.

I decreed that we all would stay in our present encampment while I pondered on where to take that army and use

it next. I had several reasons for wanting to remain for some time where we were. One was to let the Purémpe women make another considerable store of the clay-ball granadas, because they had proved so effective in Tonalá. And since we now had an appreciable number of horses, I wanted more of my men to learn to ride them. Also, because we had lost many of our best arcabuz men—partly through my own fault—I wanted others to have ample opportunity to practice with our now-numerous armory of those weapons, and to learn to employ them in the manner the late Uno had recommended.

So I delegated to Knight Nochéztli most of the workaday responsibilities of command, thereby relieving myself of having to deal with petty complaints, petitions, quarrels and other such exasperations, conserving my own time and attention for those things that only I could command and oversee in person. Foremost of those was a project I wished to commence while we were still comfortably encamped. That is why one day I summoned you, Verónica.

When you stood before me, looking alert and attentive but demure, your hands behind your back, I said what I had said to so many others before, "It is my intention to retake this One World from its unwelcome Spanish conquerors and occupiers and oppressors."

You nodded and I went on, "Whether we succeed or fail in this endeavor, it may be that, at some time in the future, the historians of The One World will be glad to have available a true record of the events of Tenamáxtzin's war. You can write and you have the materials for doing so. I should like you to start setting down in writing what may be the only record of this rebellion that will ever exist. Do you think you can do that?"

"I will do my best, my lord."

"Now, you witnessed only the conclusion of the battle at Tonalá. I will recount for you the circumstances and incidents leading up to it. This you and I can do at leisure, while we are camped here, allowing me to sort out in my own mind the sequence of events, and allowing you to get accustomed to writing at my dictation, and allowing both of us to review and amend any mistakes that may be made.''

''I am fortunate in having a retentive memory, my lord. I think we will not make many mistakes.''

''Let us hope not. However, we will not always have the luxury of our sitting together while I talk and you listen. This army has uncountable one-long-runs to march, uncountable enemies to confront, uncountable battles to be fought. I should wish to have them all on record—the marches, the enemies, the battles, the outcomes. Since I must lead the marching, find the enemies, be in the forefront of the battles, I clearly cannot always be describing for you what is occurring. Much of it you will have to see for yourself.''

''I also possess good eyesight, my lord.''

''I will choose a horse for you, and teach you to ride it, and keep you ever by my side—except in the thick of battle, when you will be posted at a safe distance. Thus you will see many things only from afar. You must try to understand what you are seeing, and then try to make coherent record of it. You will seldom have long, quiet intervals in which to sit down with quill and paper. You may seldom even have a *place* to sit down. So you must contrive some way to make quick notes—on the spot or on the run—that later you can elaborate when, as now, we are encamped for a time.''

''I can do that, my lord. In fact—''

''Let me finish, girl. I was about to suggest that you use a method long favored by the traveling pochtéca merchants for keeping their accounts. You pluck the leaves of the wild grapevine and—''

''And scratch on them with a sharp twig. The white marks are as enduring as ink on paper. Your pardon, my lord. I already knew that. In fact, I have been doing that—here and now—as you have been speaking.''

You brought your hands out from behind your back, holding grape leaves and a twig. The leaves bore minute scratches that you had made without even looking at what you were doing.

More than a little astonished, I said, "You can make sense of those marks? You can repeat some of the words I have spoken?"

"The marks, my lord, are only to nudge my memory. No one else could interpret them. And I do not pretend to have preserved your *every* word, but—"

"Prove it, girl. Read back to me something from this conversation." I reached out and indicated one of the leaves at random. "What was said there?"

It took you only a moment of study. " 'At some time in the future, the historians of The One World will be glad to have available—' "

"By Huitztli!" I exclaimed. "This is something most marvelous. *You* are something most marvelous. I have known only one other scribe in my lifetime, a Spanish churchman. He was not nearly so adept as you are, and he was a man approaching middle age. How old are you, Verónica?"

"I think I have ten or eleven years, my lord. I am not sure."

"Indeed? From the near maturity of your form, and even more from the refinement evidenced in your speech, I should have taken you to be three or four years older. How did you get so well educated at such a young age?"

"My mother was Church-schooled and convent-bred. She taught me from my earliest years. Just before she died, she placed me in the same nunnery."

"That explains your name, then. But if your mother was a slave, she could have been no ordinary Moro drudge."

"She was a mulata, my lord," you said, without embarrassment. "She disliked to talk much about her parentage— or my own. But children, of course, can divine much that is left unsaid. I surmised that her mother must have been a black, but her father a Spaniard of some fairly high position and prosperity, that he would pay to send a bastard daughter to school. Of my own father, she was so secretive that I have never been able even to conjecture."

"I have seen only your face," I said. "Let me see the rest of you. Undress for me, Verónica."

That took but a moment, because you wore only a single, flimsy, ankle-length, almost threadbare gown of Spanish style.

I said, "I once had all the gradations and degrees of mixed parentage described to me. But I have no experience of judging them on sight, except that I also once knew a girl who was, I believe, the product of a white mother and black father. As for you, Verónica, I would say that your grandmother's Moro blood shows only in your already budded breasts and dark nipples and already beginning tuft of ymáxtli down below. Your grandfather's Spanish blood, I would suppose, accounts for your delicate and very handsome facial features. But you do not have hairy armpits or legs, so your grandfather's Spanish white blood must have been later diluted. Also you are as clean and sweet-smelling as any female of my own race. It is easily apparent that your unknown father contributed some further and improving admixture to your nature."

"If it matters to you, my lord," you said boldly, "whatever else I am, I am also still a virgin. I have not yet been raped by any man and not yet been tempted to dally with any."

I paused to contemplate that forthright remark—you had said "tempted," you had said "not yet"—while I savored what I was looking at. And here I will honestly confide something. Even back then, at that tender age, Verónica, you were so womanly endowed, so physically beautiful and appealing—besides being intelligent and cultivated beyond your years—that you were a very real temptation to me. I might have asked you to become something more than just my companion and my scribe. But that notion flickered only briefly in my mind, because I was still mindful of the pledge I had made to the memory of Ixínatsi. In truth, though I would have rejoiced in a mutual intimacy, I dared not either tempt or cajole you to it, for I would have risked falling in love with you. And genuinely to love a woman was what I had sworn never to do again.

And, again in truth, it is as well that I did not, in view of what would later transpire between us.

And, still in truth, I did, nevertheless—inevitably, inescapably—come to love you dearly.

At that time, though, all I said was, "Get dressed again and come with me. We shall relieve the Purémpe women of some of the garments they pilfered from the Tonalá wardrobes. You deserve the finest of feminine garb, little Verónica. And you will need more of it, too—certainly underneath—if you are to ride a horse beside mine."

Not all of our subsequent conquests were accomplished as easily as that of Tonalá. While we remained encamped, I kept my scouts and swift-runners circulating in all directions roundabout, and from their reports, I decided to make our next assault on the Spaniards a *double* assault—simultaneous but at two separate, far-apart places. It would certainly serve to make the Spaniards ever more fearful that we were many in number, powerful in force of arms, fierce in our determination, capable of striking anywhere—not just the angry uprising of a few malcontent tribesmen but a genuine, landwide insurrection against *all* the usurper white men.

Some of the scouts informed me that some distance to the southeast of our camp lay a vast expanse of rich estancia farms and ranches, the proprietors of which had all clustered their residences close together—for convenience and neighborliness and mutual protection—at the center of that expanse of land. Other scouts reported that to the southwest of us was situated a Spanish crossroads trading post, doing a thriving business with traveling merchants and local landowners—but heavily fortified and guarded by a considerable force of Spanish foot soldiers.

Those were the two places I determined to hit next, and

at the same time, Knight Nochéztli to lead the attack on the estancia community, I the attack on the trading post. And now I would give some of our previously unblooded (and envious) warriors *their* chance at fighting, at plunder, at glory, at god-pleasing death. So to Nochéztli I assigned our Cora and Huichol men and all our horsemen—among them Verónica, to be the chronicler of that battle. With me I took Rarámuri and Otomí warriors and all our accomplished arcabuz men. We left behind all those others who had participated in the taking of Tonalá—causing the Yaki, in their customary way, to mutter mutinously. Nochéztli and I carefully calculated our traveling times, to set the day on which we would make our separate, simultaneous sieges, and the later day of our rejoining, victorious, at our present camp— and then we marched away in our divergent directions.

As I have said, not all of my war went smoothly. My attack on the trading post seemed, at first, unlikely to result in any outcome that could be called victorious.

The place consisted mostly of the huts and shacks of the Spaniards' laborers and slaves. But those surrounded the post itself, which sat secure inside a palisade of heavy, close-abutted logs, all pointed at the top, with an equally massive gate, tight shut and barred within. From narrow slits in the log wall protruded the snouts of thunder-tubes. When our forces went, roaring and bellowing, at a run across the open ground at one side of the post, I expected we would only have to dodge the heavy iron balls that I had previously seen thrown by Spanish thunder-tubes. But *these* had been charged with bits of scrap metal, flints, nails, broken glass and the like. When they boomed out at us, there was no dodging the lethal spray they threw, and a great many of our warriors in the forefront of the attack fell horribly mutilated, dismembered, shredded to death.

Happily for us, though, a thunder-tube takes even longer to recharge than does a thunder-stick. Before the Spanish soldiers could manage that, we surviving warriors had made our way close against the stockade wall where the thunder-tubes could not be turned to aim at us. My Rarámuri men, true to their name of "Fast of Feet," easily swarmed up the rough-barked logs, and over them into the stockade. While some of those began at once to engage the Spanish defenders, others rushed to unbar the gate to let the rest of us enter.

Still, the soldiers were no cowards, nor unnerved to the point of immediate surrender. Some, in ranks at a distance, belabored us with arcabuces. But my own arcabuz men, now well versed in the proper employment of that weapon, performed with equal accuracy and killing efficiency. Meanwhile, we others, with spears and swords and maquáhuime, fought the many other soldiers at close quarters and eventually hand to hand. This was no brief battle; the brave soldiers were prepared to fight to the death. And, finally, to that death they all went.

So had a lamentable number of my own men, both outside and inside the palisade. Since, on this march, we had brought no Swaddlers to attend our wounded, and since the post contained no horses on which to transport them, I could only instruct our Swallowers to bestow a quick and merciful death on the fallen who were still alive but too badly injured to make our return march.

It had been a costly conquest, but still a profitable one. The trading post was a treasure house of useful and valuable goods—pólvora and lead balls, arcabuces and swords and knives, blankets and robes, smoked or salted stores of many good foods, even jugs of octli and chápari and Spanish wines. So, with my permission, we survivors celebrated our victory to the extent that we were all quite drunk and unsteady on our feet when we staggered away from there next morning. As I had done before, I invited the local slave families to come with us, and most of them did, carrying our bales and bags and jugs of plunder.

Arriving back at our encampment beyond the ruins of Tonalá, I was glad to learn from Nochéztli that his had been a much less difficult expedition than mine. The estancia community had been guarded not by trained soldiers, but only by the proprietors' own slave watchmen, naturally not armed with arcabuces, and not at all eager to repel an invasion. So Nochéztli had lost not a single man, and his forces had killed and raped and looted almost at leisure. They too had returned with great stores of foodstuffs and bags of maize and warm fabrics and usable Spanish clothing. Best of all, they had brought from those ranches many more horses and a herd of cattle nearly as numerous as those Coronado had taken north with him. We would no longer have to do much foraging or even hunting. We had food enough to sustain our whole army for a long time to come.

"And here, my lord," said Nochéztli. "A personal gift from me to you. I took these from the bed of one of those Spanish nobles." He handed me a neatly folded pair of beautifully lustrous silk sheets, only very slightly bloodstained. "I believe the Uey-Tecútli of the Aztéca should not have to sleep on the bare ground or a straw pallet like any common warrior."

"I thank you, my friend," I said sincerely, then laughed. "Though I fear you may incline me to the same self-indulgence and indolence as that of any Spanish nobleman."

There was other good news awaiting me there at the camp. Some of my swift-runners had gone scouting far abroad indeed, and now had returned to tell me that my war was being fought by others besides my own army.

"Tenamáxtzin, the word of your insurrection has spread from nation to nation and tribe to tribe, and many are eager to emulate your actions on behalf of The One World. From here, all the way to the coast of the Eastern Sea, bands of warriors are making forays—quick strike, quick withdrawal—against Spanish settlements and farms and homesteads. The Chichiméca Dog People, the Téochichiméca Wild Dog People, even the Zácachichiméca Rabid Dog People, are all doing those raid-and-run assaults on the white men. Even the Huaxtéca of the coastal lands, so long notorious for their lassitude, made an attack on the seaport city the Spanish call Vera Cruz. Of course, with their primitive weapons, the

Huaxtéca could not do much damage there, but they assuredly caused alarm and fear among the residents.''

I was immensely pleased to hear these things. The peoples mentioned by the scouts certainly were poorly armed, and just as certainly poorly organized in their uprisings. But they *were* helping me to keep the white man uneasy, apprehensive, perhaps awake at night. All of New Spain by now would be aware of those sporadic raids and my more devastating ones. New Spain, I hoped and believed, must be getting increasingly nervous and anxious about the continued *existence* of New Spain.

Well, the Huaxtéca and others could contrive to make their sudden attack-then-flee forays almost with impunity. But I was now commanding what was practically a traveling city—warriors, slaves, women, whole families, many horses and a herd of cattle—unwieldy, to say the least, to move from battlefield to battlefield. I decided that we needed a permanent place to settle, a place stoutly defensible, whence I could lead or send either small forces or formidable forces in any direction and have a safe haven for them to return to. So I summoned various of my knights who, I knew, had done considerable traveling in these parts of The One World, and asked their advice. A knight named Pixqui said:

''I know the very place, my lord. Our ultimate objective is an assault upon the City of Mексíco, southeast of here, and the place I am thinking of lies just about midway between here and there. The mountains called Miztóapan, 'Where the Cuguars Lurk.' The few white men who have ever seen them call them in their tongue the Mixton Mountains. They are rugged and craggy mountains interlaced with narrow ravines. We can find a valley in there commodious enough to accommodate our whole vast army. Even when the Spaniards learn we are there—as doubtless they will—they would have a hard time getting at us, unless they learn to fly. Lookouts atop the crags around our valley could espy any approaching enemy force. And since any such force would have to thread its way through those narrow ravines almost in single file, just a handful of our arcabuz men could stop them there, while our other warriors would rain arrows and spears and boulders down onto them from above."

"Excellent," I said. "It sounds impregnable. I thank you, Knight Pixqui. Go, then, throughout the camp and spread the order for everyone to prepare to march. We will leave at dawn for the Miztóapan Mountains. And one of you find that slave girl Verónica, my scribe, and have her attend me."

It was the Iyac Pozonáli who fetched you to me that fateful day. I had long been aware that he was often in your company, and regarding you with yearning looks. I am not oblivious to such things, and I have frequently been in love myself. I knew the iyac to be an admirable young man and— even before the revelation that transpired between us that day, Verónica—I could hardly have been jealous if it turned out that Pozonáli found favor in your eyes, as well.

Anyway, you had already written your account of No-chéztli's assault on the estancias—since you had been present there—so now I dictated the account of my own much more difficult assault on the trading post, you writing down all the words foregoing here, concluding with the decision to move to the Miztóapan. When I had done, you murmured:

"I am happy, my lord, to hear that you intend soon to attack the City of Mexíco. I hope you obliterate it as you did Tonalá."

"So do I. But why do you?"

"Because that will also obliterate the nunnery where I lived after my mother died."

"That convent was in the City of Mexíco? You never mentioned its location before. I know of only one nunnery there. It was very near the Mesón de San José, where I myself once lived."

"That is the one, my lord."

A somewhat disturbing but not dismaying suspicion was already dawning on me.

"And you hold some grudge against those nuns, child? I have often meant to ask. Why *did* you flee that convent and become a homeless wanderer, finally to find refuge among our slave contingent?"

"Because the nuns were so cruel, first to my mother, then to me."

"Explain."

"After her Church schooling, when my mother had had sufficient instruction in that religion, and had attained the age required, she was confirmed as a Christian and immediately took what they call holy orders—became a bride of Christ, as they say—and took residence in the convent as a novice nun. However, not many months later, it was discovered that she was pregnant. She was stripped of her habit and viciously whipped and evicted in disgrace. As I have said, she never told even me who it was that made her pregnant." You added bitterly, "I doubt that it was her husband Christ."

I pondered awhile, then asked, "Might your mother's name have been Rebeca?"

"Yes," you said, astonished. "How could you possibly know that, my lord?"

"I briefly attended that same Church school, so I know— some little—of her story. But I left the city about that time, so I never knew the *whole* story. After Rebeca's eviction, what became of her?"

"Bearing a fatherless bastard inside her, I daresay she was ashamed to go home to her own mother and father—her white patrón. For a time, she earned a precarious living, do- ing menial odd jobs about the markets, literally living on the streets. I was birthed on a bed of rags in some alley some- where. I suppose I am fortunate to have survived the expe- rience."

"And then?"

"Now she had two mouths to feed. I blush to say it, my lord, but she went—what you call in your language 'astrad- dle the road.' And, she being a mulata—well, you can imag- ine—she could hardly solicit rich Spanish nobles or even

prosperous pochtéca merchants. Only market porters and
Moro slaves and the like—entertaining them in squalid little
inns and even in back streets outdoors. Toward the end—I
could not have been more than four years old—I remember
having to watch her do these things.''

''Toward the end. What was the end?''

''Again I blush, my lord. From some one of her strad-
dlings, she contracted the nanáua, the disease of uttermost
shame and revulsion. When she knew she was dying, she
went again to the convent, leading me by the hand. Under
the rules of that Christian order, the nuns could not refuse
to take me in. But of course they knew my history, so I was
despised by all, and I had no hope of being accorded a no-
vitiate. They simply used me as a servant, a slave, a drudge.
Of all the work that needed doing, I did the lowliest, but at
least they gave me bed and board.''

''And education?''

''As I have told you, my mother had imparted to me much
of the knowledge that she herself had earlier acquired. And
I have some facility at being observant and attentive. So,
even while I labored, I watched and listened and absorbed
what the nuns were teaching their novices and other respectable young girls in residence there. When finally I decided I
had learned all that they could, however viciously, teach me
there . . . and when the drudgery and beatings had become
intolerable . . . that was when I ran away.''

''You are one supremely remarkable girl, Verónica. I am
immeasurably glad that you survived your wanderings and
came at last to—to us.''

I pondered some more. How best to say this?

''From what little acquaintance I had with my schoolmate
Rebeca, I believe it was her *mother* who gave you your white
blood, and her father would have been a Moro, not some
Spanish patrón. But that does not matter. What matters is
that *your* father—whoever he was—I believe to have been
an indio, a Mexícatl or Aztécatl. Thus you have three bloods
in your veins, Verónica. That combination, I suppose, ac-

counts for your uncommon comeliness. Now, mind you, I can only surmise the rest from the few hints dropped by Rebeca. But, if I am right, your paternal grandfather was a high noble of the Mexíca, a man brave and wise and *truly* noble in all respects. A man who defied the Spanish conquerors to the very end of his life. *His* contribution to your nature would account for your uncommon intelligence, and especially your astounding facility with words and writing. If I am right, that grandfather of yours was a Mexícatl named Mixtli—more properly Mixtzin—*Lord* Mixtli.''

XXXI

Our army's progress across the countryside was even slower now than before, because of our having to herd along the stupid, stubborn, shambling, recalcitrant cattle. Because my warriors were becoming understandably restive—I having turned them from warriors into mere escorts and herdsmen—I halted the army once along the way to give them an opportunity for bloodshed, raping and looting.

That was at what had formerly been the Otomí people's chief village, named N't Tahí, but was now a town of estimable size, populated almost entirely by Spaniards and their usual retinues of servants and slaves, and renamed by them Zelalla. We left it as scorched and ruined and leveled as Tonalá, most of the leveling having been done by the Purémpe women's granadas. And we left it *un*populated, except by corpses—*hairless* corpses, courtesy of the Yaki.

I am gratified to report that my warriors departed from Zelalla with much more dignity and much less flamboyance than when they had departed from Tonalá—that is, not bedecked and bedizened in Spanish skirts and bonnets and mantillas and such. Indeed, for some while now, they had been getting ashamed—even the women and the most ignorant Moros—of all those gauds and baubles and steel breastplates. Besides their increasing embarrassment at wear-

ing such unwarriorlike garb, they found the clothes dangerously constrictive in battle, and uncomfortably heavy even
to march in, especially when sodden by rain. So all had been
shedding those white men's garments and ornaments, piece
by piece, along the way—everything except the warm wool-
ens usable as blankets and mantles—and we again looked
like the true *indio* army that we were.

In time, an excruciatingly long time, we did reach those
Mountains Where the Cuguars Lurk, and they were exactly
as Knight Pixqui had described them. With him in the lead,
we wove our tortuous way through a maze of those narrow
ravines, some only wide enough for a single horseman (or
cow) to pass through, one after another. And eventually we
did emerge into a not broad but lengthy valley, well watered,
spacious enough for us all to camp comfortably, and even
sufficiently green to provide grazing for our animals.

When we had settled down and gratefully rested for two
or three days, I summoned to me the Iyac Pozonáli and my
darling scribe Verónica, and told them:

"I have a mission for you two. I think it will not be a
hazardous mission, though it will entail arduous travel. However"—I smiled—"I think also that you will not mind a
long journey in close company with one another." You
blushed, Verónica, and so did Pozonáli.

I went on, "It is certain that everyone in the City of Mexíco, from the Viceroy Mendoza down to the least market
slave, knows of our insurrection and our depredations. But I
should like to know how *much* they know of us, and what
measures they may be taking to defend the city against us
or to sally out and find and fight us in the open. What I want
you to do is this. Go on horseback as fast and as far southeastward as you can, stopping only when you decide you are
getting perilously close to any possible Spanish outposts. By
my reckoning, that will probably be somewhere in the eastern part of Michihuácan, where it borders on the Mexíca
lands. Leave the horses with any hospitable native who can
tend them. From there, go on foot and dressed in the roughest

of peasant garb. Take with you bags of some kind of marketable goods—fruits, vegetables, whatever you can procure. You may find the city solidly ringed about with sharp steel, but it *must* let supplies and commodities in and out. And I think the guards will hardly be suspicious of a young peasant farmer and—shall we say?—his little cousin, headed for the market.''

You both blushed again. I continued:

''Just do *not*, Verónica, speak your Spanish. Do not speak at all. You, Pozonáli, I trust can talk your way past any guard or other challenger by mumbling Náhuatl and the few Spanish words you know, and gesticulating like some clumsy rustic.''

''We will get into the city, Tenamáxtzin, I kiss the earth to that,'' he said. ''Have you specific orders for us, once we are there?''

''I want both of you mainly to look and to listen. You, Iyac, have proven yourself a competent military man. You should have no trouble in recognizing whatever defenses the city is preparing for itself, or whatever preparations it is making in the way of an offensive against us. Meanwhile, go about the streets and the markets and engage the common folk in conversation. I wish to know their mood, their temper and their opinion of our insurrection, because I know from experience that *some*, perhaps many, will side with the Spaniards on whom they have come to depend. Meanwhile, also, there is one Aztécatl man—a goldsmith, elderly by now— you are to visit personally.'' I gave him directions. ''He was my very first ally in this campaign, so I want him warned that we will be coming. He may wish to hide his gold or even leave the city with it. And, of course, pass on to him my fond regards.''

''All will be done as you say, Tenamáxtzin. And Verónica? Am I to stay protectively close by her?''

''No need, I think. Verónica, you are an exceedingly resourceful girl. I want you merely to get within hearing distance of any two or more Spaniards conversing on the streets, in the markets, wherever, and *eavesdrop*—especially if they are in uniform or otherwise look like important persons. They will scarcely suspect that you can understand their talk, and it may be that you will learn even more than Iyac Pozonáli about the Spaniards' intended responses to our intended assault.''

"Yes, my lord."

"I have also one specific instruction for you. In all that city, there is but a single *white* man to whom I owe the same warning that Pozonáli will give to the goldsmith. His name is Alonso de Molina—remember it—and he is a high official at the Cathedral."

"I know where it is, my lord."

"Do not go and speak that warning to him directly. He is, after all, a Spaniard. He might well seize you and hold you hostage. He most certainly would, if he should remotely suspect that you are my—my personal scribe. So write the warning on a piece of paper, fold it, put Alonso's name on the outside and—*without speaking*, just with gestures—give it to any lowly churchman you find loitering about the Cathedral. Then get away from there as fast as you can. And stay away."

"Yes, my lord. Anything else?"

"Just this. The most important order I can give you both. When you feel you have learned all you can, get safely out of the city, get safely back to your horses and get safely back here. Both of you. If, Iyac, you should dare to return here without Verónica . . . well . . .''

"We shall safely return, Tenamáxtzin, I kiss the earth to that. If some unforeseen evil befalls, and only one of us returns, it will be Verónica. To *that*, I kiss the earth four hundred times!"

When they were gone, the rest of us rather luxuriated in our new surroundings. We certainly lived well. There was more than enough cow meat to eat, of course, but our hunters ranged about the valley anyway, just to provide variety—

deer and rabbits and quail and ducks and other game. They even slew two or three of the cuguars for which the mountains were named, though cuguar meat is tough to chew and not very tasty. Our fishers found the mountain streams abounding in a fish—I do not know what it is called—that made a delectable change from our mostly meat meals. Our foragers found all sorts of fruits, vegetables, roots and such. The plundered jugs of octli, chápari and Spanish wines were reserved to myself and my knights, but we now drank only sparingly of them. All we lacked was something really sweet, like the coconuts of my homeland. I do believe that many of our people—particularly the numerous slave families we had freed and brought along—would have been content to live in that valley for the rest of their lives. And they probably could have done so, unmolested by the white men, even unknown to the white men, to the end of time.

I do not mean to say that we all simply lazed and vegetated there. Though I slept at night between silken Spanish sheets and under a fine woolen Spanish blanket—feeling as if I were a Spanish marqués or viceroy—I was busy all day long. I kept my scouts roaming the countryside beyond the mountains, and reporting back to me. I strode about the valley, as a sort of inspector-in-general, because I had ordered Nochéztli and our other knights to train many more of our warriors to ride the many new horses we had acquired and to employ properly the many new arcabuces we had acquired.

When one of my scouts came to report that not far to the west of our mountains was a crossroads Spanish trading post—similar to the one we had earlier vanquished—I decided to try an experiment. I took a medium-sized force of Sobáipuri warriors, because they had not yet had the pleasure of participating in *any* of our battles, and because they had become proficient both at riding and at using the arcabuz, and I asked Knight Pixqui to accompany me, and we rode westward to that trading post.

I intended not really a battle, but only a feint. We galloped, hooting and howling and discharging our arcabuces, out of the woods into the open ground before the palisaded post. And, as before, from the ports in that palisade, thunder-tubes spewed a spray of lethal scraps and fragments, but I was careful to keep us out of their range, and only one of our men suffered a minor shoulder wound. We remained out there, dancing our horses back and forth, making our threatening war cries and extravagantly threatening gestures, until the stockade gate opened and a troop of mounted soldiers came galloping out. Then, pretending to be intimidated, we all turned and galloped back the way we had come. The soldiers pursued us, and I made sure that we stayed ahead of them, but always in their sight. We led them all the way back to the ravine from which we had left our valley.

Still taking care that the soldiers should not lose us in those mazes, we baited them through one very narrow notch where I had already posted arcabuz men on either side. Just as Knight Pixqui had predicted, the first discharges of those arcabuces brought down enough soldiers and their horses to block the passage for all the others behind. And those, milling about in confusion, were in a very short time destroyed by spears, arrows and boulders propelled by other warriors I had posted on the heights above. My Sobáipuri of course were pleased to confiscate the weapons and the surviving horses of all those dead Spaniards. But I was mainly pleased to have proven that our hideaway was indeed invulnerable. We could hold out here forever, if need be, against any force sent to assail us.

There came a day when several of my scouts came to tell me, really gleefully, that they had discovered a new and major target for us to attack.

"About three days east of here, Tenamáxtzin, a town almost as big as a city, but we might never have known it existed, except that we espied a mounted Spanish soldier and followed him. One of us who understands a little Spanish crept into the town behind him, and learned that it is a rich town, well built, called by the white men Aguascalientes."

"Hot Springs," I said.

"Yes, my lord. It is evidently a place to which the Spanish men and women resort for curative baths and recreations of other sorts. *Rich* Spanish men and women. So you can imagine the plunder we can take from it. Not to mention *clean* white women, for a change. I must report, though, that the town is heavily fortified, manned and armed. We cannot possibly take it without using our entire complement of warriors, both foot and mounted."

I called for Nochéztli and repeated the report. "Prepare our forces. We will march two days from now. This time I want *everyone* to participate, including—we will doubtless have need of them—all our tíciltin, Swaddlers and Swallowers. This will be the most ambitious, audacious assault of all we have yet made, hence perfect practice for our eventual assault on the City of Mexíco."

Fortuitously, the very next day, Pozonáli and Verónica returned to us, safely and together, and, though much fatigued from their long, hard ride, came immediately to report to me. So excited were they that they began speaking simultaneously in their separate languages of Náhuatl and Spanish.

"The goldsmith thanks you for your warning, Tenamáxtzin, and sends you his warm regards in return . . ."

"You are already famous in the City of Mexíco, my lord. I should say famous and *feared* . . ."

"Wait, wait," I said, laughing. "Verónica first."

"What I bring is the good news, my lord. To begin with, I did deliver your message to the Cathedral and, as you supposed, when your friend Alonso received it, whole troops of soldiers began combing the city to find the messenger who had brought it. But they could not, of course, I being indistinguishable from so many other girls like myself. And, as you commanded, I listened to many conversations. The Spaniards, by what means I do not know, are already aware that our whole army is encamped here in the Mixtóapan. So they are calling our insurrection 'the Mixton War,' and—I rejoice to report—it has much of New Spain in a panic.

Whole families from the City of Mexíco and from everywhere else are crowding into the seaports—Vera Cruz and Tampico and Campeche and every other—demanding passages back to Old Spain, on any kind of vessel sailing there—galleons, caravels, victualler ships, *anything.* Many are saying fearfully that this is the *re*conquest of The One World. It appears, my lord, that you *are* achieving your aim of chasing the interlopers—at least the white ones—entirely out of our lands.''

''But not all of them,'' said Iyac Pozonáli, frowning. ''Despite Coronado's having taken so many of New Spain's soldiers on his northward expedition, the Viceroy Mendoza has still a considerable force in the City of Mexíco, some hundreds of mounted and foot soldiers, and Mendoza has taken personal command of them. Furthermore, as you expected, Tenamáxtzin, many of his *tame* Mexíca have enlisted to fight alongside him. So have many of those other treacherous peoples—the Totonáca, the Tezcaltéca, the Acólhua—who long ago aided the Conquistador Cortés in his overthrow of Motecuzóma. For the first time ever, Mendoza is allowing those indios to ride horses and carry thunder-sticks, and he is right now busily engaged in the training of them.''

''Our own people,'' I said sadly, ''arrayed against us.''

''The city will maintain a sufficient defensive force,'' Pozonáli went on. ''Thunder-tubes and such. But I would reckon, from what I learned, that the Viceroy Mendoza plans an offensive march to rout us out of here and destroy us before we ever get near the City of Mexíco.''

''Well, good luck to Mendoza,'' I said offhandedly. ''However many his men, however well armed, they will be annihilated before they ever get to us here. I have experimented, and the Knight Pixqui was right when he said that these mountains are impregnable. In the meantime, I will be giving the viceroy further evidence of our might and our determination. Tomorrow we march east—every warrior, every horseman, every arcabuz man, every Purémpe granada-thrower, every last one of us who can wield a weapon. We are marching against a city called Hot Springs, and after we have taken that, the Viceroy Mendoza may decide to try to *hide* the City of México. Now, you two go and get some food and rest. I know you, Iyac, will want to be in the thick of the fight. And I shall want you near me, Verónica, to do the chronicling of this most epic of all our battles so far.''

XXXII

OF THE FINAL battle of the "Mixton War"—of our defeat and the *end* of the Mixton War—I will speak only briefly, because it happened through my own grievous fault, and I am ashamed of that. Again, as I had done with other enemies, and even with some of the women in my life, I underestimated the cunning of my opponent. And I am paying for my mistake by lying here slowly dying—or slowly healing, I know not which, and do not much care.

My army could still be here in the Miztóapan, entire and secure and healthy and strong and ready to do battle again, had I not taken them out of this valley. Just as we had earlier baited the Spanish trading post's soldiers into ambush here, so we were baited *out* of our safe haven. It was the doing of the Viceroy Mendoza. He, knowing that we were invincible in these mountains, almost untouchable, contrived to lure us out of them by, in a sense, *offering* us Aguascalientes. I do not blame my scouts who found that town—they are dead now, like so many others—but I have no doubt that the Spanish horseman they followed to that town was playing a part in Mendoza's plan.

I took my whole army, leaving in the valley only the slaves and those males too old or too young to do battle. It was a three-day march to Hot Springs, and even before we got within sight of it, I began to suspect that *something* was not quite right. There were army outpost shacks, but no soldiers in them. When we approached the town, no thundertubes boomed out at us. When I sent my forward scouts sneaking warily into the town itself, there was no rattle of arcabuces, and the scouts came out, shrugging in puzzlement, to report that there seemed to be not a single person in the town.

It was a trap. I turned in my saddle to shout "Retreat!" But it was already too late. Arcabuces now *did* rattle, and from all around us. We were surrounded by Mendoza's soldiers and their indio allies.

Oh, we fought back, of course. The battle went on daylong, and many hundreds died on both sides. Death, that day, was a glutton. As I have remarked, any battle is a commotion and a confusion, and some of the dyings were done in curious ways. My knights Nochéztli and Pixqui both were pierced by balls discharged by *our own* arcabuz men, too recklessly employing their weapons. On the other side, Pedro de Alvarado—one of the first conquistadores in The One World, and the only one still being an active conquistador— died when he fell from his horse and the horse of another Spaniard trampled him.

Since both our armies, mine and Mendoza's, were fairly equal in numbers and armament, it should have been a pitched battle, the victory going to the bravest and strongest and most clever. But what lost it for us was this. My men courageously engaged every white soldier they encountered, but too many of them (bar the Yaki) could not bring themselves to slaughter the men of their own race—the Mexíca and Texcaltéca and others—who were fighting on Mendoza's side. To the contrary, those traitors of our own race, naturally seeking to curry favor with their Spanish masters, hesitated not at all to slaughter *us*. I myself took an arrow in my right side, and that surely came from no Spaniard. For all I know, it came from some unknown *relative* of mine.

One of our battlefield tíciltin jerked the arrow out of me—

painful enough, that—then daubed the open wound with the corrosive xocóyatl—so much *more* painful that I actually and unmanfully screeched aloud. The tícitl could do no more for me, because next instant he fell dead of an arcabuz ball.

When finally night came down, our armies disengaged—what was left of them—and the ragged remnant of ours, those who had horses, hastily withdrew to the westward. Pozonáli, one of the few survivors whom I knew by name, found Verónica on the hilltop whence she had watched the carnage, and brought her along as we made haste to get back to our mountain sanctuary. I could barely sit my saddle, so agonizing was the pain in my side, thus I was in no condition to worry about whether we were being pursued through the night.

If we were, the pursuers never caught up to us. Three days later—days of terrible pain for me, and I was not the worst wounded of us—we arrived again at the Miztóapan, and wound our way through the maze of ravines (often losing our way, since we had not the experienced Knight Pixqui to guide us) and finally, faint with thirst and hunger and fatigue and loss of blood, found our valley again.

I have not even tried to count the survivors of the Hot Springs battle, though I could probably do that without even scribbling down the little flags and trees and dots of numbers. Several who made it safely back here have since died of their wounds, because there are no tíciltin to treat them. All our tíciltin, like all our other hundreds of hundreds, are lying dead back yonder at Hot Springs. One Yaki tícitl is still alive, still with us, and he graciously offered to come and dance and chant at me, but I would be damned to Míctlan before I would submit to that kind of doctoring. So my wound has gradually festered, gone green, oozing pus. I blaze with fever, then shiver with chill and drift in and out of delirium, as once I did in an open acáli on the Western Sea.

Verónica has faithfully and tenderly attended me, as best she can, applying hot compresses to the wound, and various tree saps and cactus juices that the old folk in camp recommend as curatives, but those things are doing no discernible good.

During one of my lucid periods, you asked, Verónica, "What do we do now, my lord?"

Trying to sound staunch and optimistic, I said, "We stay here, licking our wounds. We can hardly do anything else, and we are at least safe from attack here. I cannot even *plan* any further action until I am healed of this accursed injury. Then we shall see. In the meantime—I have been thinking— your chronicle of what the Spaniards call the Mixton War commenced with our devastation of Tonalá. It occurs to me that future historians of The One World might benefit from my telling and your writing of earlier events, of how this all began. Would it try your patience, dear Verónica, if I recounted to you practically my entire life?"

"Of course not, my lord. Not only am I here to serve you, I should myself be . . . most interested . . . in hearing your life story."

I meditated for some while. How to begin at the beginning? Then I smiled, as well as I was able, and said, "I think, Verónica, I have already, long ago, spoken to you the opening sentence of this chronicle."

"I believe so, too, my lord. I kept it and still have it here."

You shuffled among your sheaf of papers, brought one out and read it aloud:

"I can still see him burning."

"Yes," I said, and sighed. "Clever darling girl. Let us proceed from there."

And, over I do not know how many ensuing days, though sometimes I was gabbling in delirium or mute with pain, I recounted everything that you have so far set down. Finally I said:

"I have told you everything I can remember, even insignificant conversations and occurrences. Still, I suppose it is but a bare-bones recounting."

"No, my dear lord. Without your knowing, ever since we have been together, I have been making notes of your merest passing remarks and my own observations of you, your nature, your character. Because, to tell the truth, I loved you, my lord, even before I knew you to be my father. With your permission, I should like to intermingle those observations of mine into the chronicle. It will put flesh on the bare bones.''

"By all means, my dear. You are the chronicler, and you know best. Anyway, you now know all there is to know, and all that any historian will need to know.''

I paused, then went on:

"You now know also that you have a close cousin in Aztlan. If ever I recover from this wretched fever and weakness, I shall take you there, and Améyatzin will give you a warm welcome. You and Pozonáli. I do hope, child, that you will wed the lad. The gods preserved him through this last battle, and I truly believe they saved him just for you.''

My mind was beginning to waver and wander, but I added, "After Aztlan, perhaps we could go on . . . to The Islands of the Women. I was happy there . . .''

"You are getting sleepy, lord father. And you have expended much energy, talking during these many days. I think you should rest now.''

"Yes. Let me say just one thing more, and please put it at the end of your chronicle. Our Mixton War is lost, and rightly so. I should never have begun it. From the day of your Grandfather Mixtli's execution, I resented and resisted the aliens among us. But, over time, I have met and admired many of those aliens—the white Alonso, the black Esteban, the padre Quiroga, your mulata mother Rebeca, and finally you, dear daughter, who commingle so many different bloods. I realize now—and I accept—I am even proud—that *your* lovely face, Verónica, is the new face of The One World. To you and to your sons and daughters and to The One World, I wish all good things.''

XXXIII

MY FATHER DIED in his sleep that night. I was at his pallet side, and I drew the silken sheet over his face. He is at peace—I hope in bliss—in the warriors' afterworld of one of his gods.

What is to become of the rest of us, I do not know.

Verónica Tenamáxtzin de Pozonáli

ACKNOWLEDGMENTS

THIS BOOK, LIKE much else in the author's life, could hardly have been accomplished without the teachings, assistance, encouragement, patience, and toleration, over a good many years, of a good many good friends:

The late Edward Amos, Radford, Virginia
Pat Colville Anderson, New York, New York
Alex and Patti Apostolides, El Paso, Texas
The late Sadie Atkins, Paterson, New Jersey
Victor Avers, Canoga Park, California
Herman and Fran Begega, Pompton Lakes, New Jersey
Jo Bertone, Dallas, Texas
The late L. R. Boyd, Jr., Teague, Texas
The late Col. James G. Chesnutt, The Presidio, San Francisco, California
Grant Chorley, Vienna, Austria
Eva Clegg, Greensboro, North Carolina
Copycat, Feather and Ditto
Angelita Correa, San Miguel de Allende, Gto., México
Sonja Heinze Coryat, Santa Rosa, California
Dino and Martha De Laurentiis, Beverly Hills, California
Henry P. Dickerson III, Staunton, Virginia
Robert M. Elkins, Cincinnati, Ohio

Hugo and Lorraine Gerstl, Carmel, California
Robert Gleason, New York, New York
Gus Heinze, Mill Valley, California
Stephen de las Heras, New York, New York
The late Les Hicks, Hicksville, Long Island, New York
Bill and Shirley Jones, McGaheysville, Virginia
Peter Kirsch, M.D., Philadelphia, Pennsylvania
The late Elizabeth Lucas, Radford, Virginia
The late A. Louis Ginsberg-Martin, Paterson, New Jersey
Donna Marxer, New York, New York
Melva Elizabeth Mann Newsom, Xenia, Ohio
Raúl G. Oviedo, M.D., Elkton, Virginia
Ernesto Pacheco, Dallas, Texas
The late Vance Packard, Martha's Vineyard, Massachusetts
David and Phyllis Parker, Lexington, Virginia
Robert Pastorio, Staunton, Virginia
Sam Pinkus, Hastings-on-Hudson, New York
Evva Pryor, New York, New York
The late James Rutherford, Radford, Virginia
Clark L. Savage, Monterey, California
Joyce O. Servis, Caldwell, New Jersey
The late Robert Shea, Glencoe, Illinois
Lewis J. Singer, M.D., Lexington, Virginia
The late Rosalie O'Brien Smith, New York, New York
Shirley Snyder, Harrisonburg, Virginia
Gayle Tatarski, Reidsville, North Carolina
Neil Thornton, Tawas City, Michigan
Francesca Todaro, San Miguel de Allende, Gto., México
Frank Vcs, Stamford, Connecticut
The late Edie Williams, San Francisco, California
Eugene and Ina Winick, Hastings-on-Hudson, New York
Rita Yancey, McGaheysville, Virginia
Yu Ok Ki, Taegu, Korea

Available by mail from

TOR · FORGE
